MATHEW'S TALE

By Quintin Jardine and available from Headline

Bob Skinner series:
Skinner's Rules
Skinner's Festival
Skinner's Trail
Skinner's Round
Skinner's Ordeal
Skinner's Mission
Skinner's Ghosts
Murmuring the Judges
Gallery Whispers
Thursday Legends
Autographs in the Rain
Head Shot
Fallen Gods
Stay of Execution
Lethal Intent
Dead and Buried
Death's Door
Aftershock
Fatal Last Words
A Rush of Blood
Grievous Angel
Funeral Note
Pray for the Dying
Hour of Darkness

Primavera Blackstone series:
Inhuman Remains
Blood Red
As Easy as Murder
Deadly Business
As Serious as Death

Oz Blackstone series:
Blackstone's Pursuits
A Coffin for Two
Wearing Purple
Screen Savers
On Honeymoon with Death
Poisoned Cherries
Unnatural Justice
Alarm Call
For the Death of Me

Standalone:
The Loner
Mathew's Tale

Quintin Jardine
MATHEW'S TALE

headline

First published in 2014 by
HEADLINE PUBLISHING GROUP

1

Cataloguing in Publication Data is available from the British Library

978 0 7553 8560 7 (Hardback)
978 0 7553 8561 4 (Trade Paperback)

Typeset in Goudy Old Style by Avon DataSet Ltd,
Bidford-on-Avon, Warwickshire

Printed in the UK by CPI Group (UK) Ltd, Croydon, CR0 4YY

Papers used by Headline are from well-managed forests
and other responsible sources.

HEADLINE PUBLISHING GROUP
An Hachette UK Company
338 Euston Road
London NW1 3BH

www.headline.co.uk
www.hachette.co.uk

This story from the past is dedicated to the future: my grandson, Rex Masato Jardine, who joined us on February 15, 2014. On his behalf, I would like to thank his midwife Eileen McVay, her colleagues in the Simpson who helped with his delivery, and most of all his parents, Kyoko and Allan, for never giving up.

Chapter One

IF MATHEW FLEMING HAD ever been truly afraid of anyone, that man was already dead.

When he fell asleep, it was with a feeling of dread for the things he might see on his journey to the next dawn, and for those people he might meet.

Old actions, skirmishes and battles that he had fought and had thought were over.

Young comrades he had comforted, even as their blood sprayed upon him from mortal wounds; they might have let go of life, but their horror held him with an unbreakable, unyielding grip.

Relentless enemies, whom no sword cut, no musket shot could down forever, who came at him and his line in his dreams, over and over again, until finally that one, that fateful little Voltigeur bastard, broke through in the last great battle against the Emperor's armies, his musket discarded but thrusting home his short blade even as he impaled himself on Mathew's bayonet.

That nightmare was the worst, the one that ended with sudden wakefulness, and a scream that was not always stifled.

The others, while vivid, were not so fearful, not even the recollection of the sabre cut that had cost him his left eye when his company had been ambushed by a pack of outlaw French irregulars.

For that little Voltigeur, that wee, agile, leaping bauchle, was the only man that Mathew had ever killed at close quarters, the only enemy whose light he had seen extinguished, even though his own had been fading in the same moment. It was the Frenchman's ghost whose forgiveness he craved yet whose curse awaited him, he was sure, in his sleep.

As he stood on the hilltop, where a great copper beech tree marked a crossroads, and looked down upon and across Carluke, bathed in May mid-morning sunshine, he was still troubled, from his victim's latest visitation the night before, but even more by his uncertainty over what he would find there.

He had spent that night in a proper bedroom, under a roof, albeit an attic in a tavern in a place called Crossford. It had been a luxury, one of the very few he allowed himself, for one who had slept in the open air or under canvas for much of his adult life. He had made that last stop, not very many miles from his destination, because he had wanted to arrive at his native village in the fullness of the day, rather than creep in after dark.

Also it fitted his plan. He had no idea what awaited him there, whether he would be coming home to good news or bad, and so his first call would be paid on the minister. The Reverend John Barclay was the only authority figure within the small community, other than the dominie, the teacher in the parish school, but Porteous's writ ran only among those aged under twelve. Mr Barclay knew everything that happened in Carluke, and if there was bad news to be borne, he was the man Mathew would prefer to break it.

But would the minister be there himself? It had been a full three years since one of Mathew's letters home had been answered. Had some disaster struck? All too often, rumours of cholera and other deadly epidemics had reached the continent. They had been unsettling for the men, even though very few of them had been verified.

Mathew's journey home had been a long one. It had been nine months since his discharge in France, after the regiment had decided that a one-eyed soldier might be much more of a liability than an asset, but six years since he had enlisted, a raw-boned nineteen-year-old, as an infantryman in the King's Own Cameron Highlanders.

He had been not only raw-boned, but also headstrong, rejecting John Barclay's advice that he should move no further than Lanark, to complete the apprenticeship as a saddler that had been cut short by the sudden death of his father.

Robert Fleming's business had died with him, and it was also true that the profits of the village inn were much less certain because of his passing. He had left no money behind him and when the sly, cajoling recruiters had told his son of the signing bounty of five pounds sterling, it had been too much for him to refuse.

They had been less pleased when Mathew gave all of the money to his mother, since the customary practice was for new soldiers to take their windfall with them into service, there to see it disappear rapidly down the throats of the cynical, predatory old lags in their platoon.

The young man had shrugged off his initial unpopularity, winning his new mates over by becoming a first-class infantryman, the sort that they were all pleased to have alongside them in the heat of battle. The Seventy-ninth Regiment of Foot, formed in the previous century, was renowned as one of the army's finest and its First Battalion saw action against Bonaparte in Spain and in Holland, before the battle that had put an end to the Emperor.

Times had been hard, and the pay much poorer than the young man had been promised. He had signed on in the belief that he would be able to send money home to his mother, but soon found that all of his wages went on food and clothing. There had been plunder during the Peninsular campaign, but his Presbyterian upbringing had prevented him from taking any part in it, endearing him still further to his less scrupulous colleagues. Long before his grievous wound at Waterloo, Mathew's plan to support his mother through his soldier's pay had come to nothing. All that he could do was write home, to his sweetheart, Elizabeth, the Marshall girl he had grown up beside, and try to survive.

Those letters were always cheerful, hiding the reality of combat from his loved ones. Occasionally a reply would find him, usually months after it had been written. Lizzie was as positive as he was and her news of his mother . . . reading and writing had never been part of Hannah Fleming's life . . . was always good, but three years ago her responses had dried up completely.

He had done his best to convince himself that the postal service in France had broken down, but he had been beset by anxiety from then on, impatient for the end of his seven-year enlistment. Thus, when the Breton guerrilla's sabre cut had taken his eye the year before, he had seen it as a gift from God, and had felt a little sympathy for the man when he and his captured cronies were shot by a firing squad of Highlander musketeers. For a time afterwards he had worn an eyepatch, but it had been uncomfortable, and besides, the great scar across his face had been uncovered. After only a few months he had abandoned it; if his appearance scared some folk at first glance, they were soon won over by his smile and gentle demeanour.

Apart from the small bonus that his colonel had insisted he be paid on his discharge, the army had been good for him in another way. It had recognised his skill as a leather worker and had enabled him to complete his training.

Since leaving the line he had earned his way home, across France in the autumn, and then all the length of England, in the harshness of its winter. He had stopped in Rouen for a month, making light moccasins . . . a style taught him by a veteran of Canadian warfare . . . and selling them on the street. He had paid for his Channel crossing by repairing the ferry officers' sea boots. He had found well-paid employment for three months on an earl's estate near Newbury, making and renewing saddles and harnesses. When there was no more to be done there, he had moved on, avoiding the turnpike roads to save money but never going far without finding a new taker for his skills.

He had stopped off for another month in Newcastle,

working as a cobbler on the dockside, then moved on to Hexham where more saddles needed repair, until finally he had crossed the border near Gretna, at the beginning of April.

By that time, Mathew Fleming was, by his standards, a well-off man. His handmade leather purse, which he wore next to his skin, was full of notes and coins, far more than the five pounds for which he had sold himself in 1812 to give his mother some reassurance. He was ready to return to look after her properly, and to fulfil the promise he had made to Lizzie before he had gone to the soldiering.

He might have made it home a month sooner had he not come upon a stage coach station in Lockerbie that was in desperate need of a saddler, and prepared to make his purse even fatter. He smiled at the memory of his last employer's gratitude and of his willingness to help him set up in business if only he would stay in town.

That proposition was still very much on his mind as he paused on the hilltop, in the shade of the copper beech, drawing breath before the last, nervous few miles of his long journey, and allowing Gracie, the pony he had brought all the way from Orleans, to graze.

He wondered who, if anyone, was meeting the needs of his father's old customers. By far the best of those had been Sir George Cleland, the amiable baronet who owned all the countryside around Carluke. The Laird's patronage had always kept Robert Fleming's feet in the sawdust, as his father had put it . . . in other words, in the village inn.

Did he still have the man that his factor had hired, full time, to replace his father? If not . . .

His musing was interrupted by the sound of hooves on the hard track, coming from behind him. He turned, to see two young men, well-dressed, on large sleek horses, bearing down upon him. They could have been no more than fifteen years old, but they carried themselves with assurance, and were comfortable on their mounts.

'What have we got here, Greg?' one of them called.

As Mathew's one eye focused on them he could see that they were no ordinary pair, but twins, alike as green peas in a pod. And from that, he knew who they were. He had seen them on a few occasions as children; noisy little brats, Sir George's sons, Gregor and Gavin, their indulgent father's pride.

'He looks like a vagrant to me,' the other replied. 'Shall we tie him across his nag and take him to the Sheriff in Lanark?'

'Or shall we tie him to a tree and empty his pockets?' Gavin suggested.

'Empty them of what?' Gregor laughed, as he looked down at Mathew. 'Identify yourself, man.'

'No, boy,' he murmured. 'I will not.'

'Here's an impertinent one!' the youth chuckled. 'Then we'll identify you. We'll call you One-lamp. Now what are you doing here, One-lamp? This is Cleland land.'

'With respect, young man,' Mathew contradicted, 'it's a public highway across Cleland land. It leads to Carluke, and that's where I'm going.'

'You'll find nothing there to steal,' he retorted. 'We

don't want the likes of you here. Yes, let's strip him and tie him to a tree, Gav. Let him cook in the sun for a bit, while he waits for the militia.'

'No, boys,' the traveller said, with a hard edge to his voice that had not been there before, 'ye'll not be doing that.'

'And why not?' Gavin challenged.

'Because you're only a couple of cheeky laddies, in want of a good arse-kicking. Because I am a soldier of the King, honourably discharged from his service, and with paper to prove it. And because,' he chuckled, 'you don't have any rope, you daft little buggers! Now go on your way and learn yourselves some manners, or I might have to teach you. You wouldna' like that, I assure you.'

The Cleland twins tried to stare him down, their four eyes to his one, before summoning enough common sense to realise that they were facing a man of his word.

'We will see you later,' Gavin murmured, then turned his horse, in a tactical withdrawal.

'I do not doubt that,' Mathew murmured as he watched the pair ride off, 'not for one second.'

Chapter Two

BAPTISMS, MARRIAGES AND FUNERALS were all in a week's work for John Barclay, but it was a rare occasion for the affairs of his rural congregation to fit all three into a single day, even rarer for that day to be a Friday.

He had just buried old Sarah Mackay, gone to her long home after seventy-two years of constant complaints about her lot, yet unwilling to leave it when the time came. In an hour he would baptise baby Jane Fisher, three days old, but unlikely to live for a week, the doctor said. Later that afternoon, he would join together in holy matrimony James Stuart and Elma McGruther, before the result of their conjoining a few months earlier became too obvious.

The simple arithmetic of his day underlined a concern that had been with him for a few years. His community was in decline; slow, but undoubted. The wars had taken some, yes, but they had gone on throughout history, and still places like his had survived and even thrived. But the new era was different: the young men were leaving the village, many drawn east to Edinburgh or west to the upstart Glasgow whose docks were sucking labour to offload imports of cotton, sugar and most of all tobacco. Others were moving within the county, to work in the filthy, dangerous hellholes they called coal mines that were booming since the opening of those damned canals, and in the new factories that were part of what people were calling the Industrial Revolution.

Yes, the place needed new blood, but it was hard to see how it would come, or from where.

The minister was fretting over the future as he climbed up into the steeple tower. Carluke's parish kirk was in want of a beadle since old Jimmy Peebles had gone to live with his son in Monklands, in the same county but as distant as the moon to most of his former neighbours, and so the church officer's essential workload had fallen upon him. These included ensuring that the clock, a gift to the church by Sir George Cleland's grandfather, also George, was always wound, oiled and keeping time.

He reached the platform and inserted the long heavy winding lever into its slot, then turned it, laboriously, straining with the effort.

'Never force it,' old Jimmy had instructed him before he left. 'Otherwise ye'll bugger the works. Then ye'll hae tae get the clockmaker frae Hamilton and he will no' be cheap.'

Barclay was in his middle years and had never been a strong man, so forcing it was not an issue. As soon as he felt that the resistance was reaching his limit he stopped and withdrew the winder, pausing for breath before reaching for the oil can.

He had barely finished the lubrication when the loud click of a turning cog sounded in the tower, as the clock reached the top of the hour, the top of the morning. It had its own bell, separate from the one that sounded twice on

Sunday to summon the faithful . . . and those who were not, but kept up appearances . . . and when it rang, it was best to be some distance away.

The minister had no time to escape. All he could do was press his hands over his ears to muffle the twelve chimes and to lean as far as he could out of the slatted stone light vents that were set on either side of the face.

As he looked out, grimacing occasionally, he saw a figure, a man in a blue three-quarter coat of uncommon design, a grey shift and breeches. He could not see his face, not properly, but even at that distance he was struck by the quality of his black boots, so well polished that they seemed to shine in the sun.

The newcomer might have drawn a greater audience, for he was exceptionally tall, at least six feet high, but Carluke was at work and there was nobody else to be seen. He was leading a pony as he crossed the green space in front of the kirk. Its brown saddle gleamed as brightly as its master's footwear, and it was laden with two leather bags, one on either side, and two cloth-wrapped bundles. The pair paused to take water, the man cranking the village pump handle and drinking straight from the spout, his horse from the trough beside it.

Refreshed, they approached the church. The bell had finished its tolling, but Barclay realised that he still had his hands over his ears. He withdrew them, self-conscious even though he could not have been observed, and continued to watch as the stranger tied his companion to the post beside the gate, then gave it an apple taken from one of his pockets.

He glanced behind him, in a slightly furtive way that alarmed the minister, then stepped on to consecrated ground, heading up the pathway.

'Who can he be?' John Barclay muttered as he made his way down the stone steps. The newcomer bore himself with confidence and authority yet his dress, while odd by village standards, was not that of a person of importance.

The kirk was always open when the minister was there. Just as he emerged from the steeple tower, so his visitor stepped inside.

Even though the place was lit only from the outside, Barclay's gaze fell at once upon the scar. It ran from the centre of his forehead, downward, diagonally across his left eye, which its opacity showed to be sightless beyond doubt, and then his cheek, not quite reaching his ear. He was transfixed and might have looked at nothing else had the other eye not been so vivid and compelling as it fixed on him.

'So you're still here, Minister,' the man said, and then he smiled.

'Aye, that I am, by God's will,' Barclay agreed. 'And so are you, by the same divine agency from the look of you. Let's go over by the window so I can see you better, then you can tell me how I can help you. Not that I've got much time, mind; I've a bairn to christen at one.'

He moved into an elongated diamond of multi-coloured light cast by the stained glass.

'Whose bairn would that be?' the stranger asked.

'The father's name is Joel,' he replied, wondering why he should be asked. 'They're calling her Jane, after his mother.'

'That's a recipe for confusion, is it not . . . no' that big Joel was ever too clear-headed.'

'That's not likely,' the clergyman replied. 'The child is weak, and shilpit, no' likely to live. She's one of twins; the other was stillborn, poor wee mite.'

'Ah, what a shame. Big Joel the smith deserves better. He's a good soul. Still, miracles do happen, and I'm sure you'll be praying for one as you christen her, Mr Barclay.'

An eyebrow rose as he peered at the visitor; for all the light, he had his back to it and it was still difficult to discern his features beyond that great blemish.

'You would seem to know Carluke,' he murmured. 'How would that be and how would you know my name?'

'As for the latter, I can read. It's printed on the sign outside, in letters of gold. But apart from that I've known you for almost twenty years, Mr Barclay, since you came here to follow that grim old fellow Howitt, who put the fear o' God into all us weans. Am I that badly marked, sir, that you do not recognise me, after standing beside me as we buried my faither?'

As he spoke, a cold hand seemed to grab the minister's innards, and he began to fear a strange irrational fear. 'Turn around,' he said sharply, 'turn to the side, to your left so your face gets all the light and I can see it better, and no' just that scar.'

'I will,' the man laughed, 'but let me make it easy for you. I'm Mathew, Mathew Fleming. Has it taken you only six years to forget me?'

John Barclay felt his legs go weak; indeed he might have fallen had he not been able to lean on the christening font.

'Mathew?' he repeated. 'Mathew my boy, I'll never forget you . . . but son, you're dead.'

He saw that face, finally familiar, turn sombre in an instant and saw that one compelling eye turn cold. 'If that's the case, John,' Mathew replied, quietly, 'did I not just tell you that miracles happen?'

The minister pondered the question for many seconds before he countered. 'They may indeed,' he said, solemnly, 'but the raising of the dead is much more likely to be down to human error than the hand of the Almighty.'

'Whatever,' the resurrected exclaimed, 'why did you write me off as dead in the first place? Are you telling me that my mother thinks I'm gone?'

'Aye, and it near broke her heart.'

'Near but not entirely? She's still alive?'

'Of course. I think sometimes that whenever Armageddon comes, Hannah Fleming will be there, daring it to do its worst. Mathew, there was a letter, three years ago, from the Highlanders. It came to your mother; she brought it to me to read for her, and I have it still, in the parish records.'

'Where is it? Can I see it?'

'I think ye'd better. Come across to the manse with me . . . and bring your cuddy as well,' Barclay added. 'I asked Jessie to have a meal ready before the christening. It will stretch to two, and I always have some oats for travellers' animals.'

The minister's residence was set on the right of the church, built of the same hard grey stone and accessible from within its grounds, but Mathew led the untethered

Gracie the long way round rather than take her across the graves that filled them.

There was a post and a trough at the side of the manse. He tied her there, then followed his host in through the kitchen entrance.

Jessie was the minister's housekeeper, not his wife. She was ancient and had come to the parish with him. There were rumours, generated by a stranger in the inn several years before, that Barclay had been born on the wrong side of the blanket and that she was, in fact, his mother, but he was too respected in the community for that tale ever to be put to him.

The old woman eyed Mathew silently as he came in. No introduction was offered, and if she recognised him she kept it to herself. Jessie had two facial expressions, severe and less severe. There were people in Carluke who claimed to have seen her smile slightly, once, at a hanging in Lanark.

The two men ate at a table in a small room next to the kitchen; it faced south, across the green and down into the village and thus it was sunlit. The minister was in a rush to be ready for the baptism, and so there was no conversation for they both knew that Mathew's tale would be long in the telling. The stovies that had been their main course were followed by steamed pudding, and then, astonishingly to the newcomer, coffee, something he had never seen in his home village. He remarked upon the fact.

'Glasgow,' Barclay replied. 'There's all sorts of stuff coming in through that city that we've never seen before. Half the tobacco in the United Kingdoms is imported through there, so they say. Scotland is being split in two; there's the aristocracy and the lawyers in the east and the merchants in the west. Edinburgh might be our capital, but I doubt that it's our largest city, no' any longer. Our country's changing, young man, and places like this are under siege. If it wasna' for Sir George Cleland, Carluke would be full of nothing but the old and the useless.'

'I had a conversation with his sons just outside the village,' Mathew remarked, quietly.

Mention of the twins made the minister frown. 'I know those brats,' he said. 'I should; I baptised them. And I look down at them every Sunday beside their father in the Cleland pew, whispering through the sermon. Hopefully Sir George will correct the pair of them out before they're grown men.' He glanced across the table and smiled. 'Your tone suggests they enjoyed the conversation rather less than you did.'

'That might have been the case; had it been a year or so ago, in another country, they wouldn't have enjoyed it at all. Indeed their father might tell them to be careful who they cheek at the roadside. There'll be a few of Wellington's veterans making their way. If they cross the wrong one, at the wrong time and place, they could wind up in a hole in the ground and their fine horses gone for sale in some town along the way.'

'I'll pass that message on, Mathew, tho' I doubt it'll do much good. Those boys are Sir George's only weakness. Another laird might have sent them off to school, in England maybe, but he won't be parted from them, not since Lady Cleland died seven years ago. Instead he has tutors for them who teach them a'thing but manners.'

He rose from the table, suddenly. 'Excuse me,' he said then strode from the room. Mathew waited, growing impatient. Now that his fear for his mother had been lifted he was anxious to see her, and not just her either. He could almost see her house, just round the bend beyond the tavern, with Lizzie Marshall's family home a little further down the same street.

Lizzie. How would she take to the man who was returning to her, much different from the impulsive boy who had left to serve King George, for money rather than patriotism? What would she think of the scar? Would it repel her, as it repelled him every time he had to look at himself in a glass?

Barclay's return broke into his thoughts. He held in his hand a letter, in its envelope, which he laid on the table before his guest. Mathew recognised the regimental crest on the outside, above the words, 'Mrs Hannah Fleming, Carluke, Lanarkshire, Scotland'.

'I'm going to christen the Fisher bairn,' the minister told him, 'and say an extra prayer for her. Who knows? Maybe your return's a sign from God that a' things are possible. While I'm gone, son, read that. We'll talk when I get back and then I'll take you to see your mother. We don't want you turning a corner and her falling over wi' shock.'

'True enough,' he conceded.

He waited until the door had closed before drawing out the letter, and unfolding it.

It, too, bore the regimental badge and was written in the same clear copperplate as the address, but it was smudged in a few places, as if its author had been careless with the blotting paper, or had been rushed. It was dated the twenty-second of June, eighteen fifteen, four days after the Battle of Waterloo.

Dear Mrs Fleming,

I am writing to you in great sorrow, to advise you of the sad news that your son, Corporal Mathew Fleming, was a casualty in the great and decisive battle that was fought against the French here in the United Kingdom of the Netherlands.

Corporal Fleming led his company of men bravely into the fiercest of the fighting, where he sustained a severe wound, while himself killing one of a group of French attackers who were attempting to break though the line. That they were unsuccessful was due to the heroism of Corporal Fleming and his company, who played an important part in a great victory. It is now clear that the power of the French is broken and that Napoleon can no longer continue as Emperor.

Sadly, I am advised by the regimental surgeon that Corporal Fleming's wound has proved insurmountable. I knew your son personally, and admired him, so be assured that I grieve with you in your loss. It may be small consolation, but you should know that his sacrifice has not been in vain and that his nation will be forever in his debt, and of course in yours.

I am, madam,

Yours faithfully,

Victor Feather, Captain.

Mathew stared at the paper, incredulous, as he took in its contents.

'Captain Feather,' he murmured. 'What did you do, you amiable idiot?'

Oh yes, he knew the captain, a young man, no older than himself but from a very different background, the fourth son of a baron and a pupil of some English school called Harrow, of which he was always scathing.

Captain Feather had been popular with his troops, because he was a friendly fellow with no airs and very few graces, and also because he was one of those officers who listened to his sergeants and corporals, and who recognised that they knew at least as much as he did, nay, undoubtedly more, about the business of front-line fighting.

Mathew thought back to the long and terrible day, the climax of the Waterloo campaign. Yes, he had seen Feather, brandishing his sword and urging his men to hold firm as Napoleon's agile and rightly feared Voltigeurs raced towards them.

Then, a very little time later, in the confrontation that still disfigured his dreams, he had been wounded and out of the battle. Apparently out of life too, it seemed, according to his commander's letter.

It came to him that he had never seen the captain again after the field of Waterloo. A few days after the battle, he had been told, Feather had been appointed to Wellington's personal staff, plucked instantly from the line. The letter to his mother must have been written in haste indeed, a fine thing for the lad to do, Mathew conceded, even if the news he sent had been wrong . . . understandable but tragically wrong.

He cast his mind back three years to the hazy moments when he had begun to emerge from a period of which he could remember nothing but darkness and pain, sometimes severe but often reduced to a dull ache by the administration of something that he learned later was called laudanum.

'You're a hardy man, Corporal Fleming. I've known very few men to suffer a wound like that and live.'

Those were the first words he could recall during his slow awakening, uttered by the regimental surgeon as he stood, looking down upon him in his wood and canvas bed.

'Are you telling me I'm not dead, sir?' he had croaked, drawing a laugh.

'Can you feel anything?'

'A sore belly.' He had grimaced as he spoke.

'Then consider yourself lucky. The dead feel nothing.'

'What happened?'

'You were wounded, nearly four weeks ago, in the battle they're calling Waterloo. You're a hero, man, you and those that weren't as lucky as you. We've seen the Corsican off for good this time.'

As soon as he had spoken, Mathew remembered: the French infantry rush, the bodies falling under musket fire, the survivors engaging at close quarters, and that wee leaping bastard, rushing on to his bayonet yet twisting at the stroke and . . .

'You were ripped open,' the surgeon had explained, graphically. 'The blade got into your liver. All I could do was stitch you up, feed you opiates, and wait for you to die.

I told your captain as much. And yet you didn't; you must be made of leather yourself, saddler.'

'There now,' he whispered as he stared at the letter. Indeed, Feather had been told he was as good as dead; he had known that, yet he had forgotten. The stuff they had given him had muddled his mind.

They gave him more after that, more than perhaps he had needed, for he had developed a craving for the drug, and had claimed to be still in pain for many days after it had gone for good, until the surgeon had seen through him and sent him back to the regiment, with a note to the colonel that his duties should be light.

And so they had been, until they had ended altogether with his second wounding.

He was still absorbing the shock when John Barclay returned from the Fisher baptism. He stood in the doorway that led to the hall, and to the manse's reception rooms.

'Mathew,' he said, quietly, 'I want you to come with me. There's someone in the parlour who'll not believe me until she sees you for herself.'

As he stood, he realised that his heart was pounding, as if he had been thrust back into battle and the French were charging. He took a deep breath and followed the minister across the hall.

Barclay paused at a door on the right, opened it and then stood aside. 'Go on,' he insisted. 'This should be a private moment.'

Chapter Three

HANNAH FLEMING WAS A stoic, born and raised. At some point in her childhood, when she had complained about the want of possessions that other village children enjoyed, her Presbyterian father had told her sternly, 'That which Fortune has not given, she cannot take away.'

Mathew Russell was quoting his own grandfather, or so he told her, never having heard of Seneca the Younger. Whatever the source, Hannah carried the message with her into adulthood, repressing her feelings with a degree of ruthlessness, and enduring everything that life threw at her.

She was brought up on farm labourer's wages in a village called Overtown. There was no parish school and so she grew up illiterate, as her parents had been, doing light work on the farm until she was apprenticed as a seamstress at the age of twelve.

Her father had been a friend of a man named Walter Fleming, the grieve in the farm where he worked. The Fleming family were better off than the Russells, and they had four sons, a mirror for Hannah and her three sisters. One of them was a young man with prospects; he was an apprentice saddler and could look forward to a good living as a tradesman, since that skill was in short supply in rural Lanarkshire. His name was Robert, and he and Hannah were more or less forced into an acquaintance by their respective parents.

She was indifferent to him, but she had been taught to believe in Fate, and so she accepted that he was hers. They were married when Hannah turned twenty-one, and moved to Carluke, almost a metropolis by comparison with Overtown, where the local landowner had promised there would be enough work to give them a decent living.

He was as good as his word, and Robert prospered, for all his developing fondness for male company in the alehouse. Hannah minded this not at all, as it allowed her to take on part-time work in her own trade and, in addition, freed her of his company for some of the time.

Five childless years went by, and Hannah had begun to think that she was barren, when she fell pregnant. She was no more excited by that prospect than by anything else in her life . . . until her son was born. When the midwife placed the squalling, wriggling, newly washed bundle in her arms, Hannah stared at him and made a great discovery, one that had passed her by for all of her twenty-seven years: love.

Her feelings for the child were so overwhelming that she thought her heart would burst.

And yet they were hers and hers alone, not to be shared with her husband or anyone else. To the rest of the world, she remained impervious to emotion, but when she was alone with her Mathew her eyes shone in a way no one could have imagined.

At first Robert had argued over her choice of name, wanting his son to be named Walter, after his own father, but she had told him, 'When you give birth, my man, you can give the name as well, but until then . . .'

She had hoped for more offspring, but when it became obvious to her that Mathew was to be her only child, she had no difficulty in coming to terms with that situation. She focused all her attention on him, making the boy her life's work. Nevertheless, she instilled in him a deep respect for his father (she was fond of Robert, who was a kind man in spite of his tendency to enjoy a tipple), making him understand that there was one head of their household and it was he.

She was determined also that the boy would grow up literate, and numerate. Her own lack of letters bothered her not at all, for she knew everything that she felt she needed or wanted to know. However she realised that the world was changing and that it was important for the new generation to have access to books, and news journals, even though very few of those found their way to Carluke. She was encouraged in this by the new parish minister, John Barclay, who had come to the charge to replace the Reverend W. G. Howitt, a man so grim and forbidding that none of his parishioners had ever plucked up the courage to ask what his Christian names actually were.

Where Howitt's sermons were rooted in the spirit of John Knox, Barclay brought a new enlightened view to the parish, and worshippers filled his church by their own choice rather than out of duty or fear. He spoke of a new world, and of things that were happening in it, of Napoleon

Bonaparte, of the Prince Regent, of the fledgling United States of America; he was an educator as much as an evangelist and Hannah knew that she should raise her son in his image as far as she could.

She came to know his housekeeper also. The two women were two generations apart in years, but similar in nature, and so they forged an understanding, if not a close friendship. It was sound enough for Jessie to tell her, and her alone, of her true relationship with the minister. She was in fact his maternal grandmother, her daughter having married very young, to a merchant from Stirling. She had died giving birth to John and his father had left it to Jessie to bring him up, living only just long enough himself to see him off to theological college.

She knew of the rumour, of course. 'If people want to prattle, mistress, let them,' she instructed Hannah. 'They've little enough to fill their lives so let them find amusement where they may.'

The other pillar of Hannah Fleming's life, and of her son's, was George Porteous, the schoolmaster. Old Howitt had done double duty as dominie as well as minister, but when Barclay arrived following his death, he persuaded, nay instructed, the kirk elders that education was too important to be entrusted to a layman.

Porteous was appointed on his recommendation; the two men had met at university and were of the same generation. With his arrival, the village school became a place of enlightenment; he did not believe in beating children into learning, and asked only that his pupils do their best. 'If they do not,' he told Hannah when she enrolled Mathew, 'they are punishing themselves, so there would be no point in my adding to their pain.'

Under his tutelage, every child in the village and in the area around learned to read, write and count, and by the time that Mathew reached his teenage years, Carluke had more literate and numerate children than it had adults.

Through those years Hannah watched her son grow with huge pleasure, but kept it to herself, admitting only to quiet satisfaction when he won the school's dux medal at the age of twelve, even though the dominie pronounced him to be the ablest pupil he ever had.

It was then that she was guilty of the only selfish act of her life. Both the minister and the dominie were keen that Mathew should progress to Lanark Grammar School, a 600-year-old institution that was held up proudly as one of the finest in Scotland. Its alumni included General William Roy, and Robert McQueen, who had gone on to become the notorious judge, Lord Braxfield, but Hannah refused point-blank, her stoicism never more evident.

'It's ower faur for the laddie tae go,' she declared. 'Asides, we a' have our place on God's earth and Mathew has his. It's no' for him or us tae put on airs and graces, but tae be content with the station into which we're born. He'll be apprenticed to his faither and that's an end o' it.'

George Porteous was furious. He went directly to Robert Fleming and asked him to overrule his wife. The saddler simply looked at him as if he was mad and shook his head. John Barclay did nothing. By that time he knew that nothing could dent her obduracy. Instead he and Porteous made a secret pact to continue the boy's education between them, as best they could.

But the fact was that Hannah's pronouncement was a sham. Distance was no issue; the school was little more than five miles from Carluke, the boy was strong and well-shod and on days of foul weather, the minister had offered to take him there and back in his small carriage. Nor did she object to personal aspirations, for she had bettered herself by her marriage to Robert.

The simple truth was that Hannah could not bear to be parted from her boy, not ever. Her husband, while stolid, was no fool, and knew that perfectly well, but he was happy with the prospect of his son as apprentice, and so as soon as his age allowed, Mathew was formally indentured, as required by law, for seven years.

That time, or most of it, passed peacefully. News of the wider world and the wars against the French made its way to Carluke as it did to everywhere else, but with no talk of invasion it meant little or nothing to the rural community.

Until the time when everything changed and Hannah's world was shattered.

Mathew had been a good apprentice, and his father a good teacher. By the time he had turned eighteen, he had learned all aspects of leatherwork. He could make a saddle that was just as fine as any his father had ever fashioned, and the boots and shoes that he was allowed to make for his mother were, she insisted, a more comfortable fit than his. The day was fast approaching when the sign over the workshop that read 'Robert Fleming, saddler' would be changed to 'Robert Fleming & Son'.

The other side of his life was settled too. He and young

Lizzie Marshall, the daughter of a neighbour family, were within two months of each other in age; they had been through school together, and Sunday school too. She was a pretty girl, with many an eye cast upon her, but hers were only for Mathew. There was an understanding between them, of which Robert and Hannah approved heartily, even if Sadie Marshall, the girl's mother, had fanciful ideas that her daughter might marry 'a professional gentleman' rather than an artisan, whatever his skills.

Mathew was less than six months short of becoming a tradesman when his father died in his sleep.

While Hannah mourned her kind-hearted husband, quite genuinely, he had been gone for no more than a day before her focus turned to the future.

Two days after Robert's funeral she called on Sir George Cleland's factor, a Borders man named Philip Armitage. She said that she intended to employ a time-served tradesman, Hugh Hinshelwood from Lanark, to supervise the completion of her son's indentureship, and trusted that work would continue to come from the estate.

But Armitage had moved fast. He had allowed no period of grace.

'I am sorry, Mistress Fleming,' he told her abruptly, 'but I have already employed Mr Hinshelwood myself, on Sir George's behalf, on a full-time basis. Henceforth he will undertake all of our saddlery work, and that of the tenant farmers.'

In that instant, three-quarters of the business of what would have been Robert Fleming & Son had vanished. Then Armitage twisted the knife.

'Of course,' he continued, 'Hinshelwood will require somewhere to work. You will be aware that the premises that your late husband used were rented from the Cleland estate. I sympathise with your situation, but I am afraid that I will require vacant possession, forthwith.'

'Can he do that, Mother?' Mathew asked when she told him.

'Aye, son, that he can,' she replied. 'He's the factor; he can do anything he pleases.'

'Then I'll put him out of business;' he declared, hotly. 'I have faither's tools and his skills. This cheil might have the estate work, but he'll hae none o' the rest. Time served or not, I'll set up as a bootmaker and cobbler. I ken all the tenants; they'll come to me, and once I have care o' their feet I'll tak' the rest in time.'

'And where will you work from, son?'

'From the cottage.'

She shook her head. 'The Cleland Estate is our landlord. Armitage'll no' have you takin' Hinshelwood's business. We'll be on the street as fast as we're oot the workshop. Mak' yer shoes, if ye can, but mak' no disturbance.'

'Has faither left any money?' the boy asked.

'Now the funeral's paid, there is fourteen pound and six shillings. A wee bit tae be goin' on with.'

She saw the alarm in her son's eyes. 'But our leather stock is low . . .'

'Then we must do what we can,' she replied. 'I'll ask Mr Barclay tae try tae find you a place where ye can finish yer time. In the meantime, I'm still the best seamstress in Carluke.'

The very next day, the Cameron Highlanders' recruiters arrived in the village. The day after that Hannah's wealth had increased by five pounds, but her only son was gone.

And three years later, she received the fateful letter that told her he was dead.

The arrival of a mailbag was a regular occurence in Carluke; the practice was that it would be delivered to the village shop, which was owned by Sadie Marshall's family, and its contents distributed from there, even those which were intended for the ancient Bernard Scott, the village's only literate Roman Catholic, whose son was a seaman in the Royal Navy and a veteran of the great battle of Trafalgar.

Hannah had never received a letter directly; all of Mathew's mail had been addressed to Lizzie, and its contents had been intended for them both. Therefore as soon as she had opened the cottage door in answer to John Barclay's knock, and had seen what was in his hand, she had known what it would tell her. Sadie's brother, Peter Wright, the shopkeeper, had guessed too, and rather than giving the letter to his niece, had entrusted it to the minister.

When Barclay read it to her, he was the one with tears in his eyes, not Hannah. She would shed hers in private, as she had done on many lamplit nights since her boy had gone.

'Will they bring him hame?' she asked, breaking the silence that had fallen when he had finished.

'No,' he answered, quietly.

'They did for yon Lord Nelson,' she observed, 'or so I heard it said. Pickled in a barrel of brandy, he wis.' She sighed, after that unique moment of bitterness. 'But no' for the likes of us, Meenister.'

'There aren't that many barrels in the world, Hannah,' he sighed, 'not for all that have fallen over the last ten years and more. The army looks after its own; its chaplain conducts many funerals.'

When she opened her door again, almost three years later, and saw Barclay standing on the step, she had no thought of déjà vu. A visit from the minister was not an everyday occurrence, but if he had something that needed doing or saying urgently, he was not one for summoning when he could walk a few yards himself. And yet, as she looked at him more closely, she saw that this was no ordinary call, that there was no tear in his vestments that needed repair. There was something about him that she did not recognise, until she looked more closely and saw an excitement in him that he could barely contain.

'Whit can I dae for ye, Mr Barclay?' she asked, with only a little curiosity in her tone.

'You can come with me, Mistress Fleming, to the manse, and on the way there, I would ask you to look into your heart and find the generosity to forgive a young man who made a terrible mistake.'

Chapter Four

MATHEW STEPPED INTO THE minister's parlour. The curtains had been thrown wide open and motes of dust danced in the beams of sunlight that flooded the room.

'Mother.' It was all he could say.

There had been some grey in her hair when he left, and in his absence it had all turned silver. She was thinner too, about the face, but still had the olive complexion that she had given him, and still stood tall and straight.

'Come here, ma bairn,' she murmured.

He crossed the room and hugged her, tight against his chest, feeling her tears through the light cotton shirt that he had brought from France. They were short-lived though; she eased him away from her and looked up at him, appraising him, taking in the changes, the lines of manhood in his face and most of all the great vivid scar.

'What have they done tae ye, laddie, thae awful Frenchies? Yer poor eye!'

'They've done less tae me than I have done to many o' them, truth be told, though I take no pride in it. Very few come out of war without wounds to body and to soul. I've had mine, but I'm still walking and breathing. As for my poor eye, you should look in the bright side; it's the reason I'm home before my term of service was due to end. Don't worry yourself, Mother, for the other eye still sees well enough for two, and I never was the prettiest cheil.'

'You were tae me, laddie, and ye still are, scar or no scar,' she smiled, 'and even if ye seem tae have lost yer Lanarkshire tongue for some strange new accent. Ye're reborn tae me, Mathew. Ah never expected tae see ye on this side again. Ach, that silly officer.'

'Don't blame Captain Feather, Mother,' he said. 'He's a good fellow, and a real gentleman. They really did think that I was for the wooden waistcoat. The surgeon told me as much himself.'

She frowned. 'How could I blame the man for what he thought was an act o' kindness?' Then she added, 'But it's no' my forgiveness that's important here.'

Before he could respond, she carried on. 'But son, could ye no hae written tae let us know ye'd recovered?'

'I did, Mother,' he protested. 'I wrote to Lizzie from the field hospital as soon as the surgeons would let me have pen and paper; and then again, month after month after month. Yet I never had any reply. I deived the quartermasters about it until they were sick of the sight of me; every month they told me there was nothing for me. Now it seems that it was the mail in the other direction that was out of order, and my letters home that were misplaced. And if you all thought I was dead, well . . .' The sentence went unfinished.

'When I had no word from Carluke,' Mathew continued, 'for a time I feared that it might be the other way around, and that, God forbid, you or Lizzie might have passed over.

But then I realised that could not be, as I knew that somehow Mr Barclay would have got word to me if there had been a tragedy. So I trusted in him and I trusted in God to keep you safe.'

'Wis it a long journey home?'

'It was, because I made it long. I left the army with only a small bounty, barely enough to get me home. And so I worked along the way. I am now a field-certified saddler and shoemaker, Mother, officially, and a man of means.' He reached inside his shirt and pulled out his well-filled leather pouch. 'There's twenty-seven pounds and nine shillings in this bag, money I've earned in the long months o' my journey home.'

His quick frown distorted his scar. 'Is that man Armitage still here?' he asked.

'Oh aye,' Hannah replied. 'And so is Mr Hinshelwood, to the disappointment o' mony that remember the quality of your faither's work.'

'Then I will have a conversation with the factor. He's a practical man, as I remember. If Hinshelwood is not giving satisfaction, I'll give him an alternative.' He paused, and Hannah saw in his expression someone new to her; he was still her son, but more than she had ever imagined him becoming. He would never be the village laddie again, she realised, and she knew there and then that Carluke would never be big enough for him.

As if to prove it, he went on, 'But I will never be beholden to one man for my livelihood, never again. I'll work for Armitage, but it will be on my terms and conditions, no' his. If he's obdurate, I'll go straight to Sir

George. He was always a good friend to my father.'

His speech had indeed changed, as his mother had noted. He was using words that she had never heard and his accent was less country-hewn than it had been when he had left.

'I've learned a lot, Mother, and most of it from the French. They use much less leather than we do, and they have less waste. Their saddle design is much better than ours, and their footwear too, but it's the saddle that I believe can make our fortune.'

He smiled, and he was her boy again. 'Enough of that, though. There's someone else I must see, with no more delay. Will Lizzie be at her uncle's shop still?'

To Hannah's astonishment he took a pocket watch from his jacket and checked the time. 'Aye, of course she will. Mother, I will see you at the cottage. Lead Gracie there, will you? She's a biddable animal, and she'll give you no bother.' He kissed her on the forehead and turned towards the door.

'Aye,' she called after him, 'but Mathew, wait on, son.'

But he was gone, seizing the astonished John Barclay's hand in both of his, shaking it like a pump handle and bidding him, 'Thank Jessie for the stovies,' before rushing from the manse.

Chapter Five

THERE HAD ALWAYS BEEN a defiant streak in Elizabeth Marshall. From her earliest days, her mother had described her as a wilful girl, requiring obedience to be beaten into her, and defiance beaten out. She had gone about it wholeheartedly too, until her father had intervened.

The beatings were always inflicted in private with no witnesses, but Lizzie had gone crying to Mathew after one particularly severe thrashing, when she was six years old, and shown him the weals that her mother's strap had left on her body. When he saw the marks on his youngest child, after being advised by Robert Fleming, Thomas Marshall had finally put his foot down, heavily, and declared that from that time on, physical punishment was a matter for him and him alone.

In the years that followed, Lizzie came to know well enough what it was to 'wait till your faither gets home', but when he did, whatever her transgression, the worst she ever received was a reproof. In truth those hurt as much as any beating, for she loved her father, and felt guilt whenever she incurred his displeasure.

Thomas Marshall was a self-employed carter, a solid,

reliable, honest man who looked after his family well (although never quite well enough for his wife). His closest friend was Robert Fleming, not unnaturally, since he shared those qualities. Also he had great admiration for Hannah, wishing that his own wife possessed her common sense and serenity.

Thomas had never seen Sadie as a bad woman, but he had always known that she had married him for security rather than love, and that she carried within her resentment that there had been no better catch around at the time.

After all, Sadie Wright was the grocer's daughter, and the grocer was an important man in any community. While she accepted that any sons of hers might follow their father into his occupation, she had greater ambitions for her daughter, her firstborn, and as it transpired her only surviving child. Those did not include marriage into the Fleming family. She had set her sights elsewhere, on the county town of Lanark, where there were many potential matches.

Lizzie's friendship with Mathew Fleming dated from their fledgling years, and Sadie had never approved. As they grew, the boy was always about the house, or she was always about his, coming back with tales of helping Mrs Fleming make potato scones, oven scones, pancakes, floury dough balls and other treats that were rare in her household; everything there came from the family shop, where Sadie had a theoretical account, although when it was rendered it was for a fraction of what it might have been.

She would have banned Mathew from her premises, but Thomas would never have permitted that, since he was alehouse cronies with Robert Fleming, and so, all she could do was bite her tongue as the two children became adolescents and grew into adulthood: bite her tongue and hope.

Lizzie was aware of her mother's pride and prejudice all along, but she would have none of it. When she went to Lanark Grammar School and Mathew did not, she sensed a wave of relief from her mother, but it amused her more than anything else. Whenever Sadie asked her if she had met any 'nice young men' at the school, she would play her by being coy, not answering directly, and building up false hopes with the occasional fluttering eyelash.

In fact there were no 'nice young men' at Lanark Grammar as far as she was concerned. They were all town mice and she was country, as they made very clear.

Not that she was bothered for a second; she and Mathew had their lives mapped out. As soon as he completed his apprenticeship, he would speak to her father, asking for her hand. There was no doubt what his answer would be, and her mother would not defy him and parade her prejudice for the whole village to see.

It all ended on the morning that Robert Fleming did not awaken from his sleep. When he went to break the news, Mathew found her in the shop. It had passed from her late grandfather to her uncle, Peter Wright, and she had gone to work there on leaving school, not as a counter servant . . . her mother would not have that . . . but as his bookkeeper, a job that needed filling, since Uncle Peter was clumsy with numbers.

She was in the small office at the back when the door

opened and she saw Mathew standing there. He needed to say nothing.

'Your mother?' she whispered.

He shook his head. 'No, Lizzie, ma faither. He's gone.'

The days that followed were a blur. The funeral, Hannah's meeting with Armitage, and the collapse of her plan to secure Mathew's future.

'I'll ask my father,' Lizzie proposed. 'Perhaps ye could work wi' him.'

'No, love,' he replied. 'That wouldn't do. I must look after Mother as best I can, but anything your faither could give me would be taken from somebody else. Ah maun make my own way.'

And that way of his had taken her from him. There had been tears, hers and his, when he told her about the men from the regiment. The minister had been appalled. Her father had offered, unbidden, to take him in and find work for him. But Mathew had seen no other way and she had never known him so determined.

'Will you wait for me, Lizzie?' he asked. 'Seven years is a long time, Ah ken, but who knows, maybe Ah can send for you when the fighting is over.'

'Of course I'll wait, my love. I'll wait until a horse trots across the top o' Lanark Loch, if that's what it takes.'

So he had gone. But the fighting did not end as swiftly as they had hoped; instead it went on, and on, interminably. The seat of battle moved from country to country, and there was no prospect of leave for common soldiers. Yet Mathew wrote, to her and through her to his mother.

When each letter arrived from the mail coach, she

would read it alone, to make sure the news was good, then take it to Hannah . . . Mother Fleming, she called her . . . and repeat his latest story for her, even embellishing from time to time.

She read through the years and their seasons, in the cold of winter by the light of the fire and the lamp, in the damp-ness of spring, in the warmth of the summer . . . although there were years when there seemed to be none, only a continuous grey drizzle, until the days grew short again.

Mathew's tales were never of fighting and war. Instead they were like a personal diary, with descriptions of his surroundings as he wrote each one, so that the two women learned of the heat and dust of Spain, of the lush green French countryside and latterly of the flatness of the Netherlands.

There was no blood in those letters. They were warm, kind and optimistic, full of hopes and dreams of a shared future that was growing closer, letter by letter . . . until without warning that future was ripped away from her.

When Mr Barclay and Mother Fleming came to see her, she refused to listen to them at first, as if not hearing the news she had read on their faces would somehow make it go away. But eventually, it came to her that her world was at an end, and she wished that she could have been a witch, so that she could curse Napoleon Bonaparte, Captain Feather, an unknown, unnamed French soldier, curse all of them to death.

She fell into mourning, and for all that had happened since, she had never stopped, and knew she never would.

Six years, almost to the day, after Mathew's departure,

she was sitting in the small office behind the shop, when the door opened.

A man stood there. He was tall, as tall as her Mathew had been, but thicker in the chest. He would have looked like Mathew too, but for a great scar that marred his fine appearance, and but for the fact that Mathew was dead. His legs were thick in his breeches and his hands were big and used to strong work; she remembered hands like those running over her body in the last hours she and her lost love had spent together, as she betrothed herself to him in the most meaningful way she could imagine.

He stood there, almost as high as the lintel of the door, looking down on her as she sat behind the desk, in her long, enveloping dark dress. And then he spoke.

'Lizzie,' he said, 'my captain was a good but headstrong man, always wanting to charge too soon. He had the heart of a lion but the brains of a donkey. He never questioned a thing, and rarely got a story straight, so when he was told I was like to die, he took it as a given thing.

'The surgeon, he was a man of certainty too, so at least he held back from burying me until he could be certain that I was quite bereft of life,' he smiled, 'which as you can see I never was.'

Lizzie's world swam before her; her eyes lost all focus and she slumped forward across the desk. She was aware, but only vaguely, of him calling her name, and then of his arm around her shoulders, raising her up and pressing a cup of water to her lips.

'There now,' she heard him say, as she came back to full consciousness. 'It's all right. My face scares bairns the first time they see it, but it's me nonetheless.'

He was crouching beside her, his one eye engaging both of hers.

'Oh Mathew,' she sighed, and then began to cry, great heaving sobs, of pure anguish that tore at his heart.

He pressed her against his shoulder. 'There now, my love,' he murmured in her ear. 'I'm not a ghost, but flesh and blood. It took me a while to live with my scar, and with another that cannot be seen. I hope that you will too, in time, and forgive my appearance.'

'Forgive?' she mumbled, into the cloth of his coat. 'Man, it's you that must do the forgivin'.'

She eased herself away from him and stood up from her high-backed chair, so that he could see her properly as she was, her left hand with the gold ring on its third finger, and her belly, heavy with child.

Chapter Six

To the immense relief of Peter Wright, a quiet, timid man who hated any sort of fuss or upset, Mathew and Lizzie left the shop. Together, they walked the short distance to Hannah Fleming's cottage, in silence all the way until they came upon the pony, tethered to the gate.

'She's yours?' Lizzie ventured, tentatively.

'Yes. This is Gracie. She's brought me all the way from France. I got her in payment for two pairs of boots for a man and his wife. She'd probably have been their family's dinner by now if I hadn't. They eat horses over there. In truth, they eat all sorts.' He shuddered. 'Even snails.'

He wondered why his mother had left her outside the garden until he saw that what was once a small green area had been dug up and planted, with turnips on one side and potatoes on the other.

Mathew had dreamed many times of the moment when he would step across Hannah's threshold once again but never had he imagined such circumstances. Gravel chips crunched under his heels as he walked up the short path that divided what had become the vegetable patch. As he reached the door he raised his hand to knock, automatically, then corrected himself and opened it instead.

Unlike the manse, the front of the cottage faced north. Impending rain had darkened the sky and the small living room was gloomy, so Hannah had lit a lamp and placed it beside the empty fireplace. She was absent as Mathew ushered Lizzie inside, but at the sound of their entry she appeared, from the kitchen.

'The kettle's on the range,' she said, as if they were ordinary visitors, 'and there's broth in the pot. You'll hae things tae talk about so Ah'll go and mak' whatever ye'd like.'

'Tea would be fine, Mother Fleming,' Lizzie replied. Mathew simply nodded.

'Sit down, Lizzie, please,' he murmured, as his mother left them alone.

She shook her head. 'I'll stand for now. Mathew,' she blurted out, heat in her voice, 'why in the name of God did ye no' write?'

'I did,' he replied. 'As He's my witness I did, as soon as I had recovered enough. I wrote, and after that, as often as I could, for the mail service was less frequent as we were moved around after the war had ended. Less frequent,' he added, 'but no less reliable, we were told.'

'How did you come by your wound?' she asked, her earlier flash of anger dissipated.

'I was struck in the liver, in the last battle, by a French foot soldier, just as I . . .' He stopped short, not ready to confess to killing another man, even in battle.

'The surgeon told me he had never seen a man survive a thrust like that. He decided that it was either a miracle, or that the liver must be able to heal itself in some way. Being not much of a Christian he decided on the latter; I believe that I am the anonymous subject of a paper that he published in a learned journal of his profession . . . or so he told me anyway.

'It was a close-run thing, but now I'm as strong as I ever was, apart from having no taste for liquor of any kind. Even beer makes me sick.'

'Your liver?' Lizzie repeated. 'Not your eye?'

Mathew laughed, bitterly. 'That? No, that was a scratch, by comparison. France was in turmoil after Napoleon finally fell, and we were not the most popular citizens out there. Some disaffected fools attacked us, and in the process,' he reached up and touched his scar, 'I was branded. The same surgeon that mended me before sewed me up a second time, then declared me *hors de combat*, and my colonel discharged me from my service. The last letter I wrote you was to tell you that I was about to make my way home.'

'How long did you travel?'

'The best part of a year,' he told her, 'but I worked along the way, to make as much money as I could, for Mother, and for you . . . for you and me. There was a bounty, but not much. Six years at war had left me with nothing, other than the tools of my trade, and a head full of ideas.'

Finally Lizzie sat, in what had been Robert Fleming's chair, beside the cold hearth. 'A year,' she whispered. 'Then even if ye'd come straight back, by the fastest coach, it would have been too late.' She looked up at him.

'It was, what,' she frowned, 'a year and a half after the

letter that told us you were dead, that a gentleman came calling, at my mother's invitation.'

'Who?' Mathew asked, impassively.

'His name is David McGill. He's a clerk on the Cleland estate.'

'Davie McGill? I know him. He settled my father's bills whenever he presented them to the factor. He must be ten years older than you and me, but I remember him as a good man, courteous. My father often wished aloud that he was the factor rather than yon man Armitage.'

'David's those things right enough. He's good, he's courteous, he's kind, and when he asked me if I would marry him I settled for those qualities, thinking I would never know love again, thinking that you were gone.' Her brow knitted into hard ridges. 'Damn your mail service, Mathew!' she snapped. 'Damn your war!'

'And damn me for going in the first place?'

'Aye if ye' like, damn you too, for leaving me!'

His eye focused on the hearth.

'And damn me for being alive, and coming back to you?'

'No!' she retorted instantly. 'Not that! I've prayed every night for God to be keepin' you safe in his arms. You were my love, you are my love, but now I'm married to another man, and havin' his child. If only one damned letter had found me in time.'

'Maybe that was God's doing too.' He paused, and as she looked at him she saw a frown gather on his face, made oddly asymmetrical by his scar. 'But as John Barclay said to me an hour or two back, that which we might think divine is usually down to human intervention.'

'What do you mean?' she asked.

'Lizzie,' he replied, 'I have written many letters now, all to you, but I've never received one. How does the mail arrive in Carluke? How does it get to those for whom it's meant?'

'It comes to my uncle's shop,' she told him. 'The coach drops off a packet, and Uncle Peter makes sure that a' the letters go where they're intended.'

'It's delivered into your uncle's hands?'

'No, there's a box, wi' a padlock. The coachman has a key, and the other's kept in the shop.'

'Have you ever emptied the box?'

'No. That's done either by Uncle Peter or by my . . .' Her eyes widened and then filled with anger.

She rose to her feet, and would have run from the cottage if Hannah Fleming had not come in from the kitchen in time to hear their last exchange.

'No, lassie!' she cried out with enough authority in her voice to halt Lizzie in her tracks. 'You have your bairn tae think of. Sit ye back doon and tak' yer tea, an' a scone, or go hame tae your husband if ye'd rather.

'If something amiss has been done, then we've a' been wronged, all three of us. This is a matter that I will deal with, and I know how I'll go about it.'

Chapter Seven

PETER WRIGHT MIGHT HAVE been able to face down John Barclay across his counter, if he had called upon him alone, but in the face of Hannah Fleming's calm but piercing stare as she stood beside the minister, he had no chance.

'There is a concern, Mr Wright,' Barclay began. 'As you have seen, Mistress Fleming's son Mathew is returned from the war with Bonaparte, when a'body in the village thought him dead, thanks to a false report from France.'

Wright nodded, vigorously. 'In- ind- indeed,' he stammered. 'I fair took a turn when he came into the shop. No' that I recognised him, ye understand, no' at first, with that great blemish on his countenance. It was only when he demanded to see our Elizabeth that I realised who he was. I was inc- inc- incredulous, I do not mind confessing.'

'And why were you incredulous, Mr Wright?' The clergyman fixed him with the glare he reserved for the most brazen sinners in his flock. 'Was it because you thought he was returned from the dead? Or was it because you knew, in fact, that he was alive, but hoped would never be seen in this village again? One letter might go missing, sir, maybe more, yet after he recovered from his all but fatal wound,

Mathew Fleming must have written twenty times to Mistress McGill, Miss Marshall as she was, and it seems that not a single missive reached her.'

'I . . .' the grocer began, then stopped, staring at the floor.

'Did you withhold those letters wilfully?' Barclay snapped.

Wright shook his head. 'Not I,' he whispered.

'No, not you,' said Hannah, with unprecedented fury hissing in her every word. 'But your sister, that's another matter; Sadie, wi' all her airs, and her fanciful notions, who offered me nae condolence when Captain Feather's letter arrived three years ago, and who rushed her daughter intae marriage with a worthy gentleman as soon as she could.'

'You must ask her.'

'Oh we will, Mr Wright,' Barclay told him, 'but we know the truth of it already.'

'Sadie is a very determined woman,' her brother moaned.

'And you are a very weak man, and not worthy of the trust that is placed in you as keeper of folks' letters.' He looked at Hannah. 'Come, Mistress Fleming, we will call on Mistress Marshall and see what she has to say for herself.'

In any small community, word of mouth travels faster than fire. When Sadie Marshall opened her door on the minister and the brooding thunderstorm that stood by his side, it was clear from her expression that she knew why they had called.

But she was of stronger stuff than her brother.

'Yes,' she declared, defiantly, as the question was put to

her, 'I kept those letters from my daughter. It was my duty to her as her mother.'

She was much shorter than either of her visitors, only five feet high in her youth and stooped a little in middle age, but her eyes were full of sparks as she gazed up at them.

'With respect to you, Mistress Fleming, I never wanted Elizabeth wedded to a Carluke tradesman. I wanted better than that for the girl. In truth I wanted better than David McGill, but at her age, and given that she was spoiled goods, he's a reasonable match for her. But the last thing I would allow would be for her to be wedded to a cripple from the war.

'When I heard your son was dead, Mistress Fleming, I respected your loss, but in my heart I was pleased, as I had been pleased the day that Mathew went off to the army.'

'So you are saying,' Hannah murmured, 'that you welcomed the death of my husband, which brought that about?'

The other woman flinched a little. 'No, I'm no' saying that,' she protested. 'There but for the grace o' God; my Thomas is dear to me, and I wouldna be parted from him.'

'Yet you allowed Mistress Fleming to live under an even greater burden,' Barclay countered. 'You allowed her to go on believing that Mathew was dead, when in fact you knew full well he was not.'

'It was for my daughter's sake!'

The storm within Hannah broke. 'Rubbish!' she shouted. 'It was for yer own sake, for yer own jumped-up notions. Ye're a stupid, vain cratur, Sadie Marshall, and you always were. I've always kent that. My, wumman, a' the village has.

And cruel too. That was kent and a', the way you used to beat that poor lass when she was wee, until your husband pit a stop tae it.'

She saw surprise in Sadie's eyes.

'Oh aye, Ah kent aboot that. Lizzie telt Mathew aboot it; she showed him the marks you left on her erse. He telt his faither and my Robert telt your man. That's how he found out, no' from Lizzie, for she never said a word tae him. You never deserved a child as loyal as she was.

'Aye,' she raged, 'your cruelty was known, but I never dreamt it ran so deep as to let me live for three years thinkin' that my life's purpose was over, and that my boy was gone. You are a wicked, wicked woman, Mistress Marshall, but you may find that your sin has cost you dear, for when we left Lizzie she was saying that you would never speak to her again, or see your grandchild, after it's born, which I pray to God will happen safely, for as long as you live.'

'She'll know I did it for her own good,' Sadie murmured.

'No. She'll ken that ye did it for your own vanity.'

'And so will the whole congregation,' John Barclay boomed. 'You and your husband will be at church on Sunday.'

'Not Thomas,' the woman protested. 'He kent nothing of what I did.'

'But he will find out. You will tell him, and you will bring him to church on Sunday, where I will denounce you from the pulpit for the evil woman you are. After that, you will be an outcast in this village. No one will speak to you, other than maybe your husband and sons, but I cannot be sure even of them. Your brother, he'll be forced, finally, to stand up to you, if only for the sake of his business.'

'You can't do that,' Sadie wailed.

'Oh but woman, I can and I will!' the minister retorted, fiercely. 'Your daughter's first thought was to have you exposed in the stocks, to be mocked and pelted with ordure. I myself would be inclined to ask the magistrate to order that very thing.' He paused allowing her fear to take full hold.

'But you will be spared that humiliation,' he continued. 'This is not God's mercy, and it's not mine either. It's that of Mathew Fleming. He has forbidden that any such complaint be made on his behalf, and has persuaded your daughter to relent. He said that the last person to do him harm was executed for his trouble, and that now he believes that the greatest punishment is to live with the knowledge of your own self and of the kind of person the world sees you to be.'

'And my daughter? What of her marriage to David McGill?'

Barclay frowned. 'Right or wrong, that was celebrated, and pledges given, before God, but I know that He must be rightly displeased at your deception.'

Chapter Eight

MATHEW FLEMING HAD BEEN imagining his first night back under his mother's roof for most of the six years of his absence. In those dreams the place had been lit brightly, by lamps and candles, logs had been roaring in the grate and a roast bird had been on the table ready for carving. And, of course, there had been three places set.

He had never contemplated the way it transpired, he in his father's chair, and Hannah in hers, well fed on stew and boiled potatoes but afterwards staring into the hearth at a wood fire that was so reluctant to spark into life it seemed to be drawing heat from the room rather than giving it.

Over supper she had asked him about the war, but he had been reluctant to discuss it. 'Those things are not for this house, Mother, or for this village. The world is much bigger than you could imagine and much nastier than you would want to know. The prospect of possibly imminent death affects men in different ways, but it does not inspire chivalry or mercy.

'My officer, Captain Feather, was a fool in some ways, but he was sensible in others. He realised that if he looked after the men under his command, they would look after him. Sadly, he was the exception, not the rule.'

'Then be thankful for him, and for yon doctor. Those folk cared about ye, and a man cannae ask for more.'

'Can he not?' Mathew murmured. 'Lizzie cares for me, as much as she ever did, and yet look at our situation. If only I'd been less headstrong when those recruiters came calling.'

'No,' Hannah retorted, firmly. 'Ye did what ye did for whit ye thocht were the best of reasons, and that was good. If you reproach yersel' for it now, ye'll do so for the rest of your life and you will live and die an unhappy man. The money ye left me was consolation and it kept me in my home. It wasnae a' in vain.'

'But it didn't keep you for ever. How have you managed, Mother?'

She laughed. 'By workin', son. How did ye think? Did I no' tell ye I was the best seamstress in this village? Mr Barclay made sure Ah had plenty o' work, and so did Sir George, when he heard what had happened wi' the man Hinshelwood.'

'As well,' he sighed. 'My thoughts of sending money home soon came to nothing. There was no money, after I'd clothed and fed myself, and bought all the other things a soldier needs but must find for himself.' His face darkened.

'And it's how he finds them. There are things happen in war that I will not bring back here, but let me just say that if you are on the wrong side, then nothing is sacred, no property secure, no person inviolable. I would have nothing to do with any of that. At first my comrades mocked me for it, until they saw that I fought as well as they did, and better than most.'

'Ye were a corporal, thon letter said. Whit's that?'

'It's a petty rank, Mother; non-commissioned, they call it. I was discharged as a sergeant . . . not that the money was much better. In fact by the time . . .' He smiled.

'What?' she asked.

'Och,' he smiled, 'after my wound, when I could not abide beer, I used to buy it for my comrades. Hah!' he laughed. 'They drank rather more than I did, the damned sponges.'

'That's good.'

He turned his head and fixed his good eye upon her. 'Is it indeed?'

'Aye. It means ye looked after others, and that ye were a man o' respect. Amang them, amang yer own kind, ye were a leader. As you were there, at war, so you will be in peace. And if that eye is the price of you being at hame for good, then while I would rather ye had baith, Ah'll regard it as worth payin'.'

'I have never sought seek to lead,' he told her. 'I seek to serve, with the skills I've learned from my father and on my travels. But where?'

'Where?' she repeated. She was about to say more when they were interrupted by a knock on the door, just loud enough to be heard. Hannah looked at her son, lodged firmly in his chair. 'Whit are ye waiting for?' she asked. 'You're the heid o' this household now, Sergeant Fleming. You answer the door.'

'I'll never be that while you're alive, Mother,' he chuckled, but rose all the same.

The caller was a man. He stood half in shadow but catching enough of the light from within to be recognisable.

'Mr McGill,' Mathew said, loud enough for Hannah to hear. 'What can we do for you, sir?'

'I wondered if I might have a word."

Mathew wondered also; he wondered whether McGill had come for a confrontation, to put him in his place. But that thought vanished quickly, as soon as he sensed that the man was apprehensive.

'Of course,' he replied, solemnly. 'Please come in.'

He stood aside, to let their visitor enter. Hannah rose to her feet.

'Please, please, Mistress Fleming,' McGill said, 'sit down, sit down.'

'Would ye rather I left you two men alone?' she asked.

'No, Mother,' her son said, 'you'll not be banished to the kitchen in your own house. I'm sure that Mr McGill would not expect it.'

'Of course not,' he agreed.

Mathew pointed him to his own vacated chair and perched himself on a fireside stool. 'Well now,' he began, an invitation that was seized.

'First and foremost, Mr Fleming . . .' McGill began, and was waved to silence.

'Let's not make this more formal than need be. It's Mathew and David. Agreed?'

Their guest smiled, shyly, and some of his nervousness seemed to leave him. 'Yes, thank you,' he agreed.

'Mathew, whatever else, I am glad to see you, back home and well from the war. I was as shocked as anyone when that false report was received. As for what has happened since . . . I cannot find the words to describe what that woman has done. You are a victim, sir, and so is Elizabeth. I'd agree to any punishment you sought for her.'

'My mother and I are both content,' he replied, 'that retribution should be left to Mr Barclay. I think you will find when he gets up in that pulpit on Sunday that he will not be charitable.'

'What would you have done, in the army?' McGill asked.

'Hypothetical,' Mathew replied. His mother raised an eyebrow; she had no idea what the word meant and wondered where he had come by it.

'I never met the soldier,' he went on, 'who would have betrayed a comrade in such a way. All I can say is that I doubt whether such a person would have survived his next action.'

'What can I do?'

Mathew stared at him. 'You, David? Why should you do anything?'

'Because I know how the land lies. You and Lizzie were betrothed before you left, in the eyes of the whole village. When I was invited by her mother to call on her, she was in mourning for you. If she had known of your survival, she would never have accepted my proposal . . . and if I had known, sir, it would never have been made.'

'But the fact is that it was, and that it was accepted. What are you saying?'

'That if you ask me, I'll stand aside. It can be as if that awful report from Waterloo had never arrived.'

Inwardly, Mathew was close to being overwhelmed by

McGill's generosity, but he concealed his feelings. 'No, man,' he said quietly. 'It can never be. Lizzie is with child. Are you saying to me that you would let them both go, or that you would keep the child?'

'The child must be with his mother.'

'And his father, be he alive,' he said, 'and David, you look hale and hearty to me. More than that you are a man of substance, which I am not, not yet at any rate. Here is the truth. My mother raised me to believe, and my life has taught me too, that we can only play with the cards that we are dealt.

'Nobody can unwrite Captain Feather's letter, or undo Sadie Marshall's treachery. The poet Burns said, "Facts are chiels that winna ding," and that is true. If I allowed you to step aside, then you would be a victim too, and I would be less of a man than I would want to be.'

He paused. 'Tell me, have you offered the same to Lizzie?'

'No, not yet. This is between us.'

'Ah, but it's not. She has a voice and a view on what is right and what is wrong, and I believe I know her well enough to speak for her here. Your offer is noble; if we accepted it, then we would be less than noble, and neither of us could thole that. Tell me this too. If this came to pass, would you be happy, for the rest of your days? Be honest, man.'

There was a long silence before McGill shook his head. 'No,' he whispered. 'I love her, no doubt of that.'

'Then it's clear. How could we know true happiness, if ours was bought at the cost of yours? My answer, David, is, "Thank you, but no." I am reconciled to what has happened and so must Lizzie be. She'll have your child and the three of you will live happily for as long as God allows.'

'I do not know what to say,' the other man murmured.

'Then say nothing more,' Hannah Fleming told him. 'Ye've shown us the man you are, and we're both happy that Lizzie's in good hands.'

'Thank you, Mistress.' McGill rose to leave.

Holding a lamp to light the way, Mathew walked with him, to where his horse, in its carriage harness, was tethered. He examined the rig, as a professional. 'Some of these straps need renewing, man,' he said. 'You should attend to it, especially since you'll be carrying a bairn in this contraption.'

'Would you do it for me, Mathew?' McGill asked. 'It belongs to the estate, and that is the standard of Hinshelwood's work.'

'I would, if I were here,' he replied. 'But that will not be the case. I cannot stay here, David, man. I'll vanish as suddenly as I returned.'

'But this village is your home.'

Mathew shook his head. 'No, it is not. This village is where I grew up but for the last six years my home has been where I made it. It would not be right for me to stay here. Look at the havoc my homecoming has created, although I have only been here for a few hours.' He smiled in the lamplight. 'Had I known I was dead I would probably have stayed that way.

'As good a man as you are, you could never live comfortably here with me in this village. Nor would it be fair to Lizzie either. She will always be a good wife to you, but if I am not here it will be easier for her to forget that today ever happened.' He paused, then added, 'And I'm selfish enough to admit that it would not be fair to me either.'

'No,' McGill protested. 'None of this was your fault. Why should you suffer?'

'Why should anyone suffer . . . aside from Sadie Marshall. Between you and me, it's only Lizzie that stops me from pursuing her with all the rigour of the law. The stocks?' he scoffed. 'Left to me, I would see her gibbeted corpse hanging in a cage and being picked at by crows, like I saw in England on my way home.'

His face formed a distorted frown. He glanced at McGill, who was shocked by his sudden candour. 'Now you see why I must go, David. I'm not the young man who left here. I've seen bad men send good men to their deaths, then look on from their position of safety. I've seen my comrades pillage and rape, and done nothing about it.

'I tell you, and you alone, there's a part of me wants to cut Sadie Marshall's throat. I hate that man but he's been bred by war. So do not look for me in the kirk on Sunday, when she gets her verbal lashing from John Barclay, and do not look for me here again, not for a while at least.'

'Mathew,' McGill sighed. A hand fell on his shoulder, while the other raised the lamp to illuminate both men's faces.

'Look,' Mathew continued, 'I was all but dead after Waterloo. I suppose it was too much to expect that I'd return to a life just as it was, so I must move on, make another somewhere else. No' too far, though; I am still a

Lanarkshire man. My mother has people in Cambusnethan, near to where she was born, and that is where I will go. Her too, if she will come. I came back here with a plan for a future; it will go with me and if it works out, it will be the making of us both.

'Never think this means that you and Lizzie are dead to me,' he added. 'Far from it. Life is always uncertain, even in this quiet wee place. If times change and you and she ever need my help, John Barclay will always know how to contact me.'

'No,' McGill said, firmly. 'I respect your reasons for leaving, but please dinna cut yourself off from me. Write to me, let me know how things are with you. And dinna worry,' he allowed himself a smile, 'I will make certain that your letters reach me.'

Mathew watched him as he mounted the carriage and drove away; long after he was out of sight he stayed there, looking around at the place where he had grown to manhood, and to which he had returned, only to feel like a stranger. Finally, he shrugged his broad shoulders and went inside.

The very next day he left, to begin the life that he had been planning for almost a year, and to seek his fortune.

Chapter Nine

'YE' COULDNAE IMAGINE IT,' Hannah Fleming declared, as she looked around the reception room, larger and more lavish than any she had ever seen.

'In eleven years ye've come frae a Waterloo far away, tae another Waterloo here in Lanarkshire, if that's what ye really do plan tae call it. Ah'm very proud of ye, my son.'

'It is ironic indeed, Mother,' Mathew agreed, 'that two places so far apart should have the same name, with no other connection between them.'

'And a' this is yours?' She touched the fabric of a large armchair.

He nodded. 'Ours, Mother. It will be your home too.'

'But Mathew, Ah like our wee place in Cam'nethan. We dinna need onything bigger.'

He smiled. 'Mother, I spent six years of my life sleeping in a tent . . . if I was lucky; often enough we had to make do with the open air. I crave living space, and now that I can afford it, after eight years of hard toil, I will have it. If you want to stay in Cambusnethan, you may, but why cut off your nose to spite your face?'

'But this house is awfu' big, son; it's got an upstairs, it's got lamps built intae the wa's, and fancy paper on them too, and five bedrooms, and rooms tae bath in. No' tae mention places inside tae do yer business, and running water tae tak' it away.'

'And water heated by a boiler, Mother,' he chuckled, 'not a kettle, don't forget that.'

'But twa parlours, Mathew,' she exclaimed. 'Wha needs twa parlours?'

'I do. If I choose to meet with a customer or a supplier at my home, I'll have a private room for that purpose. The way we've lived until now, I can't do that.'

'And a' that land,' she persisted. 'It's only fine folk that hae hooses wi' a' that land.'

'Wars have been fought to change that situation, Mother,' he pointed out. 'There is a parliament in London to change that.'

'Aye,' she laughed, a rarity, 'and did ye no' tell me that fool Captain Feather's a member? That's a mark o' what that's worth.'

'Lieutenant Colonel Feather now; I will never forget the look on his face when I called on him on my first visit to London, and told him who I was. I told you, he remembered the letter straight away.'

She nodded. 'And he was richtly mortified,' she said. 'At least he had the guid grace tae send me his apologies. What an eedjit.'

'Victor's a fool to you maybe, but he's the right sort of man to have in Parliament, an ex-soldier with humanity in him, as is Wellington himself. They say that the Duke wept after the siege of Badajoz when he saw the bodies piled high.

I fought with these men, and I'm glad that they're showing interest in governing the country. And Mother, it is not a sin to have wealth. A man can be rich and righteous.'

'Och, laddie.' She paused, hesitated, then blurted out, 'Are we no' gettin' above oor station?'

'No, we are not,' he insisted. 'Mother, your days of taking in sewing are long since over, yet you do not seem to have accustomed yourself to that fact. Have I always been an obedient son?' he asked.

'Apart frae when you insisted on joining the army, aye,' she conceded, 'you have.'

'Then obey me, for once in your life. Let me move you in here.'

She frowned. 'If ye must. Ah'll come and live here, as your housekeeper.'

'No, ye'll come and live as my mother, I have a housekeeper in mind already.'

Hannah displayed her most inscrutable smile, but said nothing. Her son hesitated, but only for a second or two.

'We're not above our station, as you put it, Mother. I was a common soldier not an officer, but I can tell you that those commanders who were the most respected were those that had earned their rank through hard work at the military college, rather than those who claimed it through social status. I have what I have because I've worked for it over the last eight years, since we left Carluke, worked just as hard as they did. I have earned it. What would you rather I did? Hide it away?'

'Ah suppose not,' Hannah conceded, 'but ye must hae an awfu' lot o' money tae buy this.'

He shook his head. 'No, this place did not cost as much as you think. It was built by a man called Schultz, a Prussian. He was an inventor who had come to work in Glasgow, and much of what's in this house is of his creation. It has its own pure well and its water is pumped into the house by a steam engine, fired by a furnace in the cellar, then stored in a big tank in the loft. It also heats some of the water and stores it in a second tank up there. Whatever you want, hot or cold, it can be drawn within the house, not from a well-head outside. More than that, the heat from the furnace isn't wasted; there is a piping system that spreads it through the rooms. Can you not you feel it?'

She pursed her lips. 'Aye,' she said, grudgingly, 'it is warm in here for April.'

'See? I tell you, the man was a genius.'

'Then why were ye able to buy the place as cheap as ye say?' she challenged.

'Schultz died,' he replied. 'His family were all in Prussia and they instructed his lawyer in Glasgow to sell it as quick as he could. His lawyer knew my lawyer and it was offered to me, furniture and everything.'

'How did he die?' she asked, casually. 'Did he bile tae death in his iron bath?'

He smiled. 'Not exactly. He was in England supervising the building of a locomotive engine that he had designed. It exploded under pressure and he was killed.'

'Michty! So this hoose could blow up too?'

Mathew laughed. 'No, not a bit of it. Mother, I am not that daft. I had my own engineer check it over. It is safe, I promise you.'

'Mmm.' Hannah nodded. 'A comfort. It's no' that clever it'll kill us a'.' She threw him an appraising glance. 'It's closer tae Carluke too,' she observed.

'Waterloo House is within that parish,' he conceded.

'So Mr Barclay'll be oor minister again.'

'He will be.'

'And when we go tae his kirk we may see . . .'

'We may. Indeed we probably will.' He sighed. 'Time has passed, Mother; we have all become different people. David and Lizzie are happily married . . . although,' he paused, 'David's last letter had some news I wasn't going to trouble you with. Their second child, the wee lass they christened Georgina; she died last month, of the scarlet fever.'

'Och!' Hannah flinched as if she had been struck. 'Whit a thing. And after she miscarried wi' the other one. But the boy, he's a' richt, aye?'

'He's fine, from what David tells me. They call him wee Matt, on account of John Barclay making a mistake when he put his name in the parish register and spelling it with an extra "t". He's a strong healthy laddie, and good at the school too, his father says.'

'Then Ah hope they don't make the mistake Ah did. Ah hope they send him tae Lanark Grammar. Mathew, I dinnae allow myself tae say "if only" very often, but if only I had let you go there.'

'What would have been different?' he asked her. 'Father would still have died. The recruiters would still have arrived.'

'Aye, but ye'd have been a scholar then, on your way tae bein' a lawyer perhaps.'

'And away to Edinburgh, like Braxfield, to be an

advocate and maybe one day a hanging judge? No thank you. I put no trust in those people.' He put his strong hands on her shoulders. 'Mother, when I became indentured to my father, it was not only because it was what you wanted me to do. It was what I wanted to do as well. I've never regretted that.'

'No?'

'Not at all. If I was a lawyer I would still be scratching out a living. King's Counsel at thirty-three years old? I doubt it. But thanks to my trade and my skills, I was able to design a saddle based on those I saw the French and the Spanish use, and with professional help I managed to patent it.

'Now I have customers all over the nation, including the military. I have orders from America and from Europe, and even from France and Spain, ironically. I employ men, the most skilled men, to make them in a proper manufactory, not just one at a time in a wee workshop. I pay them good wages and I make a fortune myself. But to keep me humble, I still make my own footwear and yours . . .'

'And Margaret Weir's?'

His expression remained unreadable even in the face of his mother's raised eyebrow, a gesture that was for her almost coquettish.

'And Mistress Weir,' he conceded. 'She's a friend as well as an employee.'

'And she will be housekeeper here; am I right?'

'That is my intention.'

'Will she occupy the servants' quarters?'

'No,' he replied, 'one of the bigger rooms; that is my intention also.'

His mother shook her head, then lowered herself into the armchair she had admired earlier, directing her son towards the one that faced it.

'Mathew,' she declared, stiffly, 'will ye please stop using such guile. The whole o' Cam'nethan knows that ye're sharing Mistress Weir's bed. Well, ma cousin Elspeth does, and that's the same thing.

'There are some that disapprove, like that mealy-moothed auld weasel o' a minister and his dried-out wife, who probably allows him access tae her once a year, if he's lucky enough . . . or unfortunate enough, frae the look of her. But most folk say, "Why should they no?" when they finish their gossip.

'Mistress Weir's a widow woman whose late husband was a minister o' the Kirk. You are a single gentleman of means. Indeed, ye're seen as a catch.'

Mathew shook his head. 'I thought Cambusnethan was big enough to allow us a bit of privacy,' he chuckled.

'Then ye're a dreamer, son. There are no people more closely watched than beddable widow women, unless they be single men wi' a bit o' money.'

'You've told me what most people say, Mother. What do you say?'

'I say that Ah tried to bring you up tae be honourable, and Ah'm not sure ye are. If ye have feelings for this woman, ye should see that employing her and bedding her at the same time might lead the wrang sort of people tae think the wrang thing, and even to say it.'

'Meaning?'

'Meaning that one or two stupid, nasty people are calling

her a hoor a'ready,' she said. 'No' in my hearing, mind, but they are, Ah ken. If ye move her in here, what will they say? More still, if we will be goin' back tae Carluke Parish Church, will she come wi' us? If she does, how will that look?'

'Should I care?'

'Of course ye should,' she snapped. 'Ye could be in the next pew tae Mr McGill and his wife, with your fancy wumman. Wid that be richt? Better, much better, for you, and for Lizzie too, if she was yer wife. Mak' her an honest woman, Mathew. She has your respect, that I dinna doubt, but she's entitled tae the respect of a'body else.'

He sighed. 'Very well, Mother. I'll give it some thought.'

'Do that, or mair folk will be saying what some are saying a'ready, that you live in hope o' an accident or an illness befalling David McGill, so that you may slip back in where ye were before.'

Chapter Ten

MOST PEOPLE SEEING MARGARET Weir for the first time described her as handsome, rather than pretty. She had strong features and brassy red hair, a gift from an Irish grandmother, she said, and her build was solid rather than sylph-like. Those qualities underlined rather than disguised an inner strength that had drawn Mathew Fleming to her, when she had come to him seeking employment in his factory in Netherton three years before.

The interview had been brief. After she had given him her life story . . . born in Glasgow twenty-eight years earlier, to a tailor and a housemaid, educated at a parish school, married to the Reverend Samuel Weir at the age of twenty-three and widowed two years later . . . and shown him references, he had handed her a copy of Jonathan Swift's *Travels of Mr Gulliver*, and asked her to read a chapter, then given her a line of numbers and asked her to add then multiply them.

Both tasks accomplished, he had employed her as a clerk, as he had known he would the moment she walked through the door. Margaret was a highly capable woman, who would be a help to his business, and more than that, he had taken an instant liking to her, as had happened occasionally in the Cameron Highlanders, when a recruit had arrived with a personality that breathed new vigour into war-tired, jaded soldiers.

Since arriving in Cambusnethan with his mother, his tools, his skills, his plans and his pony, but little else, Mathew Fleming had become a slave to constant toil. In little or no time, he had established himself as a boot and shoemaker and repairer, at prices he knew his customers could afford. At the same time he had engaged a draughtsman to produce proper copies of his plans for the new saddle that he had already begun to manufacture, and then a lawyer to secure patents for the design.

His masterstroke had been to take a gamble on the cost of a journey to London . . . by the fastest stagecoach . . . and to run to ground his former captain, Victor Feather. Not unnaturally, the officer had been astonished to see him and even more astonished to learn how his career had progressed.

Feather retained considerable influence as an aide to the Duke of Wellington, who had been as much a politician as a soldier. He arranged field trials for the sample saddle that Mathew had taken south with him, and within two months the first order had arrived, for a quantity beyond his imagination. With money borrowed from the British Linen Bank, he had equipped his factory in Netherton, close to Cambusnethan, and had watched his business grow, working on production along with his men, and ensuring that the promised quality was maintained at all times.

Soon, the Netherton Saddle, as it became known, was in

demand not only by armies but by even more civilians, as word spread, by mouth but also by announcements placed in *The Times* of London and in the fledgling *Scotsman* newspaper in Edinburgh.

Mathew knew nothing but his business as it grew, and that suited him as it helped put the tragedy of his loss in Carluke out of his mind, although never out of his heart.

One of the virtues that endeared Margaret Weir to him very quickly was that she worked whatever hours he asked of her without complaint. They were close within six months, and intimate within another year, initially within the confines of a small bedroom that Mathew had equipped for himself above the factory, but later also in Margaret's house in Gowkthrapple, a short distance from the factory.

He liked her smile. There were few lights in his life, beyond his mother, his business, and one of whom he would no longer allow himself to think.

David McGill was a faithful correspondent, as he had promised he would be, but his letters, while usually cheery, were sometimes difficult to read, as Mathew found himself searching between the lines for hidden signs that all might not be well between him and his wife.

The growth of his relationship with Margaret eased that for him. He was able to think of Lizzie, if not less frequently, in a more detached way. There had been a second significant benefit. He dreamed no longer of the last great battle and of the Voltigeur dying on his bayonet.

'Would it offend you, Mathew,' Margaret asked, 'if I asked for time to think about your proposal?'

'No,' he replied. 'Not at all. It's a decision that any

woman has a right to consider properly.'

She smiled; a shadowy smile, under the lamplight in the drawing room of his fine new house. 'Just as you considered your offer of marriage for some time before making it?'

He laughed at her retort. 'Touché. And I apologise for that. If it means that you reject me, though, I'll be sore hurt. Please, take all the time you need, as long as you accept in the end.'

'Now I'm sorry,' she said. 'I was jesting. I know the way your mind works, and how important your business is to you; your fault, if such it be, is that you think of nothing else. Of course I accept . . . although . . . in the circumstances it might have been better had you asked me a few weeks back.'

He stared at her. 'What are you saying?'

'I'm saying that we may have a wedding and a christening in the same year. I'm having your bairn, sir. I had been about to tell you, when you surprised me.'

'Then we'll go to Carluke at once,' he exclaimed, 'and see John Barclay. The banns will be called, and we'll be married as soon as they allow.'

'A quiet wedding, yes?'

'Any kind you like.'

'That's what it will be, then.'

A thought leapt into his head. 'Would you mind,' he asked, 'if I ask David McGill to be my groomsman?'

'Why should I mind? I'll be a friend to his wife, I promise, as she should be to you by now.'

He took her hand. 'You are right, Margaret, as well as generous. My mother . . . who will be very pleased at our news, by the way . . . thinks the same: enough time's past, and our lives are what we've made of them.

'You and she have got the same good heart, my dear, and I'm proud you'll be my wife.'

Chapter Eleven

DAVID MCGILL HAD NEVER been to a wedding breakfast before. As many did, he wondered aloud about the oddity of the name, given that the meal was in fact a dinner, until John Barclay explained, 'Likely it has nothing to do with the time of day; rather it goes back to Catholic days when it was the custom to fast before the nuptial Mass.'

The ceremony had been brief, and to the point; the minister had dispensed with hymns, and restricted himself to brief prayers and to the formal exchange of promises, before declaring that the couple were man and wife. Mathew had expected no one other than invited guests to be present, and so he was surprised to see up to two dozen in the church. Most were his village contemporaries, but the most surprising was Sir George Cleland, who was seated, smiling, in his family pew. The old Laird was well past seventy and rarely left his estate, other than for occasional journeys to Edinburgh, and so his presence was seen as a tribute.

'How did he know?' Mathew whispered to his groomsman as he waited for Margaret to join them before the altar.

'How do you think?' McGill murmured. 'I told him. When I did he insisted on attending. He still has a down on

Armitage for taking the estate business away from you. It was done without his knowledge or consent; by the time he learned of it, you were gone.'

The reception took place at Mathew's mansion. A cook had been hired for the occasion, with the encouragement that if she impressed, her employment might become permanent.

The guests were few: the minister and the ancient Jessie, said to be aged well over ninety, and dressed in her inevitable black, regardless of the occasion, Hannah, her brother Hector, from Cambusnethan, with his wife, and David McGill, with his eight-year-old son. Lizzie was absent, as she had been from the marriage ceremony. Her husband had explained that she was expecting another child and with a history of miscarriage had been warned by her midwife against exercise or excitement. Sir George had been invited at the kirk, but had pleaded tiredness.

Mathew arranged the seating so that he faced his young near namesake across the table. He had never met young Matt McGill and found that he wanted to get to know him.

'I hear you're doing well at the parish school, young man,' he said as the Cullen Skink was served. 'Mr Porteous is a very fine teacher; he did well by your mother and me.'

The boy nodded, vigorously. 'We all like him, Mr Fleming,' he replied. 'He makes us laugh sometimes, at the things he writes on the blackboard.'

'Mr Fleming, is it? Well, I am all for children showing proper respect for their elders. But now that has been established, with your father's approval I give you permission to call me Mathew.' He winked at the minister. 'After all, you and I bear almost the same name; indeed they tell me we would absolutely, but for Mr Barclay's occasional fondness for Madeira wine.'

'Not true, not true,' the clergyman insisted. 'It was a moment's aberration, no more, a slip of the quill; Jessie does not allow me Madeira wine until after six o'clock, and I do the registrations in the morning.'

'It's what you had the night before that bleared your eyes, I'll wager,' Mathew laughed. 'Whatever, for all the misspelling, you and I are bound by name, young Matt McGill, and if ever you have need of my service, it's yours.'

As the dinner progressed, Hannah Fleming was bound to admit to herself that her son fitted into his new house as if it had been built for him. She was struck, too, by his natural empathy with the McGill boy, and by the subtle way he offered him respect as his father's son.

Most of all she was pleased by her son's choice. Fond as she had been of Lizzie, she had reconciled herself to their misfortune years before, and had seen Margaret, with her common sense, her skills and her resolve, as an ideal partner for him. Now that it had come to pass, to see her new daughter-in-law blooming in her new status . . . even if she was a little thick in the waist . . . warmed her heart.

The evening ran its pleasant course, until there was a ringing from the hall, where the bell at the front door hung. The champagne toast to bride and groom, proposed by David McGill, was barely over. Mathew checked his pocket watch. 'The carriages are early,' he murmured, with a rare show of annoyance that Margaret's day should be less than perfect. 'They can damn well wait.'

He rose from the table and strode from the room, ready to issue a reproof, only to find, as he threw open the door, a young man standing, cap in hand, in a state of some agitation. A small coach was standing a few yards away, its horse tethered.

'Mr Fleming,' he began, 'I'm sent by Mr Armitage for Mr David McGill. He's tae come at once. I was gi'en a note for him.' He handed over an envelope, unsealed.

'What's up?' Mathew demanded. 'Is it Mrs McGill? Is she poorly?'

'Ah canna say, sir. It'll be in the note.'

'Very well,' he snapped. 'Step into the hall and wait. I'll speak with him.'

He returned to the dining room, and from the doorway beckoned McGill to join him in the reception parlour.

'This is for you,' he said, handing over the note. 'That lad that brought it is in a fair old lather.'

He watched his friend as he opened it and read it, watched his frown grow deeper.

'Is it . . .' he began.

McGill read his mind. 'No, it's not about Lizzie. It's Sir George. The old man died in his armchair not three hours ago. Armitage wants me to go to the estate, "to help with arrangements", he says, as if I was the funeral undertaker. Still, I must go, out of respect for the old Laird, if nothing else. Mathew, can you send the boy home in the carriage with Mr Barclay?'

'Of course I will.' He sighed. 'The poor old man. I was touched that he came to the wedding, even more now it turns out it was more or less the last thing he ever did.

He was a good patron to my father, and a good friend of this parish.'

'Aye, he'll be mourned,' McGill agreed. 'We'll grieve no' just for his passing but for what will come after. Now we'll have Gregor Cleland as the master of the estate. He's the older of the twins, if only by two hours.'

'I have not seen nor heard of him for a while,' Mathew said, 'not since our paths crossed, literally, eight years ago. He must have been fifteen then. How has he grown?'

'Into a first-class wastrel,' his friend replied. 'Armitage will have his hands full now, and he never was the surest helmsman. Still, it could have been worse.'

'How's that?'

'But for those two precious hours, we might have had Gavin!'

Chapter Twelve

MATHEW CLAPPED HIS ONE eye on the Cleland twins once more, at their father's funeral. They were side by side in the family pew, where the old Laird had sat at his marriage a few days earlier. The pair were identically dressed and looked like bookends in search of a library.

Mathew's place was five rows from the front, nearest the aisle, so that they could not fail so see him as they followed the coffin outside after the service, to the grave that was waiting for it within the Cleland plot. They were clad in black with velvet trim, both of them, but their expressions were those of mere participants rather than mourners.

These boys have not grown up, Mathew thought.

He had no sure notion of which twin was which, although the order in which they had been greeted by John Barclay led him to assume that Sir Gregor, the new baronet, was on the right. Neither gave any show of recognition as they passed him, although he fancied that the presumed Gavin's blink and quick frown was a sign that a spark had been lit.

At the graveside, Mathew stood a few yards away, in an exclusively male crowd, alongside the Sheriff of Lanark,

Robin Stirling. The two had met a year before at a reception given by the Lord Lieutenant of the county. They watched as the old man's oaken box was lowered into the grave by his sons and four other, older men, family members, Mathew assumed.

As the crowd dispersed, and after he had bid the amiable Sheriff good day, the thin-faced factor Armitage approached him. 'Mr Fleming, is it?' he ventured.

'It is, as I think you knew.'

'McGill said you would come.'

Mathew felt his hackles rise. 'Mr McGill knows me well. He's the closest friend I have. I hope that his situation will be unaffected by the change at Cleland Hall.'

'There's no reason to suppose it will be, I assure you. I hear you have become very successful, Fleming. You are a credit to your late father, they say.'

'And to my very much alive mother,' he retorted, 'whose livelihood you threatened less than ten years gone. I have not forgotten that, Mr Armitage, nor will I ever.'

'Mr Fleming, upon my word, I regret that; it was a bad choice on my part. Your father did say that if anything went amiss with him you were ready to take over. I should have trusted him. If you wish the estate business returned to you, then of course I can arrange that.'

'And throw another man out of work? I thank you, but that's not my way of doing, sir. In any event, my life has followed a different course.'

As the conversation progressed, Mathew began to realise a truth that had escaped him until that morning. He saw that with his business success and his wealth had come something else. Within his own county, he was a man of influence; people deferred to him, and when their number included the factor of the shire's biggest estate, it was significant.

The man persisted. 'But if Hinshelwood was to be dismissed simply because his work was below the standard the new baronet requires . . .'

'How many ways of saying "No" do you possess, Mr Armitage? I have only one at my command, but it is definitive.'

The factor showed him a thin smile, which only made Mathew even more wary of the man. 'The saddles that you made for my new master and his brother are very satisfactory,' he ventured. 'There may be commissions for more.'

'Thank you,' Mathew replied; he had assumed that Sir George's order was for his sons, and wondered how they would react if they ever recalled that their manufacturer had once threatened to kick their privileged arses.

'In that case,' he continued, 'I trust you will see that the account is settled promptly. It was held back because of my wedding, and further because of the funeral, but my wife will be sending it to the estate within the week.'

'Of course, sir; I will instruct McGill.'

Who is many times the man you are and should be in your job, Mathew thought but did not say.

Chapter Thirteen

As ARMITAGE HAD PROMISED, the bill for the saddles was settled promptly. However the further orders at which he had hinted never materialised.

The loss of that custom was of not the slightest concern to Mathew. Indeed there might have been a marginal benefit, since he had given Sir George a generous discount, and would have felt obliged to continue it.

The emotional peaks and troughs of the two contrasting services within Carluke Kirk soon became only memories as Mr and Mistress Fleming of Waterloo House established their domesticity. In the weeks that followed, Margaret bloomed. She continued to support him in his business, travelling to Netherton with him on most days of the week to help with the accounts and with his ever-growing correspondence. When he told her that after the child was born he would need to find three people to replace her, there was little jest in his words.

For as long as Margaret was comfortable with it, they entertained. The cook had passed her test, and a house-keeper had also joined the staff. Mathew had taken to heart his lesson from his meeting with Armitage, learning from it that influence was beginning to shift from the exclusive grasp of landowners into the hands of manufacturers. Although he still regarded himself as a craftsman he realised that he was one of the new industrial breed, and he had become determined to be a significant presence among them.

Sheriff Stirling was a regular dinner guest at Waterloo House, as was Baron Dalzell, one of the senior noblemen of the county, and a few others, men of position and respect within the economic community that was growing bigger in and around Glasgow year by year. Mathew had no specific agenda, but his common sense told him that he must have a voice that might be heard in considerations that might affect his company.

While the guests were all male, that being the nature of the community that Mathew sought to address and influence, Margaret always took her place at the dinner table, as hostess, but also as a participant in discussions that ensued. This was a private and personal test that Mathew had set for his guests. Any who appeared irritated by the fact that a woman should express a view on public and business affairs, or who were patronising towards her, were crossed off any future guest list.

In the months following their marriage, he and his wife began to look at what might lie ahead for the company. He was aware that its strength lay only in a single product, and so they began to discuss also an expanded range of goods.

'People are travelling more,' she remarked, one evening. 'Did you hear what your newest acquaintance, Sir Graham

Stockley, said last week over dinner, or were you taken up with your crony, the Sheriff?'

'Probably the latter,' he admitted. 'What was it?'

'It was a vision of the future, he said, and not too far ahead either. He sees a time when stagecoaches will be replaced by carriages, with iron wheels, set on rails, and drawn by great steam engines called locomotives, that move much faster than horses, and never tire.'

He smiled. 'I hope they are safer than the one that killed the builder of this house.'

'They are. There is a man called Stephenson, apparently . . .'

He nodded. 'Yes, I know. The first proper railways are in existence already, I believe, in north England. Stockley was merely repeating what many expect: today railways are mostly for hauling coal, but soon they will carry people, many of them, and at a low cost. They say that by the end of this century all the British cities will be linked by them, but I believe that it will happen even sooner.'

'In that case we should plan for it,' she said. 'As these railways develop, travel will come within the means of folk who have never been able to afford it before. People who travel need baggage if they are going any distance. We should make it for them: cases, valises, hand baggage.'

Mathew took no convincing; he accepted her proposition at once. 'Then let us do it,' he said. 'Let us try the market, in a small way. If these products are to be successful they must be like the saddle: light, portable and easy to use. I will get to work on some designs, and have some samples created.

You are right, Margaret; the railways will mean cheaper travel and that will change the world.'

He smiled, as broadly as she had ever seen him.

'What's amusing you?' she asked.

'The way your red hair twinkles in the firelight,' he replied.

'Don't tease me. What is it?'

'Simply this. It happens that Stockley's interest in the railways is more than casual. You know his main business is mining coal in a place called Coatbridge, on the other side of the county?'

'Yes, my late husband called it "hell on earth". Coal mining is a filthy business, he said.'

'And so it is, but families are fed because of it, and Stockley, to his credit, tries to make it as tolerable for his miners as can be.'

'So he's not just a man rich from the sweat of others,' she chuckled.

'No, he is a kind man, with an eye to the future, as you said. Coal is not his only interest: he mines ironstone also. Now he has a grand plan, to use them both. There is a new process, he tells me, called hot blast, which means that iron can be made using much less coal, at a fraction of the cost. Sir Graham will use that to set up a foundry in Coatbridge, to manufacture parts for the new railways.

'And,' he added, 'he has offered me the chance to share it. He wants me to be his partner in the new venture.'

Her smile vanished, and what he called her 'business face' was set in place. 'In what amount?'

'Equal. Fifty per cent. We will provide fifty per cent of

the initial capital between us and his bank will advance the rest. He has a full order book already from Stephenson in England, and from others.'

'Why you?' Margaret asked. 'He must have other wealthy friends. The man barely knows you.'

'True, but he knows that I have acquaintances in London. He perceives an advantage there.'

'I see. But what is the cost?'

'Five thousand pounds, from each of us.'

'Mathew,' she exclaimed, 'that's a fortune. It's nearly all the money that the business has available.'

'I can borrow half of it from the British Linen Bank; that has been agreed already. What do you say?'

'Are you certain this is a good venture?'

'As certain as I've ever been. These blast furnaces and their moulded iron will be the stimulus for all sorts of things, not just locomotives.'

'Then do it. You've never been wrong yet.'

Two weeks after Mathew signed the agreement with Sir Graham Stockley, in late November, Margaret went into labour. Her pregnancy had been uneventful. He had wanted to engage a specialist doctor from Glasgow, but she had insisted that Henry Lindsay, the local physician, and Mistress Blyth, the midwife, had seen enough children into the world to know what they were doing.

The child was a boy, but he chose an unfortunate place to arrive. Margaret felt the first contractions ten days after she had been told she would, in the back of Mathew's carriage as he was driving them both to the factory in Netherton. He took another road and headed straight for

Dr Lindsay's rooms, but even as they arrived at his door, their son made his first appearance in the world.

After the midwife had done her work, Mathew carried his wife inside, while the doctor took the baby. 'That was a close-run thing,' he murmured, as he laid her on the bed in the surgery. As he spoke he noticed the blood.

He drew Lindsay across. 'Doctor. What's this?'

The physician shooed him away to admire his son then bent to examine his patient. 'She has a small tear,' he said when he was done. 'Just the one, though, and it will heal fast, wi' a stitch. He's a big bairn, your laddie.'

Mathew was bewildered. His life had been one of method, skill and organisation; everything worked to a plan. Spontaneity did not come naturally to him.

'What do we do?' he asked. 'I cannot take her home in the carriage.'

'No,' Lindsay agreed, 'that you cannot. They must stay here, until Mistress Fleming heals, then you can take them both home.'

Work forgotten, Mathew stayed with his wife and child for the rest of the day. Margaret was drowsy, and still in pain from her speedy delivery of such a large baby. The doctor explained that it would be unwise to give her laudanum, as the drug might find its way into her milk. She accepted that without complaint, and her husband watched as she put their son to the breast for the first time.

The baby had his mother's red hair, he thought, as he looked at them in the lamplight. The rest of his features were crumpled and unfathomable, but his body was long, an early sign, Mathew hoped, that he might grow to his father's height.

He stayed until after the second feed, then left them both to sleep and drove his carriage home. The business was not a worry to him. He had a good foreman, and he had sent a message to him advising him of what had happened, and that he should take temporary charge as they had planned.

Hannah was waiting for him in Waterloo House. 'Where is Margaret?' she asked as soon as she saw that he was alone.

'Taken to her bed in the doctor's hospital, her and our child. Happy day, Granny.' He hugged her to him.

Over dinner, he explained what had happened, and the unusual site of the baby's arrival. He grinned as he told the story, with relief rather than humour, but his mother did not.

'Bairns are best born in the mither's ain bed,' she declared.

'Another piece of homespun wisdom, Mother?' he suggested.

'No. A truth that every midwife knows, and maist women who've had a child will confirm. Better, too, wi' a doctor nowhere near.'

'Lindsay would be offended to hear you say that, but he did arrive very late in the day. All the work was done by then.'

Hannah drew him a severe look. 'His perhaps. Yours and Margaret's is only jist beginning, and it'll gang on as long as ye live.'

'And we'll be proud to do it, proud parents both.'

'What will ye cry' him?' she asked.

'That we have still to discuss. Margaret was too tired for any subject to be raised.'

'After you then?'

'No. After my father, perhaps, but there are many Roberts in the world, and maybe another would only add to the confusion. But I won't choose alone; it'll be Margaret's decision as much as mine. Now, let's toast them both in that fine ginger wine of yours, and then I'm for bed. I have never been so tired since I left the army.'

It may have been the ginger wine he had drunk, it may have been the blood he had seen, but that night, Mathew's dream of his newborn son was infiltrated by the return of an old enemy. For the first time in his recent memory, for the first time since Margaret, he was visited by the Voltigeur.

Forcing himself awake, he sat up in bed, bolt upright, sweat-covered, in damp bedlinen, yet cold and shuddering, with a feeling of dread and an ache in the spot where the Frenchie's sword had pierced him.

The clock on the mantelpiece showed only ten minutes past five, but he knew he would find no more sleep that night. He bathed and shaved, forcing his mind to dwell only on his new son, and running over names that he might suggest to Margaret. He was certain of one, but there was another possibility that might require a little tact when he put it forward.

The cook was still asleep when he went downstairs, so he went into the kitchen, lit the lamps, and cut a slice from a load baked the afternoon before. He spread it with his mother's damson jam . . . not only the best seamstress in

Carluke, Hannah had been, by common consent, its best jam-maker.

Still hungry he spread another slice, filled a pewter pot with milk, and set both on a tray that he carried one-handed, leaving the other free for a lamp to light the way through to his own parlour, the room he had taken to calling his study.

He lit all of the lamps and candles, so that he had enough light to read. A low fire was burning in the grate and he chose to sit beside it, putting down his tray on a small table. Before settling down he crossed to his desk and picked up a folder of papers.

They included copies, sent to him by Stockley, of firm orders from the Robert Stephenson company in Newcastle, for components and wheels for new locomotives. He had never seen a locomotive, but as he had explained to Margaret, he knew of their potential. As he looked at the orders he realised their profitability also, and trusted that the Stephensons had the funds to pay them. If they did, and the cast-iron business grew, then he and Stockley were on the verge of a new level of wealth.

He had been reading for an hour, making a note here and there, when he was startled by the sound of the doorbell. Mathew had never worried before about the relative isolation of his house, but the arrival of an infant had awakened all sorts of new considerations within him, even making him reconsider his refusal to have firearms in the place.

He picked up a heavy metal poker from the fireplace and went to answer the call, hoping that it had not awakened his mother.

Mathew did not recognise the young man who stood there as he opened the door, but he did know the look on the face of a messenger who was fearful of the reception his news might be given.

'Yes?' he said, more roughly than he might have.

'Ah'm frae Cam'nethan, sir, frae Dr Lindsay. He says ye need tae come richt away. Yer wife's been taken badly.'

Two things had made Mathew Fleming a very good soldier. He was a deadly shot with a musket or a pistol, and even more important, he never panicked. And so the feeling that swept over him was completely new to him. He felt his legs go weak, and he grabbed at the doorpost for a moment to steady himself.

'Whit is it, son?'

His mother's voice came from behind him, from the tip of the stairs. He turned and saw her standing, in her long nightgown, candlestick in hand.

'It's Margaret,' he answered. 'She's not well, the doctor says.'

'Then we maun go. Ah'll be dressed in a minute.'

'You have no need to come, Mother.'

'Oh, but Ah do. That man Lindsay's no fool, and no' one tae panic either. God forbid, but ye micht need me, and the bairn too.'

'Very well,' he agreed, 'but hurry.'

He looked at the messenger. 'How did ye' get here?'

'Ah ran, sir. It's what Ah dae. Ah'll awa' back the noo'.'

'Can you harness a horse to a trap?'

The lad nodded.

'Then go round the back to the stable. It'll be the first

box you come to, a black horse. Not the pony, mind. She's a very old lady and does nothing but graze these days. Do that and you can come back with us on the back of the carriage. You'll have to hang on tight though.'

He was waiting for them with the rig when they came out, both mother and son in heavy winter coats. He saw the look in Mathew's eye and made a decision on the safety of hanging on to the back of a coach driven by such a man. 'Ah'll just run back, sir.'

'If you insist.' Mathew locked the house then handed him a sovereign. 'Thank you for your trouble, if not your message. Call on me in Netherton and you'll have a new pair of shoes as well.'

He turned and held out a hand to help his mother into the carriage, only to have her brush it aside. Hannah Fleming was sixty years old but still supple.

'Dinna' be hard on the horse,' she murmured as he eased on beside her and took the reins. 'It's no' his fault.'

He tried to keep her caution in mind as he drove; indeed he had to, for the sun was well short of rising, the light was poor, and the road was rutted by recent rain. Even so, the animal covered the miles from Waterloo House to Cambusnethan as fast as ever it had.

There was one light shining in the room above the surgery as they arrived. Mathew secured the rig to a post and made for the door; it opened before he reached it, and Dr Lindsay stepped out to greet him, in great distress.

'Mr Fleming, Mistress Fleming . . .' he began.

'What is it?' Mathew demanded

'Childbed fever,' his mother murmured, beside him.

Lindsay nodded. 'Aye, I fear so. Puerperal fever, it's properly called, but it's the same. I've never seen its onset so fast, though, or seen it develop so quickly.'

'I knew it,' Hannah sighed. 'When I heard where the bairn was born. Cleanliness is next tae Godliness, and the seat of a carriage is far frae both.'

'Probably,' the physician agreed. 'I promise you, sir, that the midwife and I are believers in hygiene.'

'What can be done for her?'

'Nothing, I fear; it's in her blood, sepsis. She's a strong woman, but still she's burning up.'

'Can I see her?'

'Yes, you should, without delay.'

'And the bairn?' Hannah asked.

'He's well, but that's another crisis. His mother will give him no more milk and he should have a wet nurse.'

'Can ye find one?'

'I'm not sure, and yet it's urgent. A newborn baby's a fragile creature.'

'I can.' Hannah Fleming turned to her son as she spoke. 'Go tae your wife,' she ordered. 'I'll find a breast tae suckle your boy.'

Mathew felt a huge surge of gratitude. His mother had never let him down and he knew she never would. He allowed Lindsay to lead him upstairs, past the surgery, to the hospital chamber where the light shone.

Margaret's red hair was spread around her on the pillow like a halo. Her arms were by her sides outside the single sheet that covered her, and her face was flushed. Her breathing was rapid but shallow, and her eyes were closed.

Her husband had seen many a man die in the army infirmary, and could not hide from or deny the inevitable.

'Is she aware?' he asked.

'Not for the last hour, nor will she be again, I'm afraid. It's for the best, sir.'

'What?' he retorted. 'No chance to say goodbye is for the best?'

'She's out of pain. Her blood and her body are full of poisons. She will sleep away now. All you can do is sit with her.'

'How long?'

'Until she lets go.'

Lindsay closed the door, leaving them alone.

There were so many thoughts in his head, so many things he wanted to say to her, so many fervent thanks he wanted to give her for all she had been to him and would always be, but all he could do was try to will them into her unconscious mind, so that she might die in the knowledge that he had come to love her as truly and deeply as he had ever loved anyone, and that she had given him a personal fulfilment he had thought he would never know.

All that he could say as he held her hand was, 'Oh, my Margaret, you made me so happy. God's cruel, that He takes you away.'

He sat with her for two hours as the sun rose, and brightened the chamber, wiping the moistness from her sleeping face occasionally with clean cloths that the doctor had left. He listened to her breathing, until it became faster, then more laboured, until finally it stopped, and she was gone.

He stood, and folded her hands across her chest. Then he murmured, 'Goodbye, my love,' kissed her on the forehead and then on the lips, and left the room that he knew would always be burned into his brain, another nightmare to curse his sleep.

When he went downstairs, his mother was waiting. She said nothing, but hugged him, then pressed her face to his shoulder. He knew she was weeping, but would want no one else to see, and so he let her shed her tears, and looked at the doctor.

'You will please ask the undertaker to call on me this afternoon,' he said. 'The funeral will be in Carluke, of course, and Mr Barclay will conduct it.'

As he finished, Hannah stood straight once more. 'I am so sorry, ma boy,' she said. She paused, but only for a second or two, and he saw her urgency. 'We maun go now,' she told him, 'and take the bairn wi' us. His need's the greatest now, but Ah've found someone who'll look after him like her ain.'

They wrapped the baby in two shawls. One had been Mathew's own and the second Hannah had crocheted for him during Margaret's pregnancy. Then his grandmother carried him outside to the carriage. The horse had been groomed and was feeding from a nosebag.

'Where are we going?' he asked.

'Carluke,' she replied, knowing that she need say no more.

Chapter Fourteen

WHEN MATHEW CARRIED HIS son into the McGill cottage, it was the first time he had seen his childhood sweetheart in more than eight years. She was standing with her back to the fire, and she too held an infant in her arms.

'You poor man,' she said, moved by the sadness in him. 'You deserved much better. I'm sorry I never met Mistress Fleming, Mathew. David said she was such a good woman.'

'The worst things happen to the best people,' he replied, in a dull monotone that she could not have imagined hearing from the man she had known for so long.

She smiled at him, sadly. 'You should know.'

'I did not mean myself,' he sighed. 'Margaret was far too good for the likes of me, that puts his business before everything. Why did it have to happen to her, Lizzie?'

'It lies in wait for all of us who give birth, Mathew. It's a risky business, regardless of status. Queens have died from childbed fever, so I've been told.'

'But you are sound?'

'Yes, I'm among the lucky ones. It's two weeks since our wee Jean was born and I am back as I was.'

'And she is thriving?'

'Oh yes,' Lizzie said, glancing down at the bundle in her arms, 'she's the most biddable child of the three.'

'I was sorry to hear of your loss,' he said. 'Your poor wee Wilma, to be taken like that.'

'We bear these things, Mathew. I had practice at it, when I was told I'd lost you, after the great battle. All we can do is love them that are left all the more.'

'I did love Margaret, you know,' he murmured, rocking his son gently in his arms.

'I know.' She nodded. 'And I love David too.'

'You should. He's a better man than me.'

'He's a different man from you, the gentlest you could ever meet, but dinna do yourself down. There's not a soul in the Upper Ward of Lanarkshire that's more respected. You put food on people's table with your factory. You might only have one eye now, but you see more with it than ten ordinary men.'

For all his misery, he smiled. 'You are biased.'

'That may be, but it's still the truth. Where is Mother Fleming?' she asked him, suddenly.

'She is gone to see Mr Barclay, to tell him the news, and to ask him to prepare for a . . .' He broke off and gazed at the ceiling. 'Last spring, Margaret told me we would have a wedding and a christening in the same year. But she could not have known we'd be having a funeral as well. I would give up everything I own to have her back.'

'Then you'd be wishing that baby unborn,' Lizzie retorted, 'that child you cradle in your arms. She would not have wanted that, I promise you, not even as the fever took hold of her. You cannot have her back, and so you will not give up everything. Far from it, you will work all the harder, for your son. David told me of your plans for your factory, with the new products, and of your new venture.'

'There is some risk in both. If one were to fail, I would survive, but if both go badly . . .'

'Mathew, neither will fail, and you know it. Now,' she said briskly, as she laid the infant Jean in a cradle at the side of the hearth, 'let me see that bairn of yours. He must be fed.'

'This is a great thing you're doing, Lizzie.'

'Nonsense, it's what any woman would do. God knows, if Mother Fleming could, you would never get him off her.' She frowned as she took the baby from him. 'Look after her, mind. She was in a fearful fuss when she arrived here. She'd driven hard all the way from Cam'nethan. David had gone to his work by then, but young Matt was still here and he was alarmed when he saw the state she was in.'

'I know,' he admitted. 'And I will take care of her, I promise. But you, are you really able to do this, feed two babies?'

She laughed. 'Man, have you never heard of twins? Sir Gregor Cleland and his brother thrived well enough . . . though more's the pity, some would say.'

'Yes, but twins tend to be smaller babies, do they not? This lad here's a bruiser.'

'I will have enough,' she insisted.

'Then I will send you extra milk, vegetables, meat, chicken, all the extra you need. And a cot and bedding and clothing and soft napkins for the child, for both the children, and coal for the fire, and oil for the lamps . . . and I'll find a wet nurse as quickly as I can, I promise.'

'No!'

Her sharpness took him by surprise.

'I will foster this child for as long as is necessary, until he is ready to be weaned. It will be hard for you, Mathew, but he must stay here with us until then. I won't have another woman suckling your Margaret's bairn. I am fit and I am healthy; you know that. How could you guarantee that in someone else? I promise you, if I find that I canna cope, I will tell you, but I know that I can.'

'Has David agreed to this?'

'Of course. I sent young Matt to fetch him home when Mother Fleming arrived. He is of the same mind as me, be sure of it.'

'Lizzie,' he exclaimed, 'that is a great commitment. If you wish, you and David and your children could move into Waterloo House, with Mother and me.'

'And then move out again when the time comes? You are a generous man, Mathew, but this is our home and here we must stay. As you can see, it is one of the biggest of the estate cottages. Your wee man will be fine here with us, and you can come and visit him, every day if you like. "Wee man" indeed,' she chuckled. 'What will you call him?'

'That,' he replied, 'you will find out at the christening, where you and David will be godparents. If Mr Barclay agrees, that will take place the day after Margaret's funeral.'

'Then go to him,' she said, 'and complete the arrangements, while this wee mite and I attend to our private business.'

Still stunned by the day's mournful events and by the speed with which they had transpired, Mathew did as she instructed, with the promise that he would be back in the evening, when David McGill would be at home.

The cottage was just inside the Cleland estate boundary, a little over half a mile from the parish church. As if to spite him the sun had come out and was shining; it was unseasonably warm. He was perspiring within his heavy coat as he reached the door of the manse. He was about to knock when it was opened for him, by Jessie.

'My condolences, sir,' she murmured. 'The meenister is in the parlour wi' your mither.'

'The things in your life this room has witnessed,' Barclay said, as Mathew entered. 'I can hardly credit this. Of all the ladies, I'd have thought your Margaret was the least likely for this to happen.'

'My mother believes it was where the birth took place that was the cause,' he replied. 'She may be right. There are cleaner places than the bench in an open cabin, barely a yard from a horse's arse. When can you do the funeral, John?'

'In two days' time, on Saturday morning, if that is agreeable to you and to the undertaker.'

'It is acceptable to me,' he answered, brusquely. 'Margaret had no family left to need to be advised. As for the undertaker, he will do what he's told. There should be a reception, I believe.'

The minister nodded, briefly. 'Of course. The lesser hall is the usual choice. Jessie will bake for it, she's still able, remarkably, and you may have alcohol if you wish.'

'I do not,' he snapped, bitterly. 'If only there had been alcohol handy to clean that damned seat, Margaret might still be alive.'

'Life is fu' of "ifs", son,' Hannah said, gently, 'but when we're lookin' back the way, nane o' them mean a damned thing.'

'Your mother is right,' Barclay concurred. 'There was nothing to be done. Self-reproach can only harm you and your child. Speaking of whom, in accordance with what Mrs Fleming has asked, I propose that he be baptised at morning service on Sunday. He was born in another parish, but that means nothing to me.'

'I thank you for that. The McGills will be godparents.'

'Have you chosen a name?' the minister asked.

'I have, subject only to David's agreement, which I hope he will give. My son will be christened Marshall Weir Fleming, after his mother, and also his foster mother. If anyone looks askance at that, they will be welcome to discuss their feelings with me, but at their peril.'

Chapter Fifteen

MARSHALL WEIR FLEMING REMAINED part of the McGill household until he was a year old. As good as his word, his father visited him almost every day, calling in the morning, while the child was awake, before going to the factory, where he was spending most of his time. The only person in the family who felt neglected was Hannah, although she too called on her grandson in Carluke, and as he grew into his third trimester, and the weather grew milder, she often sent a carriage so that Lizzie could bring him, and his foster sister, to Waterloo House.

On her first visit, Hannah saw that she was overwhelmed by the size of Mathew's home, and by its grandeur.

'I always knew he would do well, Mother Fleming,' she said, 'but this makes me very proud of him. As you must be too,' she added.

'We both always were, lass,' Hannah replied. 'But if ye think this is fine . . . My son speaks to me about his business, now that he doesna' hae Margaret tae share with. Most of it goes ower ma heid, but that which sticks . . .'

She smiled. 'He now has another leather factory, makin' baggage o' his own design just as fast as he can sell it. As for the cast-iron cairry-on in Coatbridge . . . that Ah do not understand . . . he says fares better than he and his partner had ever hoped for.'

'That is very good, but does he have time for himself?' Lizzie asked.

'No, but he disna' want ony. He says he likes tae work, as it keeps his mind frae settling on other things.' She looked down at the sturdy seven-month-old Marshall, wriggling as he sat in her lap, as if he was ready to climb down and walk. 'Perhaps when this wee man comes hame, it will help him.'

'I think so,' the child's foster mother said. 'His face seems lighter, and younger, all the time he's with him.'

The only days on which Mathew did not visit his son were those when he felt compelled to be at Coatbridge, to involve himself in the iron foundry. Each one was something of a chore, for the industrialised ward of Lanarkshire was a place he had never known before, and he was struck by its contrast with the quiet rural community in which he had been raised. To him, the place was squalid, the air unclean and the people coarse. Every time he went there he travelled in his oldest clothes.

And yet, there was an energy about it that drew him back; he understood that it was the sort that generates wealth, and as long as that was fairly distributed, it had to be accepted. The only disagreement that he and Sir Graham Stockley had was over his proposal that the workers should be given production targets and paid a small bonus for timely completion of an order.

The mine owner had been sceptical. 'Is it really

necessary?' he had asked after the proposal had been tabled.

'No, it is not,' Mathew had replied. 'The real question should be, "Will it be productive?" In my experience, in my other companies, it has increased production by up to twenty per cent, with no loss of quality. You are confident, Graham, in the skills and commitment of our work-force? Good, I say, now let us give them a chance to demonstrate those qualities and be rewarded for it.'

In the two months that followed the introduction of the bonus scheme, production in the Stockley Fleming foundry increased by twenty-five per cent. Three months after that, the order book had doubled, and a second hot-blast furnace had been commissioned.

The return of Marshall to his family home took place the day after a party held in the McGill cottage to celebrate his birthday and Jean's, and on the same day as the memorial service for his mother, held in Carluke Parish Church. Mathew had instructed it and had decreed that it would happen annually, as long as John Barclay remained in the charge. The minister was bereaved himself by that time, as his dear old Jessie had slept away two months before.

The service over, Mathew stood at the door of the kirk, so that he could thank each member of the congregation for their attendance as they left. There had been no dinners at Waterloo House for just over a year, but his friend Sheriff Stirling was there nonetheless, along with several other prominent people in the wider community.

And two others: Sir Gregor Cleland and his brother were the first to leave. Mathew had not even glanced at their family pew and was surprised to see them. He looked more closely at them than he had on the day of their father's funeral. They were slight figures, small babies grown into small men, he thought, with pinched faces and no warmth in their eyes.

'Our condolences, Mr Fleming,' Sir Gregor said, not offering a handshake.

'I thank you,' he replied, 'although this is as much a service of celebration of Margaret's life as of grief for her passing. Since neither of you knew my wife, or myself for that matter, I'm surprised that you have graced us with your presence, but nonetheless, I thank you again.'

'Not at all,' Gavin retorted, and then gave a small mocking snigger. 'We simply wanted to cast an eye over you, Fleming, that's all. Or should I call you "One-lamp"?' As the brothers walked away, their laughter floated back to him.

The last member of the congregation to emerge was Philip Armitage, the factor. 'Did you suggest to your masters that they come here today?' Mathew asked him, having accepted his formal greeting.

'No, Mr Fleming, I promise you that I did not. I can tell by your tone that you're not best pleased to see them. Did they give offence?'

'If I deemed that they besmirched Margaret's memory,' he replied, 'they would have, and there would be consequences. But they did not, so I have no regard for them. Tell me, man, how do you manage working for toerags like those two, after the old Laird?'

'It's a change for the worse, sir,' the factor admitted, 'but in truth they do not impinge on my daily life very much, for I rarely see them. They spend much of their time in Edinburgh, and even in London on occasion. All they do is send me their bills for the paying . . . but I imagine McGill has told you that.'

In that moment he remembered why he had disliked the man. 'Why should you imagine that?' he asked coldly. 'David does not discuss estate business with me, any more than he would discuss mine with you . . . or what he knows of it, which is not much.'

'My apologies, sir,' Armitage exclaimed, obviously alarmed by his outburst. 'I meant no slight on Mr McGill.'

'Accepted.' Mathew's curiosity had been pricked. 'How goes the estate, then?'

'Not as well as it did under Sir George. Half the staff in the big house have gone.'

'I knew that some had; Ewan Beattie, the coachman, works for me now. I suppose if the brothers are absent much of the time, they have no need for as many people.'

'True, but it's not just that, sir. The tenant farmers are all having their rent increased at Candlemas. The Laird wanted it done for Martinmas, but there was no time to give notice.'

'Do they know yet?'

'No, and some of them will find it hard to pay. The brothers will not mind that; they seem to think they can farm the land themselves and make more profit.'

'Can they?'

'Candidly, no. I will find myself hiring on displaced tenants to do the same job for a minimum wage. The factor is usually the least popular man on an estate, Mr Fleming, but that will make me truly hated, if it comes to pass.'

Mathew was shocked, genuinely. 'Is Gregor that cruel?'

'In my view, no, not Sir Gregor. The brothers have the same looks, but not the same mind. Gavin is the dominant one, and between the two of them . . . and the two of us, mind . . . what he says is what happens.'

He was about to say that he had heard such a suggestion before, when they were interrupted by young Matt. 'Mathew,' he called out as he ran towards them, 'Mother Fleming says Ah've to ask you if you're coming.'

He smiled. 'That was not a question, Mr Armitage,' he said, 'it was a summons. Good luck with your task. It is not one that makes me envious.'

The two shook hands and Mathew left, with his young near-namesake, to answer the call.

'We'll miss Marshall when he's gone,' the boy declared as they headed for the McGill cottage.

'There will be no need for that, Matt. He will not be going awful far, so you can come and visit him, as often as your mother and your father will allow. That's when the school is not in term of course.'

'Can Ah bring a friend?'

The question took Mathew by surprise. 'Who would that be?' he asked.

'Jane Fisher. She and I sit together in the schoolroom. She whispers answers to me when I dinna ken them.'

He smiled, and felt a surge of pleasure. John Barclay's prayer, and no doubt the prayers of her parents, had been answered those nine years ago. The child who had been baptised on the day of his return had confounded the doctor and midwives by surviving infancy, and was growing up healthy and unblemished.

'Of course you may,' he said, 'with her parents' consent.'

Life goes in cycles, he mused. Twenty-five years earlier another boy and girl had sat side by side in that same schoolroom.

Matt and Jane did visit Marshall, often, when he was established in his nursery in Waterloo House, under the supervision of his grandmother, and under the daily care of his governess, a stout spinster named Meg Liddell, who had been recruited through the church. She had come with John Barclay's personal recommendation, but had only been hired after an hour-long interview with Hannah, from which Mathew had been excluded. She looked formidable, but in fact she was jolly, and seemed to live for the child who was her charge.

Once again, Mathew's life had a routine, even if there was a void at its heart, of which he was reminded every time he looked at his son, but most of all when he saw his red hair shining in the firelight.

His business activity became less frantic, also; the saddles continued to sell, with their international markets growing, but the baggage range soon came to rival them in terms of turnover and profitability. As he and Margaret had anticipated, demand began to spread through the social classes, leading him to introduce lower-cost items, serviceable but made from less expensive leather.

Yet this growth was exceeded by that of Stockley Fleming. Within two years, Mathew was able to repay the money he had borrowed to invest in the venture. He had done so entirely from the dividends that it paid him, even allowing for investment in the rapid growth of the mill. By 1830, the company was the biggest employer in Coatbridge, and its two founders were known as 'The Iron Barons', locally and beyond.

In that same year, a crisis arose close to Mathew. He and David McGill had both become elders of Carluke Parish Church, and met regularly at the kirk session meetings. On one of those, McGill was so unusually distracted, that the minister had to reprove him for his inattention.

Business was hardly concluded before Mathew took him into a corner of the kirk's lesser hall.

'What's ailing you, man?' he demanded. 'I've never seen you looking so vexed, other than when you lost your wee Wilma. Is Jean sick? I saw young Matt on the way in so it canna be him.' He paused. 'Or is it Lizzie?'

'None of us,' David replied. 'There's no sickness in the house, I promise you.'

'Then what is it?'

'Whatever it is, Mathew, it's my concern, not yours. I'll find a solution.'

He shook his head, firmly. 'David, man, anything that upsets you so much is my concern, whether you like it or not. Now out with it, for you know I will find out if I set my mind to it.'

His friend sighed. 'It's the estate. I have been dismissed from my position. Mr Armitage told me today that my services are no longer required. If that is not bad enough, from now on I will be expected to pay full market rent for the cottage . . . full market rent being whatever the Laird says it is. I am stunned by this, man. I never saw it coming.'

'Damn the Laird!' Mathew barked. 'I know about the Clelands; their reputation is well set among my business friends and social acquaintances. Gregor and his brother are a pair of profligate wasters, with their workers and their tenants paying the price for their excesses. They have crossed me twice, those pipsqueaks. It was of no importance to me then, but when they harm my friends, it is. Well, you can thumb your nose at them, David, for you will come and work for me.'

'No!' McGill exclaimed. 'Begging you for employment is the last thing I'd ever do.'

'You are not begging me at all,' Mathew retorted. 'How many times have I asked you if you would join my company? Tell me, please, for I have lost count myself. This is not charity; I have need of a capable man like you to supervise the managers of my leather businesses. At the moment neither of them can do a damn thing without reference to me. The pay will be two pounds a week; Sundays off, of course, and two weeks paid holidays a year.'

'Two pounds a week! Mathew, that's well over twice what I was paid by the estate. It's far too much.'

'Hah!' he laughed. 'That's something I have never heard before, a man wanting lower wages. David, it is what the job is worth to me, and whoever takes it, that is what he'll get. But I would much rather it was you than someone else, for it is you I want, for your skills and experience, not your friendship.'

'Will I have to move to Netherton?' McGill asked, tentatively.

'Not if you do not want to. I'll give you my old trap; you can ride to Waterloo in the morning, pick me up and we will go the rest of the way together. What is your notice at the estate?' he asked, briskly.

'The end of this week.'

'Good, you start on Monday. On that day I will send Ewan, my coachman, up with the trap. He will be there at seven fifteen, and you can pick me up at seven thirty. It will be the start of a new era for us both, David, and I welcome it.'

Chapter Sixteen

DAVID MCGILL FITTED INTO his friend's business empire very quickly. He won the respect of the men under his supervision and surprised himself, and in truth surprised his new employer, by the speed with which he grasped the mechanics of the company, Netherton Leather Goods, as it had been renamed.

He was more than a merely adequate replacement for Margaret, although Mathew would never admit as much, not even to himself. The closest he came to revealing his feelings was over dinner one night at Waterloo House with Sheriff Stirling and Sir Graham Stockley, his two confidants.

'It makes me laugh,' he said, although his face betrayed not a hint of a smile, 'when I think of those fools, the Cleland twins. They leave their estate in the hands of a man who does not understand anything beyond a column of figures, having dismissed the very person who was capable of using it to keep them in good fortune all their days. Mark me, it will come back and bite them.'

'I sense you do not like the brothers,' the Sheriff chuckled, his port glass halfway to his lips.

'Robin,' he replied, 'I am honestly indifferent to those

men. Our society has created them and we must accept their existence, but the easiest way to live with them is to ignore them and let them proceed on the course they have charted, towards to their own inevitable downfall.'

'Inevitable?'

'From what I hear, yes; I sound out Mr Armitage on occasion, when I see him at the kirk. Even run as ineffici-ently as it is, the estate might support the lifestyle of one profligate, but not two, gentlemen, not two. The brothers will have to change, or fail.'

'Or marry well,' Stockley suggested. 'Neither has yet found a wife.'

'That is true,' Mathew conceded, 'but I do not see a queue of comely candidates stretching from here to Edinburgh. Enough of those two, though, they are not worth our consideration. I apologise for raising their name at this table.'

The Waterloo House dinners had been reintroduced in the second year after Margaret's death. Stockley and Stirling were always on the guest list, but otherwise the events were political as much as social, as Mathew knew that his own standing and that of his business interests were inextricably linked.

Always, Mathew listened more than he spoke. He never sought to dominate a dinner table, but to allow his guests to express themselves. When his view was sought he gave it, but always stressed that he spoke from a rural perspective, with little or no experience of city life or of great affairs of state.

'You, sir, are of the officer class,' he told the Earl of

Teviotdale at one event. 'I was only a corporal.'

'So was Napoleon,' the aristocrat countered. 'He went from the ranks to rule most of Europe, until you helped beat him at the battle after which your house is named. You, on the other hand, went on to become a sergeant. But where is Napoleon now? As dead as poxy old King George the Fourth, while you, Iron Baron, are building an empire of your own, based on contraptions that might have made Bonaparte invincible had they been available to him.'

That exchange taught Mathew two valuable lessons. The first was that a wise guest at an event of influence should know in advance every available fact about every person at that table. The second was that while his saddles and his valises might have made him his original fortune, it was his position in heavy industry that gave him his status in the new society that was beginning to develop through-out Great Britain. 'Iron Baron' they called him, yet never 'Leather Baron', even though, in those products, his business had become the biggest in the land.

His new standing was emphasised in the year before his fortieth birthday, when a letter was delivered by special messenger to his home. It bore the seal of the Lord Chamberlain, the Duke of Devonshire. Hannah was looking over his shoulder as he tore it open.

'Whit does it say?' she demanded.

'Ssh, Mother, let me read it.'

The language was flowery, courtly, but he went straight to the essential paragraph.

'His Majesty, King William the Fourth,' he read aloud, 'is minded, in the light of your standing in the community, to appoint you to the office of deputy to the Lord Lieutenant of Lanarkshire, His Grace the Duke of Hamilton.'

'What does it mean?' He had never seen his mother so excited, the great knower of her station in life. 'That ye're a lord?'

'No,' he laughed, 'well short of that. The Duke of Hamilton is the King's representative in the county. He stands for him at events he cannot attend himself, which means in practice nearly all of them. The Duke cannot guarantee always to be able to perform this function and so he has deputies who stand for him as required. Sheriff Stirling is one.'

'Whit will ye have tae do?'

'Wear a fine uniform and shake hands with folk, I imagine. No more sergeant's stripes for me, Mother,' he laughed.

As he mentioned his old rank, he knew in the same moment who had put his name forward.

The deputy lieutenancy proved to be no more onerous than he had imagined it would be. The uniform would have been shared with the Sheriff, but Mathew's height and breadth of shoulder made that impossible, and so a new one had to be commissioned.

He wore it rarely but had done so on the fine June Sunday that his life changed for ever. He was not long returned from an event in Hamilton, and was playing with the seven-year-old Marshall on the lawn in front of the house, beside one of the silver birches that he had planted for Margaret, because she had said once that she liked them, when he saw a youth running up the drive, at full pelt.

'Hold up, hold up,' he called out. 'What's the panic?'

The young runner skidded to a halt, his chest heaving. It took him more than a few moments until he could catch his breath enough to speak. In that time, Mathew recognised him as Billy Fisher, from Carluke, Joel's son and Jane's older brother.

'Mr Fleming, sir,' he exclaimed when he could, 'I'm sent by Mr Barclay, to ask ye if ye'd be so good as to come to the manse at once.'

He was oddly irked by the lad's deference, but put that to one side.

'What has happened?' he asked, calmly, although he was disturbed.

'Ah dinna' ken, but they say Sir Gregor Cleland is deid.'

More to it than that, Mathew thought at once. *Men die, even young men, and while Gregor Cleland might have been the Laird, his passing alone should not be the cause of an emergency summons.*

'A few moments, Billy,' he said, 'and I'll be with you.'

Ewan Beattie was in his lodging above the stable, but he had already driven him to Hamilton and back that day, and so he decided to let him lie. Instead, as soon as he had delivered Marshall back into the charge of Miss Liddell, he put on a short jacket, went back outside and saddled his horse, a chestnut that he had named Victor. He had told Hannah nothing more than the simple truth, that John Barclay wanted to see him, at his convenience.

Mounted, he reached down and offered the young runner a hand. 'Get up behind me, Billy. She can carry two for all the distance we're going.'

The young man was not the best passenger, and so Mathew had to go more steadily than he might have wished; consequently it took them more than the normal half-hour to reach Carluke.

As soon as he arrived at the green in front of the kirk, he could see that there was something serious afoot. Villagers, men and women, were standing around in groups, and not one of them was smiling; indeed, Beth Fisher, Billy's mother, was in tears. He brought Victor to a standstill to let the boy dismount, and then trotted him forward towards the manse, speaking to no one on the way.

The minister's housekeeper, whose name he did not yet know, opened the door to him. He strode straight into the parlour . . . to find Lizzie and her children sitting on the sofa in a tight, tense group, and Barclay in an armchair, his face white.

'What's happened?' he asked at once.

Lizzie looked up him; her face was stained with tears and her eyes were puffy. She looked old, and that alarmed him. 'David has been arrested,' she replied. 'The Sheriff's men came and took him away.'

'Why? What cause could they possibly have had? And what's this about Gregor Cleland being dead?'

'The two must be connected,' John Barclay said, rising to his feet. He looked at the boy. 'Laddie,' he said, 'tell your story.'

Young Matt stood also. The boy was fifteen and on his way to being full grown. Mathew saw that there was a mark on his face, a vivid red weal that ran from his forehead down and across his cheek, as if in mimicry of his own scar.

'It wasn't my fault,' he exclaimed, in a voice that had become deeper than his father's.

'Nobody is saying it is,' the minister told him gently. 'Just carry on.'

'I was playing, in the roadway,' he began. 'Some o' the village lads and I; we were just chasing, kickin' a ball made out o' old clothes. We were doing no harm at all, Mathew, honest.'

'Fine,' Mathew murmured. 'I do not think for a minute that you were. Go on, as Mr Barclay says.'

He nodded. 'I never saw the carriage, the Laird's carriage. I had my back to it as it cam' up the road. One o' the other lads kicked the ball. It went over ma head and I turned to run after it and almost ran under one o' the Laird's horses. The beast was startled; it reared up and the carriage was shaken. Only for a second or so, mind,' he added.

'I can see that it would be rocked, but it wasn't near to overturning, was it?'

'No, not at all.'

'Did you know the coachman?'

'The Laird was drivin' himself. There were two ladies in the carriage, finely dressed, and no' from Carluke. The Laird's brother was alongside on a horse. It had one o' your saddles,' he noted, as if the detail was important.

'After startling the horse, Matt,' Mathew asked, 'what did you do?'

'I said I was sorry, very sorry, right away, and I reached out my hand to calm the animal, just to soothe it. But the Laird, he shouted something at me, words I've been told are foul, and then he lashed out, he hit me across the face with his whip.'

Mathew felt a cold rage within him. 'Who saw this?' he growled.

'Only my father. Ah never saw him, but he'd been watching us play. All the other lads ran off, but he came towards us. Ah've never seen my father angry before, but he was fair ablaze. He went up to the carriage and he grabbed the Laird and hauled him right out of his seat and down on to the ground, then he leaned over him slapping him once, twice, three times. The ladies, they were laughing, thinking it was great sport, even though my father was shouting, saying he was going to thrash the Laird within an inch of his life. And that's when the other one fired.'

'The other one?'

'The Laird's brother; Gavin, I think they cry him. He'd got off his horse, he drew a pistol, he pointed it at my father's back, and he fired. But he missed, and he shot the Laird instead.'

'And he killed him? Is that what you're saying?'

'I dinna ken, Mathew, I've never seen anyone shot before.'

'Where did the ball strike him?'

Young Matt tapped the centre of his own forehead, less than an inch above his nose. 'There.'

'Then he killed him, for sure.'

'Oh my,' Lizzie whispered, a hand to her mouth. 'But he meant to kill David.'

'What happened next, Matt?' Mathew asked.

'My father stood, but before he could even turn round,

Gavin Cleland hit him with the pistol he'd just fired, and it knocked him down. I went to help him. As I did, Gavin gathered up the Laird in his arms and put him in the carriage. Then he tied his horse to the back, got up in the seat and drove away, at speed.'

'Did your father recover?'

'He got up, but he was dazed and his eyes were funny. I asked him what we should do. He said we should go to the manse and that was what we did. Mr Barclay came out to meet us. He had heard the shot.'

'But nobody saw it?'

'No. Nobody at all, other than us that wis there.'

Mathew turned to the minister. 'John, what did you do?'

'I took them in, of course. They both had wounds; young Matt's you can see, and David had a cut to the head. I bathed them both. As Matt said, David was dazed at first but he recovered most of his senses after a few minutes. I told him that the incident had to be reported to Sheriff Stirling, in Lanark, but I deemed that neither was fit to ride. So I told them both to go home and wait there, and then I summoned the beadle, our worthy church officer. I bade him carry the message to the Sheriff's clerk, and he did. But when he got there he was told that the occurrence was already known, and by that time . . .'

'The Sheriff's officers came to our door,' Lizzie exclaimed, her voice a wail that alarmed, saddened and enraged Mathew, simultaneously.

'They burst into our home and they seized David. They treated him roughly and bound his wrists in chains, and put him in their black carriage. Then Gavin Cleland arrived, with some ruffians from the estate. He ordered the children and me out of the house. He told me we were evicted, then he had his men take all our furniture and possessions outside and smash them in the street. Young Matt would have fought them, but I held him back. I told him I could not lose husband and son in the same day.'

'Then I'll fight them tomorrow,' the boy growled.

'No, you will not!' Mathew barked. The force of his censure startled everyone, most of all little Jean, who started to cry. He knelt by her side and stroked her hair as she cowered against her mother.

'There now, wee one,' he murmured. 'I'm sorry, I should not have shouted. Your brother only spoke as I would have at his age.

'But,' he continued as he rose to his feet once more, 'what I said still goes. You cannot fight these people, Matt, not with your fists. You can only do it with the law, and that is how we must rescue your father. There is nothing to be done tonight, but tomorrow you and I will go to Lanark. We will see Sheriff Stirling, and you can tell him your story. He is a good friend of mine, and a fair man; I expect we'll bring David back with us.'

'But our home, Mathew,' Lizzie said. 'What of that?'

'Well, first and foremost,' he retorted, 'Sir Gavin, as I suppose he'll be called now, having killed his brother, will find that he is short of the rent, for John and I will let it be known in and around Carluke that anyone who occupies that cottage will incur our displeasure. And you, you'll have better lodgings. Until we can find something permanent, you and your bairns will move into Waterloo House with me. I will ride back and send my carriage for you and the effects that those people left untouched.'

'That's not much more than our clothes, but we've nothing to carry them in.'

'Then I will send cases, and tell my coachman to help you fill them.'

She made to speak, but he cut her off. 'Lizzie,' he smiled, but sadly, 'do you think Mother Fleming would have it any other way?'

Chapter Seventeen

HANNAH FLEMING'S ETERNAL CALMNESS was tested by the news that her son brought from Carluke, but by the time the three houseguests arrived, it was fully restored.

She welcomed them in and then took complete charge, allocating bedrooms, and placing Jean in the care of Miss Liddell, a proposition which the little girl accepted as soon as she saw Marshall. Hannah said nothing to any of them about David's predicament, waiting instead until the family had been fed and had retired for the night, and she and Mathew were alone.

'This is a terrible business,' she said, as they sat together in the gazebo that had been built a year before with such nights in mind. The midsummer sun was fully set but a blue glow remained in the northern sky, bathing the garden in its light.

'True,' her son agreed. 'Gregor Cleland was as big a waste of a baronetcy as there has ever been, but nobody should die like that, shot down in the street.'

'Perhaps but let's you and me no' waste oor time mourning him. Our concern must be for poor David. How will it go wi' him, do ye think?'

'As I told Lizzie, I hope that he will return with us tomorrow.'

'But ye're afraid he won't?'

'I'm not certain of it,' he admitted.

'Surely yer friend the Sheriff will see reason when he hears the boy's story.'

'Robin Stirling, the man, is my friend, but a good Sheriff can have none of those, nor show favour to anyone. I know Martin Knox, the Sheriff's clerk, too; he would not have sent those officers for David unless he saw good cause.'

'That was my thought too,' she murmured.

The next morning Mathew rose early, and rode to Netherton, to advise his managers that neither he nor Mr McGill would be available that day, and that they should take instructions from his secretary, a capable man named Gabriel Spence whom he had hired not long after Margaret's death and who had earned his trust.

When he returned to Waterloo House, Lizzie and her son were dressed and ready for the road.

'There is no need for you to come, my dear,' he told her. 'Young Matt saw what happened yesterday; you did not. It's his word that the Sheriff needs to hear.'

'But I must support my husband, Mathew,' she protested. 'Miss Liddell says that she's happy to look after Jean while I'm gone.'

He smiled. 'I understand but, Lizzie, remember, there'll be four in the carriage when we return. That'll be a tight fit, even if you are one of those.'

'I can sit with the coachman,' Matt suggested. 'Or I could ride postillion.'

'You know the word,' Mathew said, 'but have you ever done it?'

Hannah Fleming had said nothing during the exchange, but finally she intervened. 'Son,' she said, 'tak' her with ye'. If everything was reversed, if it was you that had been arrested and David goin' tae rescue ye', he couldna' keep me from goin' wi' him.'

He gave in to her persuasion. 'Very well, Mother,' he sighed. He looked at Matt. 'On the way back, I'll ride with Mr Beattie, and you three can travel as a family in the carriage.'

The journey to Lanark was neither long nor arduous. Young Matt made it every day of the school term. The county town's Sheriff Court was an old building; a replacement had been promised, but Robin Stirling had told Mathew that he did not expect ever to sit in it. Instead he had to dispense justice in a room where the public were barely separated from the accused, although in Stirling's court, that caused few problems, since the Sheriff had a reputation for dealing with rowdy behaviour on the spot.

The Monday sitting was over by the time they arrived, and the courtroom was empty. Mathew made his way to the Sheriff clerk's office, and found Martin Knox at his desk.

'I thought we might be seeing you today, Mr Fleming,' he said.

'Then you know why I'm here. I want David McGill, who should never have been in this place in the first place.'

'Nor is he any longer,' Knox replied, ominously. 'You must speak to the Sheriff. He said you were to be shown in as soon as you arrived.'

'I am not alone,' Mathew told him, wondering what Knox meant. 'Mrs McGill is here and their son, a witness to the event and to the death of Sir Gregor.'

'You may have been unwise in bringing them.'

'I had no choice. But let me see the Sheriff, and find out what he thinks.'

Knox nodded and left the room by a side door that connected to the Sheriff's chamber. He returned in less than a minute. 'You may go in,' he said, 'and you may take the boy in with you, but Sheriff Stirling would prefer it if Mrs McGill remained outside.'

Mathew frowned, but saw no point in arguing. Instead, he went back to the corridor to fetch Matt and explain to Lizzie that she should be patient.

Robin Stirling was still in his wig and robes when they entered, as if to underline a distance that was clear to his friend from his demeanour.

He took a seat at a rectangular table and indicated to the visitors that they should sit on the other side. *As if we were adversaries*, Mathew thought, then realised that was exactly what they were.

The Sheriff looked directly at young Matt. 'Knox says you have a story to tell me, young man. Is that so?'

'Yes, sir,' the boy replied, meeting his gaze, but happily, his escort saw, with no show of defiance.

'By rights you should be telling it not to me but to the procurator fiscal. However, as you are in the company of someone who is like myself an officer of the Crown, I am prepared to hear you, informally.' His eyes were piercing. 'By that I mean that I will not place you under oath, but be warned, you must behave as if you were. The truth, the whole truth and nothing but the truth. Do you understand?'

'Yes, sir.'

'Then begin.'

Mathew had given his young charge clear instructions on the way to Lanark. He was to tell his story clearly, without becoming excited or emotional, he was not to abuse Gavin Cleland verbally, and most important, he was to address Sheriff Stirling as 'sir' or 'my Lord'. He followed them to the letter, even under the judge's stern gaze, describing the events as they had happened, including his family's subsequent eviction and the destruction of their property on the orders of Cleland.

When he was finished, Stirling was silent for almost half a minute, his elbows on the table and his hands steepled, fingertips a few inches from his nose, and his eyes on Matt all the time.

'I will ask you only one thing, young man. Were you rude to the late Sir Gregor Cleland in any way? Did you give him cheek?'

'No, sir,' the boy replied. 'Although he gave me a mark on mine.'

Mathew winced at the glibness of the answer, but the Sheriff did not react. Instead he said, 'Thank you for your story. Now, will you please leave us.'

'Wait for me outside, Matt, with your mother,' Mathew instructed him.

'But my father . . .' he began.

'Wait for me outside,' Mathew repeated, firmly. 'There's a good man.'

As the door closed on him, he turned to his friend, who had removed his judicial wig. 'Well?'

'Do you believe him to be telling the truth?' Stirling asked him.

'Of course,' he retorted. 'There is no doubt in my mind. Robin, I have only one question that needs answering. Did Gavin Cleland really mean to shoot David McGill or did he see a chance to have everything for himself, and seize it?'

'That is something that you would be best advised not to ask outside this room. Mathew, for what it is worth, I do not see the young man as a liar and, believe me, I have seen scores of them in this building. However I have a great problem, and you are not going to like it.'

'Go on,' he sighed, 'test me.'

'David McGill appeared before me this morning. He was the first man in the dock, and he was charged with the wilful murder of Sir Gregor Cleland.'

'But man,' Mathew exclaimed, 'that is ridiculous!'

'I wish it were so, but it wasn't. The procurator fiscal put before me sworn affidavits by Gavin Cleland and by the two ladies who were in the carriage and witnesses to the event. They are a Miss Charlotte Smith, from Knutsford, Cheshire, a close acquaintance of Sir Gregor, and her employed companion, Miss Judith Stout.

'They all swear that the boy chased the horses and startled them and that he provoked his whipping. They said also that David McGill did nothing to stop his son. More than that, when the boy was lashed, McGill became enraged. He then, they say, pulled Gavin Cleland from his horse, seized his pistol and shot Sir Gregor through the forehead.'

'But those are lies, all lies,' Mathew gasped.

'They are still sworn testimony from three people of good character, and that is how the Crown Agent will see it. Mr McGill's version bears out his son's but with no independent corroboration of their story, his prospects in the High Court will be gloomy.'

Sheriff Stirling's face was pained. 'For that's where I have been compelled to send him, my friend. He is on his way there even now, in the keeping of my officers, bound for the Calton Jail to await his trial. Everything is out of my hands, Mathew.

'Gavin Cleland has moved fast,' he added. 'He must have friends in Edinburgh, for the Crown Office was alerted last night. Forbes, the fiscal, had an instruction this morning from the Lord Advocate himself, that the matter should be expedited. The indictment is being prepared already and the trial will be swift.

'I do not have to tell you what a guilty verdict will bring. Mr McGill will be for the Lawnmarket, and the gallows.'

Chapter Eighteen

'IT'S NOT TRUE, MOTHER!' young Matt McGill shouted. 'It happened as I said it did. I never chased thae horses; it was an accident, I swear.'

'I do not doubt you, son,' Lizzie told him. 'Be calm now; we are in the court building remember.' Her face was chalk-white as she looked up at Mathew. 'Why has Cleland done this?' she asked.

'I can see only two reasons,' he replied. 'Either he was afraid that he would not be believed if he said that he shot his brother by accident, or in fact it was no accident.'

'He meant to do it? Is that what you are saying?'

'It was a very lucrative mischance, Lizzie. Sir Gregor was unmarried, so Gavin will not only inherit the baronetcy, but the whole Cleland estate. That might not be what it was in the old Laird's day, but it is still a considerable property. Think about it; the pair were born minutes apart . . . it was a lottery which one emerged first . . . yet as the younger son Gavin relied on his brother's good grace for his position, for the clothes on his back, for everything. To find himself in a position where he could change all that in a moment, then throw the blame on to another man, that must have been a great temptation. And from what I have gleaned from Mr Armitage, Gavin has no great record when it comes to resisting temptation.'

'The two women, what of them?'

'I know nothing of them, only what the Sheriff has told me, which may be more than he should have. I must be careful with that information if only to protect him.'

'If the Sheriff is your friend, Mathew,' Matt demanded, 'how could he do that to my father, knowing that he is also your friend?'

'With what was put before him by the procurator fiscal, he had no choice.'

'Why has he sent him to Edinburgh? Could he no' be tried here, where it would quickly be sorted?'

Mathew sighed, inwardly. In his account to Lizzie and her son of his discussion with the Sheriff, he had tried to play down the seriousness of McGill's situation, but the boy was too sharp, too perceptive.

'The Sheriff's Court only has the power to deal with offenders up to a certain level of seriousness,' he explained, 'and its sentencing powers are limited. Everything else has to go to the High Court, to be tried there by one of the senators of Scotland's College of Justice.'

'But they don't know him! They don't know he's a good man.'

'Then they must be told, by you and by me and by others, if we can find them. Your friends, lad, that you were kicking the ball with, who were they?'

'Johnny Cope and Johnny Wilson.'

'We must talk to them.'

'I don't believe they saw anything. Even before my father arrived I saw only their backs. As soon as the horse was startled, they were off through the kirkyard like twa rabbits.'

'Nevertheless,' Mathew insisted, 'we must go back to Carluke, find them and talk to them.'

'They'll no' be there; they'll be at their work.'

'What do they do?'

'They labour on the land,' Matt replied. 'Johnny Cope's faither's a tenant farmer and Johnny Wilson works for the estate.'

'I see. So they're both beholden to the Clelands one way or another. But are they honest boys?'

'I believe so.'

'Then we'll speak to them today.'

'Why would the women lie, Mathew?'

He turned to look at Lizzie. 'We can only guess at that, until they are in the witness box. Then they can be asked directly.'

'But who will ask them, Mathew? How can David defend himself through there, where he knows no one? We have no money for lawyers.'

He gave a short, terse laugh. 'Oh, but you have. Cleland may think that he has a scapegoat who can be easily swept away, but I promise you both, David will have all my resources at his disposal. I'll be in Edinburgh before tomorrow is out, and I will find him the finest advocate I can to present his case and confound Cleland's lies.'

'Is his life really at stake?' she murmured.

It was that direct question he had hoped to avoid; having

been put he could only speak the truth. 'Yes, my dear, it is. But he has the truth on his side, and the fairness of the courts.'

'Who knows how fair they might be, though? Edinburgh's a far-away place, and all sorts has happened there.'

'So I'm told,' he agreed, 'for I have never had occasion to go there myself, but that will not hinder us.'

'Us?' she repeated.

He nodded. 'Aye. Young Matt must come with me; he and I will trawl Carluke for witnesses, but unless we find one or two, he is his father's only defence. There is the minister too, though. I will ask John Barclay to come if it is necessary, to speak on David's behalf, as an elder of the kirk. Come now,' he declared, 'let's be about it. The quicker we act, the sooner David will be home with you.'

The overcrowded carriage that they had hoped for on their return journey had not come to pass, but Mathew chose to ride with the coachman in any event, to give Lizzie the chance to spend time alone with her son, for once they left, Mathew had no clear idea of when she would see him again.

The travelled straight to Carluke; when they arrived there, young Matt was dispatched to find the two Johnnys and bring them to the manse. Ewan Beattie was instructed to take Lizzie to Waterloo House and then to return. Once they were gone, Mathew headed directly to the minister's house.

'You are alone, then,' John Barclay said, gloomily, as he ushered him in.

'Aye,' he replied, and then exploded with a rage so great

that it astounded the clergyman and put him in fear. 'That snivelling, misbegotten little bastard Gavin Cleland is accusing David McGill of assassinating his brother,' he roared. 'For two pins I would go straight to the estate, root him out, and thrash the truth out of him.'

'I have two pins,' Barclay concede, 'but you are not having them, for I cannot condone violence. Calm yourself, Mathew, and tell me the whole story. Once you have done, if I decide there's no other option, then maybes I'll raid my pin store.'

By the time he was finished, he was indeed calm, but the minister was as agitated as he had been, more upset than Mathew had ever seen him. 'It's grievous that Master Cleland would do such a thing. I find it hard to credit.'

His eyes narrowed very slightly. 'You are sure that the boy is telling the truth?' he murmured. 'I know David is a mild man, but that lad is the apple of his eye, and if he did provoke Gregor Cleland to whip him, well, even the most saintly among us can sometimes yield to temptation.'

'Am I sure?' Mathew gasped, astonished and shocked. 'Of course I'm sure. How can you ask such a thing?'

'I was being the devil's advocate, sir, that is all. Of course I cannot believe David to be a cold-hearted murderer. After all, he's a member of my own session, like yourself. And yet, even by the boy's story, he did drag Sir Gregor to the ground and beat him sorely.'

'John,' he replied evenly, 'I spent my first adult years as a soldier. I did my duty, and as part of that I killed people in the hot blood of battle. Yet I had comrades who were not up to that task. When it came to the press they would fire their weapons, but they would aim to miss. It never surprised me when it happened, for I had sensed that the moment I saw them. David McGill would have been one of those; he might have given Sir Gregor the battering he deserved, but he could not be a murderer. He would defend his family with his own life, but could he take another's? No, sir. I tell you that for sure. If you tell me that you doubt me, you are demeaning your ministry.'

'I'm sorry,' Barclay replied, his grey head bowed. 'Of course I do not.'

'Then if this thing goes to trial, you'll come and speak for him?'

'How will I know when that time is?'

'I will send for you. My intention is to go to Edinburgh, and to remain there as long as is necessary, until David's innocence is proved and he is released.'

'And if it is not?' the minister murmured.

'That is not an outcome I will even consider. I will not come back to Carluke without him.'

'Then God be with you. And you'll need Him, for you'll be heading into a foreign city, within your own land. It's a cold place and it can be cruel.'

'Maybe, but John, I have been in Paris, Madrid, Brussels and even London. So you see, cities are not strange to me.'

'But I doubt there's another like Edinburgh,' Barclay said. 'I was there as a young man, forty years ago. The stench of the pisspots and the stench of corruption are with me to this day.'

Any observation that Mathew might have made was

deflected by the sight, though the parlour window, of young Matt, crossing the green and entering the church-yard. His expression was not that of one bringing good news.

'They wouldn't come, neither o' them,' he said as he joined the two men. 'Johnny Cope said his father wouldna' let him; as for Johnny Wilson, he says I did try to scare the horses. I tried to shake the truth out of him but he's more scared of Gavin Cleland than he was of me. Could you make him change his mind, Mathew?'

'Possibly,' he replied, 'but you cannot rely on an unwilling witness.'

'Did either of these boys see Matt being whipped?' Barclay asked.

'I doubt it, but in any case, that he was struck is not in dispute.'

'Johnny Cope said something else,' young Matt added. 'He said his father told him that my father killed Sir Gregor out of revenge for being dismissed from his job.'

'If that is Gavin's story, it does not surprise me,' Mathew said. 'A man acting out of spite will draw much less sympathy from the jury than one acting to protect his son. But it does not worry me either. A good lawyer can dismiss that allegation, by pointing out that your father's station improved when he left the estate's employment, therefore leaving him no reason to feel animosity towards Cleland.'

He put a hand on the boy's shoulder. 'You should carry no grudges either, against those two lads. They are afraid; Cope for his family's welfare and Wilson for his own. Fear is a human weakness, so forgive them. In any case, having run off, they were of minor importance to your father's defence; we'll put the truth before the court without their help. Come on, my boy, I see Mr Beattie returning. We need to get back to Waterloo House to prepare for the long journey we have ahead of us tomorrow.'

Chapter Nineteen

BEFORE HE COULD GO anywhere, Mathew had one thing to do and that was to make sure that his business could function properly in his absence. When the two managers of his leather factories arrived for work the next day, they found him there before them.

He told them what had happened and that he would have to deal with it. In his absence, Alan Craig, the senior of the two men, would be in overall charge of both factories. If he was not back by the end of the week, a progress report should be sent to him through Gabriel Spence.

'Write to Sir Graham Stockley on my behalf,' he instructed his secretary. 'Tell him that I will be in Edinburgh for a period; you need not say why. Sheriff Stirling has told me of a new hotel in Edinburgh, a grand place, and not far from the Calton Jail, to where Mr McGill was taken. That is where I will be until this matter is resolved.

'You would scarcely credit this, Gabriel,' he said, 'but it is called "The Waterloo", in a street called Waterloo Place. How that name has woven its way through my life!'

The journey to Scotland's capital city was completed in a single day. Initially, Mathew had contemplated taking the stagecoach from Lanark, but had decided instead that Ewan Beattie should drive them, and stay with them in Edinburgh, to take care of young Matt, should he have business where the boy could not be present.

There would still be a man about the place at Waterloo House. Tam Jackson, the gardener, was a sturdy fellow and an ex-soldier like his employer, who had hired him as much for that military background as for his skill in growing the vegetables that kept them fed throughout the year.

Beattie, who had journeyed many times to Edinburgh in the employ of Sir George Cleland, chose to head for Carnwath, and then to take the Lang Whang road to Edinburgh. Most of it ran over grazing land, open desolate moorland with several ascents and no shade.

The day was unusually hot and so the coachman did not press the horses, although he was exposed himself to the full force of the summer sun. Even at that leisurely pace, they reached the Haymarket within six hours, and fifteen minutes later they emerged from Shandwick Place, into Princes Street. Mathew had seen many remarkable things in several countries, but had never been as impressed by anything as he was by the mighty castle on its great rock, that overlooked the New Town.

Eventually they drew up outside the Waterloo Hotel, at twenty minutes after five o'clock. Mathew jumped down from the coach and stepped into the entrance hall, where he found a man, in formal dress, seated at a desk.

When he introduced himself and asked for rooms, he discovered to his great surprise that his name was known.

'Would that be Mr Mathew Fleming, of Stockley Fleming?' the manager asked.

'Yes, it would,' he admitted.

'Sir Graham Stockley is a frequent guest of the Waterloo, sir,' the man explained. 'He speaks of you often, and warmly too.'

'Then I hope I will be a frequent guest myself in the future, Mr . . . ?'

'Soutar, sir, Andrew Soutar. How many are in your party?'

He nodded in the direction of his two companions, who were waiting by the door. 'We will be three; myself, my young charge, Matthew McGill, who is fifteen years old, and my coachman, Mr Ewan Beattie.'

Surprise verging on astonishment showed in Soutar's eyes. 'Your coachman will be lodging with us?'

'Of course. Where else would I put him? He and young Matt will share a room, for I do not want the boy to be alone. Do you have a place for my coach and stabling for my horses?'

'Indeed, sir. Our stable boy will take charge of them and our porter will take your baggage to your rooms. They will be adjacent, on the first floor, with a view of Princes Street rather than of the jail.'

'The jail?' Mathew repeated casually.

'Yes, sir, at the top of the rise, facing Calton Hill itself. Of course we would rather it had been sited somewhere else, but at least it is more pleasing aesthetically than the awful old Tolbooth that it replaced.'

'Does this mean that one might open the curtains to see some poor fellow on the scaffold?'

Soutar smiled. 'Oh no, sir. Executions still take place at the Lawnmarket, happily.'

'Not so happily for the man at the end of the rope.'

The manager winced.

'Tell me if you can,' Mathew continued, 'how I can reach Hanover Street.'

'Certainly sir. It's only a short walk, along Princes Street.'

'Good, I will go there tomorrow. Now, if you would be so good as to show us to our rooms. We will dine here later, but first there is a call I must pay upon a friend.'

'Do you have his address?'

'Oh yes. It is not far from here.'

Mathew had brought clothes that would see him comfortably through a week; he was pleased to discover that the hotel was properly furnished and that he would be able to hang his coats and store everything else in drawers. As soon as he had unpacked, he knocked on the door of the room adjacent.

'I am going up the road a little way,' he told Beattie when he opened it. 'Keep the boy close, but do not tell him where I have gone, or he might come after me.'

'We'll wait here for your return, sir,' the driver replied. 'I can guess your destination.'

He stepped out into Waterloo Place, taking a proper lungful of city air. He sniffed, to catch the scent of Edinburgh, trying to match it to Barclay's description, but detecting not the faintest waft of pisspots in the atmosphere. As for the stench of corruption, he knew that to be more subtle.

The roadway was cobbled, and paved on either side with flagstones. The metal segs that he always fitted to his boot heels clicked as he walked. As he approached the prison, he cast his eye to his left, looking up at Calton Hill, with its observatory, and beyond that the pillared National Monument, planned to celebrate the victory over Napoleon.

He knew the story, from newspaper accounts: the intention had been to build a replica of the Parthenon, in Athens, funded by public subscription, but interest in the scheme had waned, and it was likely that all that would be completed was the single line of columns that he could see on the hilltop.

However there had been no problem in finding the money to build the Calton Jail. Its outer walls were formidable, with a great wooden double gate set in the centre. Within that there was a doorway, a wicket gate, which Mathew struck with the side of his closed fist.

After a few moments a small hatch opened, and a moustachioed face peered at him. 'You're a fearsome one richt enough,' its owner said. 'Have ye come tae storm the jail?'

'I hope that will not be necessary,' Mathew replied. 'No, I have come to visit one of your temporary inmates, Mr David McGill, who was brought here yesterday.'

'This is no' a lodging house,' the warder laughed. 'Ye cannae call here at will.'

'I am well aware of that. Nonetheless, I wish to speak with my friend.'

'Only the governor can allow that, sir.'

'Then go at once, if you please, and tell him that Mr Mathew Fleming, a Deputy Lord Lieutenant of Lanarkshire, is being kept waiting at his gate.'

The gatekeeper's smile turned to a frown, as he weighed

up his options; finally he came down in the side of caution. 'Wait here, please, sir,' he said.

After ten minutes the wicket gate was opened, and he was invited to step inside, into a paved yard beyond which the tall grey prison stood. The bewhiskered warder whom he had seen through the hatch had been joined by a second man. He was not in uniform; instead he wore a black jacket and breeches, with a white, starched shirt, and a cravat.

'My name is Henry Stevens, Governor,' he announced. 'Do you have proof that you are who you say you are, sir?'

Mathew smiled. 'Do you?' he retorted but reached into a pocket of his coat. He had expected such a question and had brought with him various documents, among them, in its envelope, the letter from the Lord Chamberlain, with its intimation of his appointment. 'You may recognise the crest,' he said.

Stevens read carefully, then handed it back. 'Thank you, Mr Fleming,' he murmured civilly. 'I am told you have a friend incarcerated here. His name?'

'David McGill, of Carluke, Lanarkshire. He was brought here yesterday, from Lanark Sheriff Court.'

The governor's eyes narrowed as he glanced down for a second or two, then back at his visitor. 'I know of him; the Crown Office alerted me to his arrival.'

'Is that usual?'

'It is not a common occurrence, but if the Lord Advocate has a special interest in a prisoner, I am sometimes informed. Why? I have no idea, for I treat them all the same, whether they be awaiting trial or convicted.'

'Should that be the case?' Mathew queried. 'Is a man not innocent until proven otherwise?'

'Oh he is, Mr Fleming, but if he's here, he is in . . . let me just call it a situation.'

'And in that situation where exactly is David at the moment?'

'He is in a cell with various other inmates . . . all of them untried, before you ask me.'

'Then may I see him, in private?'

'Normally, my answer would be no,' Stevens began. 'You are not his lawyer and from what you say you are not his family.'

'I am his employer.'

'That would not make you an entitled visitor.' He paused. 'However, there is your rank, and while I am not bound to defer to that, I will. Come with me.'

The governor led Mathew towards the jail building; it might have struck him as grand, had he not known its purpose. It was long, built of grey stone, three storeys high, with three turrets, one at either end and one in the centre to which they were heading.

As they reached it, Stevens took a set of keys that were attached to his belt by a foot-long chain, and found one that fitted the lock in the main door. Inside, the building was gloomy, even though the evening was still bright outside.

They walked along a lamp-lit corridor; at the other end the governor unlocked a second door and the two men stepped out into a great, galleried hall, with three tiers, walkways around the upper levels, all looking into the centre. The area was lighter with a cupola above, but it was sweltering, and the smell of pisspots that had been absent on the outside was much in evidence. The only people in sight all wore warders' dark, belted uniforms and peaked caps, and carried clubs and short cutlasses.

There was a slight buzz of conversation, but no more than that. Although Mathew knew that hundreds of men were contained on the levels above, the place was unnaturally silent. He commented on the fact.

'Conversation is forbidden outside the cells; inside, when men are locked up together for weeks, months and years, they run out of things to say to each other.'

'Where are they fed?'

'In a mess hall beyond this area; they get three meals a day. They have porridge for breakfast, with milk that's as fresh as we can keep it, soup and potatoes for lunch, with a little meat if we have it, and porridge in the evening, with milk again and biscuits. Three cups of water each, per day.'

'How can men sustain themselves on such a diet?' Mathew asked.

'Poorly,' Stevens admitted, 'but they manage. I am given a budget to feed them and I do the best I can with it. Remember, Mr Fleming, they are not here to be nurtured; rather the opposite. The last thing I would want would be for this place to be filled with strong men. We keep them weak and we keep them cowed. That may sound brutal but it is the truth; any who rebel, or are insolent, are dealt with severely, with the lash or the birch if deserved, or by isolation in dark cells, down in the cellars in the rear walls. They are set on the rock of this hill. I am sorry if that offends you,' he continued 'but this is not a place of recreation.'

'And men can be here for years?'

'Yes. Not your friend, though; from what I was told of the charge against him, murdering a member of the gentry, the best he can possibly hope for is transportation for life, and then only if his judge is one of the softer hearts among the senators. Come, I will find you a private place and will have him brought to you.'

They walked across the hall, and into another corridor. There Stevens opened an unlocked door and ushered his guest into a small room. It was completely unfurnished, but had a window that looked out on to a yard and across to a strange circular building.

'That is my house,' he explained. 'To an extent, I am a prisoner here myself. Wait and I'll bring your man.'

Left alone with his thoughts, Mathew was shaken by what he had seen. He was, by upbringing and at heart, a countryman, and as such an innocent in many ways, even after his military service, which had been spent in foreign lands. One evening in the capital city had shattered his illusions, and he knew that having been introduced to the other, darker world he had avoided for his forty years, he could never put it out of his mind.

He was still gazing blindly through the window, when the door opened behind him. 'Fifteen minutes, sir,' the governor said, then closed it again.

He turned, came face to face with David McGill, and recoiled. His friend's face was lopsided; his left eye was so swollen that only a slit could be seen, and his lower lip was cut.

'Who did that?' Mathew growled. 'If it was the Sheriff's

officers, I'll make sure they're pilloried for it.'

'No,' McGill whispered, 'not them.' Amazingly he managed a crooked smile, revealing that one of his lower front teeth was chipped. 'One of my cell companions decided that I was a dandy. As you can see, he does not like dandies.'

'God, man, what sort of a place is this?'

'It is not the place, Mathew, but the people; the men I am in with are thieves and ruffians, but they know nothing else. They are not all villains either. There are six of us, and when I was set upon, three of the others restrained my attacker. He has left me alone since.'

'But I will not leave him alone,' Mathew declared, his blood boiling.

'Forget him,' David said, 'he is of no consequence. Is Lizzie safe? Are my children safe?'

'They are,' Mathew assured him. 'Cleland has evicted them from the cottage, but they are under my roof. Jean is being looked after by Miss Liddell, and Lizzie is in my mother's care.'

'And Matt?'

'He is with me. As we speak he is in my hotel, under the eye of my man Beattie.'

'Oh no,' David moaned. 'Send him back, Mathew, I beg you. I dinna want him near any of this.'

'He must be. Matt is your only witness. Without his testimony . . .' He broke off for a second or two. 'David, what do you know of the charge against you?'

'Nothing really. I could not take it in. There was a man in the court, the procurator fiscal, I think, in a wig like the Sheriff. The two were talking and then the Sheriff ordered me to be brought here. I know next to nothing. Is it that bad a thing, man, to lay hands on a baronet?'

'Not in my opinion, given what happened to Matt, but that is not what Gavin and his lady friends are saying you did. They have libelled you, man; they are calling you murderer, saying you shot Gregor.'

His friend stared back at him, one good eye looking upon another. 'How can they?' he whispered. 'Nobody believes that, surely?'

'They have given sworn evidence, David. It must be countered and disproved, in court if necessary.'

'And if not?' he whispered. His right hand went to his throat. 'My God! If there is a murder here it could be mine.'

'That will not happen.'

'You can say that and be certain of it?'

'I have faith that our courts cannot convict an innocent man. The Crown has lies as evidence; Gavin and the women will be cross-examined in court and exposed. We have Matt's true account, and John Barclay as a witness to your goodness, and me also. We will set this false charge aside, hopefully before it gets as far as a trial.'

'Pray God that you do,' David whispered. 'Man, I was afraid before, but now . . . I am not a brave man, Mathew, just an ordinary clerk from Carluke.'

'Nonsense,' Mathew declared. 'You are the best man I know, and I will not let you down. Tomorrow I will get your defence under way, and with a fair wind, by Friday at the latest we will all be back home.'

'How can you be away from business for so long?' his friend asked.

He laughed. 'You are thinking of my business at a time like this? David, man, for as long as it takes, you are my business, my only business.'

He explained what he was planning to do. Just as he finished, the door opened, and the governor joined them. 'I'm afraid that I must end your conversation, Mr Fleming,' he said.

'I thank you for the opportunity,' Mathew replied. 'But there is one more thing to be discussed,' he added, 'and that is the state of Mr McGill's face.'

'That was noted,' Stevens said grimly, 'and it is being dealt with. The man responsible is on his way to the whipping post, and after that to a dark room in the bowels of this building, where he'll stay until it is his turn to face the court. Mr McGill will be lodged alone from now on,' he added. 'I have given orders for that. You may visit him daily.'

'Thank you; as soon as I engage a lawyer I will bring him here. Sir, if I send in decent food, will he get it?'

'There will be no need for you to do so. He will eat from my kitchen. I can provide very few small mercies here, but for your friend, sir, I will.'

Two warders were waiting outside, to take David to his new, solitary cell. The two friends embraced before parting, then Stevens escorted Mathew back to the entrance to the prison.

'Good luck in your quest,' the governor said. 'There is only one piece of advice that I can offer. Be careful who you trust in this city. Here, everyone has the same motive, and that is self-interest.'

Chapter Twenty

'WILL I COME WITH you, Mr Fleming?' Ewan Beattie asked, wiping a strand of egg yolk from his beard. The coachman was far from being the tidiest eater that Mathew had ever met.

He looked back at him across the hotel's breakfast table. 'No, I think not; not on this occasion. I will need Matt with me when I find the man I'm after, but when I do, another body in the room would only make a crowd. I have been considering another task for you, now that we know the horses are well looked after. Are you ready for a spot of intrigue, Ewan?'

'Ready for it, aye, sir. Whether I'll be ony good at it, that's another matter. What would you have me do?'

'When you worked for the Clelands, did you ever drive them to Edinburgh?'

Beattie shook his head. 'Not the twins, no. Their faither I did, old Sir George, once or twice.'

'When you did, where did you take him? Did he have a town house?'

'He had small one, yes, in a street in the centre of the city; it was in a terrace, not in its own grounds, but with a lane behind for stabling. MacPherson, the old man who was head coachman afore me, said that when Lady Cleland was alive it was used often, but that after she died, Sir George had little interest in it.'

'But perhaps his sons had. I want you to find out if Gavin is there. Discreetly, mind; he need not discover our interest in him until he has to.'

Beattie smiled. 'I will do my best not to be noticed, sir.'

Mathew chuckled. 'Your best is all you can do, Ewan. I acknowledge that you were not built to be easily forgotten.' The coachman was three inches shorter than Mathew, but much broader built, with legs like small tree trunks.

'If I took my beard off, sir?' he suggested.

'Maybe that will not be necessary; to a man like Gavin Cleland, a servant's face is not one to be recalled.' The chuckle evolved into a gentle laugh. 'Given your respective positions on the coach he might well recognise your arse, but the other end will be much less familiar.'

Beside him at the table, on his blind side, Matt did not join in the laughter. 'Can I go looking for him?' he asked, but there was no humour on his face, or in his voice.

'You will not,' Mathew replied. 'Make no mistake, your father is in a bad situation, and you must do nothing to worsen it. You are in my care, and like it or not, boy, you are under my orders. Your father knows that and because of it he is content. You will see Cleland, but only in court.'

He pushed his plate away from him and rose to his feet. 'To that end, let us go. Ewan, I have no idea how long we will be; when you are done, go to the hotel salon and wait for us if necessary.'

'Where are we going?' young Matt asked, as the pair stepped out into Waterloo Place. 'To see my father?' he added hopefully.

'Not yet. When we do that I want to have news to give him.' In truth, Mathew wanted to delay the boy's visit to the jail for as long as possible, to give David's battered face time to heal. 'We are going in search of a solicitor, whose name I was given by Sheriff Stirling.'

'Will he speak for my father in court?'

'No,' Mathew replied. 'That must be done by counsel, that is, by an advocate. The solicitor prepares the case for his client, and counsel presents it.'

'Who is this man, this soli . . . ?'

'Solicitor. His name is Paul Johnston and he has chambers in Hanover Street; that, I am told, is not far from here.'

In fact it was less than half a mile, past Register House, then along Princes Street. The turn into Hanover Street was opposite the Royal Scottish Academy building, another Athenian design by the architect Playfair. It struck Mathew as vaguely similar to what the National Monument might have been, although on a smaller scale.

They had no time to admire it; Stirling had warned that after nine thirty the solicitor would probably have left for court, and Mathew's pocket watch showed twenty past. Happily they did not have much further to walk. The pavement rose up towards George Street, where a statue of the recently deceased monarch after whom it had been named looked up at Edinburgh Castle. A few yards short of that Mathew spotted a brass plate with the engraving, 'Mr Paul Johnston, Solicitor'.

'This is our man,' he told his companion, then climbed the stone steps that led to the door on which the sign was mounted.

There was a knocker. He rapped three times, and waited.

After a minute or so, the door was opened, and a man stood. He was blinking furiously, either at the disturbance or at the sunlight, they could not be sure. His age could have been anywhere between thirty and forty. He was cadaverous in appearance with a bald head, hollow cheeks, and spectacles perched on the bridge of his nose. He wore a royal blue jacket, with noticeably frayed cuffs, and he held a top hat in his left hand.

'This is not convenient,' he stammered, agitated. 'You catch me on the point of leaving for Parliament Hall. You must make an appointment. I can see you tomorrow, if you wish.'

'Our situation is more urgent than that, Mr Johnston,' Mathew said. 'You are Mr Johnston, I take it.'

'Yes, yes. In the Supreme Courts, sir, everyone's situation is always urgent. Tomorrow, I say.'

Mathew smiled. 'If you do not reach the court by ten o'clock, will someone die?' he asked.

The question provoked another bout of furious blinking. 'No,' Johnston conceded.

'Will an innocent man be put on a ship for Botany Bay?'
'No.'

'If you are a few minutes late, will anyone actually notice?'

'I am always there for ten o'clock, sir.'

'Then please break the habit of a lifetime, Mr Johnston,

if not for us, then for my friend Sheriff Robin Stirling.'

The lawyer's countenance changed in an instant. A surprised smile replaced the agitated frown; his spectacles fell from his nose but he caught them in his right hand.

'Sheriff Stirling?' he repeated. 'Why did you not say so?'

'There was barely an opportunity until now. My name is Mathew Fleming, of Waterloo House, Lanarkshire, and my young friend here is Matt McGill. We are in need of a lawyer and this is a capital matter. When I asked Robin for a recommendation, yours was the first name to pass his lips . . . although he did say that I might have to pour a bucket of water down your trousers to get your attention.'

'My old university tutor knows me too well,' Johnston agreed. 'I am sorry for my abruptness. Very few clients seek me out in my chambers; I am usually approached in Parliament Hall itself. Come inside and tell me about your predicament.'

He led them into a hallway, then into the first room on the right. It had two tables, one set against a window that looked out on to the busy street, the other against the opposite wall.

'Some people like to be seen with me,' he explained, 'others prefer discretion.'

'Then let us be visible,' Mathew declared. 'I want everyone in Edinburgh to know my business.'

'And what is that?'

'My good friend, Matt's father, is facing trial for his life. The evidence against him is a farrago of wicked lies dreamed up to cover the guilt of another man, his principal accuser.'

'But are all the liars telling the same story?'

'Yes, they are.'

'Then let me hear their side and then yours, and I will see what is to be done.'

Chapter Twenty-One

EWAN BEATTIE COULD NOT remember when last he had been so unexpectedly pleased. His master had entrusted him with a task that had nothing to do either with horses or with their equipment, and that was a rare occurrence in his world.

Yes, the evening before he had been asked to look after the boy, but as a coachman it was a daily occurrence for him to have people in his care.

He only had one problem as he set out on his mission. He had forgotten the name of the street in which the Cleland town house was located, if he had ever known it. Ten years had gone by since he had taken old Sir George there, on the occasion of a visit to Edinburgh by the late King. On that arrival, as on every other, the Laird had simply given him instructions as he had neared their destination, 'Left ahead', or 'Turn right here, Beattie', until they had reached their destination, and then he had always directed him to the stables and small yard at the rear. Unusually for a gentleman, the old fellow had never been too haughty to use the servants' entrance.

The only clue that Ewan could recall for certain was the

number nineteen, displayed in iron letters on the gatepost as he drove in. Whatever the street might be, he knew that number, even if he had never actually seen the frontage of the building. Of one thing also he was sure. If the Cleland twins had arrived in their own coach, its driver would know the main entrance, for that pair would use no other.

When he set out from the hotel he was instantly and completely lost. He had no bearings, as he was to the east of Princes Street at the outer limits of what they called the New Town, whereas invariably he had arrived from the west.

The only solution, he decided, was to walk the length of Princes Street, then down Maitland Street, if necessary, before turning on his heel and trying to recreate those earlier journeys from memory.

As soon as he set out, he experienced a strange feeling, one of being shut in by the tall buildings on either side of him. On his coach, he was impervious to anything, but alone and on foot, that was a great difference. Once he passed into Princes Street, open on one side as it was, that trepidation passed . . . only to be replaced by another.

On his earlier visits to Edinburgh, he had remained in the house, at Sir George's pleasure, never venturing out other than in the coach, and even that had been a rare circumstance. Thus he had never been conscious of the number of people in the streets, far more than he had ever seen gathered in one place. In Princes Street, as he headed west, an army hundreds strong seemed to be marching in the other direction, all of them in a mighty hurry and expecting him to step out of the way. That he did not do; as a result more than one man bounced off him, throwing him fierce looks that faded invariably as they realised how solid he was.

Before long he crossed to the other side, where the gardens were, and where the oncomers were fewer in number. As he walked, he looked for clues, familiar turnings on the other side of the road, seeing none until he reached St John's Church.

'There, I think,' he murmured, and crossed the street, mindful of the carriages, aware that if a coachman was run over he would never hear the end of it.

He had gone more than half a mile before the descent towards the Water of Leith told him he was heading out of the city. Damning his memory, he retraced his steps, and realised that he had made only a small mistake. He turned instead into Charlotte Square . . . 'Left here, Beattie' . . . and crossed it, before turning into Albyn Place . . . 'Right here, man, and gentle on the cobbles' . . . and soon he was on familiar ground, as Albyn Place became Queen Street.

Past the gardens on the north side of the street and then . . . 'Left here, Beattie.'

The coachman needed no further prompting; his sense of direction was fully in place, and his equilibrium restored. Just before he made the turn into Duke Street, he looked up and saw Calton Hill, realising that he had come almost full circle and had travelled four times as far as had been necessary.

As the road sloped away from him he remembered reining in the horses, and almost automatically glanced to his right, and saw the entrance to the lane. He crossed the street and ventured along the passageway; sure enough, he had not gone far before he came to a familiar gatepost, bearing the number nineteen. Looking beyond, he saw the door that led into the basement of the house, and above, well above, the rear attic room that had been his on his brief stays with the old Laird.

Beattie ventured no further. Instead he returned to Duke Street and walked down to the next junction, to check the name of the thoroughfare: Albany Street; the Cleland town house was number nineteen Albany Street.

On the corner, on the northern side, there was a small shop, a milliner. Beattie was standing by it when he saw a small carriage approaching from the other end of the street. As he looked he saw the driver haul on the reins, bringing the vehicle to a halt, not far from where he stood. Instinctively he looked into the shop window, then after a few seconds ventured a quick glance.

The horse was turning in the full width of the empty street. A man had climbed down from the conveyance and stood on the pavement, reaching into a pocket as if for a key.

Beattie's eyes were keen, he knew who he was looking at; even from that distance he could see that the new arrival was dishevelled, crumpled and blue-chinned, and that beyond question it was Sir Gavin Cleland.

Chapter Twenty-Two

'WELL?' MATHEW ASKED, WHEN Matt had finished his story.
'What do you think of it?'

'What did Sheriff Stirling think?' Johnston countered.
'After all, it is he who has committed Mr McGill for trial.'

'Yes, but he only heard one side of the story, the false
allegation.'

'Mr Fleming, that is all the Sheriff is required to hear at
this stage. The accused is only able to defend himself once
the indictment is laid.'

'All I can tell you is that Robin did not think the boy
a liar when he heard him.'

'No,' the lawyer said, firmly, 'and neither did I.
Unfortunately I will not be on the jury and nor will I be on
the Bench.'

'What does the Bench have to do with it? Surely the
judge is bound to try the case impartially, without showing
favour to either side.'

'Surely he is. Have you ever heard of Lord Braxfield?'

'Of course I have,' Mathew replied. 'He was a Lanarkshire
man.'

'No doubt, but he was a Crown man first and foremost.

Happily, Lord Cooper, the present Lord Justice General, sets a different example. However it is less than likely that he will take the trial; I hear he is ill.'

Johnston looked, earnestly, over the top of his spectacles. 'I am the most intrigued,' he murmured, 'by what you say of the interest of the Lord Advocate in this case. Sir Gregor Cleland was a minor landowner, a baronet rather than a baron. It may be that the murder of any titled gentleman inflames him, but even so, he has been unusually expeditious in this case.'

He raised his arms above his head, his fingers interlocked. 'The ways of the Crown Office are often a mystery to me, but I am only a humble solicitor. We will have to see what counsel thinks. Before we do that we must retain one, the best available.' He glanced at Mathew. 'How deep is your pocket, Mr Deputy Lieutenant?

'Deep enough for this purpose.'

'Then let us walk up the hill to Parliament House and see who is for hire.'

The solicitor ushered them out of his office, leading the way back to Princes Street, and then across it, along the side of the Royal Academy Building, and up the steep hill that led first to the Bank of Scotland and then on to St Giles Cathedral. The roadway was macadamised rather than cobbled, and their guide told them that it was known as The Mound.

By the time they reached the top, Johnston's breath was rasping in his chest and his face was flushed. Mathew wondered if the man was a consumptive.

'Do you make that climb every day?' he asked.

'With difficulty,' the lawyer replied. 'I had a touch of pleurisy a month ago. The physician said I should recuperate for longer, but I could not. People depend on me and if I am not there, well, some might go unrepresented or, worse, be represented by the wrong sort. There are charlatans here, sir.'

'Then guide us well. Where is Parliament Hall?'

'Follow.' He led his clients across the courtyard in front of St Giles and past a building so new that its grey stone almost shone. 'That is the great library,' he told them, 'the home of the Writers to the Signet, of which I have the honour to be a member; but it is not where we are going. We are for Parliament House, round the corner.'

The trio walked on until they reached an unprepossessing doorway, with a small, illegible sign at the side. Beyond it lay an entrance porch.

'The first call I must pay is to the Lord Advocate's office, to find out where this matter stands. You gentlemen may care to wait in here.'

He threw open a door at the side. 'This is Parliament Hall; in the days when we had one of those, over a hundred years ago, it sat here. Now it is the home of the Supreme Court. It is not in session at the moment, but when it is,' he pointed to the right, 'it sits at the far end there.'

Mathew and Matt looked as he directed, and saw a high mahogany tower, faced by an enclosure with a table between them and rows of seats on either side.

'I shall not be long,' Johnston told them. 'When I am back, we will be in a position to recruit.'

As he left, Mathew looked around the great hall; the

end opposite to the court was lit by a huge window, and set into the far wall he saw a stone fireplace, which was unlit. Then he looked up, and gasped. The roof was built entirely of great beams of wood, carved in a series of arches with gold crests, and with its supports fastened into the walls.

'Is that not a marvel?' he whispered.

Young Matt shrugged his solid shoulders. 'It's a roof,' he grunted.

They stood by the door for fifteen minutes, watching men in robes and wigs, usually in twos, occasionally in a trio, walking up and down the length of the great hall. They appeared to be conversing, but to what purpose neither of the watchers could tell.

Finally, Paul Johnston returned, carrying a document, bound in ribbon; if anything his cheeks looked even more sunken, and his face even more pale.

'You have news?' Mathew asked.

'Yes,' he replied, 'but not good. The indictment against Mr McGill is completed already and it will be put to him on Friday, in the court.'

'You mean the trial begins this week?'

'No, not that soon; on Friday he will only be asked how he pleads, guilty or otherwise. That is a formality; he will be committed for trial, and that will begin next Tuesday. I say "begin", but only a single day has been allocated for it. I have never known the Lord Advocate to proceed so fast. I asked his clerk why it was. He could only tell me that since the evidence is clear-cut and he has a longer trial to follow after, Mr Douglas wants to clear the decks.'

'Douglas?'

'James Douglas, KC; he is the Lord Advocate, and the most powerful man in Scots law, save only for the Lord Justice General himself. He leads the prosecution service, but more than that, he is a member of the Westminster Parliament and responsible there for all of our Scottish affairs.'

'Is such a rush to judgment allowed by the law?'

'The court sets its own rules; it will be for the judge to confirm the trial date. Counsel for Mr McGill may request more time to prepare his case, but it will be at the discretion of the Bench. Do not look, however, for that discretion to be exercised. Lord Bellhouse is trying the case, the Lord Justice Clerk himself, and he is the least patient of our judges. He is also well acquainted with the Lord Advocate; when James Douglas was a pupil advocate, and Bellhouse was King's Counsel, he was his devilmaster.'

'Are we helpless in this?' Mathew asked.

'Not entirely. There are a few senior counsel that Bellhouse would not cross, men who might soon be candidates for the Bench themselves. Cooper, the Lord Justice General, is an old man. When he goes, his successor is uncertain, but it is unlikely to be Bellhouse, on account of his own years.'

'Then find us one of these men to take David's case.'

'That is where we go now. We are heading for the Faculty of Advocates; its members are the only men with rights of audience in the Supreme Courts. '

The solicitor led them to a door across the hall, and opened it, allowing his clients to step into a rectangular area. It was not much of a room, more of an ante-chamber, with a stair to the right leading to lower levels of the building. In its centre a man in an ornate but predominantly black uniform sat at a desk.

'Mr Johnston,' he exclaimed. 'And what is it today, sir?'

'Senior counsel, Mr Baird, for a most urgent case,' he replied, then turned and whispered to his companions. 'Mr Magnus Baird is clerk to the advocates,' he explained. 'He keeps their diaries.'

'Do you have anyone specific in mind, sir?' Baird asked. There was something in his tone for which Mathew did not care, a hint of mockery, perhaps.

'Sir Basil Foster, KC.'

The clerk choked off a gasp. 'Sir Basil? Surely, Mr Johnston, he's a cut above your usual run of clients? And why do you bring them here? Finely dressed this chap may be, but his face tells a different story.'

'This chap, as you call him, is an officer of the King,' Johnston retorted, 'one of his deputy lieutenants. He is here to seek counsel to defend his friend, the father of the boy, on a false capital charge. I do not need to remind you that advocates have a duty to represent anyone in need of their services. I have checked the lists and I do not see Sir Basil's name on any of them for the next week. I wish to instruct him.'

Baird seemed to stiffen. Mathew wondered whether the solicitor would have spoken to him so harshly had he not been present, and whether he might pay for his boldness at some time in the future.

'Do you have the indictment?' the clerk asked coldly. 'If so, I will show it to Sir Basil.'

'Here it is.' Johnston handed him the document he had brought from the Lord Advocate's office.

'Does everyone have a little power in this place?' Mathew asked, as the man left them through a doorway that he could see led into a long room, lined with desks each with a twin candelabra.

'Very perceptive of you, sir,' the solicitor chuckled. 'That is exactly how it is, but that man has more than most, given his station. All of us solicitors come to Baird as supplicants; we have no other route to the Bar, and to those who may plead a case in the Supreme Courts, than through him. We need his favour, if we are to retain counsel of our choice, not his. His advocates are all beholden to him, even the mightiest King's Counsel, like Foster, as their work comes through him. And Baird is clever, a good tactician, ensuring that the fattest briefs go to the fattest men, the top silks, the most senior counsel, while at the same time ensuring that every junior has a worthy living.'

'He should be a politician.'

'He is, Mr Fleming, in his own way.'

Mathew gave voice to his earlier concern. 'Then, Mr Johnston,' he said, 'have you not put your own future relations with this powerful man in jeopardy by the way you treated him just now?'

'Possibly, but my first duty is to my clients, not myself. If I do fall out of favour, it will not be for long. I will tell you honestly, sir, the type of brief and the size of fee that I am used to bringing to him are the kind he needs to keep his newer members in work and in pocket. All of the advocates here are sole traders, not members of a group as they are in England. So, to keep his own position secure, Baird must keep all of them happy. He may fall out with me, sir, but it will not be for long. As you observed, each of us has a little power of a sort.'

'But what of quality? How is that assured?'

'It is not. Advocates never suffer the consequences of their failures. They may not be sued, not even for the grossest negligence.'

'Then they are lucky men,' Mathew remarked. 'If I make a saddle that falls apart, and the rider falls and is injured, or worse, or if my factory makes a component for a locomotive that fractures, then I may expect to find myself here, albeit in the civil court, rather than the criminal. '

'But you never do,' young Matt exclaimed.

'Thank you for your loyalty, lad,' he laughed, 'but you can see now why that is, and why every item that leaves Netherton or Coatbridge is inspected.'

'Mathew . . .'

The boy was interrupted by the clerk's return. He handed the folded document back to Johnston.

'Sir Basil declines your brief,' he said.

The solicitor peered at the knotted ribbon. 'Did he do me the courtesy of reading it?' he asked, icily.

'There would have been no point. Sir Basil is fishing with the Marquis of Lothian on Tuesday.'

'So a salmon takes precedence over a man's life?' Mathew suggested.

Baird tried to meet his eye, but could not hold his gaze. 'One cannot disappoint a marquis, sir,' he murmured. 'But I cannot debate with you; I may only deal with instructing solicitors, not their clients.'

'In that event,' Johnston said, 'take my brief to Michael Kerr, KC. He is listed nowhere for Tuesday.'

'As you wish.'

He was gone for only a few minutes. 'Mr Kerr is nowhere to be found. Sir Basil believes he may be at his country house in Fife.'

'Then please approach Richard Scott, KC.'

The charade continued

'Did you anticipate this?' Mathew asked, after the clerk had gone off to seek Johnston's fifth choice.

'I feared that it might happen,' he admitted, 'although I hoped that the Faculty's tradition of fairness would prevail. On the face of it, without knowledge of the boy's account, the case is hopeless, and no King's Counsel likes to have a capital failure in the court record. More than that, these men will note that the indictment has been expedited. If they know also, and they will, that the Lord Advocate will prosecute himself . . . none, not even Foster, will wish to cross him.'

After the sixth refusal of the brief, and the sixth ingenious excuse, Johnston's list was exhausted, and a smug smile rested on the clerk's face.

Young Matt's agitation was obvious. 'What can be done?' he demanded. 'Faither cannae go undefended! These men are wicked. Mathew, you told me we were coming here for justice, but I see none,' he glared at the advocates' clerk, 'only a . . .'

'Hush, boy,' his guardian told him. 'Everything you say,

I feel too, and I will not forget it. But raised voices will not help. Mr Johnston,' he asked, 'what else can be done?'

'Only one thing.' He turned back to Baird. 'Since you, sir, are unable to meet any of my requirements, I am forced to insist that you take my brief to Mr Graham, KC, the Dean of Faculty himself.'

The little clerk nodded; he seemed unsurprised by the demand, rather than outraged. He took the document for the seventh time, and returned to the reading room.

'Why should the Dean accept what the others have rejected?' Mathew asked.

'He will not,' Johnston replied. 'Man, I hope he does not. Gordon Graham may be the head of the Faculty, but he is one of the worst criminal pleaders in this building. However in these circumstances, the Dean is obliged to appoint an advocate. We can only hope for the best, but in reality, since Mr Graham is a close friend of Mr Douglas, we will simply have to take what we are given.'

The three waited for fifteen minutes, and more. 'Perhaps Mr Graham is shooting with the Duke of Argyll,' Mathew observed drily.

Finally Baird reappeared. 'You have counsel,' he declared, straight-faced but too smugly for Johnston's liking. 'Please return to the hall and he will come to consult with you.'

'How will he know us?' young Matt asked, his belligerence unchecked.

The clerk looked down his nose at him and laughed. 'He may recognise your solicitor, or he may not, but if there is another one-eyed, scar-faced man out there, I will eat the buttons on my uniform.'

I would like to feed them to you, Magnus, one by one, Mathew thought, but he stepped back into Parliament Hall in silence.

They had been waiting there for five minutes when the door to the Advocates' Library opened once again and a young man stepped out. He was no taller than the fifteen-year-old Matt but draped in a robe that might have fitted Mathew. He carried his wig on his left hand and a familiar document in the other.

He looked around the hall, which was more full than it had been when the trio arrived, until his eyes settled on them, and he approached.

'Mr Johnston?' he ventured, looking hopefully at the solicitor.

'Indeed,' he replied. 'And you are?'

'Innes Irvine, advocate.' He ticked the brief under his left arm and extended his hand to Johnston. 'Honoured to meet you, sir.'

'And I you. I confess that I have not heard your name before, Mr Irvine.'

'That is no surprise, sir. I was called to the Bar only two weeks ago.'

Johnston frowned and held up a hand. 'A moment, if you please.' He drew Mathew to one side. 'Graham has appointed the boots of the Faculty to lead the defence in a trial for a man's life. Do you want to proceed, or do you want me to raise hell here, in a loud voice?'

'Would that serve any purpose?' Mathew asked. 'Would it secure us a more acceptable person?'

'No,' the solicitor admitted, 'there is no likelihood that it would. The Dean may appoint whoever he chooses.'

'Then let us hear the young fellow out. He holds the brief as if it were a gold bar; that much is in his favour.'

They turned back to Irvine; standing beside Matt, he looked as if he might not be much the older of the two.

'What was your university?' Johnston asked.

'Edinburgh, sir.'

'A good beginning. What is your background?'

'The law, sir. My father is a solicitor in Linlithgow, as was his father before him.'

'Very good. As a pupil, to whom did you devil?'

'To Mr Nigel Sutherland, KC; sadly he is seriously indisposed at the moment or I would have offered this brief to him. I am aware of the responsibility, and of the trust the Dean has placed in me.'

'Ah, but I am not sure that you are fully aware. Do you know the Lord Advocate?'

'Not at all, sir, nor anything about him save for one thing.'

'And what is that?'

'He is in an uncommon hurry to see our client hang.'

Beside him, young Matt blanched.

'This is our client's son,' Johnston said, sharply. 'He is also your principal witness.'

'Then shall we consult on the matter as he is here?'

'Indeed,' Johnston glanced over his shoulder at other advocates promenading in the hall, in earnest conversation with other solicitors, 'but not here. I see too many friends of Douglas, and their hearing will be keen. Let us all go to the coffee shop down the way. Is that acceptable to you, Mr Fleming?'

'As long as the coffee justifies it.'

The establishment in question was in the High Street, just past the constabulary office. It was still well short of noon; there were a few other customers, but none that Johnston recognised as lawyers. They took a table by the window, where the three men ordered coffee, and scones with strawberry jelly, and young Matt asked for lemonade.

As they waited, the young advocate read through the brief once more, then looked up at Mathew, having identified him as the paymaster, and thus the person of greatest influence in the group.

'May I speak freely in front of the boy, sir?'

'You must; but please do not think of him as such. He's here on man's business, and must be treated thus.'

'Very well. On the face of it, we have an open and shut case here, one which any advocate would rather prosecute than defend. But your persistence . . . indeed your very presence, Mr Fleming, for I know who you are, and that you are a very important person in the west of Scotland . . . that tells me there is more to this matter than what is set out in this hasty libel. The panel . . . that is to say the accused . . . is said to have shown extraordinary violence and displayed malice aforethought to the deceased. Can that be true?'

'Aforethought or afterthought,' Mathew said, 'certainly not. Mr McGill was dismissed from his post by Sir Gregor Cleland, and employed by me on the very same day, on significantly better terms. If anything, he had cause to be grateful to Cleland; he and I laughed about that on more than one occasion.'

'And will you attest to that under oath?'

'Of course. As to the violence, I was not there, but if I had been, and had seen what had happened, I would have done as David did in response, only I would have disabled Gavin first, as I would not have left that man at my back with a pistol. But I was a soldier; David, on the other hand, had never been roused to such anger in his life. He was hot-blooded and left himself exposed to what has happened since.'

'Left himself exposed on the day, you mean,' Irvine corrected him.

'No, sir, I do not. I have thought on this over the last few days, so I do not say it lightly. Consider if you will the width of a man's back, and of his forehead. Even for the worst shot in the world, how difficult is it to miss a target that size from a distance of no more than three yards? Now consider the size of a man's forehead. How difficult is it to hit a target of that size, slap in the centre? Gavin Cleland is not the worst shot in the world. His father was very proud of his sons' prowess with the pistol. He spoke to me of it one day, when I delivered a saddle to him, because he knew I had been an infantryman. He even said that Gavin could hit a target from horseback, if he chose.'

'You are saying?' the advocate asked.

'Nothing. Hear Matt's story, think on what I have said and see what you think.'

He leaned back in his chair and listened as his young

charge told Irvine the true story of what had happened on the previous Sunday.

'What do you think?' he asked when he was done.

'I think, Mr Fleming, that we have our defence, one of impeachment. We must counter the indictment by accusing Gavin Cleland of his brother's murder.'

Johnston intervened. 'Even though there is no corroboration of the boy's . . . sorry, the young man's story?'

'Ah, but there is, after a fashion. As well as attesting to the lack of animosity held towards Sir Gregor by the accused, Mr Fleming is also a witness to Gavin's prowess with the pistol, as described by his father.'

'There is still the matter of the two women and their evidence.'

'Their false evidence,' Irvine added. 'What is their motive in saying what they did? What do we know of these women?'

'Other than that one is a gentlewoman from Cheshire and that the other is her servant, we know nothing.'

'A gentlewoman who is prepared to lie a man's life away, under oath? I am a brand new advocate and I may be naive, but I doubt that. I would like to know more of her and of her companion.'

'Where can they be lodging in Edinburgh?' Paul Johnston wondered aloud. 'The indictment tells us nothing, and yet if they are to be in the witness box on Tuesday, they must be close by, surely?'

'They may be on the Cleland Estate,' Mathew pointed out.

'That is true. If Miss Smith was indeed a close friend of

the deceased, she may well have remained there. After all, there will be a funeral.'

'Indeed, but when?'

'I can tell you that,' the solicitor said. 'I asked the Lord Advocate's clerk if it would be possible to view the corpse. He said that would not be possible as it had been released for burial, on Saturday. Although he did not say where.'

'There is a family plot at Carluke Kirk; he'll join his ancestors there, I am sure. I think I will go along to see him off, and hopefully the ladies will be present. Sheriff Stirling will be, I am sure. If so, I may lay a charge of perjury against them.'

'A good plan,' Innes Irvine agreed, 'but let us not get ahead of ourselves. Before any of that, young Mr McGill must give a formal precognition of his evidence, and I must visit my client. I must take his personal instruction, before lodging notice of our defence.'

'We can do the first now, and the second this afternoon.'

'Very good.' The young advocate drank some of his strong coffee and shuddered slightly at the taste.

'This case could be the making of you, could it not?' Mathew suggested.

'Indeed, sir, provided that it is the making of my client, rather than his ending.'

Chapter Twenty-Three

'WHAT NEWS DO YOU have for me, Ewan? Was your mission a success?'

'Doubly so, Mr Fleming,' the coachman replied. 'I found the Clelands' house in Edinburgh, and I have discovered also that Gavin, Sir Gavin, as I assume he must be now, is residing there.'

'Indeed? Well done, man. Is he alone, or did you see the two ladies also, Miss Smith and Miss Stout?'

'No. By chance I saw him arrive and he was alone. However,' he added with a smile, 'I did discover whaur he had been. Ah kept an eye on the coach that had carried him home and saw it stop outside a tavern. So Ah went inside myself and engaged the driver in conversation. Ah complimented him on his rig . . . the surest way into a coachman's good graces, sir . . . and asked if he worked for the gentleman Ah'd seen him drop off. He said no, that he was employed by a gentlemen's club to see its members safely home after a night at the tables, or with the ladies. In the case of Sir Gavin Cleland, he said, it was both.'

Mathew smiled and turned to Innes Irvine; he, Johnston and young Matt were seated with them in the hotel salon.

'Did you hear that, Mr Advocate? A mere three days after the death of his twin brother, and our new baronet is out carousing. Is that not something to lay before the court?'

'Indeed it is,' Irvine agreed. 'It will help our defence of impeachment to demonstrate that he was not overcome by grief, as surely he would have been if he was innocent.'

'Very good. Let us go, then, so that you can meet your client and let him see that he is in good hands with a good prospect of acquittal.'

He, Johnston and the advocate rose from the table; so did young Matt. 'You cannot leave me behind, Mathew,' he pleaded. 'I must see my father.'

'He may not wish you to visit him in Calton Jail, lad. He said as much to me yesterday.'

'Is it no' better for me to see his true situation,' he asked, 'than to imagine all sorts of horrors? I have heard stories of the Tolbooth, and what happened there.'

'You should not have been listening to such stuff. The old Tolbooth prison was from a less enlightened time, and it was rightly torn down. The new jail is still a grim place, mind, but its inmates are treated with respect. But yes, I concede that you should see for yourself, so come with us. I am sure David will understand that your will is stronger than his, or mine.'

On their way up Waterloo Place, Matt's eye was caught by the monument on the hilltop. 'What is that?' he asked.

'That is Scotland's national disgrace . . . or so they are calling it,' Innes Irvine told him, 'our way of remembering the defeat of Napoleon in the last great battle.'

'I for one,' Mathew remarked, 'would prefer to forget

that encounter, since it was almost the death of me. In fact it was, in a way.'

'What do you mean?' young Matt asked.

'Never mind. It is of no significance to you.'

They came to the great prison door. No sooner had the hatch swung back in answer to Mathew's knock than the wicket gate opened. 'Mr Fleming, sir,' the whiskery doorkeeper exclaimed, in great contrast to his first greeting. 'Please come in. Warders will take you to meet your friend.'

They waited for ten minutes before their escorts arrived but when they did, they were taken straight to the room in which Mathew had seen David on the evening before. As they reached it, he saw Henry Stevens, waiting in the lamplit corridor.

'A moment, sir,' he said, drawing him away from the others.

'You are ruffling feathers,' the governor whispered. 'This afternoon I received a message from the Lord Advocate's agent.'

'Who, or rather what, is he?' Mathew asked.

'A powerful man, third in rank in the Crown Office, after the Lord Advocate and the Solicitor General: he gave me an instruction that the prisoner McGill may only be visited by his legal advisers, and then just once per week. I am further instructed to be present at those meetings, and to report on their contact.'

'Are you saying that I cannot go in, and that David's son cannot see him?'

'I am telling you what my instructions were, Mr Fleming, not that I propose to obey them. I am the governor of this prison; I answer to the city and not the Crown. However, Douglas has influence everywhere, and so I must be careful. Yes, you may enter and of course the young man may see his father. As for my presence . . . consider it spiritual rather than physical. If I am ever asked for an account of the consultation, I will say that the lawyers spoke mostly in Latin, in which I am not fluent, and that the prisoner spoke not at all. If you are ever asked . . .'

'I will say that I waited outside in the corridor. Are your men to be trusted, though? I'd guess that my Lord Advocate must have spies everywhere.'

'And you would be right, but I know who those spies are and they are well away from us at this moment.' He frowned. 'However, Mr Fleming, it would be prudent to assume that others are watching you, wherever you go in the city. You have come to their attention, no doubt of it, so this really should be your last visit here, before the trial. If that goes well, there will be no need for others.'

'And if it does not?'

'We will cross that bridge if we reach it. Go on in now, and good fortune be with you.'

David was waiting for them, in the company of a single guard, who left as they entered.

Before a word was said Matt rushed up to his father and embraced him, in a hug that might have crushed him, for he was the broader of the two and there was nothing between them in height.

Eventually David extricated himself and held his son at arm's length. 'Let me see your face,' he said, inspecting the whip cut, which was still vivid.

'And let me see yours,' Matt retorted, seeing his father's swollen eye. 'Who did that to you? The Sheriff's officers?'

'No, they were crude but proper. A poor sap in my cell decided to pick on me. After Mathew arrived and the governor saw me, it went badly for him. Now I have a room to myself and I eat far better than the other prisoners. That makes me feel guilty, but if I refuse what I'm given it will not help either of us.'

'And as an innocent man why should you suffer?' Paul Johnston smiled and extended his hand. 'I am your solicitor, Mr McGill, and this gentleman,' he looked round towards Irvine, 'is your advocate. He will plead your case in court.'

'I have a case then?'

'Oh yes,' the advocate insisted, 'and a strong one. You have been accused by three perjured witnesses, but we will fight back against them. It is my hope that when you have been discharged, the real killer of Sir Gregor Cleland will stand in the dock himself.'

'That is a very fine hope, sir,' McGill said, 'but Gavin is one of Scotland's ruling classes, and I have learned in here already that those people stand by each other, even when they are not even close to being in the right. Just get me out of here and back to my family; that will be enough.'

'That we will achieve, I am sure,' Johnston told him. 'But to do the one we need to do the other. At the very least we must discredit Sir Gavin Cleland and his ladies as witnesses in the eyes of the jury and plant the seed of doubt in the minds of eight of them. That is all we will need; eight out of fifteen people who do not like the cut of Sir Gavin's jib and think him capable of murdering his brother. In the

High Court the jury has three choices of verdict, Guilty, Not Guilty and Not Proven. Two of those mean acquittal and a simple majority decides.'

'This does not mean, of necessity,' Irvine added, 'that Cleland will be immediately indicted himself. That is of no concern to us; if it happens, good and well, although from what I have heard today, that is an outcome that not even Sir Walter Scott could have anticipated.'

'Very well,' McGill sighed. 'To be honest, gentlemen, it's my own neck that concerns me, not his. How do we go about this?'

'On Friday,' the advocate replied, 'I will lodge a special defence of impeachment with the Crown Office. We must do that in advance for the court to accept it. We will name our witnesses as Matthew McGill, who will give the true version of events, and Mr Mathew Fleming, the celebrated Iron Baron and Deputy Lord Lieutenant of Lanarkshire, as a witness both to the panel's . . . that is you, sir . . . good character, and to the expertise of Sir Gavin Cleland with a pistol, a man who would not be as easily disarmed as he says, and who would be too good a shot to miss a target so readily presented to him, as was your back. Then there are the lady witnesses; there are questions about them, and I will expose them in the witness box.'

'Forgive me, sir,' David murmured, 'but there is still down on your cheeks. Are you confident in this?'

'Never more so; let me present this case and I will prevail. As for my youth, there is nothing to forgive, for it is self-evident. Do I have your instruction to proceed?'

The accused man frowned. 'There is only one aspect of

this that worries me and holds me back from giving you my consent; that is the part my lad will play. He will be exposed to cross-examination, will he not?'

'Yes, he will.'

'What worry is that, Father?' young Matt cried out. 'I will be telling the truth.'

'Nevertheless, we are dealing with dangerous men here, son, and you are still a boy.'

'That may be,' the husky youth retorted, 'but if you had let me last Sunday, I could have taken Sir Gregor to the ground as easily as you did, and defended myself as well.'

Mathew laughed. 'I am sure you could, but that is not a boast you will make in the witness box, cheil.' He looked at his friend. 'David, I understand your concern, but you must let us do this, for we have no other weapons in our armoury.'

'Then I will, but on one condition: at the first sign of peril to my boy, you will withdraw the impeachment, and rely on all that is left. Do I have your word on that, friend?'

'Even if it means sentencing you to death?'

'Even so.'

'Then you have that promise. God be with us both.'

Chapter Twenty-Four

MINDFUL OF HENRY STEVENS' advice, Mathew stayed in the hotel for the rest of that day and all of the next, reading and working on business papers that he had brought with him for such quiet moments.

He was visited by Paul Johnston in the early afternoon. 'The bill of impeachment is prepared,' the solicitor told him. 'Irvine will lodge it with the Crown Office tomorrow morning.'

'Why the morning?' Mathew asked.

'In truth, I do not know,' the cadaverous Johnston confessed.

'Are you happy with our counsel? Tell me straight now.'

'I confess that I would rather we had been able to instruct King's Counsel. But I like young Innes; his learning is evident and his enthusiasm for the case is in no doubt. However he is a debutant in court and he is being forced to enter the most difficult defence of all. He is also going to be facing the best opponent that could have been placed before him. James Douglas may be cunning and hugely ambitious, but he is undeniably a gifted advocate. He is also a man who knows how to pick a winner. As a defence counsel he always managed to avoid the obvious losing cases. As a prosecutor he has never failed to secure a guilty verdict. He has put the rope round the neck of many a man, and more than one woman.'

Mathew felt his heart sink.

'However,' the solicitor went on, 'I have done some further investigation and have discovered that it is also true that he has never prosecuted a case in which a special defence has been lodged. In his time as Lord Advocate, and as Solicitor General before that, every time such a plea has been intimated, the indictment against the accused has been withdrawn.'

Mathew sat upright in his chair. 'Is that so?' he exclaimed. 'Why would he be so compliant?'

'He would, because such a defence is never offered lightly and because it implies either malice towards the accused or incompetence in the office of prosecutor. If James Douglas sees even the possibility of defeat on the horizon, he cuts and runs. He is said to be formidable at the card tables for that very reason; he takes no risks.'

'Then we have a chance. Tell Innes to lodge the defence as quickly as possible, in the hope that we can have David home for the weekend.'

'There is no chance of that; tomorrow is a vacation day in the court; it will take a judge to order his release and there will none available.'

'Damn it!' Mathew snapped. 'Still, it may be no bad thing if my Lord Advocate has an extra day or so to muse on the possibility of defeat.'

Johnston left soon afterwards, bearing a banker's draft to

cover his fees and expenses and those of Irvine, as soon as a note was submitted by Baird, who also served as collector for his stable.

Mathew passed the rest of the afternoon alone, for young Matt and Beattie had been despatched on a mission. They returned just before six o'clock.

'We have watched that house all day,' the coachman told his master, as he collapsed into a chair, a mug of ale clutched in his hand. 'Sir Gavin came out in the morning, but only tae take the air. He went no further than the coffee house at the road end, and after half an hour went back hame.'

'No sign of the women?'

'None. And no sign o' him after that either. An hour ago, I sent the young man here round the back tae check the stabling. The coach and horses were there in the morning, but nae mair. Ye' say his brother's burial is on Saturday, sir? It may be he's gone hame already.'

'The chances are he has. Since I intend to be there too, and since we cannot visit David, there is no point in our cooling our heels here. We will leave too; there will be enough light this evening to see us home.'

Mathew settled their bill at the hotel and reserved the same rooms from Sunday onwards. When their rig was brought to them, it was evident that the horses had been well fed and cared for. The carriage had been cleaned also, for it bore no signs of its previous journey.

The summer weather was holding good, and so Beattie decided that they would return by a different route, along the Glasgow toll road, which ran through Midcalder and intersected with the track that linked the wards of Lanarkshire. It was not without hills, but they were less steep than on the Lang Whang, and so they made better time.

Lizzie was in the younger children's bedchamber, settling them down for the night when she saw the approaching carriage, a quarter mile off. Calling to Hannah, she rushed downstairs and outside.

When Beattie reined in the horses and only Mathew and young Matt climbed out of the coach, her face fell. 'You are alone,' she murmured.

'We are, Mother,' her son replied, 'but don't let that dishearten you. Mr Johnston, the lawyer, has given us good reason to hope for the best outcome.'

'Come inside and tell us about it,' Hannah instructed. 'Ah'll tell the cook tae conjure up some supper. Ye look fair famished.'

'We are,' Mathew agreed. 'Mr Beattie will eat with us, after we have all washed off the dust of the journey, for the countryside is very dry. He has been a great help in our expedition.'

Half an hour later, around the table, he gave the two women an account of their days in the capital city. 'The place where David is lodged is grim, but not inhumane, so you need not fear for his well-being.'

'I only fear this trial, Mathew,' she replied.

'Then rest easy tonight, for as your son says, we have a good prospect of success. We will return on Sunday, and with luck will be back the very next day, with David alongside us. In the meantime, I have a burial to attend. Sir

Gregor Cleland is being laid to rest, on Saturday, I'm told.'

'Can I go too?' young Matt asked.

'Absolutely not. I will not have you anywhere near Gavin Cleland.' He paused. 'Lizzie,' he said, 'I was precipitate; I am sorry for it. You are his mother and that decision is yours to make, not mine.'

She frowned. 'Maybe, but it is no different. Matt, a wicked calumny though it is, your father is charged with taking the Laird's life. With that unresolved, it would not be wise for you to attend the funeral. Nor me, for that matter; if I saw Gavin Cleland I could not be trusted to stay silent, any more than you could.'

'What makes you think I can?' Mathew murmured. 'I will take no provocation from that gentleman. However I will offer none either, and I doubt that even he would choose to mar such an occasion with an argument.'

The next day was a strange one for all of them; they were in limbo, unable to do anything to help David, but unable to free their minds of his predicament. After breakfast, Mathew glanced at his watch. 'Ten minutes to nine,' he said, 'ten minutes to the lodging of the special defence; let us hope that it gives James Douglas food for thought, and that he acts true to type.'

He spent the rest of the day on a hectic tour of his business, riding to Netherton to inspect the leather factories and make sure that his temporary arrangement was working, then on to Coatbridge. Sir Graham Stockley was in the office when he arrived; he was surprised to see his partner.

'Mathew,' he exclaimed. 'What brings you?'

'A desperate need to keep myself busy,' he replied. 'Also I had a need to breathe some honest air, after the week I have had.'

'On your trip to Edinburgh? What business did you have there that it disturbs you so much?'

Mathew told him the story from start to finish.

'My,' he said. 'I had heard of the death of the fellow Cleland, and that they had a suspect in charge. A violent criminal, the *Register* said yesterday. Your manager, Mr McGill, you say?'

'Yes, ridiculous though that may sound. And he is innocent, however harshly he is defamed by the Edinburgh press.'

'It is no surprise that he would be,' Stockley snapped, bitterly. 'That newspaper is a mouthpiece for the princes of the city, and be in no doubt, James Douglas is one of those. The most powerful man in Scotland, they say. I have met the man; he makes my flesh creep. Bellhouse is the judge, you say?'

'Yes. We can only hope that he is fair.'

'Do not build those hopes too high, my friend. Let's hope your impeachment does the trick and the case never gets to trail. Do you know who Bellhouse is?'

'He is the Lord Justice Clerk.'

'He is also James Douglas's uncle. There is no greater bastion of nepotism than the Scottish Supreme Courts.'

Mathew kept his partner's worrying revelation to himself when he arrived back at Waterloo House. Instead he was as positive as he could manage. 'We must plan, Lizzie,' he said over dinner, 'for the future. When David comes home he will be welcome here also, but I am sure you will both wish to have your own roof over your heads.'

'Yes, but I have no idea where that will be. I would not go back to the estate cottage even if Gavin Cleland begged us on his knees, although there is no chance of that. There is nothing within my family. When my mother died, Uncle Peter moved my cousin Daphne and her family into her house, for he owns it. He has no other property, though, other than the shop.'

'Peter cannot continue there for much longer, surely,' Mathew observed. 'He is an old man now, well past seventy, and from what I hear, getting no help from your cousin, whose dog of a husband, Cleland's gamekeeper, keeps her rushed off her feet.'

Her eyes blazed, suddenly. Across the table, young Matt seemed to stiffen in his chair. 'Gerald Grose?' Lizzie retorted. 'Please do not speak of him to me. After the Sheriff's men had taken David away, he was one of the men who threw our furniture into the street and smashed it with hammers. A kinsman of mine and yet he did that on his master's orders. Gamekeeper indeed! A brute and a bully, that is what he is.'

'Mmm,' Mathew murmured. 'I was not aware of that. Next time I see Mr Grose at the kirk, he and I will have words that he will not enjoy.' He stared into his water glass for a few seconds, as if he was anticipating that meeting.

'But back to your uncle,' he continued, suddenly. 'He has no children, apart from Daphne, who can barely run her own household, as you say. There is nobody to whom he can hand on his business, and he does not have wealth enough to be able to afford to close it and retire, although John Barclay tells me he would dearly love to do so. He has a problem, it seems.'

'But not one that worries me too much,' she said.

'Why not, Mother?' young Matt asked. 'He is your uncle, after all; should you not be sad that he is in such a predicament.'

'And he is your great-uncle, but does he ever treat you as such when you go into his shop?'

'No, but why should he when you ignore him? Only my father and I go in there, you never do. As for the man Grose, when I am a bit more grown, he will pay with his teeth for what he did to us, as will everyone else who acted against my father, but your uncle had nothing to do with it, for all that you are so against him; or my grandmother either. She died when I was eight, yet I never met her. Why?'

'Stop right there,' Mathew told him; his voice was raised, an almost unique occurrence. 'Your mother's feelings towards them,' he continued, more gently, 'they are part of an old story, one that is none of your concern; take it from me that I understand her completely, and do not fault her for them.

'As for your plans for Grose, you are speaking as he would himself. Out of respect for your parents, and for me, for that matter, you should be above his level. If I wanted, I could hire my own men, ex-soldiers who work for me in Netherton and Coatbridge, and have them beat the living shit . . . excuse me, ladies . . . out of the coward and those who were with him last Sunday.

'But that would be wrong, legally and morally; moreover,

it would not be sufficient. I have my own plans for those people, and what I do to them will not be something that will wear off in a week, as would the effects of a thrashing. It will be something that will be with them for the rest of their lives. So let me hear no more of such talk from you.'

He clenched his right hand into a fist. 'You do not fight people with this,' he paused and tapped the side of his head, just above the temple, with one finger, 'when you can do much more damage with this. All it takes is a little patience, and that is what you must learn.'

'And where did you learn that, ma son?' Hannah asked.

'From you, Mother. Where else?' He turned back to Lizzie. 'I have a solution to your uncle's problem, and to yours, if you are agreeable. I believe in investing my wealth prudently, but for the good of others when I can. I know what a fair price would be for Peter Wright's shop, as a business, and for the property. I am sure he would sell. If I bought it, would you run it for me? You helped your uncle before Matt was born, so you know how the business works. The profits would be yours, and from them you would pay me rent; your brain would be occupied and you, David, Matt and Jean would have that roof over your head.'

She stared at him. 'Are you so wealthy you could do that?'

'Of course,' he laughed. 'You have no notion of how wealthy I am.'

'Mathew, I don't know . . .'

'No, you don't, I agree. This is not a decision I expect you to make on your own, but with David, when he is released. However,' he smiled, 'I have a fair idea of his response.'

The idea of buying Wright's shop had come to Mathew out of the blue, but he retired to bed that night resolved to instruct his lawyer to take the first steps towards that end.

In the morning he rose and dressed in his best black. 'You will come to the service too, Ewan,' he instructed Beattie. 'After all, you did work for the Cleland family, and so it would be respectful. There is also the point that another pair of eyes in the kirk would do me no harm.'

They arrived at the church at one minute after noon, for a service that was scheduled to begin at half past the hour, but they did not go inside; instead they stood in the kirkyard in a prominent spot. Mathew wanted to be early so that he could observe the demeanour of those who attended, and also so that he could be observed himself.

Not that there were many people to be seen. All of the subsequent arrivals appeared to be estate employees, or workers on tenant farms. But one in particular attracted his attention: Gerald Grose, who arrived with his wife, Lizzie's cousin Daphne. He remembered her from their youth; she was two years younger than him, but had not aged well. Her face was lined and there were dark, saggy bags under her eyes.

He knew the gamekeeper also; they had been classmates at the parish school. As he approached, he beckoned to him. Grose looked surprised, but he came across. 'Mr Fleming,' he said. 'What can I do for you?'

'For me, nothing,' he replied, quietly. 'For yourself . . . you might be well advised to seek alternative employment very far away from here.'

The man stuck out his chin, in a truculent gesture. 'And why should Ah do that?'

'If you do not know, then you have become an even bigger idiot than you showed yourself to be in the classroom.'

Grose flushed; he frowned. 'I did what Ah was telt tae do by my master. Your friend McGill had just kilt his brither. His family belang in the street, and that's where we pit them.'

'And broke their belongings with hammers? Did your master tell you to do that also, or was that your own idea?'

'Ah told you; we did as we were telt. Sir Gavin was righteously angry.'

'So you obeyed his order to persecute your own wife's kin.'

'Lizzie McGill doesna acknowledge her folk.'

'And you know why that is. I can see you, man, for what you are. You took pleasure in what you did last Sunday. You are a bully, Grose, a weak man and a rogue. Even so, until I heard what you did, you were nothing to me. Now you are my enemy; see how well that suits you, then take my advice. Go away from here, never come back, and never let a day go by without reflecting on the harm you did to an innocent woman and her children. You might tell your fellow cowards to do the same, for I will find out who they are and come after them.'

'And how would ye dae that?'

'With the full force of the law. As soon as David McGill has been cleared of this false accusation, I will have you and your cronies before the Sheriff. Are you so stupid that you think it legal to evict a family without a warrant or to destroy their property? It will probably be classed as robbery with violence, an offence that my friend the Sheriff hates. Whatever else your sentence might be, you can all expect to be baring your arses for the birch.'

Mathew's smile was mocking. Ewan Beattie thought that he might be trying to provoke Grose into striking him, but the gamekeeper was not so foolish, or so brave, as to try. Instead he slunk back towards his wife, a voice calling after him, 'Far away, remember. It will not stop me coming after you, but it is your best chance of keeping your hide intact.'

'Would the Sheriff do that, sir?' the coachman asked, quietly.

'Be sure of it. When I saw him last Monday, it was his proposal that we swear a complaint against the men who forced Lizzie from her home.'

'Cleland too?'

'No. He would only plead that his rabble were over-zealous. He may also have had the right to order the eviction. I admit that I did fantasise to an extent, to gain Master Grose's full attention.'

'Ye succeeded, sir. Yon's a frightened man now.'

As he spoke the hearse came into sight, an ornate affair drawn by four black-plumed horses. The two men entered the church, which was little more than half full; this was to Mathew's pleasure. The people he recognised all had estate connections, but he saw no one who was a friend of David McGill. Peter Wright was there, though, beside his daughter and Grose, who refused to meet his gaze.

Leaving Beattie at the back of the kirk, he took his place in the elders' pew, at the front. The organist was playing as they waited; the instrument was in good condition, since Mathew had paid for its refurbishment the year before. After a minute or so, John Barclay entered from the vestry door and stood facing the congregation. He looked strangely ill at ease, as if he wished his task done with, and quickly.

'All rise,' he said, motioning with his hands, and as he did so there came the sound of shuffling feet as the pall-bearers turned into the aisle.

Sir Gregor Cleland's coffin was an ornate affair, of dark mahogany, with polished brass screws and handles and draped with red cords. The six men who carried it were all strangers to the village; Mathew wondered whether they were simply the undertaker's assistants or whether the new Laird had thought it prudent to hire bodyguards, against any popular reaction to David McGill's arrest and trial.

Gavin Cleland walked behind the coffin, pausing, and giving a respectful nod as it was laid on trestles before the altar, then slipping into the family pew, the front row to the right, beneath the pulpit; in it, he was alone. The factor Armitage and his wife were in the row behind, but no others sat close to him.

The service was formal; it began with a hymn, followed by prayers and after them the Twenty-third Psalm. Then John Barclay climbed slowly and laboriously into the pulpit. He had gained considerable weight since Jessie's death, through a stodgy diet and probably, Mathew guessed, because there was no longer any restriction upon his consumption of Madeira wine.

'Dearly beloved,' he began. 'We are gathered here on this most sad occasion to pay our respects to our young Laird, Sir Gregor Cleland, and to commend his blameless soul to God.'

Mathew's one eye narrowed.

'The Cleland family have been stalwarts of Carluke Parish for many generations,' the minister continued. 'They have blessed us with their munificence, they have been easy landlords and they have been generous employers. It is a very short time in the affairs of man since we gathered here to bury the good Sir George, yet here we are again, come together in grief to say farewell to his older son, and to extend our deepest condolences to his brother, who sits with us today as Sir Gavin Cleland, master of Cleland House and its estate. May God grant him comfort in his hour of despair over his great loss, and may He show him the way forward to guide his community.'

A spluttering cough came from the back of the kirk; Mathew thought he recognised Ewan Beattie's familiar manner of clearing his throat when it was tickled by dust from the road.

With only the briefest of frowns Barclay went on. 'It is not for me to comment on the manner of Sir Gregor's death. The matter is in the hands of the highest court in the land and we can only wait for it to dispense justice, in all its majesty, and if it is so determined with all its final severity. Make no mistake, God demands that the guilty be punished, even if that should strike at the very heart of this congregation.'

The old cleric bowed his head. 'There is no comfort for

Carluke today. A terrible sin has been committed in our village, and we all sit in its shadow; it will only be expiated when the sinner himself rests in the ground to which we are about to commit his victim. In the name of the Father, Son and Holy Ghost, amen.'

He moved on to the final hymn, and then a benediction, before instructing the congregation to remain standing while the coffin was raised once more on to the shoulders of its bearers, to be carried outside, to the Cleland plot, for burial.

Mathew was obliged, as an elder, to attend the committal, and he was at the head of the group that followed the bearers, with the three other members of the Kirk Session. As they reached the graveside, Gavin Cleland turned and approached him. 'Fleming,' he said, his voice clear enough to carry to all those present, 'there are eight cords on the coffin, but only seven of us. You will oblige me, sir, by taking the eighth.'

'If you wish,' he replied. He could have refused, he knew, but that would have been a public display of antipathy that he felt it would be better not to make at that time.

'Thank you,' the baronet murmured. 'I will be at the head; you will please take the cord at the feet.'

The eight men took their positions, John Barclay intoned the words of committal and steadily, slowly, they lowered the coffin into the ground. As they did so, Mathew could read the inscription on the polished brass plate; 'Sir Gregor Cleland, Bt., foully murdered, by David McGill.'

As their burden reached the ground and the cords lost their tension, he looked up and along, into Gavin's eyes. They shone, with what could only have been triumph.

He tossed the end of his cord into the grave and stood, then walked round past three of the pall-bearers, to the new Laird. 'Your ladies are not here, I note,' he murmured.

'No. My brother's fiancée . . .'

'Fiancée? I had heard of no betrothal.'

'It was to be announced this very day. Poor Charlotte is distraught, too grief-stricken to attend. It was a terrible experience for us all, Fleming. I was taken completely by surprise by the suddenness of McGill's attack and by its ferocity, I had no time to defend myself before my pistol was seized and the fatal shot fired.'

'Aye, sure,' Mathew replied. 'And who is the beneficiary of this mindless violence, Sir Gavin? Not David, only you. We will see what view the court makes of it . . . if it gets that far.'

'I am confident that it will, Fleming, and I do not fear its verdict. Within the next week, I expect to see your friend swinging, and off on his way to the anatomist's table. Perhaps when they look at his brain they will find whatever it was that made him act so madly.' He smiled. 'Good day, sir. I look forward to our next meeting, under the kindly auspices of Lord Bellhouse.' He turned on his heel and strode off towards his waiting carriage.

For his part, Mathew strode towards the minister. 'Your eulogy, John,' he exclaimed. 'What the hell was that about? You know David is innocent, yet you damned him!'

'No, Mathew, I did not,' Barclay countered. 'My words were very carefully chosen. The matter is with the court, and like you I have to trust that it will reach the correct verdict. As for what I know . . . well, what I know is what

David told me, and that is what you know too, for you were not there yourself. You were not a witness to what happened. The only thing that you and I have seen for ourselves is that young Matt was whipped, for his face bears that out. For the rest, I have a man dead by violence, and my first duty, God's first duty, is to him. Can you not see the truth of that?'

Mathew took a pace back, and looked him up and down. 'All that I can see, old friend,' he murmured, 'is the uncomfortable fidgeting of a man who is sitting on the fence.'

Chapter Twenty-Five

'I AM DISAPPOINTED IN our minister, Mother.'

Mathew had said nothing to Lizzie or Matt about the service, or about his encounter with Gerald Grose, but Hannah had recognised the worm that was gnawing at him and had asked him what was wrong as soon as they were alone in the garden summer house.

'Mak' allowances for him, son,' she responded. 'Ah never took him for a strong man. He's spent most o' his life in a quiet village wi' nobody tae bother him but God, and wi' old Jessie tae bolster him when he needed it and keep him off the fortified wine when he didna' need any more o' that. Now something terrible's happened, almost in his front parlour, and he finds himself wi' a duty tae both the dead and the livin', wi' a conflict between them. From what ye say he did indeed choose his words carefully in the pulpit, but that may have been more out of fear than what you see as disloyalty.'

He sighed. 'You may be right. All the same, I am glad that we will not need him to stand as a character witness before the court, with the defence we propose. The last thing we will need there is any show of ambivalence.'

'Ach,' she laughed, 'you and yer big words. Ah suppose it's tae be expected, given the folk ye mix with. Deputy Lord Lieutenant Fleming, indeed; it would never do for ye tae be speaking Scots tae the King, would it?'

'I doubt if I will ever get the chance to speak any language to him. There are many deputy lieutenants across the land, and remember, our function is to represent him in his absence.'

'Then let's hope there's nae more o' that Jacobite nonsense. Ma granny used to tell us about the forty-five rebellion. There were heids on spikes after that, she said.'

Mathew smiled. 'I think mine is secure,' he said. 'Bonnie Prince Charlie died a drunk in Rome, and any new pretenders are likely to speak Italian, hardly the language in which to rally the clans.'

'That's better,' Hannah chuckled, 'mair like your usual humour. So,' she continued, 'ye feel the next few days will go well for David?'

'That is our lawyers' hope and belief, and I am guided by them.' He rose. 'Now I am off to my bed, for I want to get back to Edinburgh at a civilised hour tomorrow.'

He, young Matt and Beattie arrived in the capital half an hour before four. The day had turned chill, and the coachman drove the horses along at good pace. Before leaving, the four, Flemings and McGills, had attended morning service in Carluke. Lizzie had insisted on going.

'I must, Mathew. If I was not seen there some might say it was out of shame, and I cannot have that. Matt and I must be there with our heads high, in support of David. The number of folk who speak to us afterwards, that will tell me how the village really feels.'

That number was considerable, although it did not include her cousin Daphne, who sat at the back of the kirk, and left as quickly as she could once the service was over. Grose, her husband, was nowhere to be seen, and the Cleland family pew had been empty also.

John Barclay's sermon had ignored the death, and David's predicament, entirely. Instead it had been a prayer for a summer of good weather and a bountiful harvest, always sure to be well received by a rural congregation. From the minister's first brief glance at the empty front row below the pulpit, Mathew had sensed his relief that at least one of the protagonists in the dispute over Gregor Cleland's death had chosen to avoid further confrontation.

His mother had been right, he thought. Events were too much for him; the old man was afraid.

Barclay's farewell to Lizzie and Matt at the door of the kirk had been effusive. 'I am pleased that you both felt able to come today,' he said. 'My prayers go with you for the resolution of your terrible situation.' He clasped Matt's hands. 'I want you to know that the entire congregation holds you blameless for what has happened.'

'That is not so, Mr Barclay,' the young man retorted. 'Sir Gavin Cleland swore the opposite in his statement to the Sheriff.'

'I am sure he misunderstood,' the minister murmured.

'There was no room for misunderstanding. His statement says that I scared thon horses on purpose and that I was insolent. I never was; it was an accident, as I told you right after it happened.'

'I have high hopes that he will think better of it,' Mathew intervened, quickly, to cool young Matt's quick temper. He looked down at Barclay. 'John, if our advice holds good, we will not need you as a character witness this week. If we do, I will send for you.'

A quick flash of apprehension ran through him as he stepped down from the carriage outside the Waterloo Hotel.

'It is going to be all right, Mathew, isn't it?' The boy's question was quietly spoken, but there was anxiety in it.

'Of course it is, lad,' he replied. 'You heard what the lawyers said; James Douglas's reputation is built on knowing when to play his hand and when to throw it in. He knows that our defence is serious, and his ambition could not suffer a public defeat.'

Mathew's optimism was boosted even higher when he registered the party, and found a message waiting for him in a sealed envelope, at the reception desk. He tore it open there and then, and saw that it was from Paul Johnston, and had been written on the previous Friday. He read it quickly and then for a second time, aloud.

Dear Mr Fleming,

I have received a summons, from the Lord Advocate himself, written in his own hand. Mr Douglas commands us to meet with him in his chambers in Parliament House, on Monday, at ten o'clock in the morning. He requests that Mr Irvine and I be present, and also

*yourself, Mr Fleming. He says that he understands that
you are the principal figure in the preparation of the
prisoner's defence, and wishes to make the acquaintance
of such a forceful person.*

*I propose that the three of us meet in Parliament
Hall, at ten minutes before ten.*

Yours . . .

'There you are, Matt,' he exclaimed, 'the news is good.
The great man wants to see us.'

'Why not me too?' the youth asked.

'Because like it or not, you are a minor, and this is men's
business.'

Matt grunted, but said no more.

When Mathew arrived in Parliament Hall, five minutes
before Johnston's meeting time, he found the two lawyers
already there and deep in conversation.

'Well then,' he exclaimed, 'you were right enough,
Innes. It seems that your bold strategy has worked.'

'Indeed,' Johnston agreed, 'it seems so. But Mr Irvine is
nervous nonetheless. He is, remember, the most junior
member of the Faculty, and for him to be called before its
foremost figure is a daunting prospect. Worry not, Innes;
I've seen Douglas in action. He won't bite you. More likely
he will offer you a position in the Crown Office.'

'You say so,' the advocate replied, 'but why is he doing
this, when all that was needed is for him to advise the court
that the indictment is deserted *simpliciter*, and that our
client should be released?'

'Who knows? He may wish to toast our success.' He

glanced to his right, past Mathew. 'We shall soon find out, I think.'

As he spoke a court usher joined them. 'Gentlemen, if you will follow me.'

They did as he asked, following him out of the great hall, along a maze of corridors and up a flight of stairs. 'One second,' he murmured when they reached the top, disappearing through a door then stepping back out little more than that single second later. 'The Lord Advocate will receive you now.'

James Douglas was seated in a huge red leather chair that served to underline the shortness of his stature. When he rose and looked up at Mathew, there was almost a foot in height between them. He was dapper, in ordinary rather than legal clothes and wigless, with dark oiled hair that shone in the light from the lamps on his desk, and from the window. He extended his hand and when the two men shook, it seemed to disappear into his visitor's.

'Mr Fleming,' he began, 'I have heard much of you; you are a power in the new world, beyond a shadow of a doubt.' He looked at the lawyers. 'Johnston, I admire your work too; welcome. And you will be Mr Irvine, advocate. When the Dean appointed you to present McGill's defence, he knew what he was doing. You and I must have a conversation later; this office is always in need of advocates with boldness and courage. Sit, please, all of you.'

He climbed into his own chair, then looked at his visitors.

'Courage, I said, Mr Irvine, because while your gambit is bold and within the law, it was not without risk, not only to your own reputation but to your clients and even to those instructing you. Mr Johnson is a fine solicitor, but he relies on the goodwill of the Faculty, and of the courts, for his living. Mr Fleming is, as I said, a coming man in the new world . . . indeed he has arrived already . . . but he is also still part of the old. Deputy lord lieutenancies can be removed as quickly as they are conferred, and those elements of his business that rely on commissions from the state . . . how many saddles do you sell to the military annually, sir? . . . they would also be at risk if he offended the wrong people.'

Mathew frowned. Something was wrong, the man was amiable and yet his words carried a huge underlying threat.

Douglas looked at Irvine directly. His eyes seemed to grow slightly, and become hypnotically piercing.

'I admire your defence, Innes, I really do, and in ordinary circumstances, I would yield to it. However,' he paused, 'this is not an ordinary case. The indictment alleges the murder of a baronet, a landowner, by a former employee, a man with a score to settle. There is an order in our society, gentlemen, and it must be preserved. The indictment demands that the panel be tried for his life.

'And then there is your defence. It avers that the murder was committed not by the panel, but by the victim's own brother, his twin no less, the chief witness against him. Is it convincing? Perhaps. But all trials are matters of whose word the jury believes, and so its success is not assured.'

He sighed. 'Before we get that far, though, it is a matter of what I believe, as prosecutor; and frankly, I believe Sir Gavin. I cannot conceive of a man murdering his own twin, and I cannot concede to a defence that implies that he did. I cannot concede,' he repeated, 'and yet if I proceed to trial, your witnesses will take to the box and give their evidence. Even if your defence failed, as I believe it would, Sir Gavin's name will still be blackened, and he will carry a weight around his neck as heavy as Mr Coleridge's Ancient Mariner.'

Douglas looked around them all again, and as he did his eyes seemed to change. Suddenly it was as if they were slitted, those of a snake.

'So this,' he seemed to hiss, 'is what I propose, Mr Irvine. If you proceed with your defence I will desert the indictment. But not *simpliciter*, sir, as you expect; no, I will desert it *pro loco et tempore* . . . that meaning "for the time being", Mr Fleming. It will then be amended; while that happens, Mr McGill will remain in the Calton Jail but he will not be alone. The new indictment will aver that his son, Matthew McGill, provoked the incident deliberately, and thus is as guilty as his father. They will stand trial together, they will be convicted together, they will be sentenced together, and be sure, Mr Fleming, whether the boy is fifteen or not, he will be liable to hang on the same scaffold as his father.'

The Lord Advocate sighed again, and some of the menace left him. 'It is possible that a benevolent sovereign might commute his sentence on my advice, rather than risk public outrage at the execution of one so young, but the very least he could expect would be transportation for life. Either way he would be lost to his mother, for ever, and to his loved ones, who include you, Mr Fleming. I know your whole story, and how the boy might have been yours.

'Well, Mr Irvine, what is it to be? Do you withdraw your impeachment?'

The young advocate held his ground; his voice was cold and steady.

'You must be aware, sir, surely,' he replied, 'that I must take instruction. The decision is not mine. May we confer alone?'

Douglas shook his head. 'You may confer, but not alone. The decision is simple.'

'Then I will make it,' Mathew declared. 'First, though, I will tell you some home truths, my Lord Advocate. You speak of the new world and the old. You may believe that you have the power to threaten me, and within this building you might. But beyond Edinburgh, you are impotent; you may speak for Scotland in Westminster, but very few listen to you. You barely know the people with whom I do business, and be assured they have no regard for you. You are a power in Edinburgh, no doubt, but do not try to flex your muscles beyond its boundaries, or you will find that I am much stronger than you.

'I will give testimony in defence of my friend, regardless of the decision we make now, be sure of that. If I left that decision to his brave son, he would call your bluff, sir, he knows what happened, and so do I. However, I cannot do that. I gave my word to his father that I would not put him in danger, and I must keep it. The impeachment will be withdrawn, the plea will be "not guilty" and we will proceed to trial in the normal way. You have seen the mettle of Mr Irvine, so you will realise it may not be as easy as you think.'

The Lord Advocate rose, indicating that the meeting was over. 'I have indeed,' he replied, 'but you may still be certain: I will hang your friend.'

Chapter Twenty-Six

'HOW DID DAVID TAKE the news?'

'Philosophically, Mr Fleming, is as good a reply as I can offer,' Paul Johnston replied. The two were having breakfast in the Waterloo Hotel, on the morning of the trial. They were alone; on Mathew's instructions Ewan Beattie had summoned the coach early in the morning and had taken a most unwilling young Matt on a trip into Haddingtonshire, with the town of North Berwick as their destination.

As he would not be giving evidence at the trial, Mathew wanted him as far from Edinburgh as possible while it ran its course, and as the youth had never seen the sea in his fifteen years, he had decided that it offered as much of a distraction as was possible.

'We still have a chance, though?'

'We are in the hands of Innes Irvine, and to an extent the judge. We are all agreed it would be too risky for the boy to have given evidence, and so all we have to rely on is our advocate's skill in exposing the three Crown witnesses as liars. If that can be done, and David gives a good account of himself under cross-examination, then with you and the minister as character witnesses, the jury may hesitate to convict him. It is a fact that many jurors as individuals do not like to take a man's life; that is why the Not Proven verdict is so popular in Scotland. That is, I believe, the best we can hope for.'

'Then let us be about it.'

They left the hotel and walked, along North Bridge Street and up the High Street to Parliament House; the distance was a little more than half a mile, but neither man said another word. Mathew was deep in thought and it was evident that Johnston was gripped by anxiety.

Just as they passed St Giles Cathedral they were overtaken by a black, armoured cab, windowless, with a padlocked door in the side. It was drawn by two very large horses, because of its obvious weight. A man sat beside the driver and two more on a board at the rear, all four clad in warder uniforms.

'God be with him,' Johnston murmured as it passed.

They had barely entered Parliament Hall before Irvine was at their side. 'They are starting already,' he said, a little breathlessly. 'Our trial was second on the list, but Bellhouse has changed the order. His macer told me he has a lunch engagement and was concerned that the other might run on too long.'

'Then let us make His Lordship's belly rumble,' Mathew growled.

He took his seat on the public benches, which were almost empty, as the two lawyers made their way into the well of the court. A door opened to his left, and David McGill was led in; his ankles were in shackles, and each of his wrists was handcuffed to a warder. They walked him past the fifteen-man jury, and into the dock, a square structure with spikes at its four corners, then freed his hands.

'Court!'

The cry boomed out; the court officials and lawyers all stood and Mathew followed suit. He turned and saw a short-jacketed, black-gaitered man, holding a ceremonial mace against his right shoulder, and leading a hook-nosed figure with a wig and a red robe, trimmed with ermine. As the small procession passed the statue of Duncan Forbes, Lord Culloden, Lord Bellhouse gave a brief nod in its direction.

The judge would be in his late sixties, Mathew estimated, as he watched him clamber stiffly on to the Bench, the highest seat in the hall. His cheekbones were prominent and his eyes were cold.

'Be seated,' the macer barked, and every person was, apart from David McGill.

Bellhouse looked down at the tiny figure who faced him on his right. 'My Lord Advocate,' he said in a high reedy voice, 'you may proceed.'

James Douglas rose to his feet; a short journey, Mathew thought, stifling a smile that came upon him almost unawares and defied the solemnity of the situation.

'Thank you, my Lord Justice Clerk. We are here today to try this man, David McGill, for the wicked murder of his former employer, Sir Gregor Cleland, master of Cleland Estate, Carluke, in the County of Lanark. The facts are clear and will be set out by witnesses, and so I need say no more at this time. Let them speak.'

Douglas called his first witness, Mr Leo McGuire, of the Royal College of Surgeons. He testified that he had examined the body of the victim and had determined that he had died from a pistol shot, the ball having lodged within his brain. As he spoke, he reached into his pocket and took out a small round pellet, which he brandished, dramatically.

'I have it here, the fatal missile.'

The Lord Advocate smiled at the jury. 'I have no further questions.'

As Innes Irvine rose to his feet, Mathew saw that he was trembling, but his voice was steady. 'How do you know it was a pistol shot, sir?' he asked.

McGuire blinked, and stared at him. 'I beg your pardon?'

'I am sorry, I thought my question was clear. How could you tell it was a pistol shot? Were you shown the weapon that was used allegedly, in this alleged crime?'

'No, sir, of course not.'

'Then what you are telling the jury is not of your own knowledge, but is in fact hearsay.'

The surgeon gulped, as Irvine pressed on. 'Sir Gregor died from a pellet in the brain, that is undeniable, given your expertise. But could that pellet not have been fired by a musket, from a distance? Might it even have come from a slingshot, such as David used to slay Goliath?'

'Mr Irvine!' Lord Bellhouse's cry cracked like a whiplash across the court. 'What is the purpose of this foolish questioning?'

'The truth, my Lord,' the young advocate replied. 'A man is on trial for his life, a good man, an elder of the kirk. Surely the jury is entitled to hear facts, not opinions?'

This is good, Mathew thought. *He is trying to muddy the water, to create doubt from the beginning.*

'It does not need to hear fanciful hypotheses,' Bellhouse snapped, 'nor a character reference for the panel. Sit down, sir. Mr McGuire, I thank you; you are excused. Lord Advocate, call your next witness.'

Douglas stood, with a small bow towards the judge. 'Thank you, my Lord, for that intervention. I call Captain Thomas Prentice, of the Lanark militia.'

The man who stepped into the witness box was around Mathew's age; he knew him, although not well, having met him on one or two occasions at functions connected to his own lieutenancy. Prentice was a professional soldier, but a soft one; he had never set a military foot outside Scotland, nor faced a disciplined enemy.

'I was summoned to Cleland House, by an urgent messenger,' he told the jury, 'on the instructions of Mr, now Sir, Gavin Cleland. He showed me the body of his brother, and told me what had happened. But that was clear; he had been shot in the head, in a fatal spot.'

'Did he tell you why he had removed the body from the scene of the murder?' Douglas asked.

'Yes, sir. He said that he had fled because he feared for his safety and that of the ladies who had witnessed the murder. However, he could not bear to leave his brother behind and so he loaded his body into the carriage and drove off.'

'Very good, thank you.'

Bellhouse glowered at the defence advocate. 'Mr Irvine.'

'Thank you, my Lord. Captain, where was the pistol? Did Sir Gavin show it to you?'

'Of course not.'

214

'Then where is it? It is not listed as an exhibit, so where is it? Did you search for it in Carluke, at the spot where the alleged murder allegedly took place?'

'No, sir.'

'Was it in Mr McGill's possession when you arrested him?'

'No, sir.'

'Was it in his house?'

'Not to my knowledge.'

'So all you are really telling the jury is that you saw Sir Gregor Cleland and that he was dead?'

'Yes, sir, I suppose so.'

'And we thank you for it, Captain,' Bellhouse intoned from the Bench. 'And you are also able to tell us, without fear of contradiction, that he was shot?'

'Indeed, my Lord.'

'But you are not in a position to deny the obvious conclusion, that McGill destroyed the pistol after shooting Sir Gregor.'

'No, sir, I am not.'

'Or did not run away?' Irvine added. 'And having committed this calumny, that McGill simply waited in his home, and waited to be seized. You cannot deny that either?'

'Mr Irvine!' Bellhouse screamed. 'You will not interrupt me, sir, otherwise, advocate or not, I will hold you in contempt of this High Court and you will return to the Calton Jail along with your client! You will be seated, and you will not rise again until you are told!'

Mathew was astonished by the Lord Justice Clerk's lack of impartiality; he hoped that the jury would feel the same, but when he looked at them all he could see on their faces was fear.

'I will now call Sir Gavin Cleland,' the Lord Advocate announced.

The baronet was brought into court from the witness room and was sworn in. 'Good morning to you, sir, on this grievous occasion.' He paused 'I understand that you buried your poor murdered brother last Saturday afternoon.'

'I did, sir.'

'Was the funeral well attended?'

'It was, sir. I was pleased that so many came to pay their respects.'

'Did their number include Mr Mathew Fleming, the present employer and benefactor of the accused?'

'Yes, Mathew was there.'

'And what was his attitude to you?'

'He was most courteous, sir. He did me the honour of holding the second cord on my brother's coffin, the one that faced me, as we lowered poor Gregor into his grave.'

'Did he indeed?' Douglas exclaimed, turning slowly to look at the public benches. 'The jury may read into that what they will.'

A ball of fury blazed in Mathew's stomach. He saw Irvine start to rise to his feet, only to be frozen by a stare from Bellhouse.

'Tell us what happened to your unfortunate brother,' the Lord Advocate continued, 'the Sunday before last, Sir Gavin.'

'He was murdered most foully, sir, shot in the head by the prisoner, in a cowardly attack. First he pulled me from my horse and seized my pistol and then he rushed up to Gregor and fired, from no more than two or three feet away.'

'The defence may suggest that he was provoked by your brother whipping his son, for scaring his horses. What say you to that?'

'The horses were startled, sir, by some foolish lads, and Gregor did react hastily, but I would ask the jury, does that justify his murder?'

'Indeed,' Bellhouse muttered from his lofty seat.

'Mr McGill was an employee of your family at one time, was he not?'

'He was favoured by my father, yes, but to be frank his work was shoddy, and Gregor was advised to dismiss him by our factor, not long after he inherited the estate. He did so, but in a kindly way; he allowed him to remain in his cottage.'

'Yet McGill still bore ill will towards you?'

'He did, Mr Douglas, as several affidavits testify.'

'Yes, I have seen them, and copies have been given to the jury. The Crown does not see the need to call them all as witnesses. What they say is clear enough.'

Innes Irvine gasped, audibly; Bellhouse heard him. 'And I agree with the Crown,' he barked. 'These folk are not vital witnesses, so we will not waste their time by bringing them here to repeat what they have already written down. Continue, sir. Did the panel say anything as he attacked your brother?'

'He screamed in rage and exultation, my Lord, but I was too shocked to remember what was said.'

'What did he do then?' Douglas asked.

'He seized the boy, his son, and ran off, towards the kirk.'

'Did he take the pistol?'

'He did, sir. He took it and he threw it down the well in front of the church. It would be there still, had not Mr Armitage, my factor, and I, while the village was at worship on Sunday, dropped buckets down until we retrieved it. If I may . . .'

The Lord Advocate nodded, and Cleland reached inside his coat and produced a short-barrelled firearm.

'This is the pistol that killed my brother. Armitage will attest to the find if the court wishes.'

'Then let's hear him,' the judge ordered.

An usher left the court and reappeared soon after with Philip Armitage in his charge. Mathew frowned. Armitage was a stern man, and his master's voice on the estate, but he had never struck him as a liar. Under oath, he repeated Cleland's story; Irvine rose to cross-examine, but Bellhouse waved him down.

'A simple matter of corroboration,' he declared.

'May I then examine Sir Gavin, my Lord?'

'If you wish,' the Lord Justice Clerk sighed.

Cleland resumed the witness box. 'Is that what really happened, Sir Gavin?' he asked.

'It is.'

'Is it not the case that while my client did remonstrate with Sir Gregor over his son being whipped, he fired no shot?'

Douglas rose to his feet. 'Then who did, my Lord?' he asked. 'There is no defence of impeachment.'

He had them, and Mathew knew it. Irvine could not accuse Cleland, nor even imply his guilt.

'No there is not,' the judge agreed. 'The question falls and so do you, sir. Sit down and let us hear the final witnesses.'

The Lord Advocate remained standing. 'In this, sir, I crave the court's indulgence. Miss Smith, Sir Gregor's betrothed, has been so overcome by this tragedy that she has been committed to a sanatorium in the north of England, in the care of physicians and of her paid companion, Miss Stout. However their testimony is very clear in the affidavits that are before the jury, and I beg that these be admitted in evidence.'

For the first time, Bellhouse seemed to hesitate. 'Do you realise what you are asking, Mr Douglas? The panel has the right to face his accusers.'

'That is true, my Lord, and he has already faced Sir Gavin and Mr Armitage, and the earlier witnesses. But I would suggest that these ladies have been so shocked by the awful thing they witnessed . . . my Lord, Miss Smith found her beloved's blood and brains on the hem of her skirt . . . that it would be cruel to inflict the horror upon them again. However, if the court wishes, we can adjourn and I will summon them.'

'No,' the Lord Justice Clerk intoned, 'let their affidavits serve.'

'Then that concludes the Crown's evidence.'

'Very good.' Bellhouse looked up at the wall clock. 'We will adjourn for fifteen minutes. Keep the panel under guard.'

Mathew wanted to stand and rail against the injustice he had seen, but with an effort he held on to his temper. All he could do was smile at David as he sat in the dock, ashen-faced.

'What can we do?' he asked, as he joined Johnston and Irvine at the far end of Parliament Hall.

'Very little,' the advocate admitted. 'They have been more clever than we could have anticipated. This is all going one way.'

'Then David must tell his own story. He is such an evidently good man that they must believe him, more so with Barclay to speak for him.'

Johnston's gaze fell to the floor. 'There we are lost, sir,' he murmured. 'I summoned your minister yesterday as a witness, but he has declined.'

'He has what?' Mathew's shout was so fierce that two promenading advocates jumped with fright.

'He sent back the message that he was unable to attend. He gave no reason.'

'Then damn him. A small part of me feared this; I believe I know the reason for his reluctance. My own testimonial will have to suffice.'

'Sir,' Innes Irvine murmured, 'I do not recommend that you give evidence. Douglas and Cleland have you hamstrung with the evidence of your conduct at the funeral . . . unless you can deny it absolutely.'

'That I cannot do, I'm afraid,' he admitted.

'Then you would be painted as two-faced, and not credible to the jury. It would deflect from any good Mr McGill might do himself.'

'Then he is truly on his own. Innes, please go to him and explain why nobody can speak for him.'

The advocate hurried off to the other end of the hall, to confer with his client. Shortly afterwards the macer's cry was heard once more and Lord Bellhouse returned.

The defence case was short and in no way sweet. To Mathew's horror, when David McGill was called to give evidence, he remained seated and shook his head.

'You have nothing to say in your defence?' the judge asked him.

'There is no point,' the prisoner replied. 'The Lord Advocate and this court, both are set against me. Any attempt to declare my innocence would do no good and would only endanger others. So I will sit silent, and let the jury hang an innocent man on the word of a pack of liars under the eye of a compliant judge.'

Bellhouse's response fell not far short of a scream. 'For that insult I would hang you twice!'

Then he turned to the jury. 'Gentlemen,' he said in a calmer tone, 'you have heard the facts in his case, and short and simple they are. Sir Gregor Cleland is dead of a pistol ball in the brain. Three witnesses have sworn that it was put there by the accused, a man with malice towards him, aforethought and evident. No form of defence has been put before you, and that silence is eloquent in itself.

'There are three verdicts open to you, as you will know, but your duty is clear. Go and do it now in the room provided, and dinna be long about it.'

Once again Mathew looked at the jurors, searching for any sign of defiance in their faces, but again he could find none. He checked his pocket watch as they filed from the court, and again when they returned. Less than six minutes had elapsed.

Bellhouse glowered at them as they sat. 'Have you a verdict?'

The largest among the fifteen rose to his feet, a slab of a man who might have been a blacksmith away from the court, or more likely a merchant butcher, given the quality of his clothing. 'We have, my Lord. We find the panel guilty as libelled.'

'Is that the verdict of you all?'

'It is, my Lord.'

'Thank you. You are all discharged from further jury service.'

The Lord Justice Clerk turned to his macer and snapped his fingers, but the man knew what was expected of him, and had already produced the black cap, which was in fact no more than a simple square of black cloth. He stepped forward, and then, in accordance with a custom imported from the English courts, he placed it on top of the judge's wig in token of the sentence about to be passed.

David McGill had risen to his feet unbidden. Bellhouse glared at him, with a cold, hard killer's expression, one that Mathew had seen in battle all too often, and, he acknowledged, had probably worn himself.

'You have been found guilty of the particularly heinous murder of a gentleman, unprovoked and in the presence of ladies. You will be taken from the Calton Jail in three days' time, to the public scaffold in the Lawnmarket, where you will be hanged by the neck until you are dead. May God have mercy on your soul, be He so minded.'

'My soul needs no mercy,' McGill replied, 'for it is blameless in this matter. As for yours, my Lord Bellhouse, if there are such things as heaven and hell, it is unlikely that we will meet again, for I expect to walk on green fields, while you will surely roast forever in Auld Nick's pit.'

'You'll be there before me,' the judge grunted. 'Take him away.'

He climbed down from the bench, and fell into step in formal procession behind his macer. As he passed, Mathew called after him, 'At least your lunch will not be served cold, my Lord. Enjoy it.'

Bellhouse spun half round to face him, only to be greeted with a smile and a courtly bow. His mouth twisted into a snarl, but he held his tongue and left the hall.

Chapter Twenty-Seven

'THREE DAYS,' DAVID MCGILL murmured, with a sad, thin smile. 'They don't keep a man hanging around, do they?'

Mathew stayed silent. Twenty years earlier, two years before Waterloo, he had stood guard over a soldier sentenced to be shot at dawn for the rape of a Spanish woman, and that victim had tried to keep his spirits up through humour. As the sun rose, though, he had pissed himself in his fear and had to be tied to the post with three ropes so that the firing squad could be sure of its target. He shuddered at that grim memory and hoped that his friend would be sustained in his courage when the moment came . . . if the moment came, for he had not given up hope.

'Mathew,' David continued, 'you will find my affairs in order. You will be the executor of my estate, such as it is. I am glad your friend the governor has allowed us this conversation, for there are things I need to say.' Mathew had gone straight from the court to the jail, where Stevens had taken the humane view that a condemned man could receive who he liked, when he liked.

'I beg you to look out for my children. Jean is young yet, but do not let her grow up thinking of me as a bad man. As for Matt, I fear for him; he has his mother's spirit and is the very boy to do something rash. Please restrain him as best you can.'

'Hah,' Mathew grunted, looking up from the table and into David's eyes. 'He may have to restrain me if the worst happens. I have power, the power that wealth confers on a man, and I will use it. The likes of Douglas and Bellhouse might be beyond me, but Cleland is not. I will crush that man like the pilliwinks; he will shit his breeks and beg for mercy before I am done with him.'

'Not on my account, please,' his friend begged. 'The Lawnmarket must not have you too.'

'Oh, it will not. Cleland has planted the seeds of his own destruction. All I will do is nurture them and help them grow. Worry not for your son either; I will treat him as my own, and Jean too.'

'And Lizzie,' David murmured. 'Look after her too. For fifteen years I've felt badly about coming between you two.'

'Then you must stop that now. You have been . . . Bugger it!' he snapped. 'I will not speak in the past tense. You are a perfect husband to her, a better match than I would have been. You have devoted your entire life to her, whereas even if my good friend Sir Victor had never written that hasty letter, I would not.

'You may believe that my business success and my losing Lizzie are linked in some way. I know that others do, but it is not so. I would have been driven in the same way even with her as my wife, and she would have suffered for it. There is a phrase I like that Stockley uses of his expensive and fanciful daughter. He says she is "high maintenance"; so, in a different way, is Lizzie, as we both know.'

David smiled. 'That she is, but she will hurt nonetheless.' He grasped Mathew's arm. 'Please do not tell her of this, not until Friday is gone and I am dead. It is better she knows nothing until everything is done. Keep Matt close to you and keep her in ignorance.'

He nodded. 'Agreed, but I will tell her nothing for I have not given up hope yet. If there is anything to be done I will do it . . . although I confess I do not know what that might be.'

'Then do it, but keep me in ignorance too. I have three days, in which I must compose myself and make my peace with God. Bring my son to see me, but that is all.'

'I will do that. Is there a chaplain here?'

'Mr Stevens says so. I tell you, that man was upset when he heard my fate.'

'If only the law in this city was as upright and honest as him.'

'Those you found for me have done their best. Mathew, I would like to pay them from my own resources.'

'That is one request I will not grant. There is no man in the world closer to me, so their efforts have been in my interests as well as yours. Now I must go to consult with them again, before Matt returns from his journey to the seashore and I have to tell him the news.'

Johnston was waiting for him in the hotel salon when he returned. 'Sir,' he said even before they were seated, 'my profession owes you an apology for what you saw today. It was judicial murder.'

'Not yet,' Mathew pointed out. 'The sentence has not yet been carried out. And even then, I would not call it murder. Yon Bellhouse is as evil a man as I've seen, but I do not believe that the Lord Advocate would collude with people he knew to be perjurers.'

'Yet he was keen to see Mr McGill convicted. That I do not understand.'

'Nor do I, or why Bellhouse was so cooperative with him. Is there any way left, Paul, by which they may be thwarted?'

'No,' the solicitor admitted. 'Before I left Parliament House, Mr Irvine asked for leave to appeal, but this was rejected. Nobody crosses Bellhouse, not even his peers. Mr Fleming, it would be dishonest of me to suggest that any hope remains. We have failed our client and the rope is as good as round his neck.'

'You have failed no one. I know how the cards were dealt against us; when the impeachment was blocked, David was finished. Bellhouse hastened the process, that was all. I will not give up hope while David is alive, but there is one other service I would ask of you, on his behalf.'

He gave Johnston brief instructions and then the solicitor left him to his thoughts, and to a reunion to which he was not looking forward with any pleasure.

Young Matt and Ewan Beattie returned from North Berwick just before six in the evening. Mathew broke the awful news in his room; he held his young ward to him as he wept, then calmed him as his fear turned into anger.

'If my father dies, I will kill Cleland, I swear it,' he raged.

'You will swear nothing of the sort, for you would be

killing your poor mother with the same blow. If this terrible thing comes to pass, your duty will be to her, and it will be best served by keeping her close, and yourself out of harm's way. When my father died, I did the opposite, and there is not a day goes by when I do not regret it.'

'Why?' Matt retorted. 'You were a hero in the wars.'

Mathew tapped his blind eye. 'This does not make a man a hero, lad. I joined the army for money, a very little money, not out of love of my monarch. I fought well, and I lived, against the odds, but I was a fool for going in the first place, and for deserting those I loved.'

'You mean my mother?' the youth murmured

'Why do you say that?' he asked, sharply.

'Daphne told me,' Matt replied, 'my mother's cousin, the one she doesna speak to. She told me you and she were sweethearts once.'

'Then she should have held her tongue, for that is in the past. Matt, your father is my truest friend, and I will do anything in my power to save him.'

'But you would not let me give evidence. You sent me away.'

'Your father forbade it. The impeachment was withdrawn to save your life, and that is the truth of it. He is sacrificing himself for you. I understand that, and so should you. If you were my son I could not love you more than I do, and in his shoes I would have done the same to keep you safe.'

'Then what can I do, Mathew?' he wailed.

'Nothing. Pray for your father and be brave when you see him, for the sight of your courage will help him keep his own.'

He waited until Matt had composed himself, and then they went down to dinner. 'Our starvation will not help David,' Mathew told him. 'I have no taste for food either but we must nourish ourselves.'

They ate in silence. Ewan Beattie passed a few remarks about North Berwick and its fresh clean air, the rival of Carluke, but neither of his companions were of a mind for conversation. When they were finished, Mathew said to the coachman, privately, 'Keep the boy close to you. I am going out to find a place where I can think. If there is another means of saving David, I must find it.' He frowned. 'That fellow you met, your compatriot who worked for the gaming club. Did he tell you where it was?'

'In a house in a place called St Bernard's Crescent, he said. There are all sorts of games on offer, and the company of ladies is available also.'

'Is it, indeed?'

He left the hotel and walked out into the bright evening. He had no clear idea of what he would do, but before he knew it he found himself at Albany Street. The coffee shop on the corner was open, and so he went inside. The place was quiet; Mathew guessed that Tuesdays were not its busiest. There was a vacant table by the window and so he chose it, ordering coffee and a selection of cheeses.

'A stranger in Edinburgh?' the owner asked as he served him.

'Yes,' he replied. 'From Lanarkshire; Carluke, in fact, in the Upper Ward. The Cleland family are our local gentry. I have been told they have a house in this area.'

'They do, just along the road. As you would expect, they

are customers of mine . . . but they have become just one now, since the murder of Sir Gregor. His brother called in this afternoon, filled with delight that they are hanging the perpetrator on Friday.'

'Delight, you say? Satisfaction I could understand, but to glory in a man's execution . . .'

The proprietor leaned closer to him. 'I did not say this, you understand, but that is Sir Gavin's way. Sir Gregor was no cherub, but his brother has no saving grace that I have discerned.'

The man stood, quickly, as if he was aware of his vulnerability in the window, turned on his heel and walked away. Mathew was left puzzled, until he looked out of the window and saw Gavin Cleland, on the other side of the street, striding out purposefully and swiftly, his eyes focused dead ahead.

He waited until the baronet had passed, and had crossed Dublin Street, then settled his account and set out after him. He walked a good hundred yards behind him, with his hat pulled down to shield his face as far as was possible. His quarry led him along Abercrombie Place, and then across Dundas Street and into Heriot Row, with its grey stone buildings on one side and gardens on the other, akin to Princes Street.

Just as Mathew was wondering where he would be led, and whether they were bound for St Bernard's Crescent, Cleland turned off the pavement abruptly and mounted the steps that led up to a fine, four-storey, terraced house, the grandest in the street. He knocked on the door and was admitted.

Mathew stepped into the gardens, concealed by a tree and waited. As he watched he saw a carriage turn into the terrace from the street beyond, and then position itself outside the very house that Cleland had entered. It had no sooner stopped moving than the door opened once more, and Gavin Cleland stepped out.

There was a lady on his arm, as tall as he, but from what Mathew could see at least ten years younger, and a great beauty. Her hair was piled high, and surmounted by a tiny hat; she looked radiant and very happy. As he watched, the couple were helped into the carriage by its driver, who then climbed back up to his perch and drove off, the horse's hooves clip-clopping on the cobbles, and the wheels rattling.

'Well, well, well,' Mathew whispered, stepping out of the gardens and crossing the street. He approached the house and saw from a distance the number, thirty-three, in large Roman numerals on the brown-painted front door. As he drew closer, he saw that there was a brass plate to the right, below the bell handle. He slowed his pace as he reached it and was able to read the name carved on it: 'Mr J Douglas, Advocate'.

'Yes, sir,' a voice came from behind him, 'that is indeed the Lord Advocate's home, if you were wondering.'

He turned to see a young man, almost as tall as he, well-dressed, in a high collar that was part of what he took to be a school uniform.

'Are you sure of that?' he asked. 'Douglas is a common name.'

'That is he, be in no doubt. I know for I live at number twenty-four.'

'Then who was the young lady I saw leave just now?'

'That would be Miss Lucy Douglas, the Lord Advocate's daughter. The gentleman would be Sir Gavin Cleland, of Cleland House, in Lanarkshire. He is said to be her suitor; my father remarked two nights ago that now he has inherited his brother's estate, a betrothal is imminent.'

Chapter Twenty-Eight

'THE WHOLE SITUATION, IN a nutshell,' Innes Irvine exclaimed. 'Cleland is after the hand of the Lord Advocate's daughter, and seems to be in favour. No wonder Douglas was so keen to see a conviction, and so determined to squash the impeachment. Had that been successful, even if it had led only to a not proven verdict, which would not have put Cleland in the dock himself, the scandal would have splashed upon the steps of thirty-three Heriot Row.'

'But what of Bellhouse?' Mathew asked. 'He was blatantly complicit in the rush to injustice. How do you explain that? The law in Edinburgh seems more than a little incestuous to me. But of course, old Bellhouse and Douglas are kin?'

Paul Johnston shook his head, as he looked out on to Hanover Street. The three had gathered in his chambers, on Mathew's summons on Wednesday morning. 'Your perception is correct, Mr Fleming. There are families who more or less control the courts. Bellhouse, he has a son, Douglas's cousin, who is not that much longer at the Bar than Innes here, yet who is being favoured already.'

'As am I,' Irvine said.

'Indeed?' the solicitor murmured, curious.

'Yes. I was summoned by the Crown Agent this morning. He asked me to act as advocate depute in the trial of a highway robber next month. I would not be leading the prosecution, but even to act as a junior at this point in my career, that would be a marker to all.'

'Did you accept?' Mathew asked.

Irvine smiled. 'I told him I would have to consult my diary.'

'Then do so, and tell him you will take the brief. You did your best for David, and you are still doing it, by being here at all. Douglas would not be offering this if he thought you a fool.'

'Some may think I was suborned.'

'Then they would be eedjits and not worthy of consideration. Paul and I know the truth, and that should be enough for you. Take your chance, man.'

The advocate nodded. 'With your blessing, I may. But let us not get ahead of this situation. Your discovery last night opens a small window of hope, sir.'

'How can we get through it?'

'There is one way. It also involves incest of a sort, I am afraid. My grandfather was a solicitor, with a considerable practice. Fifty years ago or more, he gave an important instruction to a junior advocate, Edward Cooper. It was a defence in a capital trial and, unlike myself yesterday, he succeeded. It was the making of him and he never forgot it.

'That man is now Lord Cooper, the Lord Justice General and Lord President of the Court of Session. He knows of me, for I bear my grandfather's Christian name. When I was called to the Bar and presented in court, he sent me his good wishes afterwards in a private message.'

'All very good,' Johnston said, 'but where does it take us, and how does it help our client?'

'Armed with Mr Fleming's discovery,' Irvine answered, 'I am prepared to go to Lord Cooper privately and tell him what we know. He is an old man, and he is rarely seen on the Bench these days, but every lawyer in Scotland knows of his reputation for probity. When he hears how this case has been conducted, and of the connection between Douglas and Cleland, I believe it probable that he will order a stay of execution, to give us time to petition the court and, if necessary, the King himself.'

'Is that a proper course of action?' Mathew asked.

'No, it is highly irregular and Lord Cooper may well refuse to hear us, but with Mr McGill's forthcoming appointment in the Lawnmarket, it is something I am quite prepared to do.'

'Even if it has an adverse effect on your career?'

'If I did nothing, it would have an adverse effect on me as a man,' the young advocate declared.

'Then let us see if we can squeeze through your window. You say we should call on him at home?'

'Yes, he has been unwell, and absent from Parliament House for three weeks. It may be better that we call on him informally; there will be no one to bar our way, and word will not get to Bellhouse and Douglas, as it would if we approached the Lord President's clerk.'

Mathew rose to his feet, but Johnston remained seated. 'It is almost lunchtime,' he pointed out. 'We might get a better reception if my Lord Cooper is well fed.'

The three dined themselves, in a basement tavern on the corner of Hanover Street and Rose Street, where Johnston seemed to be well known, but Mathew had little appetite and was impatient to be on the move. When, finally, Irvine declared that it was time to go, he paid the bill and led the way back up to the street, taking the steps two at a time.

'Where does Lord Cooper live?' he asked Johnston, as they waited for the advocate to join them after relieving himself.

'In Moray Place. Not a long walk; indeed, nothing in the New Town is a long walk.'

With Irvine's comfort restored, they set off, Johnston striding out in the lead, turning into George Street and following it until they reached Charlotte Square, then heading downhill, through Forres Street and into Moray Place.

For all his urgency earlier Mathew paused, to look around. It was a great circle of stone town houses: some boasted pillared frontages, and all were four storeys, piled on top of basements; he guessed that the servants were housed below street level, and perhaps also on the top floor, if the household was wealthy enough to justify an extravagant staff.

Johnston led them towards the grandest house of all; Mathew thought they had reached their destination but their leader strode on. He stopped before one of the less ostentatious buildings . . . then exclaimed, 'Oh! Oh my! I hope that does not mean what I fear it does.'

The shutters on the ground floor were closed, as were all

the others save for one above the blue-painted front door, in the centre of which there hung a black crêpe wreath.

The trio stood on the pavement outside, staring at the grim intimation.

'Should we . . .' Johnston ventured.

'Of course,' Irvine snapped. He stepped towards the door but was only halfway there when it opened. A black-clad man, who looked to be in his mid-forties, stood there; he wore a wig, and at first Mathew took him for a servant, until he spoke.

'Young Innes,' he said. 'I saw you from the window above. You will have guessed what has happened. You and your friends, please come in.'

'Who is he?' Mathew whispered.

'Lord Cooper's oldest son,' Johnston murmured, 'also named Edward and King's Counsel. He is the Vice-Dean of the Faculty of Advocates, because of his father more than anything else. He will become a judge, no doubt, but he is nowhere near the Lord President's stature.'

They followed him indoors, through a dark hall and into a room at the rear, which was unshuttered.

'My father died this morning,' he told them. 'He caught a summer cold a month back, and it saw him off. We did not broadcast the severity of his illness, in case we were overwhelmed by well-wishers.'

'I am very sorry,' Irvine said. 'Please accept our condolences.'

'Thank you,' Cooper replied, looking at Mathew. 'Mr Johnston I know, of course, and this, unless I am misinformed and there is another formidable man of similar appearance, is Mr Fleming, who has been making a considerable stir around the court these past few days.'

He extended his hand to Mathew. As they shook, he said, 'I hear you are about to lose a friend, and I guess that was what brought you here. I was at Parliament House yesterday afternoon, and heard whispers about a trial in the morning. Whispers only,' he added. 'My father has been on the periphery for some time, and the inner circle have been keeping me at arm's length.' He looked at Irvine. 'I take it you were hoping for my father's intercession.'

The advocate nodded his reply.

'Then I am sorry for you, for there is no influence left in this house. With the death of the Lord Justice General, until a successor is appointed, the Lord Justice Clerk is the highest figure on the Bench, and as you know that is Bellhouse himself. Whatever grounds you may have for further proceedings, I will wager they will fall on deaf ears.'

'How soon will that appointment be made?' Mathew asked.

'Not before my father's funeral, which will be in St Giles on Monday. But it could be today and it would not help you. It is decided already; Bellhouse is too old to take office himself, so someone else will step up. As Scotland's man in Westminster, the Lord Advocate makes the choice for confirmation by the King. Douglas intends to nominate . . . himself. He will be my father's successor; when he is done with the post, it will pass to Bellhouse's son. That bargain was struck some time ago.' Cooper frowned. 'I am sorry, gentlemen, sometimes our court shames me.'

'Yet you do nothing about it!' Mathew exclaimed,

regretting his anger as soon as the words were out. 'No, sir,' he said, at once. 'I apologise; you are newly bereaved, and you are one man. The corruption I have seen here goes very deep. Thank you for receiving us; I hope you will speak to others about what happened yesterday, and that when you are a judge yourself, you will be the better for it.'

In the street outside, Irvine was crestfallen. 'I am sorry. I had real hope that Lord Cooper might have interceded. Indeed, had he been alive I am sure he would have. Strange,' he mused, 'that house felt empty, and yet a month ago, with the old man alive, there would have been such a feeling of power about it.'

'I keep telling folk in this city,' Mathew said, 'that they do not understand power. The power of the law has David by the neck at the moment, but let us see if the power of the people can help. Paul, I want you to find me a printer, one who can work fast and, most important of all, can be trusted to keep his mouth shut, whoever comes asking. If you can, have him call on me this evening. He will be a last resort though; I have one more card to play before I reach him.'

Johnston nodded. 'I can guess what you mean, and I know the very man. His name is Blackwood and his discretion is legendary.'

'Good. I have a sense here that I may be setting out on a long campaign, but I will not give it up, even if Friday goes ill. I cannot be in Edinburgh for ever, but you know this city and I want you to act as my agent. I will give you instructions as time goes on, but here is the first. I want those women found, those two who condemned David. "Gentlewoman of Knutsford, Cheshire", indeed,' he spat. 'By her actions she is no such thing, nor is her maid. Their disappearance is too convenient and too facile. I want to know who they are, where they are, and what they are; then I want them brought before me. I have another task for them also, but that will be the priority.'

'I can employ sub-agents on your behalf, Mr Fleming,' the solicitor said, 'but it will be costly.'

'That will be nothing to me. You are all in a cocoon in this place; there are different rules outside and different values.'

'Very good, but if they are found, I am not sure I can have them brought to you against their will.'

'Oh, but you can. For there is one thing that everyone has forgotten and that I had not considered myself, not until now. With my office under the Crown I became a magistrate in the County of Lanark. I can issue you with a warrant.'

'What would be the charge?'

'Murder, by perjury. That should get their attention, and loosen their tongues. Now,' he continued, 'back to your office. I want to send a letter to London, by the swiftest means possible, and I need a place to write.'

'I can arrange that. To whom do you want to send it?'

Mathew's good eye was ablaze with the rage that he had contained, mostly, until that point. 'To Sir Victor Feather, Member of Parliament and confidant of the Duke of Wellington, lately Prime Minister, and likely to be again. I have been patronised by these bastards long enough, gentlemen. I will show them what influence really is.'

Chapter Twenty-Nine

MATHEW HAD RUN OUT of hope for his friend's life, but he kept that truth within himself as he strode along the High Street, in search of the office of the *Register* newspaper. His letter to Feather was written and in the hands of the post office, with the promise that it would be delivered by the weekend.

He found the newspaper's office almost opposite St Giles, near the mouth of Advocates' Close. He strode into the musty place; it smelled of oil, ink and metal and he pitied those who had to work there.

'I would like to speak with the editor,' he told a shirtsleeved man who greeted him.

'Mr McCulloch is not here, sir,' the other replied. 'He is on his annual holiday in Dunbar and will not be back for another week. Can I help? I am his deputy; my name is Jonathan Mackay.'

'I have a story to tell you,' Mathew began. 'It concerns a trial, or rather a travesty, that took place yesterday in yon place across the street. It has left a man facing the gallows, even though he is innocent.'

'You say he is innocent,' Mackay retorted, 'but if it is the affair I anticipate, that of the murderer McGill, our court reporter said that the verdict was unanimous. He told me that the hearing was brief and that he offered no defence. Like as no', our report of his execution will be longer than that of his trial.'

'Did your reporter also tell you of Lord Bellhouse's performance?'

Mackay's eyes narrowed. 'He said that the Lord Justice Clerk was unusually tetchy, even by his standards, and that he had precious little patience . . . as in, none at all . . . with the prisoner's advocate.'

'There is more to it than that, much more. There was collusion between him and the Lord Advocate to convict my friend.'

'Then why do you no' take it back to the court?' the journalist asked.

'We would, but there is little time, and little point now that Lord Cooper is dead, and Bellhouse sits temporarily in his place.'

Mackay seemed to turn rigid. 'Cooper is dead?'

'Yes, he died this morning. I am not long from his house in Moray Place.'

'Then take your story back there, sir. Or take it to the *Scotsman* or the *Glasgow Herald*. Take it anywhere, but away from here. I do not want to hear it. I do not even want to ken your name.'

'I beg your pardon?' He was astonished. 'Is this not the newspaper set up to fight the obsequious nature of the Scottish press, as its founders proclaimed? And yet you turn away a true tale. When did you join the ranks or the arse-kissers?'

'So they did say, sir, and so we have been. But with Cooper gone, Douglas will preside over the court with old Bellhouse by his side. Now you come in here hinting of a plot between them. We have to live in the real world, Mr Fleming . . . yes, I do know who you are . . . if we are to survive at all. Please go away, and take your scandal with you.'

'Very well,' Mathew replied, 'but know that I think you a cowardly wretch, and that you have lost a reader and made an enemy in a single sentence.'

His anger dissipated as he made his way back to the Waterloo Hotel; he did his best to drive the looming prospect of Friday morning from his mind, and to focus on the day ahead, but it proved impossible and as he walked his imagination was full of terrible images.

Matt was waiting for him when he reached the hotel. 'When can I see my father?' he asked.

'I had faint hopes that you would have seen him today, at liberty, but those are gone. We will visit him tomorrow in the afternoon, for as long as the governor will allow. If you have to say goodbye, and I can no longer deny that is likely, you must appear as brave as you can before him.'

'Will my mother not know by now? I heard a vendor calling out the story not long ago.'

'Your mother will not know, for she will see no newspapers. I gave that order before we left, in case things went wrong.'

'Mathew,' the young man moaned, 'is there no more to be done?'

'Only one thing: people must know the truth. I have

tried one way but found it blocked by cowardice, now I will turn to the other. Go to your room now, please, and wait. I am expecting a visitor.'

The printer Blackwood arrived an hour later; Mathew received him privately, in his own room, and wasted no time on niceties. 'I wish to publish a pamphlet,' he said, 'and to have it distributed to as many people as you can print copies. It will be anonymous and its source should not be obvious. It will tell the true story of an act of shame by the highest court in our land and of a man unjustly condemned to death.'

'Is it defamatory?' his visitor asked. 'I have principles, sir.'

'No, because every word is true. It will be anonymous, but those against whom it is directed will know the source.'

'Will they act against you? If its printing is traced to me and I am questioned, I must answer honestly. By that I mean I canna protect you.'

'I will not need your protection. No one will move against me; they wish this affair to end with the scapegoat, and to be forgotten as quickly as possible.'

'Do you have a text?'

'Yes. Here it is.' He handed over a document that he had drafted in Johnston's office, with the solicitor's guidance. 'How soon can it be on the streets?'

'Tomorrow morning, if I work overnight.'

'The afternoon will do, then more at the Lawnmarket, on Friday morning. I am told that hangings draw a great crowd in Edinburgh, and I want them all to have something to read while they are waiting for the drop.'

'Consider it done, sir,' Blackwood declared, confidently. 'It will no' be cheap though. Should we no' discuss cost?'

Mathew took a roll of five-pound notes from his pocket and peeled one off, then another. 'Tell me when to stop,' he said.

He had reached four, when the printer called out, 'Enough. That'll be fine, sir.' He smiled. 'If I'm asked how I came by these, I'll say I won them at the cards.'

'You are a gamer?'

'Oh aye. I love the card tables. No' that I'm very good at it. I cover my stake usually but no' much more. I have friends tho', that mak' their living from it, and a good one at that. The club where I play is full o' rich folk whose common sense vanishes as soon as they step over the door. After a glass of brandy and some time upstairs with a hoor, they're easy pickings, and they never know when to stop.'

'Where do you play?'

'In a club in St Bernard's Crescent. You'd be welcome there, sir, I'm sure, although I suspect you'd no' be as easy parted from your money as most.'

'That might be the case; or it might not. I played in the army, to pass the time, but I have not lifted a card since then. The tables cause too much trouble, even between comrades in arms.' He paused. 'However, I would be interested in meeting your friends. How many of them are there?'

'Three. Jimmy, Pilmar and Kenneth: they dinna go in for surnames.'

'Can you contact them easily?'

'Pilmar, I can; he can pass on any message.'

'Then ask them to call on me here at three o'clock tomorrow, if they would be so kind.'

'Will you be providing the cards? They might not like that.'

Mathew shook his head. 'That is not quite the game that I have in mind.'

Chapter Thirty

BLACKWOOD'S FRIENDS WERE PUNCTUAL, and the meeting with them was productive. When Mathew showed them out, he found copies of his pamphlet on the table in the salon. He picked one up, casually, and when they were gone, sat down to read it.

The printer had excelled himself. There was a headline that seemed to shout from the page: 'Innocent yet Doomed!' and below it an illustration showing the scene as young Matt had described it, a pistol being fired at two brawling men with two women watching from a carriage. The key parts of the text were highlighted in bold type, for maximum effect.

Mathew had stopped short of accusing Gavin Cleland of perjury; instead the text said that he had suffered an 'imperfection of memory' as a result of the shock of 'mistakenly' shooting his brother. As for the women, it noted that they both seemed to have suffered 'remarkably' from the same 'imperfection', but that they had been unable to describe it to the High Court in person as they had been mysteriously spirited away.

And as for the Lord Advocate, usually so meticulous in

his pursuit of the truth, it concluded that he too must have been overcome by the shock of the incident, as a result of his personal connection to Gavin Cleland, who was 'linked romantically' with his own dear daughter.

There was only a single mention of Bellhouse, screaming at the innocent man as he stood before him, 'I would hang you twice!'

Mathew stepped outside and walked slowly down Waterloo Place, pausing at Register House and looking around. Several pedestrians had stopped their progress, standing transfixed by the pamphlet as they read it. He smiled with satisfaction, then returned to the hotel.

Shortly afterwards, he and Matt left for the prison. Mathew had wondered whether he might have a visit from the Lord Advocate's officers, but none came. However, when they arrived at the gate he found that Douglas had acted there.

Governor Stevens came to greet him. 'I cannot admit you, Mr Fleming. The boy yes, but you, no. The Lord Provost has forbidden your entrance, on the ground that he does not want Mr McGill coached in what he called "inflammatory speeches". The Lord Provost is a figurehead, and as we both know, his order has come straight from the Lord Advocate, but he wears the chain of office and I must obey him.'

'I understand. Thank you for the care you are taking of my poor friend. Please give his son as much time with him as you can allow.'

Matt looked back in anguish as he was led inside the jail, back at his guardian, catching his face in an unguarded moment and realising that for the first time it was bereft of any sign of hope.

He was allowed to see his father alone, unescorted, but the officers refused to remove his shackles.

'Worry not, son,' David told him. 'Chains canna bind your conscience and mine is clear.'

'Faither, this is my fault,' Matt moaned. 'If I had seen those horses, and not startled them . . .'

'And if I had never met your mother, you would never have been born, and I would not be here. If you had succumbed to the fever you had when you were two, I would not be here. "If" is something that never happened or may not happen, and has no reality. You're my precious son and I am grateful for the fifteen years I've had you. You are faultless in this, the villains are the Clelands, and most of all Gavin, but fate has a way of rewarding sinners.'

'I will reward him, in time.'

'No. You will reward me, by looking after your mother and your sister; Mathew will stand by you. He will be your father from now on, and although he would deny it, you could not have one better. You should look after him too, and keep him safe from himself. He is, after all, a man that was made by war. He should have died, but he lived, and is all the more formidable for it. He is the best friend a man could have, but the worst enemy, as Gavin Cleland will find out. Stop him from going too far, though, for if you lost him too, then you and your mother really would be alone.'

David looked at his son, holding his hands as he sat next to him. 'Would you like to pray with me?'

'I have prayed for you, Faither,' Matt replied, 'but look,

you're still here. I put no trust in prayer, not any more.'

'Then you should; faith is important to a man. Faith is absolute belief, in the want of any supporting evidence. Without it we might be entirely alone. Mine is with me now, and it will be with me tomorrow, leading me through to the other side.'

He leaned forward and kissed his son on the forehead. 'Go on, now, while we are both strong. Give that kiss to your mother and your wee sister, and tell them I will always love them.'

Chapter Thirty-One

THE MORNING WAS COLD and it was wet, as Mathew Fleming rose to face the hardest and most painful duty he would ever have to perform. Sleep had eluded him all night.

'Be there for me,' David had asked him. 'Let me find my strength in yours. But keep my son away from the Lawnmarket if you can . . . though that task may be beyond even you.'

He had no wish for breakfast and in any event time was short. The execution was scheduled for ten o'clock, but Mathew wondered whether it would be brought forward. He had gone wandering in the evening before to try to judge the effectiveness of his pamphlet; in the taverns and houses he had visited, the talk was of nothing else.

He dressed in black, and in a long coat made of waxed cotton sailcloth, that he had found in a shop in Glasgow, then went next door, to the room Matt shared with Ewan Beattie.

The boy was ready for the day; his eyes were red from the sobbing that Mathew had heard through the wall for much of the night. 'Matt,' he said, 'you are to stay here, until I return.'

'No! I must be there!'

'It is your father's wish that you should not see him die.'

'But I want to be there. I want to see his courage, and I want to see exactly what Cleland has done to him, so that I can keep it in my heart as I make the rest of that man's short life a misery.'

'That is a task you can leave to me,' Mathew retorted. 'I repeat what you have been told, and told, and told again. Your duty is to your mother and your sister; today you become a man, a little before your time, and you will show that by acting sensibly.'

'I want to be there,' Matt muttered.

'I know,' Mathew sighed, 'but would you have me break my word to your father?' He looked at the coachman. 'Ewan, lock the door after me and keep him here.'

Outside, he found himself in a crowd of people all heading in the same direction. As he crossed the North Bridge and strode up the High Street, more and more joined, and hundreds became thousands.

The scaffold was a massive structure; it had been set up overnight and was guarded not by constables, as Mathew understood to be the usual practice, but by soldiers. He had passed by a public execution in Newbury and it had been a gala occasion, but the mood of the Lawnmarket crowd was in no way festive. The pamphlet was to be seen everywhere, and its effect was clear. It would be a poor day for the souvenir sellers, that much was certain.

The executioner was waiting on the raised platform, and he was not alone. The Lord Provost, in his chain, and the baillies in their robes stood in line. Legally, the execution was their responsibility, and the court always kept well clear.

The first apple came from the middle of the crowd, and barely missed the Provost, but the next caught one of the baillies full in the face. Within seconds the onslaught had become serious and a fusillade of fruit was flying. A mounted officer shouted an order and the troops pressed forward, but at that moment the confrontation was halted by the arrival of the black prison wagon.

Quickly, Mathew moved forward through the crowd, taking up position directly in front of the hangman. He looked all around, but saw no familiar faces, until his eye fell on a bulky figure, in sodden clothing: the jury foreman. His expression was solemn and he clutched a copy of the pamphlet.

The execution was under way and the men who supervised it were practised. They could read the public mood, and they knew without telling to be quick. David was hustled from his transport and up the steps, as fast as his shackles would allow, then positioned beneath the beam alongside the waiting rope. As it was placed around his neck, his eyes found Mathew, and he smiled.

A moment after the grey hood was placed over his head, covering his face, blocking out the last daylight David McGill would ever see, Mathew felt someone bump into him. He looked down and saw young Matt, with his appointed keeper.

'I'm sorry, sir,' Beattie gasped, out of breath. 'He'd have broken the door down and me with it.'

He shrugged his shoulders. 'His father said the task would be beyond us.'

On the scaffold the Lord Provost stepped forward. He began to read but a roar erupted from the crowd, and nothing could be heard.

Duty done, the civic leader retreated. The crowd fell absolutely silent as the hangman moved in, and words could be heard from the scaffold.

'Our Father who art in Heaven, hallowed be Thy name. Thy Kingdom come, Thy . . .'

Before the trap opened, Mathew seized his charge with both hands and spun him around, away from the scene, and looked away himself. But both heard the crack, and then the crowd's collective moan.

Then the sound of applause came from their right. Mathew looked round and found himself staring at Sir Gavin Cleland, whose smile was a mix of triumph and mockery.

'Hold him,' he said to Beattie, thrusting Matt into his grasp, although restraint was unnecessary, for the lad had collapsed.

Only a few spectators stood between the two, and Mathew brushed them aside to reach Cleland. He towered over him, consumed with a rage that was far beyond the heat of battle, and seized him by the lapel. 'You have become my life's work,' he snarled. 'I will finish you, whatever it takes, however long it takes.'

'It need not take that long,' the baronet laughed, and Mathew realised that he was slightly drunk. 'We are both countrymen; I offer you a duel on my estate.'

'Then you would be a fool. You proved yourself a fine shot when you murdered your brother, but you have never faced anyone with a pistol in his hand. Nor have you faced me. I was a soldier, sir, and I have killed far, far better men than you.'

He pointed up at the scaffold, where David's head and shoulders could still be seen, turning slowly on the rope.

'That is the fate I have in mind for you, and when it happens I will be stood right here, watching you foul your breeches when you feel the rope on your neck. Believe me, Cleland, you are as good as dead, and when it happens, this same crowd will cheer the hangman, and throw flowers, not rotten fruit, at the Provost and his friends.'

He pushed him away, so hard that the man tripped and fell, then returned to care for his fatherless charge.

Chapter Thirty-Two

MATHEW DROVE THE CARRIAGE back to Waterloo House that afternoon, with Matt behind him in the closed compartment. The young man had said not a word since his father's execution.

He ignored the heavy rain that had been falling all day. He was lost in dark thoughts, and once or twice had to restrain himself from pushing the horses too hard. He eased off still further as they came close to home. Half a mile away, just out of sight of the house, he stopped altogether and joined his companion in the cabin.

'Are you ready for this?' he asked.

Matt nodded.

'What will you tell your mother?'

'That you did everything you could but the court was set against Faither from the very start.'

'What else?'

'That he was the bravest man I have ever seen.'

'Good. There is no denying that.'

They covered the rest of the ground at little more than walking pace. As they approached the house the rain lessened, and by the time they turned into the long driveway it had stopped altogether, and the evening sun was breaking through.

Mathew had dreaded facing Lizzie, but as he approached the great house, the main door opened, and she stepped out. She was dressed in black, as was Hannah who followed her. A small movement made him glance up, and spot the children, Jean and Marshall, with their faces pressed against the glass of an upstairs window.

He drew the carriage to a halt, jumping down from the driver's bench, just as Matt emerged from cover and rushed into his mother's arms. He was taller and broader than she, and she seemed to disappear into his embrace. They wept together, for several minutes, their emotions released and uncontrollable.

Mathew stood back, looking helplessly at his own mother.

When they were spent, and had recovered themselves, Lizzie kissed her boy on the cheek and passed him into Hannah's care. She took him inside, leaving the two alone.

'So it's true,' she murmured, her eyes red and puffy from her tears. 'Gavin Cleland's lie has killed my husband.'

'That, and the weakness of men who put their own interests first. How did you know?' he asked. 'I hoped you would not find out until I told you myself.'

'Uncle Peter came to see me. He was distraught, the poor man; he had heard of the part his son-in-law played in our eviction, and he came to apologise. They are gone, he said, Daphne and Grose, vanished overnight.' She paused 'And he brought me this. It came to the shop with the newspapers this afternoon.'

She opened her hand and showed him, folded, a copy of his pamphlet. 'So you see, Mathew, I know everything,' She held up the printed paper. 'I take it this was your doing.'

He nodded. 'I published it anonymously. It was all that was left open to me. It damn near started a riot at the . . .' He stopped in mid-sentence.

'You can say it!' Her sudden, shrill, bitter laugh shocked him. 'At the hanging: there are no soft words for it. Will this man Douglas have seen your paper too?'

'I would be amazed if he had not, but he is committed to Cleland, for reasons of family and of reputation.'

'And my children and I, we must go on, must we, living close to that man?' Her voice was low and venomous.

'For now, but that will be good, for you will see him suffer. I have plans for that murderer. I told him as much this morning. He may think himself impervious, but he is not. You must keep Matt close, though,' he added. 'He is dangerous at the moment; young, hot-headed and strong. There is anger burning in him, and you must damp it down with love.'

'I could feel it there; the lad is like a volcano.' Her lips trembled. 'He said his father died well. Does that mean he was there?'

'I tried my best to prevent it, but if necessary he would have gone through Beattie, and a locked door, to get there. He did not see it, though, Lizzie, I promise you, any more than I did, for I turned his head away and mine.'

She nodded. 'Had I been in Edinburgh,' she murmured, 'you would not have kept me away either.'

'That I know. How are you now?'

'Broken-hearted, but it will mend. I will be fine, for the children. I have felt like this before, remember. When Captain Feather's letter told me you were dead, that was like being widowed too, for in my heart we were man and wife already.'

In mine too, he thought. *And like a fool I went off to war, starting a chain of events that has led us here.*

'Mathew . . .' Lizzie hesitated for a second or two '. . . where is David, where is his body? I have heard that they give bodies to the anatomists after execution.'

'They did, but no longer, I discovered, not since the Anatomy Act was passed a couple of years back. Normally he would have been buried in an unmarked grave, but Mr Johnston, my solicitor, reached a financial understanding with the undertaker. He is on his way back here now, under the guard of Ewan Beattie, who has been with him every step of the way from the Lawnmarket. I never realised till now what a good man he is.'

'Will I be able to see him?' she asked.

'If you wish. When I saw him, afterwards, he looked peaceful. But not Matt, I suggest; he needs no more images in his brain. You go inside now; tend to him, and to the wee ones, even though they will not understand what has happened. Stand the coffin in the hall when it arrives; I have a visit to make, concerning the funeral, and another matter.'

As Lizzie went indoors, he led the horses and their carriage round to the rear of the house, to the stables, and left them under the care of the groom. Then he saddled his own mount, and set off towards Carluke, with his anger beginning to smoulder once again.

Even though it was high summer and the day had brightened, there was lamplight showing in the manse parlour as he arrived. John Barclay came to the door to greet him, recoiling a little as he saw him, unsmiling and fierce in his heavy travel-soiled overcoat.

'Mathew,' the minister began, 'from your expression . . .'

He strode past him and into the parlour. Its curtains were half-drawn, and the dim light made him look even more menacing.

'How could you refuse me, John?' he boomed. 'How could you decline to come and speak for one of your own? Did you think David guilty? Was that it?'

'It was his word against that of three witnesses,' Barclay replied, tentatively.

'His word, the word of an elder of your kirk, and that of his son. And two of those witnesses have disappeared. But even so, even if he had been guilty of the crime in his anger, it was your duty to come forward and speak to his character.'

'I . . .'

'Be quiet! When David came to see you, did he have a pistol with him?'

'No, of course not.'

'Of course not, but you heard a shot?'

'Yes.'

'And afterwards when David told you his story, did you look outside?'

'I went to the place where he said it had happened, and saw nothing but a patch of blood where Sir Gregor had lain.'

'When you were out, was the well cover in place?'

'Yes, as always, to keep the children safe.'

'When the chain that raises it is wound in, it makes a noise. Do you hear it from inside the manse?'

'Always. It makes a frightful racket.'

'Between the shot and David's arrival, did you hear it?'

'No, but what does that have to do with the matter?'

'Now, nothing,' Mathew glared at him as he shouted, 'for it is too late and David is hanged. But had you done your duty and come to court as I asked, that fact, from your mouth, would have shown Gavin Cleland for the liar he is. And yet you chose not to; you stayed skulking in your big cold house and let your friend go to the gallows.'

Barclay sighed, then collapsed into his armchair. 'I could not come,' he whispered. 'I am an old man, Mathew, and not a rich one. I must be in that pulpit next door until I die, for I have no other choice. As you know, as an elder, the charge in this parish is in the gift of the Laird. He appointed me as the minister and he may remove me at will. You must realise that, surely?'

'I do, but I'd thought you a better man. You were told to stay away; I guessed that days ago, but I need to hear you say it.'

'I had a visit from Philip Armitage,' the minister admitted. 'He told me that the new Laird would be extremely displeased if I involved myself in the McGill trial, and that I would lose my living if I disregarded his wishes.'

'And you were a coward.'

'Like it or not, Mathew,' Barclay protested, 'he is my master.'

'Then I am a fool, because I thought God was your master.'

The old man winced, as if he had been struck.

'You have one chance to redeem yourself, in my eyes and before David's widow and son. His coffin will be lying in Waterloo House by now. I want you to conduct his funeral service and to bury him in the churchyard, next to his parents.'

Barclay stared at his hands clasped together in his lap. 'That I cannot do either. David is a convicted murderer; that is a fact that not even you can alter. I cannot bury him in consecrated ground.'

'You could,' Mathew countered, 'but your fear of Cleland stops you. That man is profoundly wicked, John. He has killed David, as sure as if he had shot him in the back down the road there, and now he has destroyed you. Old friend, you have lost two elders in the one day. I will send my written resignation to the session clerk, and I will not set foot in Carluke Parish Church again while you are in its pulpit. You are a fool, you know. If I had known your loyalty was for sale, I could have outbid Cleland.'

Chapter Thirty-Three

'WHAT WILL WE DO, Mathew?' Lizzie asked, her face twisted unattractively by yet more anxiety. Her son was perched beside her on the arm of her chair; he looked far more exhausted than any fifteen-year-old should.

'First, you will calm yourself, please,' he replied. 'But not with the brandy,' he added. 'That can darken a person as easily as it lightens her. After that? This is what I propose. Tomorrow, the three of us will go to the new minister at Cambusnethan; he is a young man, I'm told, and his congregation like him. I will explain to him our situation and you will ask him if he will conduct David's funeral service.'

'Is the Cam'nethan graveyard not consecrated?' young Matt asked.

'It is, but I have somewhere else in mind for your father. One of my fields, up behind the house, the one where the horses graze, and the cows that give us our milk, it rises to a hilltop. I would like to bury David there, and raise a stone to him; his grave will be fenced off, and I will leave room for others, if you wish. His soul is with God, and that is what matters; his body is entrusted to us.' He looked at Lizzie. 'What do you say to that?'

She smiled, and once again she was beautiful. 'I say, can I choose the epitaph?'

'Of course; that is your privilege. What will it say, do you know yet?'

'Oh yes,' she replied at once. 'It should read, "Here lies a good and gentle man, who died blameless, as he lived." Or will that be too long for the stone?'

'The monument will fit the epitaph, not the other way around.'

David McGill's funeral service was set for six days after his death, at noon. Those who attended would do so at Mathew's personal invitation, and the leather factories were to be closed for the day as a mark of respect. Only one person declined: Sheriff Robin Stirling sent his written apologies, saying that he was deeply troubled by the part he had played in David's death and felt that his presence there might be wounding to his widow and children, to whom he presented his sympathies and deepest regrets.

'What does that mean?' Lizzie asked when he showed her the letter on the day before, in the summer house, in the afternoon.

'It means that my friend is worried that he was deceived when he committed David for trial, for he is as just a judge as lives, and any miscarriage at all, not only a fatal one, is anathema to him.'

'He may judge this correctly, though,' she said. 'I understand his position, but Matt still bears resentment towards everyone involved. I am working on him, but it will take time. He is changed, Mathew.'

'No wonder.'

'He says he will not return to Lanark Grammar. He is afraid his classmates would taunt him. If they did, I am afraid of what he would do. I tried to reason with him, to tell him that education is a weapon in the hands of a man who knows how to use it, but he would have none of it.'

'Nor I,' Mathew chuckled. 'Its absence has done me no harm. Let him leave, Lizzie. He will be none the worse of it either, and you will spare the other boys a few broken pates by letting him have his way. We will find work for him between us. He may be too young for his father's old position, but there are many things I could have him do, and teach him. Stockley and I are building a new foundry in Yorkshire and expanding Coatbridge still further. I always have need of men; the busier he is and the more he sweats, the less time he will have to brood.'

He smiled. 'But then again, he might prefer to work for his mother. I spoke to Peter Wright yesterday; he will sell me the shop, and his house. He is going to live in the cottage his daughter has run away from. Congratulations, shop-keeper.'

Lizzie's mouth fell open. 'I did not think you serious when you said that,' she gasped.

'When was I ever flippant? The business is done.'

'Mathew,' she said, suddenly serious, 'I will not be your kept woman, or be seen to be.'

'Nor would I wish you to be. You will pay me rent, to give us each a clear conscience, but only when you are established in the business and we can both see that it can afford it. The arrangement between Peter and me is private;

it will seem that he has given you the shop out of remorse, for his son-in-law's action.' He beamed. 'Come on, Lizzie, just say yes, will you?'

'Oh, very well, and thank you, landlord.' She laughed lightly, then looked up at him. 'Did you have a hand in our Daphne's vanishing?' she asked.

'Let us just say that Mr Grose was given a choice, and took the wiser option. That was only for your cousin's sake, though. I am not inclined to be gentle with anyone who has been involved in this awful thing, even those who think they are beyond my reach.'

'The judges are beyond everyone, are they not?'

'They think they are, but it is not so simple. They have power, but our constitution, such as it is, places them apart from Government, so they cannot reach beyond their own sphere, and even there they can only judge what is brought before them. They are outside of the politics of the nation. Do you understand?'

'I think so,' she replied. 'I read the newspapers too, remember.'

'Then you may know this also. The Lord Advocate does not simply head the Crown Office and direct prosecution. He is a member of the Government in London, and its voice in Scotland. Thus, that office has great political power, and in it, James Douglas was impervious. And yet he has given it up.'

'Why would he?'

'Because his mentality is that of an Edinburgh lawyer, not a London politician. He never aspired to be Prime Minister; he always sought Scotland's highest judicial office and as Lord Advocate he was able to appoint himself into it.'

'Appoint himself?' Lizzie repeated. 'Surely not.'

'That is the way these games are played, believe me. Douglas will also believe he can appoint his own successor as Lord Advocate, through the Home Secretary, Lord Melbourne. Who will he choose? My friends are certain it will be his close friend Gordon Graham, KC. Well, we will see about that.'

'What can you do about it?' she asked

'Perhaps nothing, but . . . the Duke of Wellington may be a Tory and not a Whig, and he may no longer be Prime Minister, but he remains the towering figure in Westminster. He has the ear of King William, and everyone knows it. Retired or not, the Duke's suggestions are orders. And who is as close to him as any? Colonel Sir Victor Feather, MP, the very same headstrong young man who wrote to my mother nineteen years ago, to tell her she was childless, and who has been mortified by his mistake since he discovered it.'

He leaned towards her, confidentially, lowering his voice in case it could be overheard. 'Where do you think my military orders came from at first, those that made me rich? Where do you think they come from still? Through Victor, I have met the Duke, on my visits to London. He remains fiercely loyal to his veterans, and I am of his party. James Douglas thought he could threaten me with financial loss, but he had no idea. But it may be I can harm him. When it became clear that David was doomed, I wrote to Victor, and told him every piece of the story. We will see what comes of that.'

'These things are beyond me,' Lizzie confessed.

'Then forget them. Leave them to me. To be honest, I dinna ken how I understand them, but I do. I must have brought the knowledge back from the dead. If so, a damaged liver was a price worth paying. As for my eye, I read ten times as much with one as I ever did with two.' He paused. 'Enough of all that though, let us take care of David tomorrow, then I can move on. Once that is done, all sorts of things are going to happen.'

The funeral took place on a brisk, sunny day, in the clear Lanarkshire air. There were over fifty mourners present, including Sir Graham Stockley, three managers from Coatbridge and over a dozen workers from Netherton. They were brought on coaches hired for the occasion, as were thirty villagers from Carluke, including the Fisher family and Peter Wright. John Barclay would have been admitted had he attended, but he did not.

They all followed the coffin as it was borne up the hill on the shoulders of Matt, Mathew, the two undermanagers from Netherton and two of David's brother elders from Carluke, who had shown their solidarity by resigning from the kirk session. Andy Sutherland, the Cambusnethan minister, conducted the service exactly as Mathew and Lizzie had hoped, reverently and with a light touch. He praised David's goodness, and added, at Mathew's request, 'Only those who accused him so falsely know why they did that. They do not know the storm that is coming, but there is one thing of which they may be assured. Their sins will find them out, and when they do, they will beg forgiveness of the man they have wronged.'

The service ended with the Lord's Prayer.

As Mathew lowered his friend into the grave, he recalled the last time he had performed that office, and regretted the way he had been played. As he had done then, with Gavin Cleland, he looked up towards the head of the coffin, into young Matt's eyes. They were dry, and burning with anger.

The burial over, they left the diggers to their task, and Lizzie led the company back to Waterloo House, where a buffet lunch had been prepared. Paul Johnston had attended also, and Innes Irvine; after a while, Mathew drew them aside, from conversation with his mother, who seemed charmed by them both.

'What news from Edinburgh?' he asked.

'The surprise of the decade,' the young advocate chuckled. 'As was expected, James Douglas was confirmed as the new Lord President as soon as Lord Cooper's funeral was done with, but when the Home Secretary's delegate revealed the name of the new Lord Advocate, in Parliament House itself, as Douglas was introduced formally to the court, what a stir there was. I thought Gordon Graham would turn purple when Edward Cooper, KC, was announced.'

'How did Douglas take it?'

'Strangely, with the resigned look of a man who thought he had played a winning hand only to see it trumped. Would you not say so, Paul?'

'I would,' the solicitor agreed. 'Cooper's father could not stand our new Lord Justice General, and now his son has all the power. And I would also wonder aloud, Innes, why our patron here does not seem surprised.'

'Gentlemen,' Mathew said, 'nothing about your city will ever surprise me again. I would like to be quit of it completely, but I cannot yet. Paul, I have a further commission for you, a most urgent one. I need unimpeachable people, for however long it takes. This is what I want you to do, as soon as you are back in the capital, but Innes, given your position as an advocate, perhaps you should not hear it.'

As the advocate went off to say his farewell to Lizzie and Matt, he gave Johnston short, clear instructions. 'See it done, and as soon as you are satisfied with what you have, send for me.'

Chapter Thirty-Four

IN THE WEEKS THAT followed David McGill's funeral, Mathew ensured that no one had an idle moment. The purchase of the shop was expedited, and Lizzie went to work there at once, but when Mathew discovered that Peter Wright had neglected the fabric of the house, he insisted on having it completely refurbished and largely refurnished before he would allow her and the family to take up occupancy.

However she was able to make an immediate impact on the business. Principally it had been a grocery, selling food and essential provisions, but Lizzie decided to widen the range to include personal items of interest to mothers and their children, and others chosen to bring more men through the door. By the end of August, Peter Wright's weekly takings had increased by two-thirds.

In the meantime, young Matt had been put to work with Ewan Beattie, Mathew's thinking being that physical labour was the best way for him to work out the anger that still burned within him.

The coachman had been given a small promotion, which put him in overall charge of the upkeep of the Waterloo

House, its lands and all its livestock, not only the horses but the few cattle and sheep that Mathew had inherited from the previous owner, everything but the hens and pullets, which remained Hannah's prerogative, as they always had been. Tam Jackson, the gardener, was happy with the arrangement, as he knew his limitations and had always been a man who preferred to work to instructions rather than use his own initiative. He was happy, too, to make use of Matt's physical strength, which increased as the high summer months went on, and as his youthful frame filled out.

Finally, at the beginning of September, the house beside the shop was fit for occupancy, and the family took up residence. The only person less than pleased was Hannah, who had become a *de facto* granny to Jean as well as Marshall, and had enjoyed having them both under the same roof.

'They will always be close, those two,' she prophesied to her son, 'but never more than that. It wouldna' be richt, since they were both suckled at the same breast.'

Mathew said nothing. What was right and what was not between a man and a woman was beginning to weigh upon his mind.

'How are you finding folk in the shop?' he asked Lizzie, as they sat in the parlour, the evening before she left for Carluke. The high season was on the wane and autumn was taking its place, making the summer house too cold for that time of day.

'They are kind and courteous, in the main,' she told him. 'They are respectful, although some might be . . . how can I express it? . . . a wee bit reserved, and might be saying one thing while thinking another.'

'What do you hear of John Barclay?'

'I hear that his congregation is not much more than half of what it was, and that his Sunday School is empty altogether. His sermons are dull and lifeless, they say, and his collection plate is light in coin, unless the Laird is there, when there might be an extra shilling in it.'

'And has he been? There much, I mean.'

'One of two Sundays, that is all. Except,' she added, 'Joel Fisher told me that two weeks ago, Cleland was there, but not alone. His fine young lady from Edinburgh was with him, and her father, and her mother. Joel said that the minister was a' flustered, and kept tripping over his own tongue in the sermon and even in prayer.'

'Douglas?' Mathew exclaimed. 'You are telling me that Lord Douglas came to David's kirk, and worshipped there? My God, I did not think the man so crass. What was the sermon that John kept falling over, did Joel say?'

'Aye, he did. It was very Old Testament, the text was of the sins of the father being repaid unto the seventh generation.'

'Indeed?' he murmured. 'No wonder he tripped; old John may have recovered some of his courage.'

'Then good for him. You may be too hard on him, Mathew. He's an old man and afraid for the little future that he has.'

'Can you forgive him?' he asked.

'Yes,' Lizzie replied, without hesitation. 'Think on the prayer you told me David was saying as he died. What does the Lord tell us in it? "Forgive us our debts, as we forgive our debtors." He was telling us, you and Matt and Jean and me, to forgive him. And so I can.'

'Then perhaps I will too. If you agree with this, next time his housekeeper comes on to the shop, give her a message for him from us both. She should tell him that I would like him to visit David's grave and pray for him there. It would be a form of penance, in my eyes, and probably in his too.'

He paused, as she nodded agreement. 'But Gavin Cleland?' he continued. 'Can you forgive him?'

Her eyes darkened. 'No, never. I am not that good a Christian.'

'And neither am I. Lizzie, I made that man a promise and I plan to keep it.'

'Then I trust you to do so; all I ask is that you keep Matt out of it.'

'He will be in at the death, in a manner of speaking, but that will be all. My word on that too.'

'Good,' she said. 'Now, you have been asking me about my business but saying nothing of yours. I have noticed your absences over the last few weeks. Is all well or have you suffered for your absence in June?'

'Suffered? Far from it. Stockley and I have been increasing our foundry capacity as fast as we can to meet our orders, which grow by the day. Railways are the future, as I have said since we began, and we are bound unbreakably to the builders of the new steam locomotives that will make them. The leather business made me one of the richest men in the Upper Ward, but cast iron goes far beyond that.

'I have been re-investing much of my profit back into the enterprise, and now own three-quarters of the company, not the half I started with eight years ago. My absences, as you call them, have taken me to Glasgow and London, and also to Liverpool and Manchester. A railway is already running between those two places, with great success.

'The growth will be incredible, Lizzie. My dream is to go from Glasgow to London by the railway. I might not live long enough, but there is a chance of it. Our children, yours and mine, they certainly will.'

'You've become prophet now,' she remarked. 'Nothing you do will ever surprise me.'

'This might. I have been diversifying, investing in different areas.'

She nodded. 'Yes, you have become a landlord, in Carluke.'

'Ah, more than that, lass. I have gone into corn. Do you know, there is only one corn merchant in the whole of Lanarkshire? Well, there is, and I have bought the business. The owner wished to retire and I have obliged him; the manager will continue, with my guidance only. He has already secured a contract to buy the Duke of Hamilton's entire arable production, wheat, oats and barley, everything, for the next five years, with prices according to quality.'

'What made you think of that?' Lizzie asked. 'You're no landsman, Mathew.'

'Do not be so sure. I am a countryman at heart, and I care about the fortunes of Lanarkshire. I have done even more than that. There are two slaughterhouses in the county, that is all, one in Wishaw and one in Lanark. They are owned by a single company, and I have bought that too. Think of it, Lizzie; as the railways grow, meat, corn, all sorts of produce will move around the country at speeds we can only dream of. Demand will grow and quality will be sought. I have already spread the word to Gavin Cleland's tenant farmers that they must think of the future.'

Lizzie's eyes narrowed, and then she smiled: it was the first full-hearted smile he had seen from her in many weeks.

'Mathew Fleming,' she laughed. 'You are a terrible man, in your own charming way.'

'Me? Everything I do is for the common good, before my own enrichment. In fact of all the things I hold dear, wealth is the least, and I only enjoy that because of the things it allows me to do.'

'And what do you hold dear?'

'My son,' he responded. 'My mother. And you and yours, as I always have. Nothing much else.'

'Then we have them in common,' she murmured, her face half in shadow, even in the brightly lamplit room, 'for I would list the same things. Mathew, what is to become of us, of you and me? People will talk, you know; indeed they do already.'

He looked into the hearth, in which unlit logs were waiting for the time when they would be needed.

'Then let them do so, and let time pass,' he said, softly, 'until I believe that I have discharged the obligation that I hold to David, and the promise I made on his behalf. After that, I will believe he can rest in peace, and I will feel free to speak to you of the future. Until then, I still see you as the wife of my best friend.'

Chapter Thirty-Five

By MID-SEPTEMBER, LIZZIE McGill's shop had become the focal point of Carluke. The premises were large and so she was able to divide them into sections, with half devoted to grocery and the rest divided between haberdashery and hardware. There was a new sign over the door: 'Carluke General Store'.

The harvest had been good and the Cleland tenant farmers had all profited from the new pricing system that the grain merchant had introduced, and so there was a feeling of well-being about the village. As Lizzie's customers grew in number, so did her circle of friends. No one looked at her askance any longer, and if anyone talked about her behind her back, her shop had become too important for them to run the risk of word getting back to her.

Her hours were long and the work was hard, but Matt was there to help her, and to look after his sister when she was not at school. His summer of hard work at Waterloo House, alongside the solid and sensible Beattie and Jackson, had been good for him, emotionally and physically too, for there seemed to be no boxes or barrels that he could not lift with ease, not even the salted fish that came from Glasgow.

He was helpful in other ways; he had suggested a home delivery service for those who wished to buy more than they could carry, and it had proved popular and profitable. He had begun by using a hand barrow, but was pressing for a pony and cart, and his mother could see the sense in that it would increase his range. As far as she could judge, the fire of his anger was less intense, although there were still moments when he fell silent and seemed to be looking at a place very far away.

As for Mathew, he had never set foot in the shop since he had bought it. Mother Fleming was a regular visitor, brought by Beattie in her own small carriage, but Mathew had made a point of staying away, to give no fuel to the gossips. His purchase of the shop remained a secret, and Peter Wright was happy to go along with the popular view that he was a most generous and compassionate uncle.

John Barclay was a customer also; he and Mathew had made their peace, although the latter had made it clear that he would not be returning to Carluke Kirk, in case he and Gavin Cleland should cross paths. The old minister was beginning to look frail; he had lost much weight and Lizzie wondered whether he was eating properly. She asked his housekeeper as much, and the woman confessed that he had no appetite for anything other than Madeira wine.

'Then tell him from me,' she said, 'that until I see a bit of a belly on him again I will sell him no more than one bottle a month. He need not think of going to the tavern for it either. I'll warn Rab Inglis off serving him.'

As for the Laird, he had not set foot in the shop in years, not since Peter Wright had caught the twins stealing liquorice when they were nine years old, but his estate workers did. They were the ones with least money in their pockets, Lizzie noticed.

Her hours were long and her door was open to all, apart, initially, from two women. She recognised them as wives of two of the men who had thrown her and her children out of their home and broken their precious things. When she refused to serve them, each one asked her why, and each received the same answer: 'Go and ask your husband. When he tells you, you may come back again and we will talk some more.'

Each woman did, and came back next day, to apologise for her man's part in what had happened. Again she told each the same: 'I will only accept an apology from him . . . but I will serve you, on condition that you spit in his porridge every so often, as a present from me.'

Philip Armitage's wife, against whom Lizzie bore no grudge, was a regular customer, but she was surprised when the factor himself came through the door one morning in October. He bought snuff, soap and a bottle of brandy; they were regular items on his wife's shopping list, and so she asked if Mrs Armitage was unwell.

'Thank you for asking,' he replied, 'but no, she is perfectly fine. I happened to be passing, that was all, and we are a little low on soap.' He frowned slightly. 'I, eh, I am pleased to see you here, Mistress McGill. I have always held you in high regard. Your uncle must be a fine man to have done this for you.'

'I am glad you think so. I will pass on your compliment next time I see him, which will probably be later today, when he collects his copy of the *Glasgow Herald*. My son has a plan to start what he calls a newspaper round. Perhaps he might go as far as your house.'

'I am not a great reader of the press, I am afraid. I notice, though, that you do not stock the *Register*.'

'I do not,' Lizzie said stiffly, 'and I never will.' Then she softened a little. 'But how are things with you, Mr Armitage? I have always thought you to be a fair man, and could never imagine you having a hand in what happened to my husband, or to my children and myself.'

The factor had a reputation for being devoid of emotion, but he seemed to smile . . . or perhaps a corner his mouth merely twitched. 'Thank you for that,' he said. 'I assure you that I did not. Your removal from the cottage was the Laird's doing, and I knew nothing of it until it had happened. I am still trying to recruit a new gamekeeper, by the way. I can only guess at what prompted Grose's sudden departure, and surmise that it has one eye.'

'I do not bother to guess, Mr Armitage. I am glad the man is gone, that is all. As for my earlier enquiry, how are you faring yourself?'

And I know a pretext when I see one, she thought. *It is not snuff that brought you here.*

'Myself, I am as always,' he responded. 'As for the estate, it is becoming more difficult to manage by the day. If I see my new master for a week out of every month, I am doing well. With Grose gone, and there being no shooting on the estate, the geese are eating our crops, the pheasants are happy and the deer are running uncontrolled.'

'Then shoot some birds and butcher some deer.'

'Would you buy then from me if I did?'

'No,' she admitted, 'I would not.'

'And no one else would either. Yet that is not my greatest worry. I see our tenants with smiles on their faces, yet when I sent the estate's own wheat and barley to the merchant in Hamilton, who has always bought our produce before any other, I was told they were sitting on a mountain of those crops and the price I was offered was half what we were paid last year, well below the cost of production. Would you credit that, Mistress McGill?'

'I know nothing of wholesale markets, Mr Armitage. I have no idea how they work.'

'I suppose not,' he sighed. 'There is worse than that. Only last Thursday, when my livestock manager drove our beef cattle and our hoggets to the slaughterhouse in Lanark, they were told there was no demand and were turned away. He made enquiries of the place in Wishaw and was told the same story. We cannot take the beasts further than that, or they would arrive in no condition to be sold. So we have them back, and not sufficient hay in our barns to feed them all over the winter. That means I will have to buy enough, yet there is little to be had, and what there is commands a premium price. So, no income from their sale, plus the added cost of keeping them until next year.'

'But what of your poor tenants?' Lizzie asked. 'I see no sign here in the shop of them suffering.'

'They sold early and received the top price; all of them, as if they had been advised to.'

'I see.' She looked him in the eye. 'Mr Armitage, why are you telling me all this?'

He returned her gaze. 'I suppose I am telling you, Mistress McGill, because it is almost as if there is a conspiracy against the Cleland Estate. Can you imagine? Yet who would do such a thing? Indeed, who could do such a thing?'

'How would I have any idea of that?' she countered. 'I am only a simple village woman. But if you ask me how I would feel about such a conspiracy, if it existed, then with no animosity towards you, Mr Armitage, I say that I would welcome it with all my heart and would wish it the very best of luck.'

'I see.'

'I hope you do. Sir, I do not mean to be unkind, but factor or not, you are still only a servant. You served the old Laird, and very well, by every account. Now you have served both his sons, as best you could, I am sure also.' She paused, to be sure of her words.

'With your servant's mind,' she continued, 'you are accustomed to accept, and not to question. So when Gavin Cleland and his two fine ladies said that black was white and that my David was a deranged murderer, who used my son as an excuse to excise an old grudge, you could not even consider that your master might be a liar, even though you knew my husband well.'

Armitage frowned, and was silent for a while, as if considering his response. When it came, it took her by surprise.

'I believe you are right in what you say of me, Mistress McGill, almost all of it, but for one thing. In my mind I do not serve the baronet. I serve the Cleland Estate, and so should he, whoever he is, for his time as its custodian.

The old Laird was undeniably a fine man. My experience of his sons in his place has been too short to judge, although I did think them unsavoury tykes as youngsters. However, if Sir Gavin was proved to be what you say he is, then I would be the first to wish him removed, for the sake of the estate itself.'

'Then what do you know of the two women, whose corroboration condemned my David?'

'I know nothing,' he admitted. 'However,' he added, 'there are some who might know a little. The Laird is absent in Edinburgh this week, as usual. I will ask the chambermaids, and see what they have to say. If it is of interest, I will tell you. Or would it be better if I told Mr Fleming?'

Chapter Thirty-Six

'YOU SAY SO?' MATHEW smiled, easing his chair away from the dinner table.

'Indeed,' Lizzie confirmed. 'Two months ago now, he said he would question the staff who attended to the pair. It has taken him that long to get back. Indeed I had begun to think he might have made good on his jest and told you rather than me.'

'Thon Armitage said something in jest?' Hannah exclaimed. 'Afore ye know it water will be flowing uphill.'

'It surprised me also, Mother Fleming. It was a barb, but I did not rise to it. I had not seen him since but yesterday he came back into the shop, when there were no other customers, and told me the tale. It seems that Miss Smith and Miss Stout were given two fine rooms upstairs with a view out over the lawn.'

'Miss Stout was well-housed for a lady's maid, surely,' Mathew observed.

'So it seems, but even better housed than that, in fact. In the time they were in the house, four nights in all, the maids confessed that the ladies' bedding was never disturbed.'

'Perhaps they were considerate,' he suggested. 'Perhaps they made up their own beds in the morning, as I do, always.'

'Perhaps they did,' Lizzie agreed. 'Perhaps they also brushed the hair off their pillows. And perhaps that hair, some fair and some auburn, was carried by the wind under two closed doors and on to the pillows of Sir Gregor and Sir Gavin, for the maids to find when they changed the bedlinen.' She sniffed. 'Fair and auburn hair on the pillows of both brothers, I might add.'

'The brazen hussies,' Hannah gasped. 'And them no' married!'

Mathew exploded with laughter; his mother frowned at him, mystified until the penny dropped. If the lamps had not been turned down a little, she might have seen Lizzie blush, at a memory over twenty years old.

'Are ye sayin' they were hoors, lassie?' Hannah exclaimed.

She nodded. 'Beyond a doubt. Mr Armitage also spoke to the laundress. She told him that the bedsheets had shown clear evidence of what I will only describe as "double occupancy" . . . although that might have been an under-statement.'

'They were prostitutes, Mother,' Mathew said, his expression serious once more. 'Frankly, I do not look down on them for that; wherever our regiment went, women like them followed us.'

'Ye're no sayin' that you . . .'

'No, Mother, I am not,' he retorted quickly . . . and truthfully. 'But they served a purpose. The Iron Duke tolerated them, though not in any written order; he even had the surgeons check them for obvious infection.'

'Hmphh!' Hannah grunted. 'It's as well we're finished wir denner.'

He nodded. 'Point taken; all I will add is that there are more ways to put a soldier out of action than blades and musket balls. Those who were found to be unclean were deemed to be agents of Napoleon, then put up against a wall and shot.'

Lizzie gasped. 'Mathew, is that true?'

He grinned; that awkward sideways grin that signified he had been caught at something, that grin that had always melted her in their youth, and did so again even though she had not seen it since they were both in their teens.

'No, of course not,' he chuckled. 'But my mother always did like a tall story, and if it has a wee bit of sauce, so much the better. Anyway,' he continued, soberly, 'as I was saying, I have nothing against honest prostitutes, but these women are something different. They are the lowest of the low, worse than cutpurses and pure . . .' He had been about to say 'gallows meat', but stopped himself just in time.

'Next time you see friend Armitage, tell him to keep those maids, and the laundress, in his service, and to keep them happy into the bargain. If things go as I hope, we may not need them, but if I have to, I will put them before the procurator fiscal, or even before the Lord Advocate.'

'Oh I will,' she murmured. 'Worry not. He did not tell me their names, or I might look after them in the shop as well.'

'No, it's as well you don't. If you show them favour, it could work against us.' He rose to his feet. 'Come and have a digestive in the parlour, and then I will drive you back to Carluke.'

'Listen tae ye,' Hannah laughed, 'and yer fine words. "A

digestive in the parlour" indeed,' she mimicked. 'Yer faither had a deep sense of humour, but if he could hae heard that, he'd hae laughed his boots aff. You go on, tho', A'm for my bed. Good nicht, lassie. Ah'm pleased tae see ye well and oot the black claes.'

Lizzie had been a frequent visitor to Waterloo House, but only to visit David's grave, and often Mathew had not been there. His dinner invitation had been a gesture, an exploration of whether she was beginning to move on. When Ewan Beattie had brought her, leaving Matt in charge of his young sister, mother and son had been pleased to see that beneath her heavy cloak she wore a long blue dress and a white blouse with a high white collar.

'Mother Fleming is in good humour herself,' Lizzie said, as she left them.

'She is my rock,' Mathew confessed. 'She is not far short of seventy, but still looks for things to do. She was on at me yesterday about baking more than we need for here and giving you some for the shop. She said the oven here is far too big just to be serving us.'

'Then let her. I'll give her three-quarters of the takings.'

'Spoken like a true shopkeeper.'

'As now I am. Which reminds me of something I was going to tell you. Old Macgregor, the butcher from Lanark, approached me this week, with a proposition. He wants to supply me with meat, sausage, black pudding and the like, the kind of produce folk have to go to Lanark to buy for a treat. He had been thinking of opening a shop in Carluke, but since there are none available, he came to me.'

'Could you accommodate it?'

'With a little adjustment and perhaps a partition to separate butchery from the rest of the shop.'

'How would you keep it fresh, though?'

'Believe it or not, there is an old ice house behind the building, a deep cellar below the back boundary wall. The loch's on the other side, remember. Matt cleaned it out and I've been using it. That would serve.'

'Are Macgregor's prices acceptable?'

'They are to me.'

'Then why not try it. I'll pay for any alteration you need.'

'I can do that myself,' she replied proudly. 'And I can start paying you rent now.'

'Ten pounds a year,' he said, 'payable annually in arrears.'

'Mathew,' she protested, 'that's nowhere near enough!'

'It is for me. Pay me that or pay me nothing.'

'In that case, thank you. You are far too good to me.'

'Nowhere near good enough. I'll start being that when Gavin Cleland has been paid in full.'

'Mmm.' Lizzie pursed her lips. 'What is Armitage's game, do you think?'

'Survival. He told you, the estate is his life; he knows that change is coming and he is worried that it will sweep him away.'

'And will it, do you think?'

'Well,' he replied, after a while, 'when a man is as loyal, and as capable, as he is, I would think twice about throwing those virtues away. The estate's present misfortunes are beyond his control. However,' he added, 'Philip Armitage's future will not be decided by me.'

Chapter Thirty-Seven

IT WAS TWO DAYS after Lizzie's visit to Waterloo House for dinner, on a Wednesday, that Mathew was summoned by Paul Johnston.

He had spent much of that time thinking of the future; his own and hers. Less than half a year had passed since David's death, and he was still able to think of her as his friend's wife. But the intimacy of that dinner table, and its humour, had been a reminder of former days, and since then he had felt his resolve beginning to soften. He strengthened himself by thinking of Margaret, something he had done infrequently since the summer tragedy had exploded upon them all.

The day before he had ventured into Carluke cemetery to visit her grave. He was pleased to find it well tended, with a clematis planted on one side and a winter jasmine on the other. The same flowers grew where David lay and so he knew who the carer was, and cursed himself for his own neglect.

'Please call on me at your earliest convenience,' Johnston's note read. 'There have been developments in the matter of Sir G.'

By Thursday afternoon, he was in the Waterloo Hotel, he and Beattie in the same two rooms they had occupied in June. As soon as they were settled in, he set off for Hanover Street, taking the coachman with him. 'You were in at the start of this journey, Ewan,' he said. 'Come a little further with me.'

Johnston had just returned from court when they arrived. 'How are things in Parliament House?' Mathew asked him.

The solicitor smiled. 'They are interesting. Edward Cooper may be a dull man, but he is proving to be an excellent Lord Advocate, and is keeping a healthy distance between himself and the Bench. He and the new Lord Justice General seem to have reached an accommodation. Bellhouse has been banished, effectively, from the High Court and now sits only on civil cases in the Court of Session. There, at least, any damage the malevolent old swine does cannot be fatal. He will not put on the black cap again.

'In the High Court, there will never be another rush to judgment. Cooper has introduced new rules which say that a prisoner must be indicted within three months, but must be given at least three weeks to prepare his defence. Innes tells me that some of his brethren in the Faculty are calling it the "McGill Rule". Our unfortunate client's case has acquired some notoriety, although his conviction is still generally accepted as just.'

'How is Innes?'

'He does very well. He declined the offer of advocate depute, saying that he lacked experience, but he has been gathering that apace. He is an attractive proposition now, and Baird is giving him some very choice briefs . . . from which Baird benefits himself as clerk, naturally.'

'And the Dean of Faculty?'

'Gone. Cooper got rid of him by the simplest method of all: he elevated him to the Bench at the first opportunity.' He smiled. 'But none of this High Street intrigue has anything to do with my note.'

'Then why are we here?'

'Because, sir, the agents I employed in Edinburgh on your instruction have earned their fees. They have found three prostitutes, all of them plying their trade in the St Bernard's Crescent house of entertainment, who have all testified that Sir Gavin Cleland was a regular client.

'Their affidavits go into great detail. He is an energetic man, it seems, for they say that he usually prefers the company of at least two ladies at a time. His tastes are more than a little disgusting, and I will let you read of them rather than describe them. I have sworn statements also from the agents, detailing the days and times on which they followed Sir Gavin.

'It seems that it was his regular habit to go directly from Lord Douglas's house to St Bernard's Crescent . . . even after the announcement last month of his betrothal to Miss Douglas.'

He handed over a folder, and leaned back in his chair as Mathew read, watching his frowns, enjoying his gasps of astonishment at certain passages.

When he finished, he was grim-faced. 'I hope these women were well paid,' he said.

'Not well enough,' Johnston replied, 'for they were only too keen to speak to my men, for no reward at all.'

'Earlier,' Mathew remarked, 'you used the past tense. Was that accident or design?'

'The latter. The women were able to speak to the agents because two weeks ago Sir Gavin Cleland was ejected from the premises and told never to return. A cheque that he wrote was dishonoured and he could not cover his debts at the tables. Since then he has been pursuing his carnality in much poorer surroundings in the port of Leith. He takes his life in his hands down there, sir.'

'Then let us try and keep him safe, I do not want him to wind up on the end of a knife in some dark close.'

He brandished the folder. 'Thank you for this, Paul. Your Edinburgh men have done a good job for me. Let me have a final account for their services, and I will deal with it immediately. How of the other agents, though?'

'Nothing yet, but the last letter I had said they were "pursuing a line of enquiry", as they put it. I will advise you of any further news.' He pointed at the folder. 'You may take that with you; I had two further copies made, all signed and witnessed by an independent notary, with his seal. What do you plan to do with it?' he asked.

'I intend to settle my first, lesser, score, and I will take pleasure in it. I will not involve you, for your own sake, even though you might enjoy being there. There is nobody so grand that he is beyond humility.'

Johnston grasped his meaning. 'Be careful how you tell him, though. Douglas may have lost his political power by putting on the red jacket with the ermine trim, but there are few more formidable enemies than the Lord Justice General, whoever he might be.'

'I will step lightly, Paul, worry not. My intention is to let him see for himself the error of his ways, rather than to ram them down his throat.'

'Then good luck. But please do not give him my regards.' He smiled, and then his eyebrows rose, suddenly. 'Ah,' he exclaimed, 'I almost forgot. Blackwood the printer called on me on Wednesday, just after I had sent you my note; he gave me a message for you, although I did not understand it. Some friends of his, he said, are anxious to speak with you.'

Chapter Thirty-Eight

'Are you sure ye dinna want me to come in wi' ye, master?' Ewan Beattie asked.

'No,' Mathew replied. 'I do not believe Lord Douglas would take that too kindly. But wait outside; in his position, he must have discreet guards about him, so I am putting myself in a small hazard by going in there . . . if I am admitted, that is.'

'And if ye dinna come out?'

He checked his watch, then handed it to his escort. 'It is seven o'clock now; if I am not out by ten, then have Mr Johnston at the court first thing tomorrow, clutching a writ of *habeas corpus*.'

'What kind o' flower is that, sir?'

'A rare one, but very efficacious in cases of confinement.'

Leaving Beattie utterly bewildered, he trotted up to the steps to thirty-three Heriot Row and pulled the brass handle that rang the bell within. A minute later, the heavy door opened, slowly and only halfway. A uniformed footman frowned at him. 'Yes?' he murmured, eyeing him up and down.

'Is Lord Douglas at home?' he asked.

'That would rather depend, sir.'

'I am sure that it would,' he agreed, cheerfully. 'To put it to the test, would you please tell him that Mr Mathew Fleming, Deputy Lord Lieutenant and magistrate of the County of Lanark is on his doorstep, and would be grateful for a few minutes of his time. Be sure to tell him also that it is a private matter, one that will be of great concern to him.'

The footman invited him to wait in the vestibule, then left to deliver his message. The man was no bodyguard, but a door to his right was slightly open, and Mathew could hear faint conversation behind it.

'Please come up, Mr Fleming.' The footman's invitation came from the top of a flight of stairs. He wanted to run up, but took them slowly, one at a time.

James Douglas might have been recently elevated, but he had gained nothing in stature. He remained seated as his guest entered, as if unwilling to be towered over by him.

'This is a surprise,' he said. 'I had not expected to see you in Edinburgh again. My future son-in-law tells me you have even shaken the dust of Carluke from your feet.

'Between you and I,' he added, in a mock whisper, 'I do not blame you one bit. An undistinguished little place, I thought, not befitting the man you have become, a man with the power in London to change even my plans. I refer, of course, to the appointment of Edward Cooper as my successor, a man of no flair but numbing integrity.'

Mathew shrugged. 'I hardly know the man,' he replied. 'As for Carluke, I am not as disconnected as Gavin Cleland might think. It is my birthplace, after all, and I still have considerable interests there.'

'Then they will prosper, I am sure.' Lord Douglas waved towards the chair that faced his. 'I want to tell you,' he continued, as his guest seated himself, 'that I am sorry our last meeting did not go better for you, but it could not. It was nothing personal, you understand.'

Mathew felt his anger flare, but he controlled himself. 'It was for me,' he replied, quietly, 'and for my late friend David.'

'Who was convicted of murder, I must remind you, on the basis of the clear evidence that I put before the jury.'

'Whose number were practically directed to convict by my Lord Bellhouse,' Mathew pointed out.

'Your friend angered my uncle, I am afraid. That is never a good idea.'

'Angering me is none too clever either,' Mathew countered, then went on quickly, denying Douglas any opportunity for a riposte, 'but that is not why I am here. You mentioned your prospective son-in-law earlier. Can I ask you how you find him, as a man?'

'I will allow you that one question about him,' the judge said. 'I find Gavin witty, courteous and charming. He is obviously devoted to my daughter, and frankly, the notion that he could have harmed his brother while intending to shoot another man in the back . . . well, sir, it beggars belief.'

'Then I am sorry, my Lord,' Mathew said, 'for I do not doubt your sincerity. But I have known Gavin Cleland for longer than you. My view of him is somewhat different and it is borne out by these documents.' He handed over the folder that he had brought with him.

He watched Douglas as he read, for a full ten minutes, his own expression remaining impassive as that of the other changed, curiosity replaced by concern, then by anger and finally black-browed rage.

'Mr Fleming,' he said finally, 'if this is all trumped up, and if the accounts of these harlots have been bought, then you are finished, your family is finished, Mr Johnston is finished and indeed anyone who has ever known you is facing a doleful future.'

'My Lord,' Mathew murmured, 'I will take you on anywhere, if I have to, so do not ever threaten me again. But I assure you, these women have not been paid, and I do not believe they have exaggerated a single one of those accusations.

'The same cannot be said of the whores who condemned my friend David to death at Bellhouse's hands, but I cannot prove their perjury, not yet. In the meantime, that is the man to whom you have betrothed your daughter. Disbelieve me, and God help her.'

The Lord Justice General sank back into his chair. 'I wish I could, but I do not,' he said, with a heavy sigh. 'I know your agents, Mr Fleming, by name and by reputation. They are former constables of the city, and I have employed them myself in a similar capacity, both as Lord Advocate and before that in my private practice.' He brandished the folder. 'May I keep these?'

'Of course. My solicitor has notarised copies; I will send another to you if you wish. I am sorry to be the bearer of this news,' he added.

'No, you are not,' Douglas countered, 'nor should you

297

be, for I have given you no reason to be sympathetic towards me. You have put me in your debt now, and forced me to open my mind to some private concerns. While Sir Gavin was all that I have described around this house, I confess that when I visited his estate, I was a little concerned. It is not quite as grand as he described it; corners are being cut, and there is an air of decay about the place.

'But it was in your church that I became most worried. I have an eye for people and their feelings, Mr Fleming, and among the congregation in that place I detected no respect for him, far less any love, only fear. It even radiated from your sad old minister. You know, I think back to his sermon that day, and I find myself wondering if he was trying to tell me something.'

'There was a time when he would have told you straight out,' Mathew said. 'But you are right about the fear. He was too afraid of Cleland to speak for David in court.'

'Then you can tell him that his hidden message has finally reached its target. Cleland's betrothal to my daughter is annulled, and he is banned from this house. If I could forbid him the city, I would, but he would be well advised to absent himself in any case.'

'He can go where he likes. When the time comes, I will find him.'

The judge smiled. 'On that day, I would not be in Sir Gavin's shoes. I think I would rather have you as a friend than an enemy, Mr Fleming. Will you take a whisky?'

'Thank you, sir, but an old wound has left me with no taste for it, or any liquor for that matter.'

'My God,' Douglas laughed, 'then you really are a

dangerous man.' He rose and crossed to an ornate sideboard against the far wall. He poured himself a generous measure from a square decanter, then returned to his armchair.

'What you have told me does make me reflect on the case of the late Mr McGill. You do believe completely in his innocence, Mr Fleming? You are not simply being un-shakeably loyal to a friend, and so blind to another possibility?'

Mathew shook his head. 'I am one-eyed, but broad-minded. Have you ever been a soldier, sir?'

'Me? No,' he chuckled, 'I am hardly built for it.'

'Do not be so sure. The man who nearly killed me was not much taller than you. The Voltigeurs were chosen because they were small, fast, agile and lethal. I remember the little bugger charging on to my bayonet and being lifted clear of the ground, yet managing to thrust his sword into my guts as he died. I dreamed about him for many a year, and woke in terror.'

'Do you still?'

'I dream of him, but the horror has gone. Instead I am sorry for him, for I have awakened every morning since my recovery but he never did.

'Being a common foot soldier introduces you to many things, sir,' he said, 'and chief among them is cynicism; you are prepared to doubt the motives of any man and the word of most. Do you understand?'

'Yes, I do. You are telling me you considered the possibility that Mr McGill and his son might have been lying.'

Mathew nodded. 'I did, briefly. But David was one of

those men whose word I would not have doubted, and even if he had not been, the question of motive remained. He gave Gregor Cleland a beating for whipping his son, of that there is no doubt. If something similar happened to your daughter and you saw it, you would react in exactly the same way. Am I correct?'

'Probably to no great effect, but I imagine I would,' Douglas conceded.

'Right. But you would not have shot him for it, as Gavin and his women described? Nor would David, and why else would he? He had absolutely no reason to do so. Your case, based on Gavin's statement, alleged that he had motive, but that was not true. There was no grudge, ever. In fact, the day David was dismissed from his position was one of the best of his life, for it meant that he was no longer able to resist the pressure I put on him to come and work for me, for nearly three times the wage. The truth was that Gregor did him a favour, and David and I often laughed about it.'

'And I believed Gavin,' the judge murmured, then paused. 'But not just him, there were the ladies, and their evidence.'

'Ah yes, Gregor's fiancée, and her lady's maid . . . who have never been seen since,' he smiled, 'not even, I suspect, in your sanatorium in the north of England.'

'Hold up there, Mr Fleming,' Douglas exclaimed. 'I had a sworn statement from the physician in charge that Miss Smith and her maid were there and unable to leave because of emotional distress.'

'You did, and young Mr Irvine obtained his name from

the trial documents, and I sent people to find him. They are still trying. There is no sanatorium, and there never was. If you want to know the relationship between the brothers and the ladies, hark back to the folder you have just read and use your imagination.'

'Can that be proved?'

'Yes, but gentlewomen can fornicate too, so that of itself does not prove them liars. I need the pair before me to do that.'

'Then I will get them,' Douglas snapped angrily.

'How can you?' Mathew asked. 'You sit on the highest Bench in the land. You can do nothing without being asked by the Lord Advocate.'

'Then go to him.'

'I could, but I do not need to, not yet. I am a magistrate and as such I am entitled to raise simple proceedings. I am after Miss Smith and Miss Stout . . . or whoever they really are . . . already, and I am probably better resourced for the task than Edward Cooper.'

'And Gavin?'

The one eye darkened, making its neighbour seem even more ghostly. 'He has more to lose than an advantageous marriage, my Lord, before the shackles are locked on to his wrists and ankles, and further to fall than a few feet to the end of a rope.'

'Then good luck to you,' Douglas declared. 'If it comes to it, I think I will have Bellhouse try him.' As Mathew smiled, he added, 'You would not have a drink, Mr Fleming, but will you dine with me . . . you and the hefty minder you have stationed outside?'

'That is kind of you, my Lord, but we cannot. There will be no supper for me tonight for I have another appointment, but if that goes the way I hope, I will fairly enjoy my breakfast.'

Chapter Thirty-Nine

'WHY DID YOU NOT tell me this before?' Sheriff Stirling asked. 'Do you not trust me after what happened in June?'

'Of course I trust you, Robin. If I did not would I be telling you now, and giving you the chance to warn off my target?'

'I am not sure it is a compliment to ask whether I might be capable of any partiality, but I will take it as such. Let me consider the situation.'

He sipped his brandy; Mathew and Sir Graham Stockley watched him across the dinner table as he thought, and came to a conclusion. 'You may find these women,' he said, once his response was formed in his mind, 'but you may not. The Crown's false letter from a false physician might be enough to have the case against David McGill reopened, but not much more, I believe.

'To have his conviction quashed, yes, that will give some comfort to his family, but I can see that you want more, my friend. You want Cleland on the scaffold.' He frowned. 'And there was I thinking of you as a gentle Christian man.'

'I would like to think that I am,' Mathew said, 'but experience has taught me that those who turn the other cheek usually wind up wounded twice. I am not after Sir Gavin out of vengeance alone. He holds the livelihood of many people in his community in his grasp, and he is not fit to do so. I want him removed for that reason alone, as well as the other.'

'You might be able to do so without seeing him swing.'

'Perhaps, but I have promises to keep; those I made to Matt, and to Cleland himself.'

'Mmm,' Sir Graham Stockley murmured, fingering his port glass. 'What does Mrs McGill wish?'

'Lizzie probably believes that hanging is too good for him. His head on the spike above the Tolbooth might satisfy her, but they knocked it down, so she must be satisfied with whatever sentence the court hands down, if we can ever bring him to trial, that is. Can we begin that now, without Smith and Stout?'

'You think they may never be found?' Stirling asked.

'I have tried to put myself in Cleland's position, an uncomfortable place to be. For his long-term protection, he would have been better killing them than sending them away.'

He paused. 'But would he have the ruthlessness? I looked into his eyes before the scaffold in the Lawnmarket and I doubt it. I saw a coward in there, an opportunist, but a coward. I believe that in an instant he saw a chance to have the estate for himself, and he took it. But to kill the witnesses once their false statements were sworn? I did not see that in him.'

'But what if you are wrong,' the Sheriff countered, 'or if the pair have been sent abroad, or to Ireland even? You ask if you can make a case without them. Well, first you must precognose those chambermaids and the laundry woman, take their statements formally and under oath. If you have that, you might have your man Innes petition the High Court for an appeal against conviction, but still you would be short of indicting Cleland.'

'It would be risky too,' Mathew said, 'for Cleland has been spending much more time on the estate these last few weeks, since Lord Douglas banned him from Heriot Row, and let it be known that anyone seen speaking to him in Edinburgh would be no friend of his.

'That meant automatically that his membership of the New Club was revoked. So all he can do in the city is lurk in Albany Street, or go down to Leith and the rough trade there. Philip Armitage's questioning of the staff was discreet and private. Formal statements would not be so, and would even put the factor's position in jeopardy. That is something I do not want, for I need the good Mr Armitage.'

'I did not think you were fond of that man, Mathew,' Stockley said. 'Being unloved is part of a factor's lot, is it not?'

He shrugged. 'Whether I like the fellow or not is irrelevant, Graham. As I said, I need him, for reasons that will become clear soon, when certain matters have made their way through the Court of Session, as they will, for the Lord President is taking a keen interest in their passage, and also keeping them out of the public eye.'

'I am intrigued.'

'So am I,' Stirling added.

Mathew smiled. 'Then you can both stay that way, until

I have further news for you. In the meantime, Robin, let us hold fire on the estate maids for a little longer at least. I am not without hope that the owners of the blond and red hairs on the Cleland pillows can yet be found.'

Chapter Forty

A<small>N HOUR AFTER MIDDAY</small> on a December Monday morning, three days before Christmas, a messenger on horseback arrived at Waterloo House, and delivered an envelope.

Mathew was in Coatbridge on business, driven by Beattie, and Hannah was visiting Lizzie in Carluke, and so the man was received by Miss Liddell, who chided him over the condition of his hard-ridden animal, even as she took possession of an envelope bearing the name, 'Mathew Fleming, Esq. DL'. It was written in a spidery hand, not that of a professional clerk, and sealed with red wax on the reverse.

'Who is the sender?' she asked.

The travel-worn rider shook his head. 'Cannae tell ye', for Ah dinna ken. An officer gied me it. Confidential for Mr Fleming is a' he said.'

'And where was this officer? Or is that secret too?''

'Edinburgh.'

'Then you'll have a long trip back. Go round to the back of the house and find the kitchen. Get some warmth in your bones, and some hot food inside you for the journey. The groom will take good care of your horse.'

The letter was on Mathew's desk, in his private parlour when he returned home, just after six that evening. He turned up the lamps to their brightest, but even so had to use his monocle to make out the detail of the wax seal. He smiled as he recognised it, then slit the envelope along the top with a knife, to preserve it.

Inside was a single page, a note that read:

It is done, decree is granted and the consequent order is issued. The documents will be with Mr Johnston this afternoon for delivery to the pursuer, through you; I imagine you might wish to make the enforcement in person.

In all the circumstances I do not imagine that I will ever be invited to visit, for although I beg forgiveness for my transgression, it is too much to expect that I might receive it. All that I can do is send the beneficiary my humble good wishes, and extend my hand to you, sir, in friendship.

Douglas.

Mathew gasped as he slumped into his chair. The plan had been a wild one, a gamble, literally, but its success had been beyond his most optimistic hopes.

He strode out into the hall, and retrieved his waxed cotton overcoat.

'Mathew,' Hannah called after him as he opened the front door. 'Where are ye gaun? It's freezin' the nicht, and ye're only just hame.'

He stopped and turned towards her. 'I have to see Lizzie,

Mother, and now. It can't wait. Quickest for me to go myself than tear Ewan away from his dinner.'

'Aw, son,' she sighed, sadly, misinterpreting him completely. 'Ah know this has always been hard for you, but gie the lassie time. Let her see this terrible year oot, and wash her hands of it. She and her weans are comin' here on Thursday, mind, for Christmas. Ye can talk tae her then about the future, if ye must, although for propriety ye might want tae talk to young Matt first.'

He smiled at her misunderstanding. 'Mother,' he chuckled, 'am I that impetuous? Lizzie and I are not children; we are agreed that if anything happens between us it will be in the fullness of time. Tonight I have to see her on urgent business. It affects her more than me, but I want it done before Christmas and for that to happen, everything must be in place . . . and everyone, including her.'

'Then tak' my pony and trap, no' yer horse. It's too cauld for that.'

'That was my plan.'

He went round to the stables, and harnessed one of the horses, rather than Hannah's pony. She was called Gracie, the second to bear that name since his old friend, who was buried by then at the foot of the hill where David lay, and he was too fond of her to take her out in the dark on a frozen road. He lit the lamps on the carriage and set out, grateful for what little moon there was.

He reached Carluke without mishap, at quarter past seven, and secured the horse, then rapped Lizzie's door knocker, hard. When he heard footsteps inside he called out, 'It's Mathew,' lest she was anxious.

She opened the door and let him into the warmth, leading him through to her sitting room. She was alone. 'Jean has a snuffle, so I sent her to bed early. Matt is out visiting Jane Fisher. I encourage that; when he's with her he can't be angry.'

'He still is?'

'Of course he is. I still am and so are you, but we are of an age to be rational. Don't worry yourself though; he is under control and he is kept busy. What a worker the laddie is. If I did not have him, I would need three in his place.'

He smiled. 'Perhaps I should take him to Coatbridge. He would fit in well there.'

She stared at him. 'Don't you . . .'

'Never in a million years,' he assured her. 'Sometimes when I go into our foundries, I feel like Satan, it is so damned hot. There may come a time when Matt does work with me, if he chooses, but it will be on no factory floor. He and Marshall will be treated the same way. I hope that my son will go to Glasgow University. That is open to yours too, if he wishes, and he might well once we have flushed out the hatred.'

'Will we ever do that?'

'Yes, we will, we will cleanse the anger in all of us when the cause is removed.'

'Then perhaps you should duel with Cleland,' she muttered. 'I have no scrap of doubt as to its outcome.'

'Your wish is my command.'

'No!' she said, at once. 'That was a bad jest. I would never put you in peril. Mathew, what a thing for me to say. What sort of a woman have I become?'

He wrapped his arms around her, enveloping her in his open raincoat. 'One after my own heart,' he murmured, 'as you have always been. And probably a wise one too, if you forbid me. The last fatal duel in Scotland, a few years back, was between a former soldier, a hot-tempered bully of a man, and a coward who was no sort of shot. The coward panicked; he fired too early . . . and he was lucky. His wild bullet hit the marksman in the throat and killed him.'

'Then you must not give Cleland even that chance.'

He held her a little away from him, so that he could look into her eyes; then he leaned forward and put his lips to her forehead.

'Right enough,' she whispered, 'you missed.' She rose up on her toes and kissed him, full on the mouth.

'No,' he breathed, 'like a good duellist I was choosing my moment. But let us sit down now, or I might have to lie to Mother Fleming when I get home.'

As they settled on her settee, facing the blazing fire, he said, 'The fact is, Lizzie my dear, I have been duelling with that weasel Cleland for the last six months, but he has been unaware, as I have been using weapons that he does not understand. Indeed he is mortally wounded, but does not yet know it. When he discovers, I want you to be there.'

'Me? Why?'

'Because you deserve to be, simple as that.'

'When will this happen?'

'In two days, on Christmas Eve. I want you to be ready for me when I come for you around noon, to pay a call on him. I know the shop will be busy, but Matt can take over.'

She looked at him. 'I really have to face that man?'

He shook his head. 'No. He really has to face you, and on his ground at that.'

'How do you know he will be there?'

'I know everywhere he is. Anyway, he has nowhere else to go. His Edinburgh house is closed and the small staff dismissed. Now it belongs to the National Bank. He is cornered, like a badger. He has no friends left, not even Philip Armitage.'

'No,' she conceded. 'I do not believe that Mr Armitage has any friends either. Friendship requires a degree of emotion in a person, and it is hard to spot in him.' She turned half round, to face him. 'Should I dress in my finest for this encounter on Wednesday?' she asked.

Mathew gave her question some thought before replying. 'No,' he said. 'I do not think so. Wear your long shopkeeper's apron and your cuffs; I want to twist this dagger.'

She grinned. 'I am intrigued, but I will do as you ask; I might even rub some flour on them. You never come here during the day; you might not recognise me.'

He squeezed her hand. 'No matter what you wear I would always recognise you, for I know what lies inside.'

'That is changed since last you saw it,' she said, quietly. 'I have had three bairns since then, and another stillborn.'

He threw his head back and laughed softly. 'I was talking about your heart, my darling lassie. For the rest, I hope to make my own judgement in due course. Perhaps around Valentine's Day, should you do me the honour?'

'You ask me now?' she exclaimed, surprised. 'I thought

312

we had agreed to wait until the year was out before thinking of ourselves.'

'I want it resolved before Wednesday,' he replied. 'I doubt that David would be concerned about timing, but we can keep the secret until banns have to be called. If you consent, that is. Do you, Elizabeth?'

'Of course I do.' She leaned close and kissed him again. 'There, that is it sealed . . . although not as emphatically as when we were younger. Yet, I do not understand the need for haste.'

'I will explain, after Wednesday . . . if I have to.'

Chapter Forty-One

HANNAH FLEMING COULD NOT recall ever having seen her son as impatient as he was the next morning. He had arrived home at nine the night before in high spirits that he would not explain, possibly unwisely, as her imagination had not diminished with her age.

Having had nothing but respect for David McGill, his tragedy had hit her as hard as anyone. In its aftermath a new worry had emerged; Mathew and Lizzie had been made for each other from their early years, and after David's death, she had no doubt, when she allowed herself to think about it, that they would be together sooner or later.

But she had a question in her mind that she knew would occur to others: would they be coming together in the aftermath of a shared loss, or with an element of relief that the way had been cleared.

If David had died of typhoid it would have been no issue, but the fact that he had been taken unjustly by the hangman's noose would raise any future marriage between his friend and his widow to a completely different level of gossip.

She surmised from his demeanour that a pact had been

reached the night before, but his impatience made her wonder what other business they had discussed. Her mind was busy, but her face gave no hint of it. To the entire household, she seemed as calm, as much a stoic as ever.

She was about to call him to lunch when she saw, through the parlour window, a coach approaching, one whose like she had never seen before; it was closed and bore a red insignia on the outside.

Mathew saw it also, and rushed to the front door. When he returned, he was carrying a sealed box, which he carried into his private parlour.

'What was that?' she asked him, when he came into the dining room.

'Business,' was his brief reply.

'Business doesna' usually have ye buzzing like a wasp at a jeelly jar,' she remarked quietly.

He smiled, but offered no further explanation. He ate lunch quickly, then excused himself to his mother, his son and the boy's governess, then left the room. A little later, Hannah heard the front door close. She went to the dining-room window and looked out, discreetly, hidden behind the curtain, and saw him stride past, in that ugly waxed-cotton coat he loved so much. He carried the box, and was heading towards the stables, where Beattie and his carriage were waiting.

A hand tugged at her sleeve. 'Where's my father going, Granny?' Marshall asked. 'I was going to play the piano for him this afternoon. It was going to be a surprise.'

She slipped her arm around the red-haired boy's shoulder, as they watched him climb on board the carriage without a backward look. 'Ah'm sure he'll be back in time for ye tae do that, son. At the moment, Ah'd say he's planning on surprising somebody else.'

Chapter Forty-Two

MATHEW BARELY SLEPT THAT night; it was cold and so he stoked the fire in his bedroom, but that made it so warm that he had to discard his duck-down quilt. Finally, at half past five, he gave up the effort; he rose and put on his dressing gown.

He peered into Marshall's room; it was lit only by one small night lamp, but he could see the shape of his head in the pillow and hear his gentle snoring. Every time he saw the boy asleep he thought of Margaret, and how, to his surprise, he had come to love her very deeply, just as he knew that Lizzie had loved David.

He had been surprised also the evening before by his son's skill on the piano. Neither he nor Hannah were any sort of musicians; the instrument had come with the house when he bought it, and had been ignored until Miss Liddell's arrival. She had been Marshall's tutor in music as in everything else, but the process had passed his father by for he had never been around when it took place, or when he practised.

This had filled him full of guilt; for much of the time, he thought, his boy might as well have been an orphan. He made himself a promise that when he and Lizzie were married, no matter how busy they were, there would be certain hours in his every week set aside for the two younger children, and maybe for another, if that transpired, for she was surely still a few years short of the change of life.

He went down to the kitchen and put a kettle on the range to make a pot of tea, then set himself to making French toast . . . or 'Poor Knights' as the Prussian soldiers had called it; two of them had shown him the trick in the army, to make meagre rations less boring. He was almost done when the door opened and his mother joined him.

'Is that you at thon fancy bread again?'

He nodded. 'Aye. Be quiet and have some; I know you like it. I'll make some more.'

'Ah'll tak' syrup on it.'

He smiled. 'You always do, Mother.' He spread the slices with golden syrup, then poured her a mug of tea, adding three spoons of sugar. That done he took three more eggs from the larder and cracked them into the bowl he had used before to beat them then soak the bread slices.

'This is Christmas Eve,' she said, when he joined her at the kitchen table. She peered at his plate, then observed, absently, 'Ah dinna ken how ye can tak it like that, wi' salt.'

He smiled. 'Easily,' he replied. 'The Frenchies call it "lost bread". They take it sweet too, but in the regiment we were not oversupplied with syrup and sugar, so we made do with what we had. And yes, Mother,' he continued, 'it is indeed Christmas Eve.'

'Do ye mind them when your faither was alive?'

'I remember Christmas Day,' he said. 'As I recall it, on

Christmas Eve, Father was usually in the tavern.'

'As he'd a perfect richt tae be,' she retorted, defensively, 'for he wis a hard-workin' man.'

'I'll never deny either. What about our Christmases?'

'They were special, for you were young and we were an entire family. We've never been that way since, and it's a shame for wee Marshall. He's never kent it either, no wi' poor Margaret bein' taken like that when he was born. Miss Liddell's a fine wumman, but yon laddie's missed his mother even though he's never kent it.'

'You're rambling, Mother,' he laughed. 'All that syrup's addling your brain.'

'Maybe, but what Ah'm saying is this. Ah want tae be part of a family again, and Ah can see what's happening wi' you and Lizzie. It wid please me very much. But Ah fear for ye. Some people are fated, Mathew. Ah pray you're no two of them, that's a'.'

'I see.' He finished his egg-rich bread and took a mouthful of tea. 'I pray that too, Mother,' he told her. 'But I would like to think that God might have finished shiteing on the pair of us, and that we might be allowed to enjoy a few peaceful and happy years.'

'Blasphemy, boy!'

'I know, I know,' he chuckled, 'God doesna shite.'

'Stop it! This chirpy mood o' yours is disturbin' me. If Ah didnae ken better Ah'd think ye'd been at the Madeira wine like auld Barclay. Whit is it? Whit's pit the cream on yer scone?'

'As you said at the very start, it's Christmas Eve, Mother. And this one will be different, I promise you, for me and for two other people. It goes beyond a dream and into the realm of miracle. I swore revenge for David, but this . . .'

'Whit?' she shouted, her calmness finally cracking. 'Dinna tease me, boy!'

'It is no tease, but the truth. You will know by the end of the day. Now I'm away to make ready.'

He left her in the kitchen and went back upstairs, just as the household was starting to awaken. There he bathed, shaved, and dressed in his most magisterial clothes. At eight fifteen, he had breakfast with Marshall and spent an hour discussing Christmas with the boy, and telling him his favourite stories.

They were all about a brave woman called Margaret Weir. He made up adventures in which she was the heroine, fantasies, stories of journeys to faraway lands, France, Spain and those places called the Low Counties. Marshall loved them and they all had happy endings.

He spent the next ninety minutes in his private parlour, reading reports from his Netherton managers, and an end-of-year review prepared for him and for Stockley by their accountant. He did some calculations of his own and was staggered to realise that in spite of all the expense he had incurred that year, his personal wealth had almost trebled.

At the foot of the pile he found a letter, one he had read before, but which still awaited a formal reply. It was from Sir Victor Feather, asking whether he would consider standing as a candidate for the Westminster Parliament.

'As always your timing is at fault, my old captain,' he whispered to the lamp-cast shadows in the room. 'You are a year too late. Besides, the last time I went south for any length of time, it cost me an eye and a lot more.'

At eleven o'clock, his impatience overcame him. He pulled on a brass knob set in the wall of his room. It rang a bell in the kitchen, one whose message was, 'Summon Beattie, we are on the move'.

The road was icy, and the sky was heavy with the promise of a snowfall. On another day Mathew would have been concerned about the coachman in his exposed position, but he could think of nothing but the visit to come.

The journey took longer than usual, but less time than in the darkness, and so they arrived in Carluke at five minutes before noon. The shop door was ajar as he arrived, and there were several customers inside. Beyond them, he could see Matt at the counter, smiling and nodding as he served them, each in her turn.

Lizzie was waiting at home and she was ready for the road. She was wrapped in a heavy cloak; she smiled as she opened it to show him what was underneath, an ankle-length, flour-caked apron, worn over a plain, high-collared dress.

'I have been more beautiful,' she chuckled.

'You are radiant, my dear,' he said, kissing her softly then drawing her hood over her head.

The entrance to the Cleland Estate was no more than half a mile away, but Beattie drove them at a gentle pace. When they arrived at the great black-painted iron gates, they saw that they were open. A man was waiting there, on horseback. He wore a long riding coat, a tall hat and there was a scarf wound round his face.

Mathew pulled down the carriage window. 'You are ready? You know what is to happen?'

A muffled, 'Yes, sir,' came from within the scarf.

'Then let us go.'

Horse and rider fell in step with the carriage. The mile-long road that led to the great house had been macadamised in the time of the old Laird, Sir George, but it had begun to crack in places, and with the ice that had formed on its surface it was unstable and the horses were unsure of their footing. Before they had gone very far, Beattie, and their companion, followed the example of an earlier visitor, whose tracks were visible on the frosty grass between the road and the tall trees that lined it.

'Do you know,' Lizzie murmured as she peered through the window, 'I have never been here. I have never ventured past those gates, even though my husband was employed on the estate.'

'I am sure that quite a few others in Carluke can say the same,' Mathew replied. 'I have only ever been here a few times myself. First with my father, and later in connection with the sale of saddles to Sir George.'

'Then why are we here now?'

He squeezed her hand, gently. 'Patience, my dear.'

'That is not my strong suit, as well you know.'

As she spoke, the carriage cleared the last of the wooded approach and Cleland Hall came into sight. 'Oh my!' she gasped.

'Yes,' he agreed. 'It makes Waterloo House look like a way station on the turnpike road.'

Cleland Hall was a vast country house with three storeys

and attic windows that ran its entire width, and above them a castellated top, suggesting that there might be a roof terrace beneath the towering chimneys. It was a rectangular building that was at least one hundred and fifty yards wide, with curving arches on either side, concealing stables and outbuildings, and was built of hard yellow stone taken from a quarry near Lanark.

The entrance was not at ground level, but on the first floor, accessed by a broad flight of twenty steps, at the foot of which the party drew up, alongside a small coach that both Mathew and Lizzie recognised.

'Why is the minister here?' she asked.

'He is, you might say, our advance guard,' he told her. 'I asked John to arrange an appointment with the Laird and to make sure he kept him occupied until our arrival . . . which is not on Sir Gavin's schedule for the day.'

He helped her down from the carriage and took her hand as they climbed the stairway. It had been salted, but there were still icy patches apparent. Their companion dismounted also and followed behind them.

Close to, the building was less impressive than from a distance. Weeds grew in some of the corners of the building, while the pale grey paint on the double entrance doors, and on the windows on either side of them, was faded and had lost its original lustre.

That outer entrance was open, revealing a vestibule with a glazed doorway behind. Mathew pulled on the bell rope; a minute passed, and then they saw a servant approach, not rushing but at a sedate pace. He was clad in a black tailcoat and his shirt had a high wing collar, an elderly man, but still tall and straight-backed; Lizzie knew him as an occasional customer. 'Mr Marston,' she whispered.

If he recognised her, he gave not a sign of it as he opened the door, looking at her only briefly, then focusing his attention entirely on Mathew. 'Yes?' he boomed. If he was matching his voice to the grandeur of his surroundings, that was fitting, Lizzie thought, for they had both known slightly better days.

'Mathew Fleming, Deputy Lord Lieutenant. My companions and I are here to see Sir Gavin Cleland.'

'I am not aware of any appointment, sir,' Mr Marston replied.

'I do not believe I need one. We are here on magisterial business.'

The butler frowned, his nose wrinkling. 'The lady too?'

'It is the lady's business we are about. Now please, sir, tell Cleland we are here.'

'Sir Gavin,' he emphasised the name, 'is currently occupied, sir.'

'I think you will find that his earlier meeting is over,' Mathew said. 'Now do as you are told, and quickly please.'

Mr Marston's back went so stiff that it seemed about to snap, but finally he gave a curt nod, and turned, slowly on his heel, before departing to his right.

He left the glass door open and so the trio stepped into the great entrance hall; its floor and straight staircase were made from reddish-toned marble, and were carpeted in dark blue, although a few bare patches showed in the areas that were walked most often. A chandelier hung above their heads, but only a few of its candles were lit.

'Down-at-heel,' Mathew murmured.

'And not too thoroughly cleaned,' Lizzie added running her finger along the wall table on which the two men had laid their hats, and leaving a line in the dust. 'The place is near freezing too.'

Mr Marston was gone for some time, but he did return. 'Sir Gavin has graciously agreed to receive you,' he announced. 'Please follow me.'

He led them through a long reception room, furnished with various chairs and tables, some set around a high, empty fireplace, and then into a library, also without heating. Its shelves were no more than half full.

'I have been here,' Mathew murmured, slowing his pace as he looked around. 'This was Sir George's favourite room; he liked to receive his visitors here, for he had a great collection of valuable books. I doubt that either of his sons has read them to destruction, so they must have been disposed of in another way.'

'If you please,' Mr Marston said, from another doorway.

The old servant stood aside, allowing them to enter another chamber, then closed the door behind him as he withdrew. The room was smaller than the others, and it was heated. Sir Gavin Cleland stood with his back to the fire, and John Barclay, in clerical clothes, was alongside him.

'This is a surprise, Fleming,' the baronet drawled, 'but at least you have spared me from any more of this old fool's prattling. How can a man go on for so long about the content of a watchnight service? It defeats me. You can go now, Barclay. Do not look for me in your kirk tonight.'

'The minister may remain, if he pleases,' Mathew said. 'He should hear what we have to say.

'You know me, Cleland,' he continued, 'but you may not ever have met Mrs Elizabeth McGill.' Lizzie smiled, made a little curtsy and opened her cloak. 'Our companion is Mr Andrew Dunlop.'

'That is very good, if a little disrespectful to a baronet. Now please tell me, what is this about? Or have you simply come to beg a goose,' he sniggered, 'for the poor widow woman's Christmas table?'

Mathew ran his fingers though his close-cropped salt and pepper hair. Lizzie had seen him do that before, in their youth; it meant that he was making a decision.

'Mr Barclay,' he said. 'Please close your eyes in a moment of prayer. Mr Dunlop, please look out of the window.'

'Certainly, sir.' The man turned slowly.

One long stride brought Cleland within Mathew's reach; he seized him by the lapels of his coat, lifted him up, and butted him with his lowered forehead, hard, between the eyes. Then he let him fall.

'That,' he murmured, 'is what Napoleon's soldiers came to call the "Scottish Kiss". Some were said to prefer being shot.'

Blood poured from the baronet's nose as he struggled unsteadily to his feet. He grabbed a handkerchief from a pocket to staunch the flow.

'There will be a duel,' he mumbled. 'I will have satisfaction.'

'I have told you before how that would end. Gentlemen,' he called out, 'you may look on once more, having seen nothing. Anyway,' he added, 'duels are about honour and you have none to defend, Gavin. Now sit down, plug your nose, and your trap along with it.' He pushed him, with just enough force to send him backwards into a chair.

'The fact is, sir, you are the most dishonourable man I have ever met. You are a murderer, twice over to my knowledge. You are, forgive my language, Lizzie . . .'

'Do not mind me,' she said, bewildered but cheerfully.

'. . . a hoormaster, a rake, a drunkard and a general all-round dissolute. You are also extremely stupid, to practise all these vices on the very doorstep of the exalted man whose daughter you were hoping to lure into marriage. You really were very easy to unmask; it took my people no time at all.'

The wounded Cleland stared up at him. 'You?' he mumbled, clutching his bloody handkerchief. 'I thought it was . . .'

'You thought Lord Douglas had you followed?' he laughed. 'No, no, you had him fooled at home as well as in the court . . . or perhaps he persuaded himself that some stones are better left unturned, for fear of slimy creatures underneath. Oh yes, it was me, Gavin. I promised you I would bring you down, and I have done.'

'Then fuck you! And your woman!' Mathew looked at Dunlop, who began to turn slowly. 'No!' the baronet screamed.

'Then mind your tongue. You'll have need of it, for your future will require a great deal of glib talking. You see, Laird, there is one other vice of yours that I have not yet touched on. You are a gambler. You are as governed by the tables as you are by the drink, and probably by the laudanum as well. But like everything else in your life . . . apart from murder . . . you do it very badly.'

Cleland's eyes began to narrow, and curiosity joined the fear they displayed.

'You may think that the cards are games of chance, but they are not. They are in the main games of skill, and they are commonly played by professionals. By the very name, those are men for hire, men like the three against whom you have made such catastrophic losses since last summer. You know them as Jimmy, Pilmar and Kenneth: so do I, for they have been playing with my money and under my contract.'

Sir Gavin went white, pure chalk white.

'Those losses of yours were so large,' Mathew continued, 'that you could not come near covering them, but still my three friends kept extending you credit. And you kept on losing. When eventually they called in your account with them, and you could not cover your debts, you were barred from the gaming house . . . but not before you had granted a floating charge to the aforesaid Jimmy, Pilmar and Kenneth, against this estate and everything in it, on the promise of future repayment. Am I right?'

Cleland made a small gurgling noise as he nodded.

'Then it is a pity you had fallen out with James Douglas, for if he had looked over that charge, he would have found it as full of holes as a piece of fancy foreign cheese. For example he would have found that without your knowledge it could be assigned, transferred, at the discretion of the holders, and that it could be foreclosed upon at will.' He paused, to let the Laird's numbed mind catch up with him.

'And assigned it has been,' he said, 'under the terms of my contract with your three opponents. They will keep the original stake money, of course, which was considerable, and as was agreed at the outset they have received between them one-tenth of the value of their winnings. That has turned out to be more money than they had ever heard of, far less dreamed. They are three happy men, blessing the days when they met the pair of us.'

He smiled. 'Honest to God, Gavin, I expected them to strip you of all your money, and probably the Edinburgh house, but to play away your entire damned estate . . . man!

'What a fool, what an eedjit! You know, I really should have kicked your arse when you were fifteen; you might have been a better man for it.' He turned to his silent companion. 'Mr Dunlop, the floor is yours.'

The man stepped forward, unrolling a document, from which he read.

'Sir Gavin Cleland,' he announced. 'I am an officer of the Sheriff of Lanark, in the service of the Supreme Court of Scotland. I have to advise you that in accordance with the floating charge that you signed over this entire property and its contents, and with its subsequent transfer, ownership has been transferred, by decree issued by the Lord President of the Court of Session himself, to the assignee of that charge, Mistress Elizabeth McGill.'

Instinct made Mathew reach out to catch Lizzie's elbow, to hold her steady.

'What have you done?' he heard her gasp.

'Justice,' he replied, almost as quietly. 'He took away your nearest and dearest; now you have his in return. Not a fair exchange, I will admit, but the best I could do.'

'Lord Douglas has ordered,' Dunlop concluded, 'that you render vacant possession of the estate by no later than January twenty-fourth. He further instructs that a full inventory of the estate be taken immediately, and that any attempt by you to destroy or sell any of the property from this moment on will be treated as a gross contempt of court and will lead to your prosecution for theft.'

The Sheriff's officer placed the document on a table beside the shocked and trembling baronet. 'You are duly served with the order of the court,' he said. 'People will come this afternoon to begin the inventory. If you obstruct them you will be arrested and held until they are done. Until Mistress McGill takes possession, the factor, Mr Armitage, I believe, has charge of the estate. I am going to speak to him now to advise him of his responsibility.'

As the officer withdrew, Mathew stepped across to Cleland's chair and leaned over him, holding his bloody face, roughly, in his right hand, and staring into his eyes.

'I would almost wish you long life,' he whispered, 'to suffer all the indignities of your change of fortune, but I made you a promise in June and I still intend to keep it.'

Chapter Forty-Three

'MATHEW,' LIZZIE EXCLAIMED AS she took off her cloak and hung it on a row of hooks behind her front door, 'have you gone raving mad?'

She had said nothing, from leaving Cleland Hall until their arrival back in Carluke. All she had done was stare out of the window of the carriage, gazing at the snowflakes that had started to fall as Beattie eased the horses into a canter, and had grown heavier along the way.

'Possibly,' he admitted. 'When my man Pilmar and his two friends came to me with that outcome, I thought that they had, but they were serious. As it turned out, Cleland was the lunatic, not having the sense to cut his losses until he had no more to lose.'

'And you paid them one-tenth of the estate's worth?'

'One-tenth of the debt, which is the same, in theory.'

'That is still a huge amount of money.'

He laughed. 'Yes, but a bargain. My dear, had the estate come on the market in the normal way, I would have bought it for you, although it might have cost fifteen or twenty times more.'

'But Mathew, what in Heaven's name am I to do with

an estate? I have no money, so how will I run it?'

'The estate runs itself; it is self-financing. The first thing you will do is send all the cattle and hogget back to the slaughterhouse that turned them away. I think you will find they are accepted this time and at a damn good price, given the scarcity of fresh meat in winter. That will fill the coffers.

'Then I suggest that you send some art to auction. In that reception room we passed two paintings by the Venetian artist, Titian, that Sir George pointed out to me when I visited him. The idiot Gavin had no idea of their value when he signed them over, but if he had sold them, I suspect that he could have cleared most of his debt. Instead he sold his father's books, which are of relatively little value.'

'Oh Mathew,' she laughed, 'you are mad, really. I like being the village shopkeeper. That is what I am cut out for.'

'Then carry on. You can live in Cleland Hall and go to work every day, as I do from Waterloo House.'

'This is too much for me,' she protested. 'I am over-whelmed.'

'Think of it as a fine new dress. It will grow on you. Lizzie, it is done. You are mistress of Cleland Hall; that is your station now.'

'Ohh!!!' she cried, then hugged him to her, transferring flour to his fine magisterial suit. 'On one condition,' she said. 'We, not I, will live in Cleland Hall and you will be the Laird. Otherwise . . .'

He grinned. 'Go on,' he chuckled. 'Twist my arm.'

She gave it a gentle tug.

'Very well, I agree. Do you know what my first act will be as master of Cleland?'

'Tell me.'

'John Barclay will be dismissed from his charge.'

Her face fell. 'Oh Mathew. I thought you had forgiven him.'

'I have. He has served this village, its folk, and its masters for long enough. He deserves a happy retirement. He will have a pension and he will live in Waterloo House under my mother's care when I move here. Cleland Hall would be a step too far for her, and she has always carried a secret fondness for the minister.'

'Will people talk?'

'Certainly. Let them. When they are done with it, both of them, the place will be Matt's. By that time he will fit it well. His father is buried there, so that is only right. Before then, once he is grown a bit more, in years if not in size, I plan to take him into the leather business, for I see him as my successor there. I like his enterprise and his enthusiasm. Even now, I believe that Marshall's talents will lie elsewhere.'

'My love, that is even more generous of you.'

'Not at all; soon Matt will be my stepson, and will be treated as such. Besides, I promised his father I would keep him out of harm's way, and giving him responsibility is a good way of doing that.'

She released him from her hug and stepped back. 'This is all . . . mind-spinning. Does Mother Fleming know yet?'

He shook his head. 'She suspects that something is up, but she has no idea what it is. I must go now and tell her, before I find myself snowed in here. Indeed I would like you three to come with me, just in case the road is not passable tomorrow.'

'Yes, that would be sensible. I will go and fetch Matt and Jean from the shop.' She made for the door, then paused. 'How do you think Mother Fleming will take the news when you tell her?'

He shot her that sideways grin, and she felt herself go liquid inside. 'Stoically, as always . . . until I get to the news about John Barclay.'

Chapter Forty-Four

ONCE SHE HAD TAKEN time to think it through, Hannah Fleming concurred with her son's proposal. The news of the Cleland Estate did shake even her composure, but the time was long past when anything that Mathew did truly astonished her.

'I am sure the lot o' you will be very well suited, even though the place is so big that ye'll tak an age findin' Jean and Marshall if they ever play hide and seek. As for me, ye're richt, I'm content here, and if it suits ye tae have me keep auld Barclay aff the drink, that'll be fine also.

'I think Ah'll always need tae be lookin' after someone, laddie. Ah was only ever unhappy when I thocht that you were gone, and even then Ah had Lizzie tae tend to for a while, for her own useless mither was no help tae her in her grief.'

As for the minister, who joined the family for Christmas lunch after his morning service, his reaction, when Mathew told him, in private, of his intentions, was to break down in tears.

'You are too generous, sir,' he gulped, 'and Mrs McGill also, after the way I failed you this summer.'

'No, John,' he replied, 'I failed you with my anger. I should have seen how exposed you were, with your living at the mercy of that wicked man.'

'I wonder what sort of a Christmas Day he is having,' Barclay pondered.

'Indigestible, I hope. Before we left the hall yesterday I suggested to Armitage that he should have the cook prepare the biggest goose she could find and pile it high on his plate.'

Christmas Day at Waterloo House was a joyous festival, and yet it had a sombre beginning. At noon Lizzie and Matt led the household through the snow and up the hill to David's grave. As they stood around it, John Barclay intoned a prayer, and Lizzie laid a bouquet of red-budded holly, cut from a tree in the grounds, before the memorial stone.

At that point, the young man did not know what had happened the day before, but when they were back indoors, Mathew and Lizzie took him into the private parlour and told him that his family's fortunes had changed, and how it had happened. Lizzie described the confrontation with Cleland with relish, and in detail.

Matt was as stunned by the development as his mother had been but he smiled broadly when she told him how Mathew had repaid the baronet's insult.

'You did that?' he exclaimed. 'Where did you learn such a thing?'

'Lad, I did not become a sergeant in the Cameron Highlanders by being a milksop,' he replied. 'Times I had to stand my ground, and some things, once learned, are never forgotten.'

'Will you teach me?'

'When your mother is elsewhere, perhaps.' Mathew held the young man's gaze. 'That brings me to a question I would put to you. If she and I were to marry at some point in the near future, would you have any objection?'

The smile left Matt's face. 'I would only object if you did not. The night before he died, Faither told me I should look after you both. It will make it a damn sight easier for me if you are man and wife.'

Mathew shook his hand, formally, man to man. 'Thank you,' he said. 'We were thinking of a time around St Valentine's Day.'

'I was thinking of tomorrow,' Matt countered, smiling once more. 'If we are all to move into Cleland Hall in a month, I would rather not have to stand outside my mother's door to keep to propriety.'

'Hey, boy,' Lizzie chided, 'would that be to keep him out or keep me in? Make no male assumptions about your answer.'

That was forestalled by Mathew. 'The banns must be called on three Sundays,' he said. 'That means,' he did a quick mental calculation, 'any time after January the eleventh. You have time to be measured for a suit, but not that much.'

Their news added the final touch to the celebration. Mathew found goose too fatty for his taste and so he had ordered the cook to prepare roast beef, preceded by broth, and trout, fresh caught from Lanark Loch, and followed by a rich dark pudding, flamed in brandy and served with cream.

When it was over, and young Matt had driven off to

Carluke in Hannah's little coach, to take Jane Fisher her present, Lizzie and Matt returned to the private parlour.

'Is all this haste too much?' he asked, an arm around her waist as they stood by the window, watching Marshall and Jean playing in the snow in the last of the fast-fading daylight.

She turned to him. 'Too much?' she murmured. 'Draw the curtains a little, lock the door and I'll show you. What Matt doesn't know won't hurt him.'

Chapter Forty-Five

MATHEW FLEMING AND LIZZIE McGill were married by John Barclay, in Carluke Parish Church, on January the fourteenth, before a small, invited congregation that included all those who had attended David's funeral, with the addition of Sheriff Robin Stirling, in response to the bride's personal invitation.

Philip Armitage was there also; there had been several meetings with the factor in Waterloo House during the days since Christmas. He was sixty-three years old, and had come to the first meeting fearing for his position, but as soon as he had been reassured he was helpful, giving a summary of the financial position of the estate, which was not as bad as Mathew had feared.

The man had been a prudent manager and during Sir George's tenure he had built up a capital reserve, which he had managed to keep out of the sight of his sons.

'I knew what they were from the beginning, Mr Fleming,' he said, 'but the old Laird would not be told. He knew of their imperfections but he trusted me to keep the estate safe from their bad habits, as I did, if only just . . . with, I might add, David McGill's considerable assistance.'

'Explain to us, in that case,' Lizzie said, 'why David was dismissed?'

'Sir Gregor ordered it; I argued against it, but I was given no leeway. It is my belief that Gavin made him do it. You should understand that while Gregor was the older and the heir, he was always under Gavin's control. Gregor had a wee bit of his father in him, but Gavin has only the devil. It is my belief that he saw David's dismissal as a blow against you, Mr Fleming. He has a hatred of you, and an intense jealousy, that strikes me as quite irrational.'

'And how is he now?' Mathew asked.

'Brooding, I would say. He is keeping to his personal quarters, for I have forbidden him access to the rest of the house while the inventory is completed.'

'Including the wine cellar?'

'He is allowed one bottle of wine a day and one bottle of whisky, my theory being that he is easier to manage drunk than sober.'

'And the inventory?'

'There are several items missing,' Armitage replied. 'Principally the books, but also a few small paintings and some statuary. The major works of art, the Titians, a Canaletto, a Holbein and three paintings by Rembrandt, they are all safe and locked away, to avoid the risk of vindictive damage. What would you have me do with them when Sir Gavin is gone?'

'Are they very valuable?' Lizzie asked.

He nodded.

She looked at Mathew. 'I have no appreciation of art. What do you say?'

'Is there a need to sell, Philip?' he asked the factor.

'Given the projected income from the livestock sales, and the quarterly rents being due soon from the tenants, I would say no.'

'Then we should keep them, Lizzie, apart from one of the Dutchman's which we should sell at auction in London, to pay for the necessary refurbishment of the hall. The rest will never become less valuable than they are, and if our heirs are taxed on our estate when we die, they will be a useful nest egg.'

'I am glad you understand these things,' she sighed, 'for . . .'

He laughed. 'I know . . . for you are only a simple village shopkeeper. Thank you, Philip,' he said. 'I look forward to our new relationship.'

Two days after the wedding, and eight before Gavin Cleland was bound to leave the estate, Mathew had a lunchtime visitor. Paul Johnston had been a wedding guest, but without news to relate, so his reappearance on the following Friday came as a great surprise, not least because he had braved the howling winds that were sweeping across the countryside, so strong they had even persuaded Mathew to work at home that day. Lizzie, however, new bride or not, had opened the shop as usual.

'They are found,' the solicitor exclaimed, as soon as the two were alone. 'The women are found!'

'Great news!' Mathew exclaimed. 'How and where? Tell me.'

'They were a little careless,' Johnston replied. 'Only a little but it was enough. They used their own names not the aliases they normally went by around Leith docks . . . English Lottie and Fat Judy, apparently . . . and Miss Smith does indeed come from Knutsford, in Cheshire.

'An agent made enquiries there and was told that the city of Liverpool might be a place to look. He searched there for some time, until he met a man, an iron worker, to whom the names were familiar, and was sent to another port nearby, called Birkenhead. It took him little time to find them there, the owners of a cathouse which they purchased with money given them, they said, by a gentleman acquaintance in Scotland.

'My man showed your warrant to the local constabulary, and asked that they be held. They are now under lock and key, and awaiting your pleasure. What will it be?'

'Paul, you are the most tenacious man I know,' Mathew exclaimed. 'Eat with me now, and then we must go to Lanark to see the Sheriff. When he hears your story, he will issue his own warrant, and send his own men to bring these tarts before him.'

Chapter Forty-Six

MATHEW SAID NOTHING TO Lizzie, but on the following Tuesday morning he was so preoccupied that she had to tell him twice that her monthly visit from an old acquaintance was four days overdue.

'How sure is that?' he asked, his attention finally captured.

'Not at all yet, but give it another four weeks and it will be. My God,' she grinned, 'if you had rung the bell as quickly in eighteen twelve, what would have become of us?'

'Mother would have coped and in time David would have had a stepchild,' he replied, 'for I was bound into the army, and could have been shot if I'd run away in wartime. Look after this one, if it is to be. Here,' he exclaimed as the consequences struck him, 'Matt may have to take over the shop.'

'Let us just be patient though,' she said, '. . . if that is possible for you, for you're like a hen on a hot griddle this morning.'

'I am,' he admitted. 'I have a meeting with Robin, in Lanark, at ten o'clock, and I must not be late. Will you stay home from the shop today?'

'No, not at all. There is no need yet, nor will there be for months.'

'Then I'll take you myself, in the wee carriage and go on from there.'

He drove her briskly to Carluke. Matt was still living in the house beside the shop, with his parents' blessing. He was beyond his years in maturity and they trusted him completely not to engage in any foolishness, not that there was anyone to lead him astray. He had never forgiven the boys who had deserted him on the day of Gregor Cleland's death, and they were all sensible enough to avoid him like the plague. Jane Fisher was his only close companion, and she was well chaperoned, with her family home close by.

'Keep an eye on your mother,' Mathew told him, quietly, as he dropped Lizzie off. 'If she seems faint in any way, insist that she sits down.'

'Is she unwell?'

'Far from it, but do as I ask anyway.'

He left for Lanark and was there within three minutes of the appointed time. The Sheriff's clerk showed him straight into his chambers, where Stirling was waiting, wearing his shrieval gown and wig.

'You are very formal,' Mathew remarked. 'Will you see them in court?'

'No, they will be brought here, but I want them to know that this is a judicial matter.'

'Do you want me to leave?'

'Hell no, I want you to question them, as aggressively as you like. The clerk will bring them from the cell they have been in overnight, now that you are here.'

He had barely finished speaking when the door opened and the two women were bustled into the room, announced by their escort, each in turn. Charlotte Smith was the blonde, Judith Stout the redhead, although the former's hair had an unnaturally brassy tinge. They were untidy and smelled the worse for their night under lock and key, and for their long journey.

'Stand before the Sheriff and the King's Deputy Lieutenant!' Martin Knox barked. They did as the clerk ordered, facing the two men across the table. Fat Judy looked uncertain, but English Lottie had a defiant gleam in her eye.

'Good,' she said. 'Now we will find out why two honest women have been taken from their 'ome without rhyme or reason or just cause.'

'Be quiet!' Stirling snapped. 'Your role here is to answer, mine to judge you.'

'And this gen'leman? Gawd, he looks like a pirate we 'ad in our house last week.'

'I am your inquisitor, Miss Smith,' Mathew said. 'I will begin by commiserating with you on your loss, but congratulating you on your obvious recovery from the shock it caused you.'

'Well, thank you, sir.'

'For how long were you affianced to Sir Gregor Cleland?' he asked.

'Two weeks,' she shot back.

'Two whole weeks? That is strange, for normally betrothals of people of substance are advertised in the newspapers and gazettes, and yet I have found no mention of that engagement.'

'Poor Gregor,' she sighed. 'He was so in love he must 'ave forgot.'

'Are you sure it was Gregor to whom you were pledged, and not Gavin? After all they were twins, and you did fuck them both.' He fixed his eye on the other woman. 'Is that not the case, Miss Stout? You should know, you were there too.'

'Sir, I don't know what . . .' she stammered

'That is a wicked bleedin' lie!' Smith shouted.

'Spoken like a true gentlewoman,' Sheriff Stirling said, coolly. 'That is how you described yourself in your affidavit to the Crown Agent, is it not?' He picked up a folder, bound in pink ribbon, then slammed it back down on the table. 'I know, for I have your statements here, the description of the murder of Gregor Cleland that condemned a man to death. Do you stand by them now?'

'Every word,' the blonde insisted, stubbornly. The redhead said nothing.

'That's what happened, is it, Judy?' Mathew asked. 'Gregor Cleland whipped a young man for insolence.'

'Yes, sir,' Stout replied.

'And at that the boy's father attacked Gavin Cleland, seized his pistol, and shot Gregor dead, leaving both of you fine ladies in fear of your lives?'

'Yes, sir.'

'How long have you been Miss Smith's maid, Judy?'

'Err . . . two years.' Her answer sounded more like a question.

'So all the time that the pair of you worked in a brothel in Leith you were actually in disguise. She played the part of

English Lottie and you were Fat Judy, yet really you were gentlewomen in disguise?'

'Mmm.' Stout's face seemed to freeze.

'Do you know what perjury is, Judy?'

'N- no, sir.'

'It is making a false statement under oath, and it is a crime. The punishment is severe in normal circumstances, but when perjured evidence causes a man to be executed, that is another matter entirely. Where does the perjurer stand then, Sheriff?'

'At the bar of the High Court,' Stirling said solemnly, 'indicted on the charge of murder.'

Mathew began to rub his neck, slowly. 'Will I tell you what happened to the man that you accused, ladies? They sentenced him to death. Three days later they took him up to the Lawnmarket and in front of a great crowd they hanged him. And that man was a friend of mine, a very good friend.' He looked back at English Lottie, and saw that she was licking her lips, and massaging her own neck.

'Do either of you think,' he asked, 'that we are too humane in Scotland to hang a woman, or even hang them two at a time on the same scaffold?'

Judith Stout began to cry.

'The Sheriff believes that there is enough evidence to bring such a charge against you two, and that you will be convicted. Here and now, in this room, you have the chance to save your lives, but it may not come again. So tell me, Lottie, where did you get the money, the two of you, to buy your whorehouse in Birkenhead?'

She nodded. 'I know when I'm beat,' she said. 'If we tell you, what will happen to us?'

'You will be Crown witnesses and immune from prosecution for that crime,' Stirling told her.

'In that case, Gavin gave us the money, for saying that the man shot his brother.'

'Who did shoot him?'

'Gavin did, 'imself, of course. The young lad, he did nothing; it was an accident that the 'orse got spooked, but Gregor whipped 'im across the face anyway. The man, 'is father you said, pulled him off the carriage and set about 'im. He wasn't 'itting him very 'ard; you could see 'e wasn't a brawler. That was when Gavin shot him.'

'By mistake? Was he aiming at Mr McGill?'

Lottie smiled. 'No. Even I'd 'ave hit him from that range if I'd meant to. He took careful aim and he shot Gregor. Then he hit the man with the gun and bundled Gregor's body on to the carriage, tied his own 'orse to it and drove us all off.'

'Did he take the pistol with him?'

'Of course.'

'You are certain of that?'

'As certain can be.'

'And do you agree with that, Judy?' Mathew asked.

'Yes, sir,' she snuffled, 'that's what 'appened.'

'How much did he pay you to lie?'

'Two hundred and fifty pound,' Smith said. 'That buys you a lot in Birkenhead.'

Mathew looked at Stirling. 'Well?'

The Sheriff nodded. 'Ladies,' he said, 'I am going to

summon an official called the procurator fiscal. Under oath you will give new statements, and then you will be held in custody until you have given evidence in the High Court. You may sit now.'

He turned to his friend. 'You have what you promised, justice for David McGill. Gavin Cleland is for the Lawn-market, no question about it. As soon as I have drawn up the warrant, I will send Dunlop now to arrest him.

'I hope he enjoys his lunch, for it will be his last decent meal. He will never breathe free air again, and fairly soon, no air at all, after the noose draws tight.'

Chapter Forty-Seven

As he left the old Sheriff Court building, and climbed into the small covered coach, Mathew experienced a strange feeling of emptiness.

Over half a year's pursuit was over, and all of his goals, save one, had been achieved. He had expected elation but none came. Instead he contemplated the fate he had secured for Gavin Cleland, and saw for the first time how cruel his pursuit of vengeance had been.

Yes, he had been more successful than he had dared to dream. Yes, the murderer was utterly ruined. Yes, the pledge he had made before the scaffold would be fulfilled.

He had done it for Lizzie, he had done it for Matt and Jean, and he had done it for himself, but what of David? Would his friend have wanted to be avenged in such a ruthless, obsessive and downright ungodly manner?

Then a truth came home to him. Just as Gavin Cleland had bought the perjured evidence that covered up his own crime, so had he bought the means of the man's certain conviction.

No bribes had been paid, but his funding of the three gamblers had been a conspiracy of sorts. On the other hand, without his resources, Lucy Douglas would have become Lady Cleland, while English Lottie and Fat Judy would have gone on undisturbed in their whorehouse in Birkenhead, rewarded for their part in David's judicial murder.

On balance he had done more good than harm, and won even more powerful allies along the way, but would David have wanted any of it? He doubted it; his peaceful friend would have wanted him to look after Lizzie and leave Cleland to ruin himself as undoubtedly he would have, given time.

He knew then that he would not go to the Lawnmarket in a few weeks' time to watch a terrified man stand before a festive mob that would cheer every last kick as he danced on the end of the rope. There would be no point, for even if he did, he would only look away and feel guilt at his part in a man's death, even a man so thoroughly reptilian as the baronet.

He remembered David McGill's last words, and how the Scottish form of prayer continued: 'Forgive us our debts as we forgive our debtors.' That is what his friend would have done, but forgiveness came hard to Mathew Fleming.

Tickling the horse into action, he left Lanark at a much more gentle pace than he had come, and drove back to Carluke, wondering how Lizzie would take the news, and whether he should even tell her, given the possibility that she had raised with him that morning.

As he reached the village, and the shop came into sight, he saw a small group of women outside, gathered in conclave. Unusually, there was a man among them; even from that distance, he had no difficulty in recognising Joel Fisher, the blacksmith. He was never away from his forge during the day, and so the sight of him raised concern and brought a frown to Mathew's face.

He rapped the horse to speed it up.

'Why the gathering?' he asked, as he pulled up beside the group, jumping out of the cabin as he spoke.

The women looked at him, fearfully. 'It's Lizzie,' Fisher said, quietly.

He would have run straight into the shop had not the smith caught his arm. 'She's a' right, Mathew,' he said. 'My Beth's wi' her. Let me tell you what's happened first. It was the Laird.'

'Cleland, what about him? If he has hurt a hair on her head, Joel, so help me God I will disembowel him.'

'You may no' be the first.'

'Tell me, man,' Mathew hissed, 'quickly.'

'It must be twenty minutes, now,' Fisher said. 'Beth wis in the shop. Wi' a few others, when Cleland burst in. He wis drunk, she said, and he wis ravin', goin' on about jumped-up rabble takin' ower his estate, and that they'd die first. Beth said he'd've struck her, but young Matt jumped in and hut him first, knocked him richt across the shop flair, and then when he got up, he nutted him.'

The blacksmith imitated the action. 'That wis enough for Cleland,' he continued. 'He scrambled oot the door and on tae his horse, but Matt went after him in that cart o' his. He'd just been deliverin', so it was harnessed at the door.

'The Laird went aff along the Crossford road wi' the lad followin'. He'll never catch him though, Mathew. Thon's a thoroughbred Cleland was on, even tho' it's gelded. Ah've shod it mony a time. It's a richt spirited bastard, wi' a temper too.'

Mathew had calmed down. 'Thanks, Joel. Twenty minutes you say?'

'Aye; the chances are the lad'll be back soon. As for the Laird . . . Whit was he on about, Mathew?'

'It's a long story, friend. I'll tell you later, but first I must see to Lizzie.'

She smiled at him, weakly, as he came into the shop. 'Joel told me,' he said.

'I'm fine, love. I'm not hurt and I am as sound as I was last time you saw me.' She grinned again. 'As for that stepson of yours,' she murmured, 'you have taught him some bad habits. Go after him, Mathew, and bring him back. Cleland will be halfway to England by now.'

'He will need to go further than that,' Mathew told her. 'The whores have been found, and turned on him. He is bound for the Calton Jail and what happens after that.' As he spoke he felt renewed enthusiasm for watching Cleland swing. 'I'll go for Matt. We dinna want him flogging that pony to death.'

The group outside had dispersed, apart from Joel Fisher, who was waiting for his wife. Mathew thanked him again then climbed back into the small coach and headed up the Crossford road.

Many years had gone by since he had taken it, sixteen, he realised as he cantered out of the village. When he had returned to Carluke from the war, that was the way he had taken. He had chosen it because it was quiet, old Gracie having been a slightly nervous animal, easily startled by passing traffic.

On that rough track, at the copper beech crossing, where it intersected with another route that led ultimately to Ayr, he had met the Cleland twins, and the seed of a grudge had been planted in Gavin's mind.

He smiled, sadly, at the memory of the two threatening to tie him to the tree the place was named after. 'Whelps,' he murmured. 'Bound for an early death for all their privileges.'

The road was rough and had many rises and dips. As he reached each crest he expected to find Matt returning, having given up a fruitless chase, and yet he did not, not until he reached the top of the hill where the track took a curve and the copper beech came into sight for the first time.

He reached the summit, where the road levelled out, and he saw it, and he saw his stepson . . . and his heart seemed to drop into his stomach.

The great old tree was bare of leaves, but it had borne fruit. Sir Gavin Cleland hung from it by the neck, swinging and twisting in the January wind. Matt stood alongside, holding the reins of his pony, while Cleland's gelding, in a Netherton saddle, grazed at the roadside.

Mathew lashed his horse, startling it into closing the last hundred and fifty yards at a gallop. If he had any hope of reviving the baronet, it vanished as soon as he saw his blackened, bruised, bleeding face with its dead but still desperate eyes, and its bulging tongue.

'Oh laddie,' he cried, as he reached the scene, 'what in heaven's name have you done?'

'What needed doing,' Matt replied; he sounded exhausted and not entirely convinced by his own words. 'The dog killed my father, and might have done the same to my mother if I had not been there. What would you have done, Mathew?'

'I would not have put my own life in jeopardy,' he retorted, angrily, 'for something as worthless as this, otherwise I'd have killed him myself, months ago. Tell me what happened.'

'I was almost ready to give up the chase,' the young man told him. 'I told old Meggie here, just one more hill, and if he is not in sight, we turn back. And there he was; his horse must have thrown him, for he lay on the road, quite still. I hoped that he was dead, but when I got close I could hear him breathing, roughly.

'I knew what I had to do,' Matt said. 'I have my old tea chest in the cart, the one I use for delivering orders, and I had the rope I use to bind it securely. I heaved him up from the road. When he came to his senses he was lying on the upturned chest, there was a noose round his neck, and the rope was over the bough above. I pulled it up, drawing him to his feet, and when he was at full stretch I tied it off.'

His eyes narrowed, with his frown. 'He shouted at first, as if he thought it was a bad joke. When he realised I was serious, that became a plea, then a whimper, and finally a coward's tears; so unlike my father. I led Meggie on, and left him swinging.'

Mathew closed his eye.

'It took him a while to die,' the young man added, quietly. 'Quite a few minutes went by before he stopped kicking and twitching. I never thought it would be like that, Mathew.'

'And do you feel the better for it?' he asked, sharply.

'No. I thought I would, but no.'

'Thank God for that, at least. If only you had kept your anger in check, son, and contented yourself with chasing him out of the shop. As of this morning, the law was ready to do this to him, although more humanely. Even now, Andrew Dunlop, the Sheriff's man, will be on his way to Cleland Hall to arrest him. When he cannot find him, he will come looking.

'Do you know what I should do?' he asked, his tone one of despair. 'As a magistrate I should hold you and take you to the Sheriff myself. No matter what this creature's crime, this is murder. Even at your age, you are liable to be sent to Australia for life.'

Matt squared his shoulders. 'Then so be it.'

'No it will not,' Mathew snapped. 'Your mother will not have that to endure. Listen, I was never here, and neither were you. Old Meggie never did crest that hill and I met you further back along the road. We will leave Cleland here with his horse. Dunlop will find him, and with any luck he will report that, having seen no way out of his troubles, and knowing his lying whore witnesses would one day be found, he chose to end his own life, using his mount as a platform.' He nodded, to himself. 'Yes, that will be his assumption and he will look no further. The Sheriff's verdict will be suicide.'

Barely a second later his satisfaction vanished as an old memory came back to him.

'Unless,' he exclaimed, 'Dunlop asks himself one question. "Where did Cleland get the rope?" If he does . . .' His voice trailed off, but his meaning did not need speaking aloud.

'Matt, I believe in the law, but I love your mother more, and you. I will lie for you, or better, say nothing, but if a single honest person says when asked that Cleland had no rope on his saddle when he left Carluke, then the procurator fiscal will have no choice but to investigate, and a true system of justice will put you in the dock.'

Even as he spoke he realised what he had to do.

'It may never happen,' he said, 'but I must guard against it. When I was not much older than you, I went away, for six years. You must do the same, for a while at least, otherwise none of us will have a moment of certainty. It will be hard for all of us who love you, but this way, at least you will have the prospect of return. From Australia there is none.

'Now,' he said, 'let us get ourselves clear of this place, in case Mr Dunlop moves faster than I give him credit for.'

Chapter Forty-Eight

'MATHEW,' LIZZIE ASKED, AS they stood on the Glasgow quayside, 'can you not talk him out of this, even at this last minute? Cleland is dead, by his own hand they're saying, to beat the hangman. The cause of Matt's anger is removed. I thought we could settle down to a calm life, yet the boy insists he is determined to travel, to see the other side of the Atlantic.'

He had not told her the truth of what happened under the copper beech, nor would he ever. 'I could talk him out of it,' he admitted, 'if I chose to. But if I did, the hankering would return sooner rather than later, and he might even go further away.'

'Is there anywhere further away than Massachusetts?' she murmured.

'Oh yes, my love,' Mathew said, 'and a lot less hospitable.'

'This is all so sudden.'

'Maybe, but a passage has come up on a ship bound for Boston, and the opportunity is too good to miss. He will not be alone, though. Ewan will go with him and stay for a year at least, until we see how he settles down. They are not short of money, nor will they ever be, so they may live and travel in comfort.'

He laughed. 'I have a notion, too, that he will pay his way over there. America is a vast market for saddles, and he carries with him drawings and prices for mine, with testimonials from across Europe. And for the luggage too: those United States are vast, and folk have no choice but to travel distances. You know how good at selling Matt is in the shop; I fancy we will have orders coming back soon, from far away.'

'Not only leather goods,' Matt added. 'I have read that they are already starting to build railways to link the states. One day they will cross the continent. Mother, this will be an adventure.' He came to her and hugged her, then bent to kiss his sister and ruffle young Marshall's hair.

'I know what you are thinking,' he told her. 'You are remembering when I was your age and Mathew went off to the army. Well, I am going to fight no one,' he said. 'I am going to travel, and I am going to study on the way, and when I come back in a few years, I will have learned more than I would at any university. Jane knows that and she says she will wait for me. Look after her as Granny Fleming took care of you and trust me to come back safe and sound.'

'I trust you, son. It's the other buggers in the world I will worry about.'

'Then do not, for I will be fine.' As he spoke a whistle sounded. 'I have to go now, or Ewan will be crossing the Atlantic on his own.' He laughed. 'The poor man! Weeks without looking up a horse's arse. How will he manage?'

'You have your passport document?' Mathew asked.

Matt nodded.

'Good. You are called Matthew McGill Fleming on it

because my name may open doors, even over there, but you know who you are, Matt, and you always will. Go on now.' He hugged him close, and whispered, 'I will send word when I believe it safe.'

'God keep him, Mathew,' Lizzie whispered as she watched him jog up the gangplank. 'He is so young.'

'That lad will get by on his own,' he assured her. 'He is the sort that new nation needs. I have a feeling that we may go and visit him, before he returns to us. Be honest, now. Did you really want him stuck in Carluke for the rest of his life?'

She thought about his question for a while, as the ship cast off and eased away from the quayside. As it moved to midstream, heading for the Firth of Clyde and the great ocean beyond, she whispered, 'No, not really. Our old world is not for him.'

Her husband laughed aloud. 'Master and mistress of Cleland Hall,' he exclaimed. 'I am not sure that it's for us either, but let us go home and find out.'